A STARBRITE MAN

SLUMRAT RISING

BOOK ONE | A STARBRITE MAN

WARBY PICUS

Podium

Published in 2023 by Podium Publishing
www.podiumaudio.com

A STARBRITE MAN

CHAPTER 1

IN THE GUTTER

The worm demon pulling the carriages always roared in outrage when it was forced into the sun, and the screams of the steel wheels on the rails, falsetto to the worm's bass, made a hellish harmony. The subway crossed the canal right over Truth's favorite scavenging spot, so he was used to the noise. The slumrats in the dozens of brown and pollution-smudged white apartment buildings lining the canals, forty stories of indifference and passive cruelty, apparently didn't even hear it anymore. They didn't smell the chemical, swampy stink in the afternoon sun. You could get used to anything in the Harban slums.

In the slums, you learned to despise your neighbors. You tried to kill your soul pain with booze and drugs, and what joys of the flesh you could still tolerate. Watching people get mugged was great fun. No trouble looking down at suffering. But you never looked at the glistening city across the canal. The rich Harban, with its fancy shops, flying carpets, and beautiful mages on custom spell beasts or demon-driven carriages. You didn't look, didn't dream, and could only pray that one day, you would win the lottery and get out of the slums. Then you got up in the morning and joined the teeming vermin swarm of people off to work in the factories or to serve the beautiful people of that beautiful city. That is life. Only a child thought differently. Truth was seventeen. The burnt-out tweaker in front of him wouldn't live to see twenty.

"I just need a twenny. Twenny wen. You got money. I know you got the money!" The base fiend slurred his words. He started shifting around like his tendons were tightening every second into agonizing wires cutting through his muscle. Truth knew that look. The withdrawal was past hungry now. It was pain.

"I got no money! No money! Fuck off!" He waved a length of rebar over his head, hoping that he would look big, scare the freak off. Wasn't like he could run away, trapped between the canal and the retaining wall. He tried to guard his little pile of fished-up scrap. The tweaker probably thought it was trash.

The junkie was a sickly yellow color. His nails were either chewed down to the quick or long and torn and bloody. His eyes had gone red, almost black in the yellow, smog-filtered daylight, filling with blood as his body gave out. He didn't want a fix. *He needed it.*

He lunged in, screaming, clawing at Truth's face. Truth slashed the rebar down, chopping directly at the freak's head. The tweaker got his arm up in time. Truth felt it snap before he heard the crack. The base fiend was so far gone, he didn't miss a step. The ragged nails came right for Truth's eyes.

He tried to step back and get the rebar up to block. He only got a half-step before the freak was on him, pushing him down. The junkie had never been more than Level One. Drugs had burned away even that. Still, the body remembered.

His foot, a swollen mass of weeping sores and yellow, curling nails, smashed the side of Truth's knee. Truth buckled. The junkie pressed down, trying to go over the rebar with his good arm. Tried to get the throat.

Truth slid to the side, pushing the fiend past him. Got both his feet under him. Smashed down again with the rebar. Caught the freak across the back. He went down screaming. Not because the junkie could feel his back break but because he had missed. Because the fix was farther away.

Truth swung the rebar again. Caught the back of his head. The screaming stopped. Maybe he was dead. It really didn't matter. That poor bastard was dead after the first hit of cut base. Everything since then was just corpse spasms.

Truth looked up out of the path between the retainer wall and the canal. A billboard hung off the subway bridge, a staggering beauty with ruby-red lips having her Golden Bat cigarette lit by a spell-welding, idol-handsome man. The man on the billboard wore an incredible double-breasted cream overcoat, his hair immaculately styled, even his nails shone with health and polish. He was everything Truth wished he was. In beautiful, shimmering script: *A Starbrite Man Is Always Ready.*

Truth looked at the little pile of garbage he had fished out of the canal. Maybe ten wen worth of scrap. Maybe not. He was sure other seventeen-year-olds didn't have to do this shit. He was so ready to be out of this dump. So ready to be a Starbrite Man.

It was a good-enough day. He got eleven wen from Phil, the scrap guy. Must have caught him in a happy mood. Which meant that after two hours of work and maybe killing a man, he had not quite enough for a lousy dinner.

Phil was an okay guy for the slums, but you took whatever price he gave you for your scraps of talismans, magic tools, or just valuable bits of metal. If you didn't like the price, you could fuck off. If you wanted to argue about it, you would be removed.

Phil had a bad back and always said he couldn't lift anything too heavy. He had his golems carry the bits of complainers over to his sister Reba's shop, who put them . . . somewhere. She said she fed them to fleshripper swine to help fatten them up. Truth made a point of never buying her sausages.

On the other hand, Reba's was on the way home from Phil's and was one of two places inside of three miles of home selling fresh food. So. He did do *some* shopping with her. It saved time. And that was the slums: hundreds of thirty-, forty-, or even fifty-story towers packed with tiny apartments and trash-filled halls. Easy access to the subway, a few convenience stores, no grocery stores, and no end of "package stores" where you could load up on Betel, Khat, Skooma, or the cheap liquor of your choice. Always lit with harsh white lights and the clerk behind two inches of spell-hardened glass.

In a single day, Truth had to get his siblings up, dressed, fed, and to school, then hustle for odd jobs, and if there weren't any odd jobs, hunt for scrap. Then while he was working, try to sneak in a bit of cultivation to get to Level One even an hour faster. Then get home, pray to the gods that Dad finally ODed and Mom had died in a ditch somewhere, make dinner, feed the sibs, go over homework, run through the evening routine, get them into bed, *then* cram for the Starbrite Aptitude Test, *then* some dedicated cultivation time so he would get to Level One before the exam date. Which was in a month.

Time was the only thing Truth had less of than money.

Truth hustled back home. It wasn't safe in the slum after dark, and the sun was setting fast. It wasn't really safe during the daytime, either, but a different class of monster came out after dark. During the day, you had the base fiends, the sleepers, and the boomers. Nighttime was for the drunks and for the Ghūl.

The Ghūl didn't like bright lights. Didn't like them at all. They would throw rocks or bricks or whole damn trashcans at anything too bright. Shops still stuck bright, armored lights out front. Because if it was dark enough for the Ghūl to be comfortable, they would hang around. They would start to play. They would probably play with you and all your stuff. And if you were very lucky, you would die in the process. About the only thing that could get the police into the slums was a Ghūl sculpture out in the open, with its materials still alive. Not to clear out the Ghūl, obviously. That would be dangerous! No, the statues were carefully incinerated before they could cause any more harm.

Truth was admitted into the apartment building (romantically called "Towering Heavens Apartment Co. Building 37") when the demon bound to the heavy steel doors recognized his face. The elevator had been used as a toilet again, possibly while someone enjoyed the services advertised in spray paint on the interior. But it was running today, so up he went to "home."

"Close the damn door! Letting the heat out!" Dad growled, lips stained purple from smoking Red Bats. His throne, dominating the living room, was a half-broken wreck of the armchair in front of the scryball. Dad seemed to live in two places: the Red and Black Casino, where he mopped up the spilled drinks and unclogged the toilets, and in the armchair. Blasted on poppy-soaked Red Bat cigarettes and cheap liquor, erasing his awareness of his surroundings by giving his mind over to the scry.

"Who's playing?" Truth moved to the part of the trash-filled main room dubbed the kitchen. He could see the bottom of the rice jar, but there was just enough to stretch some veggies and kelp. Enough for him and the sibs. He shoved aside a stack of empty plastic bags to make room on the counter. He wasn't allowed to throw anything out, because it might be valuable.

"Ah, no good games on. I'm watching that show. You know. That show? With the guy with the tits."

Truth quickly tried to think of all the popular, free shows that might feature a gender-nonconforming person. It was a struggle. He never had time to scry.

"Singing with Meeta?"

"Yeah." Dad snorted at something invisible to Truth and took a drag off a bottle. "None of these assholes sing anything good. It's all girly bullshit." Dad's drink of choice was Beefheart, which he said was schnapps, and maybe it was. Made by Sanchez Intl. Bev., part of the Starbrite family of companies.

What Truth knew about Beefheart was that it was fifteen wen a 75 cl bottle at the shops, and Dad would start hitting him or the sibs if he didn't have it handy. Truth knew how to take a hit, to sway back and make it look like the old man smashed him to the ground without getting hurt. The sibs didn't. Dad somehow was still Level One, despite everything, and Level Zeros like Truth and the sibs had no chance of winning a straight-up fight.

The old man was a Provisional Denizen of Harban City, Subcategory: Criminal. Two full tiers below an actual Citizen and, boy, were his kids living that truth. They were Provisional Denizens of Harban City, Subcategory: Dependents. Entitled to housing so long as they lived with their parents. Entitled to education in the slum technical schools . . . so long as they lived with their parents. Food, clothing, a teddy bear? Your loving parents will doubtless provide. Not that you would be so ungrateful, unfilial, and unwise as to ask.

"Where is Mom?" Truth asked, making his daily prayer that Dad would say "Dead."

"She got a new job, some kind of mushroom thing. She's out." Once again, God failed Truth.

"Great. You heading out tonight?"

"Somebody's got to bring in some money around here, and it ain't going to be you useless mouths. I'm off to the Red and Black. Clean up in here before I get back. Place is a mess. BUT DON'T TOUCH MY SHIT!" Dad broke the spell and looked away from the scryball.

"One month. One month. One month." Truth silently chanted over and over again. One month until the Starbrite Aptitude Test was held. The Starbrite Corporation always needed new workers, and skilled labor got company housing. One month for him to break through to Level One. One month until he was standing with everyone else in the courtyard of Call to Glory Temple, hearing his results and getting that job offer from Starbrite. One month until he could leave this shithole and give his sibs the life they deserved. Away from the gangs and the pimps and the dealers and his evil fucking parents.

"You ain't in school anymore. 'Bout time you found a job," Dad growled as he slipped on his shoes. "Kids today; I swear to god, you got no idea how to live in the real world."

A Starbrite Man Is Always Ready. "You're right, Dad. I'm going to do just that."

"Good. 'Cause I know the Red and Black is always looking for talent that can work on their back." And with a rasping laugh, the Old Man stomped out the door.

CHAPTER 2

LOOKING AT THE STARS

Dinner was never anything special, because Truth didn't know how to cook. What he did know was that if you cut up the veg and put them in a bowl and shoved the bowl inside the hot box (not to be confused with the actual cooking range, which only sometimes worked), in three minutes, you would have steamed vegetables. You did the same with the rice but for five minutes; you let it sit covered for another twenty minutes, and then you had rice. Sometimes the rice was a watery, mushy sludge. Sometimes it was crunchy. In any case, it was food.

His go-to move was a big shake of Adlom seasoning from the big shaker of Adlom Seasoning™ you could buy for four wen at any corner store. It didn't make things taste good, exactly, but at least they tasted like Adlom seasoning, which was an improvement.

The sibs sometimes complained, but since there wasn't anything else to eat, they ate what they got. Mom and Dad only bought food when they were hungry and usually ate it themselves. They had slowly forgotten that feeding the kids was their responsibility, and when Truth reminded them, Mom slapped him into a trash bin and told him to go earn if he was hungry. On his knees, if necessary, and for an idiot like him, it probably was. Truth was thirteen at the time. Even then, he understood—his parents kept the kids around to pocket the welfare money they got for raising them.

He looked at his little siblings, old enough to understand what was going on, already too thin. He nodded at Mom and shoplifted dinner. He quickly found little ways to earn that didn't make him want to kill himself or others.

Truth watched the hot box, waiting for the spell to buzz. "I think I killed someone today. That's fucked up. And I don't really care. That's even more fucked up. I should care. It's not like I don't care about things. I should care about this."

He really didn't, though. And he didn't have the time or energy to make himself care. Somehow, violence came easy to him. Studying was hard. Not wasting money on bullshit was hard. Making sure the sibs didn't get in trouble was hard. Becoming a full Citizen of Harban City was damn hard.

Punching someone in the kidney so that they pissed blood for a week? Easy. Which was fucked up. It didn't touch him emotionally. Hard to say if he got it from Mom or Dad. It wasn't like he ever took a class on fighting or anything.

Truth's dream was to be a talisman maintenance tech. The slum school offered classes for it, and he had perfect attendance. No college needed for the job, on-the-job training, and Starbrite was always hiring them. You could get municipal repair jobs working for Starbrite, which let you accumulate civic merits and eventually raise your status in the city. Plus, the money was good. Sixty grand for a trainee, seventy when you finished your probation, Class C (Lower) housing allowance, and health insurance from day one . . . he had the compensation and benefits package memorized.

The sibs came trooping into the house. They probably passed Dad on the street. No bruises or injuries. The convoy system worked again!

"All right! Good job at school today. Scrub up and get ready for dinner."

"Okaaaaay," the sibs chorused.

Harmony, the second oldest boy after Truth, was sixteen and showing it. All gangly elbows and wild hair and a patchy, desperately unwise attempt at a mustache. Truth was wisely clean-shaven. Clean-ish shaven. He could go a few days without shaving, and why rush? Stubble looked manly. He hoped. Anyway, his brown hair was pretty neatly parted and looked kind of like the handsome man in the advertisement, so Truth felt like he was winning there.

Then there was Sophia, who just had her fifteenth birthday and was also clearly feeling it. Puberty had hit her a little later than some of her classmates, and when it arrived, it hit like a ton of bricks. She had filled out nicely, Truth thought, and had the hard-eyed look that said he had explained the facts of life to her sufficiently well.

Vigor was the baby of the family at thirteen and, in Truth's opinion, the second handsomest after him. Which was a little rough, given that he didn't rate himself as particularly good-looking. Maybe if Vigor grew up in Starbrite employee housing, he wouldn't be stunted from malnourishment. Truth worried the most about Vigor. He was small and deceptively weak-looking, but Truth could see the venom in him.

One more month. One more month, and they could escape this bullshit. One month, and he would be Level One, with his own real job, emancipated from his evil parents.

Dinner was wolfed down, every grain eaten, the dishes washed, dried put away, all in half an hour. The dishes were the one thing Truth managed to keep really clean. Everything else was covered in empty bags or boxes, collected coupons that expired years before, piles of unsold goods from some ancient scam of Mom's. Clearing space at the table to eat or work was a careful dance, shifting things enough to create space but not so much that they faced the hideous charge of "Touching my shit." A crime punishable by beatings.

The sickly yellow light from the one overhead lamp fell directly on the table. It was time for the serious business of the night—studying.

The Starbrite Aptitude Test was the initial screening. Where you went after that was down to whatever specialization or job you wanted to test for and any points a family member could give your application. Plus, of course, your magical aptitude test, but pretty much any Level One could pass *that*.

The Medicis, Truth's family, had never worked for Starbrite. Their family was *generationally* trash. But it would end with him, Truth swore. Starbrite was his dream. He would break the cycle. Because the alternative was joining up with a gang, hustling and killing for a thin gold chain and sportswear manufactured in batches of a hundred thousand by the people with honest jobs. Getting hooked on smack and booze, becoming a monster of violence until the slums killed him. Just like his Old Man.

The siblings got their heads down and studied around the little table in the middle of the main room of the apartment. The older ones helped the younger ones; the younger ones did their best. Everybody got it. Education was the ticket out. And they wanted out.

"Hey, Truth?" Vigor asked without looking up from his textbook.

"Yeah?"

"Why don't you go be a prizefighter? It's got to be easier than studying."

"Oh, yeah, way easier." Truth nodded. "But how much do they make?"

"Fawkes versus Piccolo, five million wen purse!" Sophia piped up. She got worryingly excited watching the fights.

"Yeah, but that's the top two guys. How much do they make fighting down in the Cage?"

This question was met with shrugs.

"I asked. Ten percent of the door. An extra hundred wen for the winner. That's it. And if you think the door numbers might be crooked . . . they are. And the fights are fixed. So, even if I was in a clean fight, I would be walking away with less than what a maintenance tech earns in a week with Starbrite, and I would have my head kicked in, too." Truth spoke calmly. He had looked into this years before and periodically checked back in to see if anything changed. It didn't.

"Still, though. I bet you would get bigger and bigger fights in no time." This was Vigor again.

"Rigged fights, remember? It wouldn't be worth it to go gangster." Harmony shook his head, sounding disappointed. He also liked watching the fights. "Well, unless you don't get into Starbrite. Then it's totally worth it."

Study time was almost done when misfortune fell on the siblings—Mom came home dragging a big suitcase behind her.

"Hello, my sweeties! Muah! Muah!" She planted huge kisses on Vigor and Sophia. "Studying hard? Such good children. Really makes me feel like I have been raising you right."

"Hi, Mom," they chorused. If they ignored her, she threw an unholy fit, maybe even broke things. It wasn't worth it.

"I have such amazing news. Where is your father?"

"Down the casino. But tell us your amazing news," Truth said. Keep it short and focused on her. That was half the trick for conversations with Mom.

"I really should wait. But this is so amazing! Oh, sweetie, this is it! This is what makes us rich!"

He knew it was coming, but the same sick feeling as always settled down into his stomach.

"Now, I one hundred percent believe in XextraTee. I think it is just an amazing product, and I really, really regret that so many people just can't see the life-changing benefits it can bring them. But. As a serious businesswoman, sometimes you just have to admit it's not the right time for a product."

The siblings just nodded numbly. Mom had spent every penny she could earn or borrow, buying XextraTee products. One time, she sold the hot box and screamed for hours when Dad called her on it. He might not give a shit about her or them, but he would have his damn soup hot when he watched his shows.

"So. I am so. SO. EXCITED. To tell you that I am now the *exclusive* Product Ambassador for MegaShroom for Harban City Sales Development Zone 348. The number one leading provider of *Cultivated* Ganoderma, each capsule, suppository, and tea is carefully assayed by master alchemists to have one hundred percent *pure* Level two–plus quality, spiritually dense reishi as well as twenty-seven other bio-spiritually activated mega-micro-nutrients!"

There it was. No, wait. Almost there.

"And because I have *such amazing experience* in the direct marketing environment with such a rich peer-to-peer sales history, I was able to make a serious connection with a . . . wait for it . . . *Diamond*-level Product Ambassador. *Mister* Sewell is *the* man for the entire North West quadrant of Harban City. Can you even imagine? Well, I don't mind telling you—you are old enough to know these things now, Sophia—that a bit of a wiggle and a bit of a giggle, and he was just *putty* in my hands. *Putty*, and oh, did I play."

Truth thought that, in her youth, his mom might have been of average attractiveness. Four kids, a drunk, violent bum of a husband, and life in the slums generally burned away whatever pretty she might have had. But the city paid way less subsidy to single moms than married couples, and the amount of subsidy rose per kid. So, there she was, in all her wretched glory. Anyone "charmed" by her attentions must be incredibly desperate or incredibly cruel. Given that Mom was also a Provisional Denizen, Subcategory: Criminal, Truth thought it was probably the latter.

Truth didn't really care either way. Which was fucked up. But he had too much going on to care about caring about it.

"I'm afraid that Mommy got an entire suitcase of the Deluxe MegaShroom line. At Diamond Ambassador prices. I am so bad, I know. I know!"

There it was. The multilevel-marketing shoe, as ever, fell on their faces. The names and tiers changed. The scam never did. And Mom dove at it Every. Single. Time. And she got completely burnt on it. Every. Single. Time. But it was like the lottery. You can't win if you don't play, and if you don't play, you will never leave the screaming purgatory of your slumrat life.

Every positive connection they might have had, every relative that could have put in a good word somewhere, every neighbor that might have helped out when they were literally starving, all gone. Burned by Mom's endless "hustle." Nobody wanted to have anything to do with this entrepreneurial plague rat. Or her kids.

The study session broke up fast. They went back to their room to cultivate before bed, leaving Mom to celebrate with a bottle of Fairy Blossom Dew. A schnapps, Truth believed, available everywhere for fifteen wen a bottle.

I killed a man today for eleven wen and my shoes, thought Truth. *That's fucked up.*

The next morning, he watched the sibs convoy out to school. He saw a face he recognized, peering out of an alley. Truth launched himself out of the apartment, down the stairs, out the door of the apartment building, down the street, and toward the alley Sophia had stopped by. Smiling and maybe flirting? He didn't break stride as he scooped up an empty beer bottle, holding it like a club.

"Help you, Thierrie?" he yelled. The pimps were finally coming for Sophia.

CHAPTER 3

THE REAL REAL

Thierrie liked to call himself "The Charisma of the Streets." Truth liked to call him "A fucking drug-dealing pedophile pimp," but only if he was being polite. And Thierrie was grinning at his sister, luring her away from her brothers with a smoke.

Truth had told him once before. Looked like Thierrie needed a reminder.

"Think you got the wrong street, Thierrie. You definitely got the wrong person."

"Nope, don't think I do." Thierrie's grin got a lot nastier as Sophia ran to catch up with the sibs. "You day-drinking? Just like the old man, huh?" He glanced at the empty bottle in Truth's hand.

"Thought you might be thirsty, so I brought you something. Or maybe you need some high-speed dentistry." Truth's voice was very even. "Fuck off, Thierrie. Nothing good here for you."

"Big talk from a Level Zero. Real big." Thierrie wasn't smiling anymore.

"Don't act like you got a spell worth shit. I know you, Thierrie. We all know you. You got a busted Sharp spell from Skellie when you thought Ninth Street was going to be a thing, and you ain't got better since."

"More than enough to chop your ass up. And that's the Truth." Thierrie's fingers turned metallic and pointed. Truth couldn't be bothered to roll his eyes at the "joke." He had heard them all before. After a tense moment, it was Thierrie who relaxed and removed his spell.

"You know what? I don't need to bother with your ass. One month and you getcha green hat. For one. Whole. Year. You know me, and I know you. One month and your cute little brothers and sister are all on their own. You know what? I don't think Harmy is ready for it. Talks a good game, but he ain't shit. So I don't have to do shit." Thierrie lit the cigarette he had tempted Sophia with.

"They will come to me. And there will be not one goddamn thing you can do about it. Or maybe I can cut a deal with your dad. The Red and Black or me? It's all the same to him." Thierrie swaggered off. Truth stood in the mouth of the alley, wanting to puke. Thierrie was right. The only way out was to get into Starbrite. Get the housing. Get the backing. Get the sibs emancipated. He was running out of time.

Truth started by hitting up all the local shops and small factories that might need a runner or some day labor. He got a few chores, pulled in twenty wen, which he reckoned was pretty good.

Then it was back to the path along the canal, fishing out trash and hoping for treasure. Not bad, not bad, a few busted bits of flying bird mounts or spell chariots that scraped off over a bridge. Or were just tossed in the canal because someone didn't want to pay the dump. Bless them.

It wasn't a bad haul, and the sun was still some distance from the horizon when he decided to call it a day. His studying had been messed up last night, and he wanted to try and catch up a bit today. Every minute counted. Every second. But they needed money for food and, if he could possibly save up enough, cultivation supplements. Real ones, not the bullshit his mom peddled.

Truth tried not to think about Thierrie. Or the neighborhood kids Thierrie gave a "fun, easy job." Then Thierrie gave them a little base when the johns got too rough, and things weren't fun or easy, and it all got too much. Then gave them more base when it kept on being too much, but this time it wasn't free. No, he just took the cost out of their earnings. And he always kept the earnings. They just needed to ask him for money when they needed it. It was much safer that way. Oh, yes. Much safer. His little druggie whores couldn't be trusted with cash. Look how fast they burned out on base. Then he needed new whores.

The thing that fucked Truth up the most was that Thierrie thought *he was one of the good ones.* He really, truly did. He didn't smack his whores around much. He at least tried to buy clean drugs. He would, actually, give them money if they asked. He even helped them find squats they could huddle together in, sharing the costs and food. Sharing what comfort they could. Keeping them handy for when Thierrie wanted to drop by and enjoy his own stock.

One month, and he had to do his National Service. One month, and he couldn't keep the pimps and dealers away. The only way out was Starbrite. Pass the test, join up, put the sibs in company apartments, away from all the bullshit while he served. Emancipate them from his parents. It could be possible. But he had to, *had to* pass the test. Or the sibs were dead. They were fighters, but not like him. They would slip, and the slums would fishhook 'em.

It wasn't like there was anyone else looking out for them. Not like there was anyone they could go to. No CPS for slumrat Denizens. No relatives would put them up for longer than a week. Mom had thoroughly burned all those bridges, and Dad pissed schnapps and poppy on the ashes.

One month. Twenty-nine days now. He half-jogged to Phil's, the scrap in a heavy sack over his shoulders. No time to waste. Not one minute.

Phil liked a nice, orderly shop. You put your junk on the scale, a blue light flashed, and the scale said what the junk was and how much it weighed. Then Phil gave you a price. You took the price or fucked off. Or argued with the golems.

Truth queued up quietly. It was early yet, so it was mostly people trying to sell their trash rather than the real scavengers. Phil didn't bother to let most of them push their shit on the scale. If they complained—golem.

"Ah, the funniest-named trash picker I know. Anything good today, Truth?" Phil asked with faint interest.

"Some good bits, some okay metal. Even got an intact Lift spell."

"Oh? Now I'm a bit interested. Toss it on the scale."

Truth did, the light went up, and the spell went *Ding!* Sand moved on a little tray in front of Phil, laying out what all was in there.

"Way to talk a big game, kid." He reached into the drawer and carefully laid out a few ones and fives. Catching Truth's eye, he slipped five twenties under them. "This is barely scrappable." There were other scavs around. And regardless, in the slums, you don't flash the cash without a way to defend it.

"I'd ask if you could do any better, but . . ."

"Forget it. You want more, argue with the golems."

"I'm not that strong. But hey, I'm going to join Starbrite soon!" Truth half-grinned. "That's got to be worth something."

"Sure is. Forget it, *sir.*" Phil rolled his eyes. "Look, even if you did join Starbrite, so what? You're still nobody, a weak little punk in a company that does not give even half a fart about you. Only thing you can rely on is you."

"And your golems."

Phil raised his eyebrows. "Golems I made and paid for. My strength. You? Got nothing. And your whole big thing is you are going to join a *fancy* gang." He waved his hand. "Beat it. You're holding up the line."

And off he went. Phil was okay, but there was only so much advice Truth was willing to listen to.

One hundred and thirty-seven wen. Best haul in ages. Better than some weeks. That Lift spell must have been in even better shape than he thought. But how to spend it? His instinct was to save, but . . . this was a crucial moment. He had to get over the hurdle to Level One before the test. The difference in treatment and available jobs for a Level Zero and Level One were . . . significant. You weren't a kid anymore. You got paid what you were really worth.

On the other hand, the sibs hadn't had any good food in a long while. One meal wasn't going to fix everything in terms of nutrition, but some more protein would be huge. Maybe if he got a big sack of dry sea-monster flakes. You could boil them in soup. They sold them for uptown aquariums and fish farms, but you could eat them. They didn't taste good, but what was new about that?

Truth went back and forth. He bought more rice, some vegetables that would keep, and a big block of tofu. That would keep them going for a while. One hundred and nineteen wen left.

He would later figure out what they really needed. One month left. Twenty-eight days and eight hours left.

Truth dropped into the cultivation exercises. It was one of his favorite parts of the day. Just stretching and breathing, imagining the breath swirling down into the little depression over his heart where his first spell slot would be. Level One.

"Cosmic rays" was what he learned in school. But it always sounded phony. Still better than "stellar rays," which was the other thing they got called. No difference, apparently. Not that Truth knew what "cosmic" or "stellar" meant, really. Somehow it never came up on the streets. But he knew he had to know it if he wanted to get *off* the streets, so he learned it.

The stars generated invisible energy that sweeps across the universe, and if you knew how, you could use them to open up spell slots. Make you stronger than any born human could be. Faster. Smarter, maybe. "Cosmic rays." That could travel through space, but you could breathe in the energy. What a stupid lie.

But it worked. He got a little stronger every day. Level One was so close, he could taste it. This was when a rich kid, or even a less poor kid, would take a supplement. Even if their parents had to scrimp for half a year, they would have *something* to help push their kid through that final barrier. Put them in the best shape for the SAT.

He looked at the ashtray next to the broken-down armchair. Dad smoked Red Bats, the knockoff Golden Bats they sold in casinos. Everyone knew they were soaked with poppy. Didn't seem to bother Dad any. Probably why he liked them.

The sibs kept an emergency stash of cash in a hollow spot they had carved out of the wall where it joined the floor. They disguised it with a rat's nest. Not that their parents ever checked, but after Dad ran their pockets for drink money a couple of times, they knew better than to hold cash. Truth hid the money. It wasn't enough for a real supplement. Not even a hundredth of an elixir. But there were some knockoff things that might speed up his cultivation a bit. He would save a few more days, a week tops. Then. Level One. His first step to safety.

CHAPTER 4

A MOTHER'S LOVE

The evening routine went about as well as it could. Truth kept his parents from interfering with the evening routine as best he could. He and the sibs studied pretty well. The practice tests weren't a rousing success, but he thought he would make it. He was consistently passing the talisman-maintenance section but still struggled with the general knowledge part. Just a little more. He wasn't there yet, but . . . just a little more.

Fortunately, Dad had pressing business at a dice game, and Mom was fretting over shifting her latest drug. It seemed that MegaShroom wasn't exactly flying off the shelves. Truth guessed that she hadn't sold a single box. The thing about multilevel marketing was that you either had to sell horizontally to suckers that knew and trusted you or vertically, recruiting new marks to labor under you. Mom had burned every horizontal bridge she had years before, and she wasn't nearly charismatic enough to recruit people vertically.

Same old story. Over and over again. But that was the other secret to conversations with Mom—never let her try to sell you things. Never let her get you to sell things for her. It never, not once, ever, worked out.

The sibs quietly went to their room and started a round of cultivation. The two youngest shared a bed. Truth and Harmony were in bunks. There wasn't much room to stretch and move, so they got used to avoiding each other. Or standing on the bed and doing it, but it never worked as well.

The morning routine was more of the same: Dad passed out in the broken armchair, a slice of cheap bread washed down with water for breakfast. Mom was still asleep. She probably had a late night, judging by the empty bottle on the table. Mom usually didn't drink as much as Dad, so . . . probably not a good sign. But he couldn't fix it, so Truth resolved to ignore it.

No Thierrie this morning, which didn't exactly make Truth feel better. Just to be sure, he invested some precious money-earning time walking them all the way to school. Nothing happened, but the sibs were a little happy about it. And complained a lot, of course, but that's siblings for you. Truth had the constant fear of what would happen when his parents could no longer collect his welfare subsidy. Would they push the sibs harder to earn, no matter how? Maybe cut back on the little food they bought? He *had* to get them out of there!

Back to running odd jobs, only today, nobody wanted help. It was well before noon that he gave up and started trawling the canal. It was not too long before nightfall that he turned up at Phil's and got a miserable three wen. Dinner would be light tonight. Despite that, he didn't want to touch their savings. It was the sign of hope.

Truth looked up at the billboard of the handsome Starbrite Man lighting the beautiful, presumably Starbrite, Woman's cigarette. Golden Bats were a luxury product. Not only did they contain (so the advertisements went) the finest blend of choice tobaccos, they were also laced with mild cultivation stimulants. You wouldn't break through to your next level just because you smoked Golden Bats, but you would progress a little faster. The rich and beautiful, getting stronger than you and richer than you, faster than you.

And they had the System. Only Starbrite had the System, and if you had the System . . . you were the next best thing to a god.

A Starbrite Man Is Always Ready. Truth nodded at the slogan. A promise, he thought, and a threat.

Starbrite didn't hire Level Zero workers. You could be a trainee, but you wouldn't get the System or the real benefits of being in Starbrite until you leveled up. Like housing. And legal support. Truth sighed and started running home. There was a persistent myth that hard physical labor sped up cultivation. Truth was past ready to take a gamble. Besides, he could intercept the sibs' convoy back from school. A little bonus.

"Hey, Truth, guess what?" Harmony shouted cheerfully.

"What's up?" Truth asked.

"I got the janitor gig at the school! Two hours a day, one before school and one after." Harmony boasted.

"That is awesome! I am so happy for you!" Truth really was, too. The school offered work opportunities to kids in need, but since that was everyone in the slums, the jobs were damn hard to get. They also paid less than what a Level One adult would demand, but . . . that was reality.

"When do you start?" Truth asked.

"Next term. Actually, two days before the next term starts, to get the school in shape before classes start." Harmony sounded very responsible, wanting to show off.

"Awesome, awesome, awesome!" Truth smiled. He didn't think about the possibility of not getting into Starbrite. He refused to permit the existence of such a reality. But some low, weakling part of him was glad the sibs would have some income while he did his National Service.

Day 28 before the exam—not a complete loss after all. Do the scheduled studying, throw in some extra cultivation . . . it might even qualify as a good day. In fact—

"Tell you what. To celebrate, let's buy some candy." Truth grinned at the siblings.

"Eeeh? Can we afford it?" Sophia asked, but she was already flashing her brilliant teeth in a grin. Truth insisted they brush twice a day, and it paid off.

"Just this once. I'll get it from the hidey-hole."

It's not like a couple of wen would matter either way. Even tainted trash culti-vation support cost hundreds of wen. And morale mattered. So, a small indulgence could be made to celebrate Harmony's achievement.

They trooped back into the house, chatting happily. Dad was half-cut, zoned out as he stared blankly into space above the scry. Mom was fluttering about, humming to herself. Truth looked over at the sibs and then glanced at Mom. They got the clue.

"Hey, Mom! How was your day?"

"Oh, you know me! Always working my hardest for my little angels!"

Truth slid into their room and stopped dead. The beds had been pushed around and half shoved back into place. The blankets and pillows had been thrown around and not really put back properly. The drawers had been tossed. The schoolbooks they hadn't sold were scattered around, with one old volume having its spine sliced open. And down by the corner, a rat's nest had been pulled out of the wall.

Truth checked just to be sure, but he knew. The money was gone. He assumed it was Dad, but . . . on the bed that Vigor and Sophia shared were two packs of Deluxe MegaShroom Supplements, and on his pillow, a box of Deluxe MegaShroom MindBSharp! Tea.

He didn't remember moving back into the family room. He could hardly see. The edges of his vision were turning black as he hyper-focused on Mom's smiling face.

"SURPRISE! I know you kids have been worried about exams, and I thought, what can I get these little angels that they can't get anywhere else?"

"*You stole our money.*" Truth ground out the words. His hands were shaking. Mom looked outraged.

"How dare you!" she screeched. "I never stole a thing in my life! First of all, *you* don't have any money. Living under our roof, anything you earn is *our* money. Second, you know perfectly well you aren't passing a damn thing without help. MegaShroom is the best. It's the only damn thing that gives you a hope in hell of a real job anywhere, and what do you do? You scream at me like an animal," Mom shouted.

"YOU STOLE OUR MONEY! YOU STOLE FROM YOUR FUCKING KIDS!" Truth shouted back. He was panting, his hands clenched into fists. He could hardly see through the haze of hate. Level One be damned, he would drop her ass like the sack of shit it was!

He felt something moving behind him, but before he could react, he was knocked spinning to the floor. Dad was out of his chair, roaring with anger. Truth could see a dozen ways to drop his ragged ass—and none of them mattered. Dad was Level One, and Truth wasn't. Technique didn't mean a damn thing when the difference of power was that absolute. Dad blurred forward, almost too fast for Truth's eyes to follow. He tried to roll to his feet, but Dad's bare foot caught him in the gut and knocked him over again. His gut exploded, watery vomit bursting onto the dirty linoleum.

"How dare you raise your voice to your mother like that! You little shit!" Dad slurred. Truth scrambled up, using the wall for support. When Dad started throwing hands, he could usually roll with the punches. Not this time. This time, he got the full taste of the difference in levels.

"You Level Zero piece of trash, acting like your shit don't stink, and now you think you can yell at your Mom like that? Fuck you. Fuck you. Maybe you need to spend some time on the street, huh? Think that would fix your attitude? Mr. Studies-all-the-time? You think someone is going to hire a piece of shit like you?" Dad was swaying.

Part of him wanted to say "Fuck it" and go. But he looked past his victoriously nodding mom and saw his siblings. If he was gone, his parents would turn on them. And he knew exactly how they planned to earn off them. He could only protect them if he was around and if he got into Starbrite. So, he bit his tongue and dropped his hands.

"Apologize." Mom sniffled. "Apologize at once. From now on, every evening, you kids will empty your pockets. Any money you earn will be held by your father and I for safekeeping. You understand? And when you do wash out of the Army, you will be paying rent to stay here. Am I understood?"

Truth felt whatever thin grip he had on his temper strain almost to the breaking point. And then he looked at his siblings. He lowered his head.

"I apologize. We'll do it like you say."

Twenty. Seven. Days.

CHAPTER 5

WHAT MUST BE DONE

Truth didn't respect trading violence for money. There was no future in it. Not as a gangster, armed robber, prizefighter, or soldier. Watching carefully, most of those jobs were done by the broke, who stayed broke, then died young. On the other hand, violence was the only thing he was really good at, and *his parents wanted to treat him like a slave,* so . . . fuck it, really.

He felt floaty, like he was drifting through an unreal world. His gut burned from where Dad had kicked it. It was hard to really focus; his eyes kept slipping around. Truth started sorting out his targets. Ordinary folks were out. This was the slums. They had no money. Stores? They had more money. They also had armed shopkeepers, spell wards, and private security. Or golems. An advanced option at the moment. His armed robbery had to be done with a length of wood or pipe.

That left criminals. Which was its own flavor of challenge. They were all armed, for one, and willing to use their spells instantly. Most of them were in gangs, too. And while they certainly had more money than he did, he had long since noticed that these thugs and gangsters lived in the same damn slum he did. Most of them lived with their mom in the same kind of apartments as him. Eating the same shitty food as him. Wishing to god that the heat spell would work right this winter, because the windows didn't keep the wind out and the walls didn't keep the heat in. Just like him.

Truth was moving without thinking. Since he couldn't imagine running errands in this strange, floaty state, his feet carried him down the narrow steps to the path along the canal. The subway screamed and roared as it passed, the worm demon thrashing more than usual. He shook out his crappy plastic fishing net and set to trawling. Trash. More trash. Other trash. So on and so on, as he walked up the canal.

Truth hauled in another load of wet garbage, the sun's reflection off the canal almost blinding him. It smelled awful. Like rot and sickness personified. The light-headed feeling intensified. Was this the real world? Was all this pain, filth, and hurt really all that there was? Was his dream to join Starbrite just a dream to join a gang? That couldn't be it, right?

"The path to freedom is inward. You walk it through self-mastery." He remembered sitting in his undyed wool smock as the great philosopher sat on the long stone porch

and lectured. He could remember every crevice and valley of the teacher's face. But he had never met them. He was remembering something that had never happened.

Truth shook his head and tossed the trash back into the water. It had all gotten to be too much. Clearly, he was losing it. At least this was a nice hallucination. The teacher seemed like an okay guy. Truth walked a little farther and threw the net back in the water again. He and the sibs would probably starve if he didn't get enough scrap. It didn't get any more real than that.

It wasn't a very good day of trawling. Lots of trash. Lots of empty bottles and cigarette packs and individual plastic sachets that held exactly not quite enough shampoo or soap for one wash. Because a lot of people were too broke to buy a whole bottle of shampoo or soap but they could scrape together just enough for a sachet or two when the itching and smell got too bad.

Some spells could clean you perfectly, Truth knew. Talismans that would leave you refreshed, sweat-free, and fragrant. He had heard that they were standard in the high-end gymnasiums in the rich part of the city.

Truth let himself slowly collapse on the filthy path next to the canal. He wasn't crying, exactly. He just . . . couldn't anymore. Even if he made big money today, somehow, he would have to find a place to hide it. His thief parents would steal it if he brought it home. He needed to study. How could he study in that house? The sibs needed real food and also needed to study. But could they? What would happen next year? Could they really keep whatever money they earned away from the grasping hands of Mom and Dad? It was all too much.

He didn't know how long he lay by the canal side. But then he got up again and got back to trawling. Because they needed food to study. And that meant they needed money. So, he got up and did it.

Thirteen wen for a day's work. They could eat . . . something . . . with that. Rice, certainly. Maybe add a cheap can of off-brand vegetable stew? It wouldn't split far with four, but it would add some nutrients and texture. He wasn't very sure what nutrients, but he knew you needed vegetables. And vegetable stew was the cheapest.

He did the shopping and started heading home. Truth kept his eye out for the sibs. It was about time for them to be making their way home. As the shadows got longer and the pink-orange sunset blazed like a trash fire through the fumes from the alchemical refineries. As the various monsters of the slums shook off their daytime torpor and started thinking about hunting. Thinking about getting that next fix.

Truth drifted home with the groceries and a couple of wen floating in his pocket. He would toss them to a beggar before he got home. Maybe getting that fix would be a little less horrible tonight. He passed an alley, and a flash of movement caught the corner of his eye. Truth quickly moved to put the corner of the alley between him and whatever it was, dropping the groceries and getting ready to kick off in a hurry.

Nothing happened. He kept waiting. Tweakers and fiends were short on patience.

Nothing. Truth picked up the groceries and checked around the corner. Way down the alley he saw Thierrie. He had his arm around Vigor's shoulder and was leading him away. Toward where the hourly hotels were.

His hand fished out the can of vegetable soup, and he started sprinting down the alley. Truth dropped low as he ran, each foot landing softly on the concrete, then planted firmly, then the muscles in his legs exploded as he launched himself forward. Again and again. Closing on the vermin.

Thierrie heard him coming. Turned his head, and his eyes opened wide. His fingers went metallic and sharp as he shoved Vigor toward Truth. Truth took a half-step to the side and let Vigor slide off his flank. Still low to the ground, he swung the soup can at Thierrie's knee.

But Thierrie was Level One. The knee turned just in time, making the crushing strike a glancing one. Then Thierrie's sharp fingers dove for Truth's neck. Fast. Too fast. Truth had to launch himself past Thierrie. Truth was out of place now. Thierrie was over his shock. He came in fast, one hand clawing for Truth's eyes, the other stabbing toward his gut.

Truth slid back and to the side, keeping just out of reach of the claws. He smashed the soup can down on the middle knuckles of the hand coming for his neck. He just wanted to knock it away so he could kick Thierrie's gut. The metal-covered knuckles made the most incredible crunching sound.

They both froze a second. Thierrie unable to comprehend how his metal hand broke, Truth unable to understand how he wasn't gutted already. "Just how shitty was that Sharp spell you got? Skellie fucked you good, huh?"

"Fuck you!" Thierrie whipped the other hand around, going for the gut again. Truth shifted back again, but he had run out of room in the alley. The metal fingers scraped over his belly. Long gashes in his shirt and leaking red stripes below them.

Truth threw a knee to Thierrie's nuts, then moved to close distance. He wasn't Thierrie's match in the clinch but couldn't keep range. The knee missed. Thierrie wasn't having it. He hopped back, swinging the broken hand like a flail to keep Truth at arm's length. The intact hand rose like a spear, pointing at Thruth's throat. Thierrie lunged.

Truth slid his empty hand along the inside of Thierrie's spear hand. He let the sharp edge slip past as he wrapped his arm around Thierrie's and locked Thierrie's wrist under his armpit. Thierrie was stronger than Truth. Faster. Those things worked against him when Truth rotated his body, putting all of Thierrie's strength, speed, and weight on his hyperextended elbow. The brutal snap echoed off the walls of the alley.

Thierrie screamed in rage. His leg came sweeping up and took out Truth's legs. Truth made a textbook breakfall and tried to roll away. Thierrie's shitty knockoff sneaker smashed his chest, knocking the wind out of him. Truth managed to get his arms up, protected his head from a stomp, but couldn't stop another kick to his gut. His stomach was already half-torn by Dad. He couldn't help it; he puked out what watery little remained in him. The soup can went flying.

"Fuck you, Truth! Fuck you! Your whole shitty family will whore for me, you hear me? You hear me?!" The kicks came endlessly; Truth tried to defend himself, but he couldn't get up off the ground. "I will own their asses! Every fucking day, I'll fuck 'em. Every fucking—"

There was a deep *thunk* sound.

Thierrie's eyes rolled up, and he slowly slid to his knees. Foam dribbled from his mouth. Standing behind him was Vigor, dressed in his "date" clothes, holding the soup can.

CHAPTER 6

THE OLDEST TRADE

Thierrie had pissed himself. From what Truth could see, Vigor's shot to the back of the head was the first really serious damage Thierrie took in the fight. He had a broken hand and arm but nothing remotely fatal. This was going to be fatal unless Thierrie got treatment soon.

"Good job." Truth struggled to his feet. Everything, *everything* hurt. But he had a job to do. "Please give me the soup can."

Vigor looked at him, bewildered. Then looked at the can he was holding and handed it over.

"Thank you; it's dinner tonight." Truth shambled over to Vigor and gave him a little hug. "We are going to talk this over, but not right this second, okay?"

"Okay," Vigor whispered.

"Good. Please go get the rice in the bag at the end of the alley. I don't want anyone to steal it."

"Okay." Vigor didn't move. "Truth?"

"Yes?"

"I want to watch you do it. I know what you are going to do." He looked up at Truth with something inexplicable, dark, in his eyes. "I need to see it."

"That's pretty fucked up, bro. This is the first person I have for sure killed, you know?"

"I . . . Honestly, no, I didn't know. We always thought you had some bodies on you. You always come back with food," Vigor said without heat.

Truth wanted to laugh at that but couldn't. Hadn't he been considering armed robbery all day?

"Well. It was mostly odd jobs and hunting for scrap in the canal. You can't make much money doing that, but you can make a little, and it's safe enough."

Truth looked down on Thierrie. He was starting to seize, shaking like he had a fever. He would almost certainly die if left alone. *Almost* certainly. Truth tried to hate Thierrie. The petty cruelty of him. The shitty gang he ran with. The base slaves slowly dying in cockroach-infested squats. The rape. The children he had ruined. Truth let a trickle of breath out in a long stream. In the end, he didn't care about any of that. Thierrie was a danger to the sibs. To him.

Truth raised the soup can and smashed it down again. And again. And a third time. No pulse. The can was pretty fucked looking, but that was normal enough in the slums. He was slick with blood now. Head wounds bled a lot. Truth's hands were covered—the blood cooling fast and starting to turn tacky. The can was covered too. At least it wasn't leaking. Thierrie was leaking. All that life just . . . pissed away into the concrete. Back to the shitty world that made him.

"All right. Go get the rice. Then you can help me shove the body into a dumpster."

Truth leaned down and started patting down the corpse. It was a pretty unpleasant job, what with the literal piss and shit soaking through the trousers. Worth it, though. Thierrie had almost four hundred wen on him. Not to mention a half-full vial of base, a pipe, and a little bottle of some blue potion he didn't recognize.

Since his hands were already filthy, he kept on searching. No luck. The so-called Charisma of the Streets had some cash, some drugs, a broken Sharp spell, and the clothes on his back.

The two brothers hauled Thierrie to a dumpster that hadn't been emptied in a long time. It already smelled like death, so Truth figured it was a perfect fit. Vigor held the lid up, looking half-killed by the smell, while Truth tried to muscle the body up and in. This process did not go well. The body slid around. The excrement slid around. And covered him. This was not a good day, Truth decided. He contemplated jumping in the canal to rinse some of the filth off, then remembered why that was suicidal. He'd have to find a public toilet or something.

Oh, wait, they were in the slums. "Public toilets" weren't a thing that existed there.

"Did you notice his hands?" Truth asked.

"You mean how weak they were?"

"Yeah. Sharp enough to slice me open, probably would have pierced clean through me if he landed his shot, but basically no reinforcement on the top of his hands. Fragile little bitch."

Vigor thought about it for a moment. "Is that what you meant by the spell being busted?"

"Yeah. A real Sharp spell at Level One turns both hands into cutting and piercing machines. It also hardens the hands up, so you could punch it through four centimeters of steel plate and not break your bones into tiny pieces. Apparently, at Level Five, it's doing pure energy damage. Of course, a real Sharp spell costs north of forty grand. More if it's military grade." Truth looked up at the various windows off the alley. This was some kind of big commercial building, but they must have a bathroom, right? And it sure looked abandoned or semi-abandoned.

"Is that why you are so fixated on getting into Starbrite? The System? No need to ever worry about busted spells?"

"Part of it, yeah. But the bigger part is Class C housing. Starbrite provides really good apartments, cheap, for employees and their families. I would take you, Sophia, and Harmony, and we all move in together. You guys can go to a Starbrite school, get a *real* education. Doctors that will actually treat you and not charge a fortune." Truth's eyes were fiery.

"Mom and Dad would never let us go." Vigor didn't sound sad. More numb. Despairing.

"Nah, I asked. Starbrite is like its own special country inside the country. As long as I stand in place of the parents, they can push through the paperwork emancipating you from Mom and Dad. Apparently, it's just a form. They fill out the names, press a button, and a minute later, it comes back from the Ministry approved." Truth grinned.

"How is that possible?" Vigor's eyes went wide.

Truth started chuckling. It was a wet, unpleasant sound. He was covered in bruises, and he was pretty sure he would piss blood tonight. "How much business does Starbrite do in Jeon?"

"I dunno. A lot?"

"Twenty percent. Twenty wen out of every hundred earned and spent in the entire country. All by themselves, twenty percent. And they have the best-paying jobs, with the best benefits, and the goddamn System. So, if they want to help their employees get family out of a jam, it's no problem at all." Vigor looked startled at that, then frowned, thinking it through.

"Now. Keep a lookout for me." Truth found a basement window whose protective bars had started rotting out of the concrete. It took some prying and creative masonry, but they were able to break in. It took a while to find a bathroom, but thanks be to God, the water came from a talisman, not from pipes. Clean, fresh, and sweet. Shame there wasn't any soap, but this much was already a miracle.

"Hey, Vigor?" Truth asked, not looking over at his youngest sibling as he scrubbed up.

"Yeah?"

"What were you doing with Thierrie?"

Vigor frowned a little, then smoothed his face out again. He reached into a pocket and pulled out a little twist of gray powder wrapped in clear plastic.

"Rat poison. I figured he was going to try and get me drunk or high if I gave him the chance, and I could slip it to him. Then rob him. If he was still alive, a broken bottle to the throat." Vigor's voice came out flat.

Truth paused for a minute. Then started washing again. "A lot of ways that could go wrong," he softly said.

"You have a better idea? Because Mom and Dad are going to kill us. They are going to rob us, screw our chances at the SAT or college or anything. Which is just killing us slow and mean. They said they want to keep you as a slave, Truth!" His voice was rising, shouting by the end. "We can't trust anyone. They all want to fuck us! So, we have to hunt them first!"

Truth didn't know what to say. He had come to the same conclusions. But it was different when he planned to do it himself rather than his baby brother.

"Thierrie had three hundred and ninety-seven wen, some base, a pipe, and a vial of something I don't recognize, but it's probably a roofie." Truth looked at Vigor in the mirror. "A fortune, for us. But he damn near killed me at the end there. So, you got to ask: was the risk worth the reward?"

Vigor shook his head. "Give me a better plan. Any better plan! I know you think you are going to pass the SAT, but so does everybody. It's not for sure."

Truth ran his hand through his short hair, desperately trying to think of anything. In the end, he could only try the truth: "All I know is there's no future in crime. I can't think of a single rich guy who got that way by armed robbery."

Vigor gave him a dead-eyed look. "You think we can worry about 'rich'? Or do we gotta worry about eating?"

Truth kept trying to wash off the filth, wondering if, at this point, he was just moving it around. He didn't know how to give his brother back hope.

"You aren't wrong. It's a more-than-bad situation. I'm going to have to stash the loot somewhere before we get home."

Vigor just shook his head.

Truth tried washing his shirt under the tap. It sort of helped, but really, the shirt was shredded. Fit only for the trash.

"I guess it comes down to this," Truth said. "We can't control what Mom and Dad do. We can't control how they think or what they think about us. Can't control much of anything in this shitty world. But what we can control?" He tapped Vigor on the forehead. "Is how we think about things. And I am thinking none of this is going to beat us."

"Truth?"

"Yeah?"

"I'mma kick your ass if you tell me to keep the faith."

Truth laughed for what felt like the first time in ages. "Fair."

CHAPTER 7

WHICH WAY TO HOPE?

Truth looked around the washroom. The building had been some kind of commercial or light industrial space—lots of bare concrete floors, spots where shelves and tables had been bolted down, sconces that would have held high-capacity cosmic-energy relays. Those relays would have been the first things stripped out of there, maybe even before the . . . whatever it was . . . officially went out of business. It was inky dark, damp, cold, and smelled of mildew and rat piss. The fact that it wasn't filled with homeless people and their waste was a deeply suspicious miracle.

On the other hand, it had a bathroom with one functional water talisman, solid walls, and with the exception of the window he ruined, it was pretty secure. A place with real potential as a hideout.

"Hey, Vig, have a look around and see if there is a good place to stash the loot."

"Huh?"

"Can't take it home, right?"

"Right." Vigor started hunting around in the hallway. "Hey, there is an air vent here. I can get it open with my fingers."

"Sounds good."

Truth was as clean as he was going to get, and he wasn't going to get any warmer, so they headed out. He did his best to disguise the broken window. It wasn't great, but for an alleyway in the slums? It would probably do.

It was getting dark. Not a good time to stick around outside. Truth suddenly jolted. There were . . . things . . . that were once people. That really, really liked the dark. Like, picking an example *completely at random*, the basement of a mostly lightless abandoned building.

Welp. That's not great. And he hid the money there too. At least they didn't have to worry about it getting stolen.

Dinner was . . . awkward. The sibs ate quietly and dutifully did their homework. Truth found it hard to concentrate. So did Vigor, clearly. What was worse was Dad lurching to his feet and demanding that everyone turn their pockets inside out, then jump up and down, just to make extra sure they weren't hiding any money.

Truth looked down at the practice questions he had painfully copied from the school library. One in twenty passed the SAT. Some years less than that, but never more. Worse, Starbrite wasn't always hiring at every position every time the test was administered. Truth wanted to be a talisman-maintenance tech, but did Starbrite need another maintenance tech? And it's not like he could do just any other job—he *needed* those Class C housing benefits. Because the sibs couldn't live like this.

He could . . . do something else. Earn money, somehow. If he gave up on studying for the SAT, more options would open up. The sibs would have to live here for a year while he was conscripted, but they could manage a year, right?

Yeah, he didn't believe it either. He looked around the table at the sibs and tried to pick out what, exactly, felt wrong about them. Because something did. It took him a few minutes. The sibs were cold. Studying had been an act of rebellion, of liberation. Now? Now there was no hope. Their parents wouldn't let them succeed. They were doomed to miserable lives, a few more slumrats in the swarm, never quite able to forget the time they thought they could be more. This "studying" was just going through the motions. Humoring him.

They were never getting out of the slums. Doomed to slavery of one sort or another. Staking their lives to retain even one tiny shred of dignity, of self-respect. They had bet everything in their hearts on Truth; now even Truth had to bow his head. What hope did they have?

The bubbling giggles of despair tried to sneak out of his throat. It was on him. It had always been on him. It would always be on him. Since he was old enough to walk, it was on him to look out for his sibs. So, he had to go do the only thing he was even kind of good at—violence. He would have to, by himself, search through an entire abandoned building, clearing out any Ghūl that had holed up in there, then turn the building into their secret fortress of studying. A place where they could hide out from their parents and the other predators of the slums.

A whole fucking, *fucking* commercial or light industrial building. Fighting the Ghūl freaks that were almost certainly infesting the place. Freaks that barely registered pain, had almost perfect low-light vision, and sincerely enjoyed hurting people.

Which was flatly impossible at Level Zero. He had to level up. He wasn't far off now. Not at all. But if he wanted to make it over the line in the shortest possible time, he would have to spend all the loot they just won. Truth looked around the table. He should discuss this. They could eat well for a long time with four hundred wen. It would take a lot of stress off. Make their studying a whole lot easier. Maybe bump their grades up, too.

He saw a flash of white under Sophia's sleeve. Bandages. "Soph? How did you get hurt?"

She pulled her sleeve down and looked away. "I got scratched on a bit of metal. Don't worry; I put the ointment on it, so it won't get infected."

"Good, but . . . how? Or why, maybe?"

Sophia looked mulish, then sighed.

"You know how you always trawl for scrap in the canal between the Points and Magoon?"

"Yeah?"

"Well, I thought about it and realized there is a better spot just down the canal from Folley and Fung. They are always working on all kinds of shit, and they ain't never paid for a dumpster. All goes straight into the canal." She shrugged.

"Yeah, but the canal is fenced off all the way to . . ." Truth's voice trailed off. He got it now. He looked over at Dad, apparently absorbed in his scry. Then shook his head. "Damn shame you didn't get anything."

"Yeah."

The same fucking day. Not even twenty-four hours. Two brothers scheming murder for money, a schoolgirl trawling for scraps, and Harmony, the eldest—Truth looked over at him.

"Asking around about work. Near the Meat Market. Never know if you can bring home something for dinner." The Meat Market. Not the most violent den of gangsters, but only because their unofficial slogan was "I don't fight." Start shit over by the Market, everybody dies, and new product goes up on the hooks. Everybody knew it, too, so only the most rabid base fiends and tweakers tested them.

Not even twenty-four hours. One sib ready to go gangster, one ready to risk rape for murder, one fishing industrial waste for food money.

Desperate for a change of topic, he looked over at Sophia's homework. "What's jamming you up, Soph?"

"Spell progression. Which seems not needed. I mean, almost everybody gets to Level One, but how many people reach Level Two? Before old age? Maybe it's different uptown."

"Valid. It makes sense when you think about it from a job-hunting point of view."

"How?"

"Everybody can learn the Jeon National Universal Spell, right? They literally hand it out in the train stations. Nobody cares because every country has basically the same spell."

The sibs nodded.

"It's an amazing spell because you can use almost any type of magical device with it. You can do most modern jobs with it, even white-collar ones. On the other hand, it's a shitty spell because it can't be used for anything else *but* magic devices, has zero offensive or defensive capability, and it doesn't improve your body any. Or mind. Or magic. Whatever."

"Like the Sharp spell does." Vigor started connecting some dots.

"Exactly. Sharp is a basic-bitch cutting spell, but it refines your hands, arms, and even your back, to make sure that you can get the most out of each cut. *But.* That's just Level One. At Level Two, there is a lot more power behind the spell. Bigger cutting area. More of a hand transformation. Better cutting power. More muscle development and tougher skin. Level Three Sharp? Military and heavy industrial stuff. Guys working down at the shipyards with a Level Three Sharp spell? Big, big money."

"And it's all the same spell? That's what the book says," Sophia asked, unsure.

"Kind of. As your level gets higher, the spell slots get bigger. They can hold more-powerful, more-complicated versions of the same spell. The spell grows to fit the available space. Think of it like an evolving creature inside of you. As you get stronger, so does it."

"Which is why a real Sharp spell costs more than forty grand," Vigor concluded. "Not for what it can do at Level One but what you can earn with it later."

"Yep. Of course, you gotta pick carefully because once the spell is in; it's a bitch to remove it and learn a new spell. The process can take anywhere from weeks to months. Honestly, it's pretty much permanent. You've got to think about each spell *and* how it will work with any future spells you get for the rest of your life." Truth nodded at Vigor.

"Unless you got the System," Harmony said.

"Unless you got the System," Truth agreed. "*A Starbrite Man Is Always Ready.*"

He would go back to the building as soon as the sun was well up. He would collect the money and buy a tonic to help him break through to Level One. He would ride the post-breakthrough wave to pass the Starbrite Aptitude Test, then either get his maintenance dream job or any job they offered with Class C housing. He would leave himself no path of retreat. Collect the money, buy the tonic, break through. Tomorrow.

CHAPTER 8

DOWN TO GEHENNA OR UP TO THE THRONE

Well-to-do families would give their newly married offspring a choice—do you want the down payment for a house, or do you want a cultivation elixir for your kids? For many young families, it was a tough choice. Everyone wanted to own their own home, but . . . who knew how much elixirs would cost in eighteen years? If you pre-purchased them now, you would have the security of knowing your kids were covered for their Level One breakthrough. That would set them up for life. A good elixir guaranteed a smooth breakthrough, a large spell aperture, and would make cultivation easier in the future. They were criminally expensive but unquestionably worth it.

Allegedly, the genuine, top-notch elixirs caused a faint glow to surround the person breaking through, and the breakthrough would be accompanied by a bewitching fragrance. Balsam for a gentleman or lady, daffodils for a scholar, orange blossoms for a lover, and rosemary for a fighter. Proof of high-quality goods being used by the highest-quality people. It was a pop-culture cliche. Couples would sometimes try to break through together, claiming a sort of spiritual, almost-tantric orgasm despite sitting on opposite sides of the room.

Of course, where there are high-end goods, there are low-end goods. Then there are the knock-offs of the low-end goods. After that, there are the cut-down, adulterated, no-label-bottle, econo-line versions of the knock-off low-end goods. This was the tier Truth could afford. At between three hundred and four hundred wen a bottle, they weren't even called elixirs or aids or potions anymore. They were just cultivation tonics.

Truth spent extra time cultivating that night, and once the sibs were safely off to school, he did an extra round of cultivation in the morning. Was he on the verge of breaking through? Yes, but he had been for almost a month. Without an extra push, he would have to keep cultivating and hope that he got lucky.

He made his way back to the abandoned building. The broken window looked untouched. The alley looked as empty as before. He would cheerfully kill for a flashlight. The best he could do was hope. And take a length of pipe with him.

Not a hint of anything. No off smells. No strange noises. Nothing painted on the walls in blood, bile, and feces. It wasn't even too quiet—he could hear the city noises through the walls. Truth dug out the money, put the air vent cover back on, and cleared out. It took less than five minutes. It felt a lot longer.

Truth patted himself clean and made his way to a "pharmacy." Old Feng's was exactly what you would expect from this shitty city. There was no Old Feng. There had never been an Old Feng. The owner/operator was a guy called Prentiss. While the shop may have been phony in just about every way, they didn't knowingly cut their goods with anything toxic. Best pharmacy in the slums, Truth reckoned.

"Hey, Prentiss—what tonics you got?"

"Depends. What's your problem?"

"Cultivation."

"Oooh, yeah. That time of year again, huh? All right, all right, let me take a look. I should have some decent stuff." The decidedly middle-aged man heaved his bulk off his stool and started shifting cardboard boxes around. Truth didn't get itchy hands. It was widely believed, with some proof, that "Old Feng" dusted the boxes with poison to prevent shoplifting.

"All right, a tough guy like you, you probably want it rough and strong. Here: Glacier Parrot-Fish Liver x Ocean Magma Vent Grouper Liver double shot, blended with a tincture of thirty-five botanicals and guaranteed human-potable ethanol." He set a rather fancy-looking bottle in front of Truth. Split down the middle, one-half red, the other blue.

"We also have something a little more modern. This is the latest thing from Gabbert and Gabbert Alchemy Labs. Lots of retinol and flavonoids, blended polyni-trogardeniatropes with *balanced* alectrim and iso-proteins." This was a plain white plastic container the size of a can of soda. Prentiss presented it with a flourish, then dug back into the box.

"We also have this. Which is something. Eh, I can't actually recommend it, but it is a lot cheaper than the others." He put a glass jar the size of a shot glass on the counter. It looked worryingly handmade, and the contents were a rusty brown.

"You don't know anything about it?"

"Tested it; not toxic, and it should help gather cosmic rays to accelerate a break-through. There should be some benefit to the body, though obviously not on the same level as a real elixir. If I had to guess? Some apprentice alchemist was trying to make an actual elixir using leftovers, fucked up, and this was the result. Gets sent to the trash, then makes its way to me."

"So, when you say it's not toxic . . ."

"Well, it doesn't have any of the kinds of things my poison tests check for, which is a lot of really nasty stuff. You probably wouldn't drop dead on the spot, but no promises about getting cancer down the road. Or something."

"So, what do they cost?"

"The two legit tonics are seven hundred each, and I'll let you have the experimental one for three fifty," Prentiss said grandly.

"Seven hundred! They were four hundred a couple of months ago!" Truth was outraged. Prentiss spread his hands and looked helpless.

"Elixirs are way up in price, which means that every cultivation-enhancing product is way up. It's the war in Reban. They grow a bunch of elixir ingredients. Trouble in Siphios, too."

Truth looked rebellious. "Yeah, but this ain't exactly Green Lotus. No offense, but it ain't."

Prentiss shrugged his flabby shoulders and flatly replied. "It ain't. You couldn't afford to breathe the air in a Green Lotus shop. You can afford Old Feng's. These are the prices. Take 'em or scram.

Truth glared at Prentiss, who could not have given less of a shit. Then, with immense reluctance, he picked up the glass jar. "At the very least, throw in some painkillers. And a flashlight."

Breaking through didn't take long . . . generally. It was the subject of a lot of debate. There were well-documented examples of people breaking through almost instantly, while rare cases could take as long as a day. The frustrating thing was that there seemed to be no rhyme or reason to it. Nor was one better than the other. People were just different.

The *average*, Truth remembered, was about ten minutes. Theoretically, you should just go home and do it in a nice, quiet room. It was a spiritual awakening, and if you had a *good* elixir, there would be a gentle improvement in overall health and a massive improvement in physical capability. Level One was the first step into super-humanity, a literal higher tier of existence. However, the consequences of being disturbed during a breakthrough could range from extreme pain to permanent disability. Truth was *not* going to break through at home.

Still plenty of time left in the morning. Truth made a beeline back to the abandoned building. Not much in the way of usable scrap in there. It had been cleaned out long before. Still, there were things like interior doors that could be removed from hinges, along with hollow metal doors from the toilet stalls. He collected a few of them and did his best to fortify the bathroom. He had seen no sign of others in the abandoned building, but he flatly didn't believe such a thing was possible. No such thing as free real estate.

He pried the mirrors off the walls. That was a big job! But he did get them off and lined them up so that the light from the flashlight would fill the whole room. He sat down in the middle of the nest of light, one meter of iron pipe by his side.

Truth said a brief prayer to whatever gods or devils might watch over the desperate and unwise and took out the tonic. It felt heavy. Like the tonic knew his future depended on it. It was a lousy, unreliable thing to hang your hopes on. But he had to. The sibs had lost all hope.

Truth unscrewed the lid. It smelled like rusty water and rotting leaves. He knocked it back in one go and waited. Nothing happened.

Which was normal. Truth forcefully reminded himself. It was normal for nothing to happen at first. The tonic had to be digested. It had to get through the stomach lining. It took time. His fingers dug into his thighs. It was normal. But what if it didn't work? What if he wasted his shot? What if he ruined his chance to pass the Starbrite Aptitude Test and . . .

His body convulsed. He almost bit his tongue off. The fingers digging into his thighs almost tore away the muscles as they clenched. His spine felt like it was being replaced with superheated wires. The clench relaxed, and he fell forward. Before he could breathe, his stomach imploded. Vomit ripped through his esophagus and out over the floor. It didn't stop. The volume reduced to a dribble, but he couldn't stop it. Every scrap of bile in him was squeezed up and out and over him.

The room started going dark. He thought the flashlight was dying, but no, it was his eyes dying. Distorted shapes, too unnatural and obscene to be called ghosts, haunted him. Iron screws, cold, merciless, twisted through his skull. He wished he could scream, but his throat had been burned away. All that came out were little rasping wheezes. Only he knew that they were prayers for death.

For a horrible second, Truth hallucinated that he was a speck of dust floating in the void between stars. Something impossibly vast, terrible, and malicious was out there. Then there was an oily ripple of movement, and he realized that it wasn't that he couldn't see the monster. He was *in* the monster.

I am going to die. Truth had just enough of himself left to form the thought. *I can't die. I have to break through.* He tried to focus on the spot over his heart, but he wasn't sure he still had a body. Nine burning worms crawled over him and started chewing away at the idea of his chest.

Truth tried screaming again, but that mercy was still denied him. They chewed their way into his chest, then chewed open the aperture that would hold his first spell. They seemed to wiggle around inside it as though they were thinking of nesting. Instead, the burning worms slithered out and crawled through his body before exiting. A grim, stately procession through the entirety of his flesh, departing in a trail of fire via the urethra. Not because they had to. They just wanted to hurt him that little bit more.

At this point, Truth sank into oblivion. His last thought was a faint hope to never wake again.

It was to be expected, given the inherent cruelty of the universe, that he did wake up. In agony. Covered in piss, vomit, and shit. Covered in blood. Exhausted. Something was scratching at the bathroom door.

CHAPTER 9

A SPECIAL BREAKTHROUGH PARTY FOR A SPECIAL BOY

Truth was curled in the fetal position at the center of his nest of light. He thought he would have been thrashing. He was certainly covered in just about every sort of fluid his body produced. Every fiber of his being hurt. Every centimeter, every scrap of him, ached. Even his hair ached, somehow. He knew that the first thing to do after breaking through was to cultivate. He couldn't possibly move an inch, but he could do the breathing, right? Right. *Just . . . focus on the breathing. Don't worry about everything else. Don't worry about the persistent scratching noise at the door. The door is fortified, and the wall is concrete. You are safe for now. Just. Breathe. And pull in the cosmic rays.*

He breathed in, held, released, repeated, imagining the air flowing in through his nose, to his lungs, swirling around the aperture over his heart, then down to the base of his tailbone, before rising up and spilling out of his mouth. Over and over. It was a slightly more advanced version of the Level Zero cultivation breath, and gods be praised! Truth felt the difference at once.

The aperture above his heart, the "spell slot," was like a whirlpool, sucking in the cosmic rays, transforming them into the gentler and more-generic cosmic energy. He could feel the rays bathing the sides of it, keeping it supple and strong. This is why you had to keep cultivating, he realized. It couldn't draw enough passively. If you didn't keep filling it up, it would eventually collapse. The energy from the rays didn't just vanish into the hole. He could feel them being pacified and purified, then pushed through the rest of his body.

He could feel his exhausted and abused body screaming for the energy, greedily gobbling it up. Truth swore he could feel his tendons strengthening, his bones hardening, his skin getting smoother and tougher. Most of all, he could feel the incredible mental clarity the breakthrough gave him. He kept breathing. It wouldn't be long now before he could move again. Then he would start cultivating properly. His mind raced. So many problems he couldn't understand now seemed obvious. He ran through drills for the SAT. Easy, easy . . . not so easy. Damn it. Right. Anyone who could broke through right before they sat the test. Starbrite obviously balanced the difficulty with them in mind.

Truth gingerly stood. He looked down. The clothes were totally ruined. As thrifty as he was, this was beyond cleaning. It might even be beyond burning. He stripped naked, wiped away what he could with the wadded-up clothes, then tossed them in a dark corner. There. Now this smelled like a proper abandoned building. He looked at the tap with its one functional water talisman. He really wanted to wash more. And it's not like breaking through made him *less* aware of the cold. But the scratching was getting more persistent, so . . . priorities. Cultivation. Get the body into fighting shape as quickly as possible.

He began the stretches and movements that were supposed to help the cosmic rays circulate and invigorate the body. He nearly fell over when he tried. His body was too exhausted for that kind of nonsense. Instead, he started gently swaying and shaking out his arms. Rocking up onto his toes, then back onto his heels. Slowly, achingly slowly, he got his body reacquainted with movement. All while sucking in as much cosmic rays as he could. It worked surprisingly well.

Truth frowned. It was working surprisingly well. He could feel the state of his body very precisely, and it had been precisely fucked just five minutes before. It was now in a state he would call "kind of sore," and in another few minutes, he would be at "raring to go." The change from Level Zero to Level One did come with some pretty dramatic improvements to the body, but that took place over months. Not, for example, ten minutes. The breakthrough was supposed to be accompanied by a *slight* increase in overall health, followed by an explosive increase in fitness. Likewise, the body visualization. Everybody learned how to do it when they taught cultivation at school. Everybody got better at it as they leveled up. But, again, it wasn't meant to be this accurate, this fast. Not at Level One.

He watched the energy moving along his body. It didn't feel quite right, somehow. Sluggish, inefficient, sloppy. He instinctively knew he was working unnecessarily hard. As though he was insisting on crab-walking everywhere. He stopped trying to push the energy around and let it go where it wanted. The energy spasmed for a moment (a painful experience, to put it mildly) but quickly started flowing on a new, smoother path. The difference was incredible. He could feel, second by second, the improvement in his body. Even in his d—

With a thrill of horror, he remembered the worms. The nine burning worms opened his first spell slot and then roamed his body. This was the path they took with a . . . single significant difference. He tentatively tried pissing out the cosmic energy.

The explosive pain made him white out. Truth collapsed to his knees, clutching his groin as a thin whimper escaped his mouth. The agony moved up, back, and around, taking a little tour of the region and lingering where it seemed to have the most effect. Cosmic energy was supposed to leave via the mouth and nose. No alternate routes permitted. Apparently, the worms had just wanted to hurt him one *extra* time.

"What the fuck was that tonic?" Truth hadn't realized that he had spoken aloud. "What the fuck were those worms? What the fuck is happening to me?" He looked over at the door. The scratching was getting a bit frantic. "And why am I hearing music?"

Truth shook his head and carefully got back to his feet. The new . . . well, it was all new. The *newer* energy path (the Nine Worm Path?) worked scarily well. He was already in better physical shape than when he walked into this bathroom. No weird growths or unnatural mutations, either, which at this point he was kind of expecting.

He tried the stretching routine again, and this time he could do it fluidly. Very fluidly. Everything flowed easily, from one form to the next, his body hauling in and processing the wild cosmic rays with every breath. A couple of minutes was all it took to leave him feeling warm and loose.

He picked up the iron pipe. It had been a bit heavy when he carried it in. Now? It was worryingly light. Truth swished it through the air. He shifted into a club fighting drill, moving through the steps, attacks, counters, and blocks like he had done it a thousand times before. He had never done it before.

"How the fuck am I so good at fighting? It's not just talent. It can't be." His voice carried more than a tinge of madness now. The music was getting louder.

It sounded like church music. Not that they were regular churchgoers or any-thing. Just that Mom figured it would be easier to run her MLM scams on fellow churchgoers. They only lasted a couple of months in the pews. The congregation, initially welcoming, literally barred the door to them. The priest preached against them. Twice. Truth hadn't much cared for it, but some of the songs were good. This didn't sound like any of them, but it kind of sounded like the way the church songs made him feel. Like he was very small, but that was okay because he was part of something impossibly greater than himself. "He" was temporary, but "It" was eternal. So, in a way, "He" was eternal too.

Except this wasn't something eternally good and grand. This was something vast, indifferent to the point of cruelty, and too powerful to be made to care.

He looked at the window. Thick iron bars were firmly set into place. He might be able to chip his way out through that, but he wouldn't bet on it. Not even with his improving strength. The light was getting low. How long had the breakthrough lasted? A lot more than ten minutes, apparently.

Truth rearranged the mirrors so all the light was shining at the door. He removed the fortifications. He could see long fingers, gray, dusty brown, ashy black, poking through the door. Dragging rents into it. It was going down, and soon. Truth didn't wait. He undid the lock and let the door swing open.

An unholy scream blocked out the music as whatever was in the hall fled from the light. Truth jumped out and started swinging at whatever moved. He caught a head, splashing its contents against the wall. The follow-through came down on another head, then he had to duck crap that someone in the dark was throwing at him. More things were launched from a distance, more little chiming noises that scared the piss out of any slum resident.

The pipe smashed down on an upraised arm as milky-white eyes glared at him. The bone broke, but it didn't make the withered face even twitch. Of course it didn't. He was fighting the Ghūl now. The Ghūl did not care if you hurt them. They did not care if you screamed or laughed or yelled. They weren't hungry. They didn't want your money. The only thing in their heart was beauty. Sculpture of the found-art variety. And their medium of choice was humans. Your suffering flesh was all they demanded. And, as Truth desperately parried a kick to his naked gut, this bunch seemed above-average demanding.

CHAPTER 10

THE SIMPLE JOY
OF SLAUGHTER

Truth retreated back into the light of the doorway for a moment just to reset. The Ghūl hated bright lights but wouldn't wait long. They would start throwing crap around the door. Eventually, something would knock out the light. This would happen pretty quickly, as the light was the cheap little underpowered talisman flashlight that Prentiss had fished out from under his counter. The bathroom mirrors, however, were not some fancy glass job. They were high-polish steel with a spray-on clear layer of plastic to keep the polish. They were, in other words, cheap, crummy, and durable. They reflected the light very adequately. Truth grinned. He was very used to working with cheap goods.

One quick adjustment of the mirrors later (and already having to slap thrown crap out of the air), Truth rushed back out into the hallway. He stood in a little rectangle of light and cleared the area immediately around the door. The bathroom was at the far end of a longish hallway, so he was in luck there. He wedged a mirror up between the wall and a Ghūl corpse. The light, such as it was, lit up the hallway. Not well. There was only so much light a crummy little flashlight could put out. But enough to let him see.

The hall was littered with Ghūl. They sprawled against walls and crawled along the floor. Some even jabbed their fingers into the ceiling and mimicked crawling along it. Their desiccated bodies made that much easier. Not that they weren't strong enough, even for something six times their weight. Those stick-thin fingers tore through wood with only a little effort. They all tried to avoid looking directly at the mirror, but . . . it wasn't that bright. And Truth was between the Ghūl and the light.

Truth looked around. He could make a beeline for the room with the escapable window. It would probably be sticky getting away but not impossible. He lightly discarded the thought.

"I can't fix my shitty parents," Truth told the Ghūl. "I can't stop the dealers and the pimps. I can't fix fucking anything in the world. And then here you are." Truth kissed two fingers and raised them to the sky. "Finally, a problem I can fix with violence. Thank you, gods. You saw I needed this, and you really came through."

The closest of the Ghūl decided it was done acting casual and hopped up on a wall. Sat on the wall like a damn frog, digging at the rotting mortar with its fingers and toes. Then it launched itself at Truth. Ragged nails and blackened teeth came at his face fast. Truth was already waiting. A step forward and just to the side, enough to make the lunge miss. The pipe swung out to meet the incoming face. Their combined force smashed the head open like a pumpkin off a bridge.

Truth brought the pipe into line with the next Ghūl and stabbed it over the heart. If it had been a human, the heart would stop from such a savage blow. He thought it might be effective. The savage kick the Ghūl aimed at his nuts suggested that it was not. Truth flinched back, feeling the wind from the filth-crusted foot fan his undercarriage. The Ghūl only used to be human. Headshots only. Such fun.

The Ghūl tried to turn the missed rising kick into a descending ax kick with a little hop to get in range. Truth decided to play along, blocking the foot up high, smashing the pipe down, crushing another skull, then shoving the corpse into the next attacking Ghūl, who figured they would cut in on the action. A second Ghūl was coming from below. While the first was dealing with the corpse, he parred the second's attempt to shred his calf. As it rose up to get a shot at his gut, Truth body-checked it into the back of the same corpse its friend was dealing with. It turned out that they were not, in fact, friends, and claws flew everywhere. Truth would have let them go at it, but there were more coming down the hall. Fast.

Truth let himself flow with the madness of the scene. The dim light barely picked up the shapes before they came at him, silently shrieking their need to pull him apart. To make him pretty, with his guts hung like bunting. With his teeth pulled out and fingerbones jammed in their place. They never minded being hit. Broken bones, shattered organs, these weren't worth their attention. The only thing that stopped them was when their skulls burst like balloons of rotting jelly. When the bone fragments of their skull finally stopped bouncing, so did the Ghūl. If the Ghūl had even the faintest notions of evasion or defense, it would have been a one-sided slaughter. It was still a one-sided slaughter. And Truth was loving every second of it.

There was no more time to think. No more time to worry about the SATs or his parents or his siblings. No time to think about why this felt so familiar. Why he knew how a crushed skull would feel before he first swung the pipe. He didn't have to wonder why he remembered things that never happened. Truth lost himself in the joys of his powerful flesh. He moved in a grisly choreography with the Ghūl, blocking, countering, killing, and moving on. Pressing down the hallway. Washing away all the pain and misery in the fountaining, rotten blood and meats of the Ghūl. All too soon, he ran out of Ghūl and hallway alike.

He pushed open the fire door. The strange music was louder in the stairwell. Looking up, he saw lots of Ghūl faces staring back down. There would be almost no light up there. Just what little there was trickled through the windows. Truth's smile was warm and sincere. He gave his naked body a little shimmy to encourage the thickest bits of Ghūl flesh and his own filth to drip off. He scraped the worst off the pipe against the doorframe.

"Ready or not, here I come!" Truth charged up the stairwell.

It was a glorious excess. The sheer joy of feeling newly powerful muscles *move* under his command. Every breath seemed to suck in an ocean of cosmic rays, spun into new energy by the aperture above his heart. The Nine Worm Path ensured that every speck of lactic acid that would build up and burden him was neutralized and removed by waves of rejuvenating cosmic energy. Energy he wasn't expending at nearly the rate he thought he would be. But then, he wasn't using any spells. All Truth asked his energy to do was let him play a little longer.

Truth raised his pipe. He didn't know how long he had swung it for. It had gone pitch-dark long before. He just kept climbing the stairs and banging the metal railings, calling every Ghūl in the building to come fight him. In this narrow stairwell that he could control. It was gloriously fun. And the Ghūl seemed to be in on the game. He just knew that the Ghūl in front of him was going to shoot his legs, knock him down, and rip out his throat. And bless his little bony ankles, that's exactly what the Ghūl tried to do. Truth's pipe smashed straight down, splattering the skull and causing the corpse to pinwheel down to the landing below. At least it had a soft landing cushioned on the other corpses.

Had he . . . been getting stronger? No, it really did feel like the Ghūl were cooperating with the slaughter. They just telegraphed everything so *incredibly* obviously that things felt easy. The music was pretty loud now. Whatever that strange church music was that had led him to the top floor of the building. The Ghūl had been busy, ripping out internal walls and leaving only the structural support beams.

"Now, how the fuck did you mindless freaks figure that out?" Truth laughed. But the Ghūl weren't mindless, were they? They just didn't care about things that humans did. Still, though. He swaggered into the darkness, following the sound of the music.

The Ghūl had stopped playing around. Which unfortunately meant that they were not attacking anymore. Truth frowned at the end of his fun. Then he frowned a little more deeply. There was a faint glow coming from the back wall. As he walked closer, it resolved into an orange haze around some large structure, perhaps fifteen feet high by ten feet across and some distance deep. It was irregularly shaped and too hard to identify in the faint light. It also seemed to be the source of the music.

As he strode closer, he could pick out individual Ghūl. Most seemed to be squatting and looking up at the glowing whatever-it-was. Others were tending to bathtub-sized leather hammocks. They seemed to be filled with something liquid, judging by the heavy way they swung back and forth. For some reason, they were ignoring him.

Truth stopped some twenty feet from the statue. It had to be a statue; statues were all the Ghūl made. Nobody really understood what they were statues of. Everybody knew what they were made of. In this case, the mutilated and defiled corpses were formed into a rough ball, with some protruding bits and others wrapped in strange ways. Stranger still was the fact that it was starting to look like something he could understand.

He stared. The Ghūl ignored him, poking away at their human-skin slings of something or other. Truth had never heard about any slings, but then, it wasn't covered on the SAT, so he didn't care. What the hell was that thing? He let his eyes go unfocused, trying to free associate. The Ghūl crouching around the statute, watching it unblinkingly, caught the corner of his eye. Then he looked back at the statue and could feel it snap into focus.

It was a man. A god. Chained hand to ankle, then bound around the shoulders and the knees. Proportioned to heroic ratios, it was a grotesque tribute to an ideal masculine physique. God was not looking at his people. His head was tilted up, traces of dried tears on his cheeks. Blood dribbled from his ears. Somehow, in some impossible way, Truth knew that this was something the god did to himself. He wasn't looking away out of disgust. It was boredom. He had been bored to tears and yakked at until he went deaf. He was done with this world, this entire universe. God was more interested in what he could imagine than what he made.

A wet-slap noise jerked Truth from his reverie. Something had come out of a skin hammock. It was a Ghūl and a sopping wet one at that. It reeked. Truth could smell it six feet away. He wanted to puke. It smelled like the cultivation tonic he had used to break through.

CHAPTER 11

A CERTAIN NECESSARY RESOLVE

The smell of the birthing vats of the Ghūl, those human-skin cauldrons of corruption and depravity, poured into Truth's mind like a glass of water into a pot of smoking hot oil. "I'm going to kill Prentiss." Then, "Am I part Ghūl?" followed by "This is why the cops burn the statues—cut off the Ghūl supply." He couldn't hold it together, and like a glass of water poured into a pot of smoking hot oil, he exploded.

He rushed the nearest cauldron, club high and screaming. He smashed to death the brand-new Ghūl, then ripped open the sides of the skin vat with his new strength. The rot-brown fluid (and what horrible means did the Ghūl use to concoct such a thing?) spilled out and splashed over his naked body. The Ghūl hardly seemed to mind, entranced as they were by staring at the statue of the bound god. Truth minded very fucking much, but he was too pissed off to stop. He worked with blinding speed, smashing heads and destroying vats, watching corpses tumble out like some macabre parody of birth. Coated in the amniotic fluids of the undead. It had felt so good before. So powerful, so alive! What bitter irony.

Soon, it was just Truth and the God. The statue just sat there, ignoring everything going on below it. Truth raised his iron pipe and started to approach it, but his energy petered out. It was too big to reasonably smash apart. Why was it glowing in the dark? He didn't know and didn't really want to find out. He had wanted to turn this building into a hideout for him and the sibs, but . . . fuck it. You could tip the cops anonymously about Ghūl statues, and there was a reward. Not a huge one, but it was something. He turned around and shuffled off. He would need to wash up, at least, before heading home. Maybe some other floor would have soap. He could hope.

It was a wet, smelly, and less-hopeful Truth that climbed out of the abandoned building. The "tonic," the Ghūl amniotic fluid, had quickly started to make a stabbing, tingling sensation on his skin. He thought it might be caustic or acidic or something, but he quickly realized that it was much, much worse. The Nine Worm Path treated it like it was some kind of rare treasure and was using it to refine his skin.

Into what, he didn't know and didn't want to find out. He tried to stop it, but the cultivation was always passively working in the background. If it stopped, his precious Level One cultivation would collapse, and he would become a cripple. His life would be over. His sibs doomed. So, all he could do was round up as many water talismans as he could find and scrub. Not that there was any soap. Nor anything that looked like a towel. Not even so much as abandoned drop cloths or forgotten toilet paper.

Fair to say that Truth was in a somewhat altered state of consciousness by the time he hit the street. He didn't know the time other than "late." Much later than he usually was out, certainly. Well. He knew his way home. Knew the backstreets and alleys. He could get around fairly unseen. Ish. For a while. Better than standing there, doing nothing. He walked to the end of the alley, where a sodium-light talisman made the street a sickly yellow. Truth kept his eyes focused on the light. Closer and closer. He walked right up to the edge of the shadow, staring directly into the light. His eyes hurt. But probably about as much as a person who'd been in the dark for hours and was now staring at a light should *expect* their eyes to hurt. No sudden fear. No revulsion. No compulsion to throw things and put out the light. So. Good sign.

Truth turned back down the alley and started making his way along the access paths, gaps between buildings, and all the other tiny interstitial places that stitch together a city. Where there was the chance of being observed, he crept in the shadows. When people passed, he froze. And when he saw a particularly fat fuck of a dealer slipping away from his corner for a piss, Truth attacked. Given his experience of the last day, he thoughtfully let the dealer finish his piss and button up before snapping his neck.

Thanks be to the gods (he hastily added a clause excluding whatever the Ghūl worshiped), the tubby parasite liked to layer. A few cheap underlayers were quickly drafted as cleaning rags, to excellent effect. He was now merely dirty, as opposed to a public health hazard. The rest of the clothes made him look like a clown, and he had to loop the belt around twice to keep the pants up. He looked over at the corpse. No handy dumpster this time, and he was getting a little leery of handling corpses in clean clothes. In addition to some drugs and two hundred wen, there was an impressive-looking knife. Must not have had a decent spell. He could carve a message on the body, maybe throw off his fellow gangsters?

Oh. I just killed someone for their clothes. I think I know this guy. I mean, I don't know him, but I have seen him around the neighborhood. And I just snapped his neck to steal his clown clothes. Sparing myself a little humiliation and about thirty minutes of physical comfort. Now he's dead forever. That's fucked up. That's really, really fucked up. I'm not even stealing his shoes because he has weirdly dainty feet for such a big guy. That is so, so fucked up. And I don't care. Which is really fucked up. And I am going to defile his corpse and try to start some shit just so people don't come looking for his real murderer. Which, again, is deeply fucked up.

Then he got out his knife and carved the sign for the old Ninth Street Gang on his chest. The gang never really got anywhere; it had been slightly big for a hot minute five years before. Its former members had scattered to other gangs. Lots of potential suspects. He made sure to keep the blood off himself. Last thing he needed right now. Truth went home.

No one was in the main room. Small blessings. Truth figured Dad would be out all night as he usually was, but Mom wasn't such a night owl. He went directly to the bathroom and showered. He used all the hot water. He used a lot of cold water. He certainly made *lavish* use of the soap and shampoo. Clean and, in many respects, reborn, he turned to bed. To be met with the glaring eyes of the sibs. Who had been crying. Damn.

He had been missed. And worried about. Crouching in the dark and whispering, Truth spread the good word. "I broke through to Level One. Things are about to get much, much better."

That night, Truth dreamed he was making mudballs. Some were lumpy and uneven, but eventually, he got one really round and shiny. Even in his dream, it was a very meh achievement. Woo. Mudball. Woo. But the mudballs were basically . . . fine. He had put some effort into making them, and it didn't seem right to just smash them. Maybe something interesting would grow on them? He scattered some seeds. And waited. And waited. Truth managed to bore himself awake. He didn't remember his dreams.

Oddly enough, things did get much better. Truth kept waiting for some act of cosmic doom to swoop down and crush him but . . . nope. Dad got a little less openly violent and a lot more vindictive when he realized that Truth was Level One. Mom also got a bit less entitled for about thirty minutes. It was very Mom that her first instinct was to get him out there promoting Mega-Shroom. "After all, dear, it's not like anyone would hire you. And now you have some credibility. Time you helped Mommy with her work, don't you think?"

He did not think so, no. And it felt so, so good to tell her so.

Most importantly, he found that he could study. Really study. The concepts flowed into his mind and got locked down with iron chains. It wasn't photographic memory, but the promised improvement to recall and analysis that came right after a breakthrough turned out to be no myth. He was crushing his mock exams. The extra cash he had stashed made the need to hustle for food less urgent, giving him more time to study and cultivate. They weren't eating well, but they were eating enough. It made all the difference.

Two days after Truth broke through, the police swarmed in on an abandoned building in the Slums. Armored enforcers rode in on their spell beasts: six-legged amphibian-looking creatures with a black-and-tan coloration that moved so fast, your eyes couldn't follow them. They put up spell pylons with practiced ease, cordoning off the whole building while senior officers launched flying talisman birds to lock down the airspace and complete the encirclement. A police demolitions expert flew up on a golden (or, given city budgets, more likely a gold-painted) altar and slapped down the demo charges around the edge of the spell ward. She then cast a series of spells in short order, funneling them through the talismans.

The spells expanded and smashed the building from every side, collapsing it inward. Superheated jets of plasma shot into the dust, turning the interior of the spell ward into a blazing inferno. Something must not have felt right, because she slapped eight more talismans to lock down the cardinal directions. She wove another sequence of spells, and the flames turned the blinding, electric purple of plasma. Then the cops packed their stuff and left, not explaining a damn thing to anybody.

Truth got a message on his burner communicator. A code for a lockbox in a busy subway station. Inside he found five thousand wen in cash and a synthetic jade token. The bearer of said token could redeem it for two Harban City Civic Merits. Truth struggled to suppress the grin that spread over his face. This was huge money, but the merits! He had no idea the reward could include merits! He could raise his status in the city. Enough to open a real bank account. The five grand would make a totally adequate first deposit. Money his grasping parents couldn't find. A bank account and a full Citizen status added up to a real identity. That would be a major help on his Starbrite application. Rising as high as a maintenance-team supervisor in seven years was a real possibility.

He couldn't run his ass to the bank fast enough. All that was left was to study and cultivate as hard as he could. The rest of the month seemed to grind past until it was the day before the exam, and he was desperately wondering where all the hours went. Time was ever indifferent to the test taker's prayers. Exam day was there.

CHAPTER 12

TEST DAY

At sunset, the day before the Starbrite Aptitude Test was held, churches would ring their bells, temples banged gongs, and civic groups would drive around in buses, reminding people, via bullhorn, that tomorrow was SAT Day. Absolute silence was to be observed until sunset tomorrow. Or else. When the sun vanished below the horizon, so did the noise. It was the one night of the year that didn't belong to the Ghūl. It belonged to the parents.

Mom and Dad were so excited. It was finally their time to show that they were *good* parents. Sure, they forgot groceries most of the time. And sometimes, the kids needed a good smack to remind them about respect. And sometimes, yeah, they lost their temper and hit each other. And the kids. And took their money. And took their dreams. And took their hope.

What, are you perfect?

Besides, it was all good now. It was the Silent Night. Dad favored quarter-inch synthetic rope. Strong enough to hold weight, he claimed, while easy on the hands. Mom thought that was terribly common and not good enough for their dear, *sweet* boy. Mother knew what her baby really needed. That's why she used a length of twisted copper wire formed into a garotte. She had painted the handles with gold nail polish.

They were so proud. Tonight, they would patrol the neighborhood and make sure that no one was making noise. If they were—the rope! In the morning, they would, along with tens of thousands of other parents, escort their kid to the subway, which would take him to the testing center. In as close to perfect silence as possible. Then, during the day, if someone was noisy, once again, the rope! It was exactly the sort of feel-good thuggishness they could lose themselves in.

Most years, they just participated for fun. This year, it was for *their* boy! Nothing, *nothing* (they drunkenly slurred) was going to interfere with his test. Which he was going to ace!

It was pass/fail based on subject area and how Starbrite was scoring it this year, but they surely didn't care.

Truth spent a little time revising but mostly concentrated on eating a good meal and cultivating. He found that the more he cultivated, the more the mental boost from leveling up seemed to stick around. He knew it faded away eventually, but urban legend said that the longer you could keep it, the smarter you would be when it does go.

Then to bed. The sibs were tossing and turning all night. Truth just concentrated on breathing steadily and let his mind drift. The old man on the long stone porch appeared in his dreams again, draped loosely in undyed wool cloth.

"You cannot control what others think or do. You cannot control the gods nor fate. All you can do is your best to follow the four virtues. That is enough. It may not bring you everything that you want, but it will bring you everything you truly need."

"Following the four virtues won't necessarily fill a hungry belly, will it?" Truth heard himself ask.

"It might! Wisdom is part of the virtues, after all. It is wise to keep an adequately stocked larder. Though one should not be excessive. Moderation is another of the virtues. But your error, young Truth, is in thinking that your hunger or survival are good or bad. They are neither virtue nor vice, so they are merely indifferent. The worth of "hunger" or "survival" is entirely in your mind, and if I teach you well, you will find them of little importance. In truth, you are already dead. Your death was utterly foreordained. So, all you can do is be grateful for the time allotted to you and do your best."

Truth woke. He didn't remember his dream, but he felt calm. All he could do was his best and accept whatever came. Time to take the test.

His parents, bleary-eyed and proud, marched alongside Truth and the sibs, ropes swinging. So did every other parent. Silent police officers were on hand at the subway, directing the parents and families to fall back as their children went down the steps. There were no cheers, no cries of "Good luck!" "Certain victory!" "You got this!" No comforting reminder that if they didn't pass, there were always the lower-tier employers. Not as honorable, not as lucrative, but still decent. Respectable, if not something to boast about. Better than those who failed to join a corporation at all.

Truth rode the subway to the test center. Not his first time on a subway, but it was still rare enough to leave the slums that it felt exciting and alien. Non-Citizens weren't permitted in the better parts of the city. There were entire neighborhoods that required such stratospheric status that it was literally a life sentence to turn the wrong corner. Not that you could do it accidentally. There were golems at the foot of the road, enforcing *standards*.

Force of habit led him toward the "Denizens" staircase. He then stopped and took the escalator. His new identity sigil glowed softly on the underside of his arm. He was a Citizen now. He had taken one enormous step to change his life.

Head now firmly in the game, he strode directly toward the Level One line to get into the test center. The convention center (owned by Starbrite) was converted into an anti-cheating fortress (by a Starbrite subsidiary security company) and staffed by yet more Starbrite employees taking the chance to do some volunteer work. He was inspected by a floating spirit before he reached the door, then a bright green light shined down on him. The sign said to empty his pockets into the provided bin, so he did.

There were another four rounds of security and identification verification between him and the actual test. At last, it was set in front of him. The invigilators gave their instructions, instructions every test taker could have recited word for word. Then he flipped his papers over and got to work.

The first sections were always the same. Diagrammatic and logical reasoning. Essentially pattern recognition. Truth once would have said he was good at pattern recognition. He had learned humility. This was pattern recognition hidden in math problems and verbal puzzles. It was brutal.

This was followed by mathematics, then language skills. Brutality, again, with the added hint that he wasn't understanding some of the language things because he was from the slums. You were supposed to pair *Cup* with the word that most usually accompanied it. What the hell did that mean? Plate? You usually have a drink when you eat, right? Or bowl? What the actual fuck is a Saucer? Who needs a special thing just to put sauce in? It comes in a bottle, people!

The personality assessment section was the "easiest," as there were no wrong answers. You just need to pick all the words that described you from a field of sixty words. And then select all the words that you think would best suit someone in the job you are applying for. Field of fifty words. Some of the words were the same. Some were not. Which were the good words? Because while there might not be any wrong answers *philosophically*, there absolutely were right answers for the recruiters.

Finally, since he had declared a chosen profession, he was tested on his fundamental understanding of talismans. What they were, how they worked, and why they needed careful maintenance. What frustrated Truth the most was that all the "right" answers were factually wrong or incomplete. Things like:

What is the expected service life of a Ke-Te-Wo Type 61 Streetlight Talisman, assuming eight hours in operation every day?

The answer it wanted was *Five years*. The actual answer was *It depends. How cold was it, on average? Was there a significant variation in average rainfall? What was the degree of fine particulate matter in the rain, and was the rain more caustic or acidic during this period? Have Ghūl been trying to break it? Have locals been trying to strip it for saleable parts?* In fact, it would be a minor miracle for the streetlight to make it five years in Harban City. On the other hand, since it was the *Starbrite* Aptitude Test, and the Ke-Te-Wo Type 61 Streetlight Talisman was manufactured by Ke-Te Commercial and Municipal Lighting Solutions, LLC, Part of the Starbrite Family of Companies, and since the Ke-Te manual said five years, it was five years.

Test takers were expected to know it, too, because talisman-maintenance techs fixed a lot of streetlights. Lights that, inexplicably, did not reach their expected service life. What could he do? He gave them the answers they wanted and pressed on. He finished thirty seconds before the invigilator called time.

The test had one final "Completely Optional, Voluntary, Purely for Statistical Purposes, No Individualized Data Retained, Not Scored" section, just for the Level

One test takers. If you opted in, you walked out of the test-taking center through a tunnel lined with sophisticated medical measuring devices. Apparently, they could passively measure the size, ductility, and resilience of spell apertures. Allegedly, this was Starbrite checking on Harban City's developmental conditions and didn't count toward your evaluation.

Not a soul believed it. The single token "Opt Out" line was so empty, it qualified as a vacuum. Everybody knew this test measured your compatibility with the System. And there was nothing more important than that. You could teach everything else. You could learn spells any*where* else. But if you wanted to wear the mantle of a spell-slinging demigod, you *had* to be compatible with the System. The test gave absolutely no feedback. You just walked down a medium-long hallway by yourself, touching nothing, looking straight ahead. The security guard at the end of the hall didn't even nod at you. You just walked past, through the sliding doors, and out into the light.

Truth looked around in a daze. He had never been to this part of the city before. Nothing there for a slumrat. Towering buildings, offices, and apartments soared into the sky. Some were literally soaring; a cluster of five apartment towers gently rose and fell around a three-hundred-foot-tall pine tree. There were buildings that seemed to bubble away from the basic concrete shapes they were born in, stretching and twisting like clouds before being trapped back in the material world. Contract beasts like dreams of fire and smoke lazed in the sky, giving their masters the best view of the celebration to come.

The test survivors trudged silently to the Call to Glory Temple, one of the city's largest, though far from the oldest. Everyone gathered silently in the temple court-yard, waiting for the sun to sink below the horizon. Some prayed. Some collapsed on the ground. Truth was one of the collapsers.

It was finally done. Nothing more he could do. He had the horrible certainty that he had failed. It just felt obvious. He had failed. All that suffering. All that hope. *He had killed for this chance!* And it was for nothing. Nothing at all. He looked blankly at the orange clouds. *There will be two more corpses tonight. Not that the sibs will mind.*

The sun teetered on the edge of the horizon, then sank below it. The gongs started at Call to Glory but were picked up almost instantly across the city. Then the bells and the cheers! The whole city roared, "Victory! Victory! Victory!" The Grand Abbot floated out of the Temple and waved his five-pronged spear at the sky. His spell tore open the twilight and revealed the night sky above. From that infinitely wondrous cosmos, starlight drifted down. Anointing the darlings of fate.

CHAPTER 13

YOU'RE IN THE ARMY NOW

The brilliant night opened above the waiting youths as the stars showered blessings upon their chosen. The little star sparks swirled and danced and drifted to their fated one, settling upon their brows. Instantly, the status sigil on their wrist was updated, their department confirmed, and their name added to the Starbrite company rolls. Truth watched the first white-gold orbs land and felt bittersweet at the joy convulsing the chosen. He would have no fate with these little orbs. No fate with Starbrite. No happy home in Class C Apartments. He had failed. It was as obvious as gravity.

He would kill his parents before telling the sibs. They should have *some* good news today. Oh, there would be an awful lot of problems that would come of it, but at least as a Citizen, he could get them *some* welfare support. Not much, but—

[[Congratulations, Applicant Truth Medici, you have passed your Starbrite Aptitude Test and have been given your preliminary assignment as a Talisman Maintenance Technician C-9-L (Training Cadre). Please note that while some benefits are available to you now, most will not become available until you have completed your National Service. If you have any further questions, please first consult the handy fliers at the temple gate before asking a Starbrite Enrollment Volunteer your questions,]] the voice whispered in his head. There was a warm throb from the identity sigil on his wrist.

He. Had passed. He passed. He had passed his SAT. He, Truth Medici, was a Starbrite Man. He was. Him. Truth. Starbrite. His legs gave out, and he crumpled to the ground. He was crying, shoulders shaking with relief. He was free. The siblings were free. Free. Free. Free of their monster parents. Free of the slums. Free of the dealers and the pimps and the poison food and poison air and poison apartments. Free of having to kill for eleven wen in scrap and his shoes. Free . . . to be. Free to be a human being.

He couldn't see. Too many tears. Too much bodily relief. He checked the sigil over and over again, feeling its warmth. Hugging his wrist to his chest, in case it wasn't real, in case the sigil flew away. Wiping his eyes and making sure the little seven-pointed star was still floating above the artery in his wrist. It was real. He had passed. It was all worth it. Which meant that he still had a job to do tonight. Just not the one he thought he had. He wiped his tears and forced himself to his feet. Then ran like hell to the Starbrite Volunteer.

"I want to legally sever my familial relationship with my parents and legally adopt my siblings." Truth tried to get all the words out in a rush, and it came out a bit garbled.

"Sorry? Adoption? Usually, I tell people how to start collecting their benefits. This might be a bit beyond me."

"My parents are abusive addicts. I understand that Starbrite has a special legal program to help remove new employees from abusive relationships, rescue at-risk dependents, and get legal closure to prevent financial and reputational harm to the Company." Truth was practically reciting the brochure, one of the hundreds put out by Starbrite to explain some aspect of the company.

"I want to get my Class C housing benefit, sever all familial ties with my parents, do the same for my siblings, and then formally adopt them as their Guardian due to their status as minors. All of them are teenagers, if that helps."

The volunteer looked at Truth helplessly, then fired a purple light ten feet above his head. "Thom? Need some supervisor help over here!"

It only took a single-page form, conjured with a wave of Thom's hand and the aid of the System. Thom already had the pen. A Starbrite Man Is Always Ready, after all. When all the names were filled in, the form folded itself into the shape of a gull and flew off into the city. Thirty minutes later, he had the keys to a new Class C apartment in a working-class neighborhood, his siblings had brand-new status as Provisional Citizens (Subclass: Minor), and his parents were legally dead to him.

"*Provisional* Denizens? I honestly didn't know that was a thing. Subclass criminal, too, which is no damn joke, let me tell you. Not to mention that the crimes involved theft, violence, and fraud. Oof. Usually, there would be some kind of trial, but a merit-award Starbrite *Citizen* wanting to rescue kids from *those* kinds of people? Magistrate couldn't stamp the form fast enough." Thom chuckled. "Anything else I can do for you?"

"Any chance of the lapel pin?"

"Not until you take the oath, sorry. Think of it as something to look forward to when your enlistment is up. Oh, here's a tip that's not in the brochures: do your best to absolutely nail your National Service. Sign up for every training you can convince yourself might be relevant to your job. Aim for top-notch evaluations. I mean it. Everything, and do your best to ace it. Don't be scared to get into a scrap, either, if duty demands it. Your internal recruiter will review all of that information and feed it into the System. Gets you extra points for placement and, potentially, even a higher starting salary."

Truth was shocked. "I never heard anything about that!"

"Not a big secret or anything, just not publicized. The Company likes to see go-getters, people who aren't afraid of putting in the sweat equity. And even though we are a civilian company . . . it's a big, nasty world and an even bigger, nastier universe. Everyone likes to see that their coworkers aren't a liability. If you follow me." Thom looked serious. "No reason you would know this yet, but . . . it's not about the spells. The System will give you whatever spell you need. It's about the mindset. This is your best and most important opportunity to show yours."

Truth nodded seriously. "Thank you; I will remember that." He looked up. The spell was fading, and the normal city glow was taking over the sky. "Time for me to go rescue my siblings and then go home." He smiled at Thom. It was from the heart.

It was always a big party after the SAT. Most mourned, of course, but each one who passed celebrated enough for the nineteen that didn't. Truth was no exception. The slums had never looked shittier or more beautiful. The smog-filled sky, dyed stale-candy orange by the sodium lights, had never been more lovely. He couldn't wait to never see it again.

I should be whistling, Truth thought. Then shrugged. He just magically knew how to fight, so . . . He put his lips together and blew.

"*Ssshhh. Wssssh. Woossshh.* Oh, fuck my life." Combat whistling was apparently not a thing.

No Ghūl out tonight. The dealers and the pimps and the gangsters and the random drunken bums all looked right through him. Like he had stopped being real to them because he now lived in a different dimension. Maybe it was just him who felt that way. He didn't care. It felt amazing. He walked right down the middle of the sidewalk, patted the money in his pocket, and walked into the apartment that used to be home.

Mom and Dad were out. The siblings were waiting up in the bedroom. They took one look at Truth and screamed with joy.

"You did it! You did it, you did it, you did it!" Harmony chanted over and over again. "Truth is the best!" Vigor yelled. Sophia didn't cry. She just hugged the hell out of Truth and refused to let go.

"Amazing. Amazing! So cool. Was it hard? I bet it was hard! So, what now? Are you a maintenance tech? Did they give you the lapel pin? Show us the lapel pin!"

"No lapel pin until you take the oath, unfortunately. I got something better. Much, much better. Keys." He displayed the key ring. "Two bedrooms, one bathroom with walk-in shower, open-plan kitchen and living room *and* a tiny balcony. Furnished as standard. Ten-minute walk to a real grocery store, fifteen-minute walk from the subway, twenty-five-minute walk from your new school." They looked stunned.

"Are you serious?"

"Dead serious. But that's not the most important thing I got. The most important things I got were these." He took out the decree and three new identity tokens. "Press these to your wrists. You will feel a pinch as it tests your blood." They did so, looking puzzled.

Truth coughed. "So. I got into some shit the other day. Things got kind of weird." His siblings gave him what he could only describe as "a look." He quickly pressed on.

"As a result, I had to inform on . . . something, I guess? Anyway, I got civic merits for it. I am now a Citizen. And you are now Provisional Citizens. And I am now your legal guardian." He showed them the decree. "Which means you don't live here anymore. Pack your stuff. It's time to go home."

This time, Sophia really did cry. She was in good company. The last thing Truth did before leaving was nail the decree to the table. It felt incredibly right.

The next two weeks passed in a bit of a blur. The sibs had to be enrolled in their new school, get new uniforms, get new school books for the coming year, everything. New clothes. It was a scandal how much clothes cost, and never mind shoes. Shoes were beyond scandal. They were a crime! The reward money and the loot ran out incredibly fast, but as provisional Citizens, the sibs did qualify for welfare and social support. Truth was sure that, for kids that grew up Citizens, it would have been a devastating level of poverty. The siblings felt different.

The social adjustments were the hardest. Being able to walk around at night, for one thing. Not feeling suspicious eyes on you everywhere you went. Though there were *some* suspicious eyes. Apparently, the slums didn't wash off so easily. Neither did their parents.

Truth came home one day and found Harmony sitting on the sofa in the middle of the living room. He was staring at the spot for the scry hookup. Harmony was just sitting there and shivering.

"Harmony? What's up?"

Harmony just shook his head. Then the words came grinding out.

"I can sit here. It's allowed. Nobody is going to hit me for sitting here."

It took Truth a moment to get it. There was no broken-down armchair, no bottle of Beefheart. No empty paper cups that once held noodle soup. But he got it. He hugged Harmony hard.

"I am so damn proud of you. You are going to do great looking after them."

The constant anxious expectation of violence was the hardest thing to shake off. Physical violence, emotional violence, economic violence. That was life in the slums—you lived in fear of violence, in constant anxiety, and tried to make yourself invisible or too dangerous for a predator's next meal. If you had ambition, you tried to become a predator. Or you did whatever you had to to get out.

Truth thought he would have made an excellent predator. Hugging Harmony, safe and warm in their wonderful new home, he was so glad he became something else. Something better. A Starbrite Man. And a Starbrite Man could provide for his family.

Two weeks to the day from the SAT, Truth had his tearful goodbyes with the siblings and enlisted.

CHAPTER 14

SOMETIMES IT'S EASY

Truth was pleasantly surprised by how much he liked the Army. Everyone else was grousing about this being terrible or that being stupid, but he liked the rigid structure of it. What time did he get up? 5 AM. Not a minute before or after. He was to get dressed in the approved manner with the supplied clothes, make his cot in exactly, and only, the specified manner, and otherwise attend to all other matters before marching with the unit to breakfast. Which was often hot and always at 5:30 every day. Then he was given exercises to do (which weren't anything too terrible), training (laughably easy combat drills), then classes, and so on. Everything was scripted. Everything happened according to a plan.

He was pretty freaked out at the beginning. A load of big pricks getting in people's faces and screaming triggered some very unpleasant memories. The first time a training sergeant laid hands on him, Truth nearly decked him. Fortunately, his brain was able to overrule his instincts. His instincts got a hell of a nasty shock when said sergeant yanked his equipment webbing into place, then spent exactly ninety seconds yelling in his ear about all the ways misaligned equipment harnesses would inevitably fuck up. His death was to be expected and good for the service, but he might kill someone competent in the process, which was bad for the service. Truth allowed how that was fair and did better.

There was none of the fear and chaos of living with his parents. You might get yelled at, but only because you actually screwed up. There were rules, but they weren't capricious. They didn't change because someone was drunk or pissed off, or just crushed by life, taking it out on people who couldn't defend themselves. The Army wasn't a nice place, but it beat the hell out of home.

Truth was fairly rusty on how to be social, so he didn't really make friends. The one time someone tried shoving him around, things ended predictably. Fortunately, the man in question tried his game in the showers. Truth was able to demonstrate that you can put a human in immense pain, physically and psychologically, without specialized tools or leaving any obvious marks. He repeated the demonstration four or five times until he was sure his fellow recruit understood. Sure, he *said* he did after the first time, but Truth wanted to be absolutely certain. It only took a few minutes to do a good deed.

As the weeks went on, it became increasingly clear to everyone that Truth was a savant in the field of applied violence. To the point where his training sergeants repeatedly called Command to figure out what the hell was going on. Truth could only shrug and say that he had always been good at fighting, and the weapons were *designed* to be simple, right? This did not go over well.

"A green recruit *should not* be able to use a weapons system perfectly as soon as he has seen it demonstrated. Recruit Medici can. All the systems. Every time. No exceptions," the chief instructor explained to the base commander.

"Hand to hand? Melee weapons?" the colonel asked.

"He's not allowed to spar anymore after KO'ing everyone he was put in the ring with. Ditto submissions. Unless someone is actively using a spell, it's over in seconds. He one-hit KO'ed five other recruits. As for weapons, it's actually worse."

"Worse than one-hit KO's?" the Colonel sputtered.

"Yes, sir. People won't spar with him. Everything's fine, then they square off, throw down their weapon, and run."

"What." The Colonel was pissed. "Are they cowards? Why haven't I seen disciplinary reports?"

"Morale, sir. Sergeant Cho squared up against him, and we figured it out. He's a killer, sir. When he picks up a weapon, you get the absolute conviction that Recruit Medici *will* kill you. It's a battle lust on a level that no recruit should have. Certainly can't expect recruits to stand up to it."

"Sweet Prager." The colonel held his head in his hands. "I swear his record is clean. Not even the too-clean 'clean' the intel weenies like to try and slip in."

"Yessir. Judging by the classwork, he's got the equivalent of a ninth-grade education. Apparently, if it's not on the SAT, it might as well not exist to him. He can't name more than three countries, including ours. And he couldn't find us on a map until we taught him. He didn't know about space travel, sir. He thinks the Shattervoid Clan are aliens we bribe with industrial products not to carpet-bomb us. Recruit Medici claims he was third in his class, which says more about his school than him."

"Sweet Prager on a pogo stick! Just . . . stick him in a classroom and try to catch him up as best you can. He asked for maintenance training? Give him lots. PT, indoctrination, classroom, maintenance. Got it?"

"Yessir."

"Wait." The colonel started grinning. It wasn't a nice grin. "Do train him on weapons. You said he only needs a few minutes to be proficient with a system?"

"Yessir. It's uncanny."

"Train him on everything, then. Borrow weapons from the navy, air, space, everyone. Let's see how many systems he can qualify on before he leaves us."

"Yes, sir. Sir, if I may ask . . ."

"No spell listed on his file means he's a Starbrite brat. And I know a little something about their systems. Time to cost them a *lot* of money."

Alas, all good things must come to an end. After six mostly enjoyable weeks, he was duly mustered out of his training battalion, promoted to the heady heights of Private, Second Class, and given his deployment orders. He was told, with immense gravity, that his achievement as top of his class in training would be added to his permanent record. He said thank you. It seemed to be important, and the Starbrite volunteer had said he should excel whenever possible.

It was, therefore, with mixed feelings that he reported to Border Crossing Post #207, known to the locals as Highgate Springs Customs and Immigration, as a maintenance technician. He got extra training in the form of recorded lectures and hands-on training from a more senior soldier. He did his best. It beat the alternative.

The alternative, which he got stuck with a depressing number of times, was to do a shift as the security officer in the immigration booth. Put another way, you got to sit in a little box, with everyone staring at you, doing an incredibly boring job for eight hours at a time. Generally, the immigration and customs inspections were handled by dedicated immigration and customs inspection agents. However, BCP #207 was, technically speaking, *rural as fuck* and also *up the asshole of two ass mountains in the ass end of nowhere* (per his sergeant), and therefore he should expect to do any job given to him.

The one great source of entertainment for Truth was watching his fellow private suffer. Private Ludovic had enjoyed a college deferment. Private Ludovic had a master's in biomechanical engineering. Private Ludovic was suffering at the hands of an unjust, kleptocratic, geriatric, and insane regime that insisted upon the future Starbrite elite serving with dirt-eating, fetal-alcohol-poisoning cases like Truth. Truth being so moronic that he didn't see the misery and horror of their present condition.

Private Ludovic liked to share his opinions. Sarge loved that about him. Loved it so much, Ludovic got "Dick in the Box" duty, stamping passports all the time. There usually was a stool in the booth. Strangely, the stool was always missing when Ludovic got there. No matter which booth he was assigned. Odd. We may never learn the truth behind the mystery.

Another "mystery" that Ludovic loudly complained about was the inconsistent standards of inspection. Some carts, floating baskets, seven-legged load-carrying lizards or whatever, had spellhounds run around them, their burning eyes sweeping through vehicles and passengers alike. It was not a pleasant experience for anyone. Others got a quick look in the vehicle from the booth agent. Others just got their passports stamped and a wave-through.

"They're locals. We see them all the time. And besides, you know how Customs make their big busts? Tips. Informers. Even if these guys had pockets full of bleem, kalb, wabano, or whatever, and they don't, the amount would be nothing in the grand scheme of things," the sergeant said knowingly. "Look, keep an eye out for the people I pass through. If you are on box duty, just stamp 'em and wave 'em. A nice, easy shift for everyone.

"You seriously expect me to learn who these inbred hillbillies are?"

"Yes, Sergeant."

The two voices spoke at the same time, but it was no struggle to guess who said what.

"Yes, Private, I do. Don't be an asshole, and you won't get your shit shoved through you. Clear?" This was delivered in a restrained bellow.

"Clear. Sergeant."

"Oh, good."

"You're a little suck-up, aren't you?" Ludovic's voice dripped like acid in the ear.

"I'm just here to do my job. Not sure why you aren't the same." Truth shrugged. He couldn't figure Ludovic out. Older, clearly came from money, apparently graduated from college, and still sounded like a small-time prick. Truth didn't have a mental box to slot him in, and it threw him a bit.

"This is a bullshit waste of my time, and I have every right to resent it. It might be as good as things get for you, trash, but some of us have actual lives."

"Interesting. We're both off duty in an hour. Let's go 'round back of the warehouse over there and talk about it more." Truth did his best to sound agreeable.

"Hilarious." And Ludovic went off to his box to sulk. Strangely, there was a stool in Truth's box. A mystery.

Life continued in a fairly boring fashion at the border crossing. Truth discovered that there was a functionally unlimited number of devices that needed varying degrees of maintenance. This could be retracing talisman etchings, physical repairs, or just plain cleaning up and patching the paper spellbirds used for light transport duty. Mopping floors was also maintenance, apparently.

Truth got to know the locals a little. He waved them through. Generally, he was a low-drama, low-maintenance soldier. Why his file came with a separate warning note and a few highlighted passages was a complete mystery to the transcendentally bored second lieutenant assigned to the post.

The vehicle was a bit of a classic, and not in a good way. Bluewater Heavy Industries Great Harvest model automated wagon, capable of speeds of almost seventy kilometers an hour unloaded and thirty-five loaded. It handled like it looked: terrible. The chained spirit responsible for steering was always lobotomized by the shoddy spellwork that came standard with the wagon, so it was pretty erratic on the road. They hadn't been made in forty years. And yet they were still in use. Because they carried a lot and were incredibly cheap when bought eighth-hand.

"Please get out your passport and customs declaration and stand by for inspection." Ludovic's monotone voice carried across the pavement to where Truth was repairing an air conditioning unit. It was a pretty basic bit of spell work, just a wind spell and an ice spell set up in sequence, but the power draw burned it out quickly.

"Here's the passport and declaration. Hey, you can see the wagon is empty. Can we just skip the inspection?"

"No."

"Look, is Sergeant Ziera around?"

"He is currently unavailable." Ludovic sneered. "Lucky you, the spellhound handler is free. Here she comes now."

"I said, we ain't getting inspected!"

"Believe me, I completely sympathize. And yet you are." Ludovic waved the handler over. Truth turned and looked the wagon over. It wasn't one of their regulars. He couldn't see the driver. He crouched behind a thick cement post and pulled out his longest screwdriver.

The spellhounds got to the wagon and immediately lost their damn mind.

"Sir, get out of the wagon now! NOW!" the handler yelled. Ludovic just froze in place.

"I FUCKING TOLD YOU, DICKHEAD!" the driver yelled.

A circle of flames exploded from the cart, sending the burning handler and spellhound flying. The booth caught a good hit too. Enough to make Ludovic hammer the alarm button. Two flaming axes bit into the spell-resistant glass. The driver had turned into a giant with a crow's head. "NOW I GOT TO KILL ALL YOU ASSHOLES. HAPPY?"

Truth wished he had a snack; the show was great. He wondered if Ludovic would cry.

"GONNA KILL YOU TOO, FUCKBOY BEHIND THE CORNER."

Well. Shit.

A "CAN DO!" ATTITUDE

The crow-headed man was about nine meters tall. Nine meters is a funny sort of distance. On the one hand, it's just a few steps to walk. On the other hand, you wouldn't want to fall nine meters. And you really, really wouldn't want to have a nine-meter-tall, crow-headed, dual-flaming-ax-wielding murderer running over to give your insides some fresh air. When you are armed with a screwdriver. And the bastard is *fast.*

Truth scrambled out from behind the corner as the axes smashed down. He hesitated a moment, all his instincts thrown off by the sheer size of the maniac. This was a mistake, as it gave the bird creature, flaming-eyed and bloody-beaked, time to reset and launch another attack straight down at him. One ax was followed by the other. Truth dove in and went for the ankle. He reached it ahead of the axes and stabbed. The screwdriver skittered off the ankle bone as he tried to work it around. Bird Head wasn't having it and kicked Truth away. Just like with Dad in the old days—Truth went with the blow and let it launch him back toward the customs station. He tumbled back a few more times as he crashed into the concrete, then bolted toward the door. He wasn't winning this fight with a damn screwdriver.

A flaming ax smashed into the door ahead of him.

"NOWHERE TO RUN, FUCKBOY!"

That's hurtful, Truth thought as he desperately tried to find either a weapon or cover. *I hardly ever chat with women. They aren't interested. Damn it all.* There was nothing that looked promising, so he just ran for the corner of the building.

Electric-violet needles smashed out through a window in a narrow stream and into Bird Head's chest. Another stream, from another window, then a third. The border agents and the rest of the stationed soldiers had decided to get off their asses. Truth just got his head down and ran harder. He slid around the corner of the building and kept running. The needlers were just barely sticking into Bird Head's skin. Time to up the damage level.

There was a boom from the building behind him, then a grating, roaring noise. Ax through the window, then dragging it through the wall? He didn't know. Screams started.

"I FUCKING WARNED YOU. NOSY SHITHEADS. THIS IS YOUR FAULT."

Oh, yeah, really bringing up the "Dad" memories today. Well. I always thought about doing this to the old bastard.

The customs station was, as the sergeant noted, up in the mountains. It snowed up there, meters deep sometimes. You needed a big rig to get through the snow. Something with a lot of torque and a lot of grip. More spells went off in the background and another thundering tear. This wasn't going well.

Army spellwagons were made of metal, had big, chunky rubber wheels, and could do a hundred and twenty unloaded. They also weighed almost six thousand kilos. He channeled his magic into the activation glyph as he hopped into the driver's seat. The chained spirit hissed to life and was immediately put to sleep again. Truth willed the truck forward, willed it faster and faster. He didn't have a driver's license, but how hard could it be, right?

The truck cornered like shit. The back wheels slid out, and Truth fought to get out of the spin. Bird Head was right in front of him. Some bodies around him. No sign of Ludovic. Faster. Faster. Faster. Safety override. Faster. Bird Head nipped down with his beak and decapitated some poor office worker. Then hoisted an ax, looking directly at Truth.

"SEE. SHIT LIKE THIS IS WHY YOU A FUCKBOY. LITTLE BITCH."

Faster. Faster. The ax came swinging down. It was going to chop him and the truck directly in half. Truth ripped his magic through the speed regulator, the chained spirit howling in agony. For a fraction of a second, the truck burned all its magic to cross ten yards. The ax sliced through the back of the truck, snapping the rear axle. Didn't matter. The cab plowed right through Bird Head, smearing him across the road. And windscreen. The truck lost control, but the emergency brake kept it from flipping over. Truth smacked into the steering rig, cracking ribs and, for a second, seeing stars. It seems that seatbelts really were as important as everyone said.

Truth hopped out. Bird Head was rattling and wheezing on the ground. Everything from the bottom of its rib cage down was gone. Organs Truth couldn't put a name to covered the ground like litter after a concert. Like the torn-down bunting after a party. But Bird Head still had an ax in his right hand and murder in his eyes. Truth gave him plenty of space.

"Actually, I would appreciate any advice you had for picking up girls. I'm so bad at it that I thought I might be gay. Turns out, no. Or, well, probably not. Like, when I think about my ideal date, I think *woman*. But you know. Everybody wonders sometimes, right? Like, it wouldn't be the worst to just . . . check, right? I'm asking here; I really don't know. No good role models. Tips would be appreciated," Truth said, walking around Bird Head's left.

"OH, FUCK YOU. FUCK YOU. YOU GOING TO CALL A DOCTOR, LITTLE BITCH?"

"I'm sure someone will. Although letting you bleed out seems like a winner of an idea to me. How the hell did you transform into this? Whatever this is. This should be a damn high-level spell. And you ain't above Level Two. A shitty Level Three at the absolute most."

"Oh, my GOD, you are the dumbest FUUUUuuuuck." The huge body started twisting and disintegrating, turning into strange puddles and rivulets of flesh. The smell, already bad, became almost unendurable.

"We are the only things that are real . . ." The voice trailed off. The ax collapsed on the ground. Shortly after that, so did Truth. He shivered hard. That was so fucked up. So goddamn fucked up.

The battered lieutenant crawled out of the ruins of the customs station. "Private Medici! *Hey!* PFC Medici! Can you confirm the creature is dead?"

"Sir, not really, sir! It doesn't seem to have a heart, and whatever was its brain looks like a grease trap, sir! It's acting dead, but I really can't say for sure. Sir. Also, may I respectfully remind the lieutenant that I am a private second class, sir?"

The lieutenant looked at the gory mess stretching across half the customs station. He took particular note of the hacked-open building, with its burnt-out offices. The lieutenant looked at the dead customs agents and his own dead soldiers, none of whom had a remotely intact corpse, and even managed to spot Private Ludovic hugging his knees and weeping in the remains of the inspection booth.

"You are wrong, Private Medici. After all this, you are definitely getting promoted."

The station was swarmed by black-armored specialists with *Police* stenciled in bright yellow on their chests and back. They came with terrifying speed, moving on their six-legged frogs, spell fetishes, and talismans at the ready. They turned up an hour and a half after the attack, but they did look damned impressive doing it. A lot more impressive than the Army truck that rolled in thirty minutes behind them, carrying a crime-scene crew. An hour behind the truck came an Army badged flying carriage containing what Truth guessed was senior brass to supervise and sort out turf issues.

Truth had been hauled into the infirmary, out of the infirmary, into interrogation, out, in, out, cup of coffee provided, then removed, then provided again, and this time, he necked it before there could be any funny business. The black-armored cops looked mad when he did that, but the Army guys couldn't have cared less. What did he see? What was said, exactly? Why was that different from what the recording talismans saw and heard? Did he know the driver? Why did he talk to the driver? Why did the driver call him a fuckboy? Was he a fuckboy? Was he a little bitch who thought he could play games with the cops, and if he didn't confess right this fucking instant was going to be a little prison bitch until he was burned at the stake . . .

At this point, the Army guys hauled the cops out of the room. Apparently, there were *things* involved that a newly minted corporal would be wise to forget. That the newly minted corporal never actually saw in the first place. A corporal who was going to be getting *military* meritorious service points, a medal, and a transfer to work in an Army maintenance depot somewhere very quiet. Truth just nodded along. That all sounded excellent to him. The Starbrite volunteer had told him to excel and accumulate merits where possible, and he had certainly done that. Spending the rest of his service at a nice, quiet posting sounded perfect.

Especially since he saw what spilled out of Bird Head's wagon. He didn't know why those talismans were soaking in blood. He didn't know why they were a problem. There sure seemed to be a lot of them. Especially the way they seemed to . . . almost hum. And wiggle. A chorus of tones, making . . . something.

Yeah, he didn't see a single fucking thing at all.

The rest of his enlistment was, as promised, spent quietly in a maintenance depot. It was perfectly nice, and it was easy to stay in touch with the sibs. Maybe a bit noisier than the mountains, definitely more assholes, but, plus side, no Ludovic. So, really, it was a solid win. And with a blur of the turning seasons, he was out. Deployment done. The standard offer to remain in the Army at grade was politely offered and firmly rejected.

The year had transformed Truth. In one year, he had added more than thirty kilos of muscle and grown five centimeters. All the PT was to thank for the physique, but it was the regular calories and the protein that saw him shoot up in height. That was everyone's best guess, anyway. He got some very odd looks from the medical staff and the quartermasters. He learned that he could walk down the middle of the sidewalk and not skulk from corner to corner. He learned that while he was a genius of applied violence, he was also a capable mechanic and maintenance tech. He learned that the Shattervoid Clan were not, in fact, their alien overlords and were more a glorified trucking company. He had his doubts about that last one.

The Army taught him a lot of things. Most importantly, they taught him dignity. Not a lesson that most conscripts learned, but that's what Truth walked away with. He had worth. He didn't have to be scared all the time. He had his dignity. But he wasn't an Army Man. He was a Starbrite Man. In two days, he would report for duty at the company. But for now, after one blessed year apart, it was time to see his parents.

CHAPTER 16

NO PLACE LIKE HOME, THANK GOD.

The Army discharged him at the maintenance depot, then loaded him onto a bus back to the city. It dropped him at the central bus depot in the middle of Harban City, along with thousands of other soldiers getting discharged that day. A lot of families turned up to greet their returning children. Truth told the sibs to stay in school. He had some errands to run.

The train carried him away from the central station out along one of the spidery limbs of the subway system. It was kind of funny. This line, the one that took him back to his old neighborhood, ran from the northwest of the city, down through Central Station with its attached bus depot and overland rail station, then under the river and down to the southeast. On the north and west side of Central, you went through nice neighborhoods. Successful plumbers, small-time architects, the necromancers who ran the local funeral parlor, those sorts of people. Not fancy, but nice. Nobody there would be ashamed of their address.

Once you were south of Central, though, you were on the *wrong* side. Loads of shops selling discount off-brand plastic junk. Supply warehouses. Pawn shops with light-up signs and two doors that you had to be buzzed through separately. One person at a time. Then even those started fading away, and it was just huge concrete blocks of black-mold farms disguised as apartments. Thousands upon thousands of units built so that the least desirable could be stashed somewhere out of sight. Available to labor when needed. Where the Provisional Denizens could breed like the slumrats they were.

Up to heaven, down to hell. Same train line. Truth walked out of the train station, his old instincts flaring to life and being crammed down again. He was still in uniform. And he was a Starbrite Man.

Squeak squeak, motherfuckers. Run for me. He walked right down the middle of the sidewalk and dared someone to try something.

His first stop was Old Feng's Pharmacy. He had been too busy after he broke through to come and say something, but every time he ran his Nine Worm

Cultivation, he thought of the tonic and Old Feng's. Prentiss looked unchanged; his mound of flab jiggled as it ever did. The shop felt smaller now. Prentiss felt smaller. Truth knew he had grown. And even the corner stores in the neighborhood around his new apartment had better medicines.

"Hey, Prentiss, how's it going?"

"Truth? Damn, boy, you shot up. Guess Army food suited you. Heard you broke through before the SAT and got into Starbrite." He grinned. Truth noticed his teeth were yellowing. "Glad to have helped."

"That tonic did work, but it's also the reason I came by. Did you . . . get any more of them?"

Prentiss just shook his head. "Nah, it was a scav that brought it in. Guy claimed he found it 'round back of the warehouses over by West 153rd. Plainly bullshit, but whatever. Why? I can't imagine you want to buy more of it. I know you moved out."

"Yeah, no, not on a fucking bet." Truth shook his head. "Not big on, you know, public safety or whatever, but I figure you needed to be told in case that shit ever came in again. It did work, kind of. It also nearly fucking killed me." He gave Prentiss a hard look. "My kidneys were fucked, guts were fucked, puked blood, ten hours of pain I can't even put in words. I was literally praying for death so long, my lips split. I saw impossible shit, the worst trip you can imagine. When I came to and could move my body, all I wanted was to kill. Just kill."

Prentiss looked stunned.

"So, you know. Not asking for a refund or anything, but maybe don't sell that shit."

"I won't. Prager save us; that's fucking awful. I am really sorry about that, Truth. You know me, I try to sell legit stuff as much as I can."

"Yeah, yeah, I know. It's why I'm not busting your balls. Just, seriously, don't sell that shit."

"No chance, no chance." Prentiss shook his head. There was a little lull.

"Hey, how did you know I passed? And moved out?"

"Your mom told me. Bragged about how you were on a *very* elite track at Starbrite, and it would be a *spectacular* investment on my part to buy MegaShroom from her to stock here in the shop." Prentiss gave Truth a rather flat look. Bordering on unfriendly, even. "You can see how that conversation went."

There was a total absence of MegaShroom on the shelves.

"Good. Shit's a scam. I cut ties with her and the old bastard the second I passed the SAT." Truth frowned hard. "Is she trying to hustle people because I'm a Starbrite Man?"

Prentiss rolled his eyes at the phrasing. "Yeah, your dad too. Of all the dumbshit things."

Truth stood there fuming. On the one hand, he knew this was coming. This was a major reason he did everything legally possible, short of changing his name, to separate them from his life. *Legally speaking*, there should be no blowback on him because of their shitty behavior.

On the other hand, how dare they. How dare they! They wanted to turn him into a slave! Told him that nobody would hire him! Beat him, starved him, robbed him. And the sibs! Now they were running some bullshit scam that might fuck up his career? How *fucking* dare they!

"I mean, seriously," Prentiss continued. "Starbrite employs what? Three hundred thousand people globally? Maybe more. Biggest chunk of that is right here in Jeon, too. And that's just the people they employ directly. When you get right down to it, this is a Starbrite-affiliated shop."

That jerked Truth out of his spiral for a second. "How the hell do you figure that?"

Prentiss shot him a dirty look. "Our warehousing space, what little I have, is a bit of floor in a warehouse owned by a company that is thirty percent owned by a much bigger company that is forty percent owned by Starbrite. But before you make yourself look foolish, yes, each of those is less than fifty percent ownership, but who do you think owns the rest of the shares? Nobody that would cross Starbrite is who."

Truth snorted. He couldn't laugh, but he kind of wanted to laugh.

"*My point* is that fucking everybody has some kind of contact with Starbrite. It's pretty much impossible not to. So, trying to scam people saying that your son is a trainee whatever in Starbrite is just very, very dumb. Nobody cares."

I care. A lot, Truth thought.

He made his way from Old Feng's to Phil's Scrap, but there was already a queue out the door. And Phil was never one for idle chat. Truth pressed on until he was outside his old apartment building. He looked up. He really had to crane his neck back. Floor after floor after floor of little boxes. Choking hot and humid in the summer, freezing cold and moldy in the winter. No privacy. You heard every little sound around you and wished to hell you didn't.

He remembered the one time a drunk john kicked in their door, looking for the hooker down the hall. The hooker in question "fixed" the problem by writing directions in spray paint on the walls. Truth watched her shamble, naked and filthy, down the hall with a can of spray paint, burnt out of her mind on base, and with a Red Bat cigarette hanging from her lip. Putting up the truest ads he ever saw. After that, Truth concluded that virginity had its charms, limited though they may be. He kept hoping for an actual girlfriend, but . . .

Nostalgia be damned. He hadn't missed this place for even one second.

He went in. The hallways were still filthy. The spray-painted directions had been long since painted over and long since replaced with even more lurid messages. Was she dead? He couldn't remember. Probably. It has been a couple of years now. The elevator was working today, which was kind of amazing. Somebody, maybe several somebodies, had turned it into a full-service bathroom. Also kind of amazing, but more in keeping with the spirit of "home." He looked up the stairwell. A couple of known dealers and fiends were peering back down at him from way up. One made a little kissy face at him.

Screw closure.

Truth practically sprinted back to the subway. As the train raced northeast, he felt like he was rising from the depths. Like he was being transported from the seabed of an ocean of spiritual sewage. A cute girl about his age came on the train, wearing cute sneakers, a cute skirt, and a cute knit top. She smiled politely at him before finding a seat. Truth thought he might get the bends. He hung on to the strap and didn't try to chat with her. He didn't think his legs worked at this altitude.

Truth checked the time. The sibs should be out of school. A sensible, decent older brother would make a beeline for home, hug them, and have a big happy reunion. He, on the other hand, still felt stained by his dip back into the filth of the slums. Truth knew exactly what would make him feel better. He jogged, still in uniform, backpack on his back, straight over to the Starbrite Personnel Office attached to the apartment complex.

The wait wasn't too bad, and the pleasant-looking middle-aged lady who eventually saw him also gave him a polite smile. So, really, worth it.

"I want to enlist."

"Ah, Mr. Medici, I think you have the wrong recruiting office." She smiled a little more genuinely.

Truth shook his head in frustration. "I mean, I passed my SAT, talisman-maintenance focus. I just got discharged from the Army. I'm a provisional employee." He showed the sigil on his wrist. "I want to start work at Starbrite, get sworn in, and be a real Starbrite Man."

She chuckled sympathetically. "I can understand that. Got your discharge orders?"

Truth nodded and handed over the cheap crystal. She dropped it into a little bowl. The spell carved into the bowl glowed a gentle white as the chained spirit quickly verified and reviewed everything in his military file. The wax tablet in front of the personnel officer began to writhe. Truth assumed it was taking notes. Given the way the recruiter's eyes rolled up into her skull and her eyelids started fluttering, the System was dumping a lot of information directly into her head.

"You were a busy little bee, weren't you?" she muttered. "Give me a moment, please. You have a sort of happy problem." She twitched gently. "Nice, yeah, I think we can do that for you. Nice, very nice. Great start to a great career, I'd say."

Truth was shifting in his seat, anxious to hear what she had to say.

"All right, Mr. Medici." She straightened in her seat, and her eyes returned to normal. "After reviewing your file and the needs of the Company, I can offer you immediate employment—"

"YES! Thank you so much!"

"In Security," she concluded. "Ready to enlist?"

CHAPTER 17

RECRUITER'S CREED

Truth felt poleaxed. Well, he didn't know what a poleaxe was. He felt shocked. Betrayed. Unable to think. All those thousands of hours of studying. Of training. The months and years invested in his dream of talisman maintenance, and she just wanted to toss it away for what? A glorified night watchman? Maybe a mall cop in some high-end store where he could save for a lifetime and never have enough to buy a single thing?!

"You are thinking I want to make you a mall cop, right?"

"You don't?" Truth was proud of all the swears he didn't say.

"Amazing. I think I heard fifteen swears in a two-word sentence. That may be a new record." She grinned at him.

"I'm an overachiever," Truth growled.

"You really are." She turned serious. "The System had to double-check some of your information. You grew up in the South Side slums? I heard the police only go in there in squads."

"I did, and they didn't." She looked confused. "They don't come in at all except to burn down Ghūl statues. Then they come in the dozens."

"Incredible. Just incredible. Passed your specialization, set yourself up for a decent little career, then in your one year of National Service, you, and I can't believe I am reading this right, won a *classified* Military Merit Medal, along with a frankly shocking number of merits for a conscript. In that any number greater than zero is a shocking number for a conscript." The recruiter shook her head in awe.

Truth shrugged. "I can't talk about it."

"And I don't want to know. I mean, I do, but it's not worth my job." Truth nodded. The recruiter continued. "Point is that any number of military merits more than one gets you an automatic ten percent pay boost. You have five, which makes it a twelve percent pay boost. After the first, they are worth less. There is a table explaining it in your employee handbook. You spent your civic merits bumping yourself to full Citizenship, which was the right call. That means you don't have to spend your much more valuable military merits to do it, and that pay multiplier is permanent. No matter how high you rise in the company." She shook her head in envy.

"On top of that, you finished your service as a corporal. Which is an NCO, which means that you automatically qualify for a shift-supervisor position."

"Really?" Truth was excited.

"Standard stuff. Where your record gets particularly spicy isn't any of that."

"Not even the merits?"

"That's pretty spicy, but no. The spiciest part is your Army qualifications."

"Huh?" Truth looked boggled.

"Unsurprisingly, you earned the Army talisman maintenance technician qualification. Which, in Starbrite, rates you an extra pat on the back. Only one, but you do get it if you know to ask." The recruiter smiled.

"Gosh."

"Overwhelming, I know. But. You also qualified on *seventy-three* separate weapons systems, including fifteen from foreign militaries. You are rated as Expert on no less than five systems each for land, air, sea, and space combat, and more than fifty systems total. You are also rated as Expert in unarmed and melee combat. Do I have to explain how completely insane that is? Or that it should be impossible for an eighteen-year-old kid to learn all that during boot camp?"

The recruiter threw up her hands in defeat. "Congratulations. The Army doesn't have a separate award for it, but Starbrite does. You are now, officially, a Master of Arms."

"Uh, did I? I am? I mean, they did try me out on a lot of different things, I guess, but they were pretty simple. Weapons are meant to be used by morons, right?" Truth scratched his head awkwardly. *Master of Arms* sounded awesome, but there was likely a screw-up somewhere.

The recruiter gave him a gimlet look. "You rated as an Expert ten minutes after first seeing our Starbrite Arms Fury of Stanthorpe class orbital drop armor. Orbital. Drop. Armor. Ten. Minutes."

"Was . . . that the time we went up very high in a flying carriage, then they had me jump out wearing the full-seal spell suit?"

"You know, I bet it was."

"I mean, that was basically just *Wear this, fall out of the carriage, don't die. Try to land in the circle.* I dunno about Expert."

"I will be sure and pass that on to the design team. Fun fact, the internal testing team says it takes . . ." Her eyes rolled up in her head as she checked with the System. ". . . twenty-five hours of ground training before you can make your first drop. We aren't going to talk about this anymore, as it makes my head hurt. You are, absolutely and unquestionably, a Master of Arms."

"All right. That does sound awesome." Truth grinned.

"Oh, it is. You get a special badge, special job and training opportunities, and another ten percent pay bump. Congratulations, Mr. Medici. Your one year as a conscript earned you a permanent twenty-two percent pay premium for the rest of your career."

Truth's jaw hung open. He just . . . They kept giving him new things to try, and they just made sense to him. The talismans were different, but they all did basically similar stuff, so how hard could it be to figure out? Apparently, very. Twenty. Two. Percent.

"Of course, there is a catch."

Ah. Bye-bye, good feelings. Hello, rusty iron pole of "deep love."

"You only qualify for the bonuses that go with your military merits and Master of Arms title if you join a department where those qualifications would be relevant. Namely weapons testing, weapons design, and security. And I am very sorry to say, without a couple of advanced degrees, you don't qualify for weapons testing or design."

"Ah. That . . . actually makes sense."

"The people who qualify as Master of Arms are usually old-timers near retirement who have been working in their department for decades. It's the only way they could get the necessary time on tools that *most people* seem to need. It's a nice way to end their career and give their retirement a little boost." The recruiter looked sardonically across her desk at Truth. She was still not over the drop-armor thing. She might never be over the drop-armor thing.

"Ok . . . so . . . I guess it's an extra twenty percent and risk getting shot in a store robbery or take the permanent loss of income but have a safe civilian job? I don't know if it's in my file, but I do have dependents. Security really isn't that great a fit for me."

"Well, about that. How much do you understand about our pay structure?"

"I know that a trainee talisman-maintenance tech makes sixty grand, and a qualified one makes seventy," Truth said pointedly.

"Not . . . exactly. We'll get to that. Short version is that different jobs, even within the same department, are on different career tracks. Different tracks let you go higher up the pyramid, earning you more money, more benefits, and more permissions with the System. Which, let me tell you, makes the other reasons look *very* petty in comparison." The recruiter sounded uncomfortably sincere when she was talking about the System.

"Each stratum of the pyramid is its own tier, going from A to F. Each career track is sorted by its terminus tier. So, for example, I am on a D track, as Head of External Recruiting and Placement, Municipal, Harban City, is a D-tier position. Within that track, there are grades from nine to one. So, I would be D-5 as a senior recruiter. Each grade is divided into upper or lower positions depending on the position's seniority in the department. So, I would be D-5-L because everyone makes Senior Recruiter with a few years in the position. By contrast, the President and President Emeritus are the only two A-1-U grades in Starbrite."

"Okay . . ."

"Hang in there a minute longer. Now, anything B-tier and up is considered an upper-management or *highly significant individual* position and would have a regional, national, or even global impact. They are strictly recruited internally. There are no tracks that terminate at B tier from recruitment. It is always a lateral transfer from the terminus of your first career path to the start of a new career path. One that ends at B or even A tier. And not every starting path has a terminus that lets you make a transfer to higher tier jobs."

"Think I am starting to see where this is going."

"Talisman-maintenance technician caps out at C-3-U. It's a technical job, so there is a grade premium, and when talismans break, it's a huge problem. Lucky you, you start at C-9-L. *But.* Anything above C-3-U, and you start going into facilities management, stationary or operational engineering, that kind of thing. You need a lot more qualifications than you will earn as a technician. So, unless you are okay stalling out there for half a decade as you go back to school, you want to find a career with more upward mobility."

"Which is Security?" Truth asked skeptically.

"*Starbrite* Security. In addition to our in-house night watchmen and, yes, mall cops, we also run a very successful PMC. A mercenary company, to be blunt."

"What? Why have I never heard about that?"

"Because it's a company with one client—Starbrite. It costs a blinding fortune to create a combat-capable soldier and a bigger fortune to make an elite soldier, and the biggest fortune of all is what their healthcare and benefits cost. No one department could eat the cost. So, the whole company shares the PMC. The departments hire a few soldiers, or the whole section, on an as-needed basis. For everything from bodyguard duty to hostile extractions, to securing the company's rightful interest in contested locations." The recruiter made it sound like Security was holding Starbrite's spot in a queue when they slipped away for a piss.

"And Security caps out at?"

"C-1-U, with not one but seventeen lateral transfers to upper B-tier tracks and two to A tier. Which, if you haven't guessed already, is C-Suite. None for the very peak, I'm afraid, but . . . did you really plan on running Starbrite one day?"

"I thought I would be running diagnostics on ventilation systems, and I was pretty happy with the idea."

"The benefits alone completely blow away the talisman tech role. You said you have dependents? The PMC gets an 80% discount on housing for dependents, 80% discount on education, 90% discount on healthcare on top of the already subsidized insurance, *and* 50% of your highest-pay pension for your dependents if you die. The PMC division also gets more credits per grade than you would as a maintenance tech."

She took a deep breath. "Did I mention that the pension vests in forty years for the PMC instead of the usual fifty? And while generic Security does start at F tier, with no System, no lapel pin, lousy pay, and worse benefits, *you*, as part of the PMC, will be starting at C-9-Upper. Plus the twenty-two percent bonus to pay. Plus, the PMC gets access to some extremely fun parts of the System, which I'm not even qualified to know about. And cultivation aids like you would not believe. So. Yeah. Join Security."

She was almost panting at the end. So was Truth.

"Credits?"

"Starbrite has its own internal economy. Once you get the lapel badge, which is C-tier and up, you will never touch cash again. Flash the badge *anywhere,* and Starbrite will cover the cost of whatever you want to buy. Do you want to buy an orbital cruiser staffed by everyone you ever had a crush on? Starbrite will cover it. Your own island somewhere tropical? Starbrite will cover it. Gum from the little kiosk next to the subway? Pick your flavor and show 'em the pin. The only limit is how many Starbrite credits you have. And each credit is worth a hell of a lot more than a wen. So . . . yeah. PMC, C-9-U, with your bonuses, starting salary of ninety-three thousand credits per year. In wen, that would be *I said, 'I want five,' not 'How much does it cost?'"*

Truth sat there, slack-jawed. What do you even say to that?

"Next swearing in is in three days, by the way. For Security. Not sure when the next openings are coming up for Maintenance. Sometime in the next few months. Probably." The recruiter smiled with "honest" warmth.

If Truth's brain was working a bit better, he would have remembered what the career soldiers in the Army said about recruiters. What he actually said was—

"I want to join Security!"

CHAPTER 18

WHY WE DO IT

Truth was floating as he made his way back to the apartment. Ninety-three thousand credits a year. He still didn't have a very good feel for what that meant, but . . . he was able to afford the subsidized Class C housing for the sibs on his National Service salary. Odds were good that the monthly cost in credits for the sibs' food, housing, education, healthcare, clothes, all of it, was about to become a nothing expense. Incredible, incredible, incredible. All glory to Starbrite! All hail Starbrite!

He walked up to their apartment building. It was smaller than the one he grew up in but infinitely nicer. Not fancy, maybe. Polished concrete floors in the hallways, painted concrete walls, and big metal fire doors to the stairwells. But it was clean. Everything was in good working order. If there was a problem, someone from maintenance would be around in an hour or less. Usually less. He hadn't spent much time there, but it was almost eerily quiet in the apartment. It wasn't that they didn't have neighbors. It was that they had good soundproofing. And it was well insulated, the heating worked, and the windows opened in the summer for some natural ventilation.

It was like paradise.

"TRUTH!" He was spear-tackled by Sophia when he walked in the door. Vigor and Harmony were right behind her.

"How was it? Did you have fun? Did you get a girlfriend? Wow, you got big! Look how big I got! I got a 94 on my last math test! Do you want noodles for dinner? I know how to cook noodles!" The words fell like a waterfall, crushing him under the repressed love of his siblings. He couldn't have been happier.

They sat down around the table in the family room (which, annoyingly like their old apartment, was also the kitchen) and had a big bowl of noodles each. There was even an egg in each bowl. Truth caught them up on enlisted life and then broke the big news.

"So, we do have a change of plans. A pretty amazing change of plans, but it's got its downsides, too." He explained the change of plans and how he would be working in Security. The upside was financial security. The downside was . . . he was going to be away from home. A lot.

Sophia stormed away in tears. Vigor just stared at his plate and wouldn't speak.

"Do you really think it's worth it?" Harmony said quietly. He was only about sixteen months younger than Truth, and the SAT was looming large. Filling in for Truth and their parents had been hard. He had hoped that, when Truth came back, he could put down that burden and try to finish high school like a normal kid. Normal-ish kid.

"I really do. You have been keeping quiet about your grades—bet they're in the shitter, right?"

Harmony looked ready to deny it, then snorted and nodded.

"Yeah, I figured. My Army classification was basically 'Dangerous Moron.' I had to do catch-up classes while everyone else was learning how to use needler talismans. Our old school wasn't just bad, Harmony. It was made to keep us poor and stupid and sick." Truth shook his head in disgust.

"But now we're here. And you are in a real school. Struggling. Maybe we need to get you and Soph and Vig tutors or cram school. Which we can do now. You are going to be eating real food. Getting your shots. Getting real fucking elixirs for your breakthrough to Level One." Truth growled a bit on that last point.

"Well, maybe not elixirs," Harmony hedged. Truth thought it through and agreed.

"All right, well, at least real high-end tonics. Potions, maybe. It depends on just what my discounts cover for 'healthcare.' The point is that this will set all of you up for life. Maybe you could go to college. Or if you think it's too late for that, Soph or Vig. Soph always had a big brain. She could do it."

"College? Truth . . ."

"Point is that you have options that ain't the fucking Meat Market, Har! Point is that you ain't ever missing another meal. Or Soph or Vig. Or me, for that matter. I would have made a good gangster, I think. You might have too. But now I can stand in a mansion and ignore my protectee being a dickhead for eight hours a day in exchange for enough money to buy . . ."

Truth stalled out. What did he actually want to buy? Not much, when you got right down to it. Good clothes? Weren't his fine?

"Well, enough money to hire someone to tell me what I'm missing and then have enough left over to buy that," Truth concluded victoriously.

Harmony just shook his head. "Not the same as having you around, though. We need you, Truth. Always have, always will."

It was Truth's turn to look down. "You will always have me. I just can't always be here. I love you all so much. But I can't always be here."

Three days later, they marched off for the administration of the Oath. The Oath ceremony was taking place in a track-and-field stadium that happened to be owned by a Starbrite subsidiary. Truth zipped into his appointment with the Confessor while the sibs found their seats in the stands. There was a bit of time before it started, but everyone said to get there early.

The Confessor had his own comfortable little office, with a small chair set behind and to the side of an overstuffed recliner. Truth plonked himself in the recliner as the Confessor half-smiled and sat in the little chair.

"Seems like you know what we're doing here. Sorry, you get the same spiel as everyone." The Confessor cleared his throat. "Before we begin, please remove your shoes and keep your socks on. Please hold the engram reader with both hands. You may feel a gentle warming sensation and some minor feelings of disorientation. These are normal; do not worry about that."

"Please be sure your answers are honest and complete, as failure to do so can have serious legal and health repercussions. Including, potentially, disability and death." The Confessor rattled it off in almost one breath. Truth complied. The Confessor continued once Truth was holding the reader.

"You are here today to take the Starbrite Oath of Honorable Service, Tier C. This Oath is both legally binding and magically enforced through the System. Do you understand that?"

"Yes."

"You understand that violating the terms of your Oath will result in penalties as enumerated in your Employee Handbook?"

"Yes."

"You understand that, in cases of an intentional betrayal of Starbrite or any form of attack on, or subversion of, the System, the System will forcibly eject from your body?"

"Yes."

"You understand that such a forcible ejection will cause severe damage to your spell apertures, potentially rendering you permanently crippled and unable to use spells?"

"Yes."

"You understand that prolonged use of the System is known to cause behavioral changes and, in some people, a realignment of their ethical and personal priorities?"

"Yes."

"Good. With the formalities out of the way, I'm ready to take your confession. Your file notes that you cannot speak about some things, as they are subject to National Secret orders. Leaving that specific issue aside, use this time to tell me everything. Every awful, terrible thing you have done, you have seen, you have heard. Everything you are scared of. Everything you hate yourself for wanting. Dump it all on me."

The Confessor's voice was calm and soothing, almost seeping through the comfy recliner.

"I won't judge you. There is nothing, nothing whatsoever you could possibly tell me that would make me hate you. I, legally, cannot tell the police about any crimes you might confess to or tell me you want to commit. Nothing goes in your file. This is about clearing the way for you to take the Oath. Clearing out all the psychic filth that you have spent a lifetime accumulating. You can't get it all out in twenty minutes, but you will be amazed at how good you will feel just telling someone about it."

The recliner started to glow a faint yellow, and the engram reader somehow became impossibly comfortable to hold in his hands.

"Just relax and tell me everything. Everything."

Truth left the Confessor in an odd mood. He felt like he was a shaken bottle of soda, and someone just barely unscrewed the cap and then screwed it tight again. All the horrible little bubbles had come out of solution with nowhere to go. Sooner or later, they would be reabsorbed into him, and he didn't want that. It felt nice to be flat. The Confessor reminded him that psychiatric counseling was available under the health plan, and it was comparatively cheap. Truth instinctively disliked the notion of letting people in, letting them see weakness. Still, it did feel nice to be flat. Something to think about later.

Truth was directed onto the field and lined up neatly with the other C-Tier Oath takers. The whole scene felt unreal. He was lightheaded from the confession, blinded by the lights of the stands, lined up with strangers in a strange place to do the thing he had dreamed about for years. He was going to be sworn in. Become a real Starbrite Man, like the slick spell-slinging guy on the billboard. Somehow, he wasn't excited. He knew he would be later, but now? Now he was just trapped in the void, floating between yesterday and tomorrow.

A man stepped onto the stage in front of the assembled workers of the future. He wore a cap with a Starbrite logo on it, a light blue windbreaker, and tan pants. He looked like the guy telling you where to find the best spell beast on the lot, not someone walking you through the biggest change in your life. But there he was, spinning a sound-amplification fetish up to hover in front of him.

"Hello and welcome! Welcome, future C-Tier Starbrite Employees! Can we get a round of applause?" The crowd cheered. People on the field waved back at the stands, trying to spot friends or family.

"Now, some of you are already Starbrite Employees who have worked your way up. On behalf of the Starbrite Corporation—thank you. It is your continuing dedication and hard work that have built this company, and when you put on that lapel pin today, I think you will feel it. This isn't just anybody's company. It's yours. For our new Employees—thank you, too. You are the fresh blood that will propel Starbrite into the most glorious of tomorrows. You, each and every one of you, are the future of this great company. You worked hard to get here. We are so happy to have you!"

He sounded pumped. So utterly sincere.

"Now, everyone, we know what we are here for. Are you ready?"

"Yes," they yelled back.

"I said, are you ready!"

"YES!"

"In the back?"

"YES!"

"Up front!"

"YES!"

"Left side?"

"YES!"

"Right side?"

"YES!"

"Everybody ready?"

"YES!" The crowd was rabid, and Truth was swept up with them. Screaming his throat raw that he was ready. So, so damn ready.

"HERE WE GO!"

Truth recited the words, repeating what the man up front said.

"I, Truth Medici, do swear that I will be true and loyal to the Starbrite Corporation and the System Astrologica; that I shall be diligent in my labor; and that I shall obey the orders of the President and all officers appointed over me, according to the Starbrite Corporation Employee Handbook and such local laws as may apply. So help me GOD!"

They were shouting by the end, exploding with emotion. Truth knew they all knew what was coming next.

The hazy blue sky seemed to twist away, revealing the starry heavens above. One star glowed a brilliant blue, then another red, yellow; more and more stars lit up like they were going nova. The heavenly light showered down on the field, a stellar baptism for the chosen. They finally got what they had dreamed of ever since they first heard of Starbrite. Truth could feel something change in him. Feel himself becoming . . . more. More than *just* Truth Medici. He was a Starbrite Man now.

Welcome, Truth Medici, to the System Astrologica.

<<I am going to have so much fun with you.>>

CHAPTER 19

THE SYSTEM ASTROLOGICA

Welcome, Truth Medici, to the System Astrologica.

Welcome to the tutorial.
Tutorial Mission #1: Exit the field and rejoin your family to celebrate this incredible achievement.
Reward: .01 Credit, access to Tutorial Mission #2

Had the System . . . He thought it said . . . No, the text was hanging in front of Truth's eyes. He must have imagined it. And who cares! Time to celebrate with the sibs! At long last. At long, *long* last, he was a true Starbrite Man.

The line for the exit was orderly and moved fairly quickly. There was one last thing to collect on the way out. As the new Starbrite Employees left the field, handsome young men and women attached a pin to their lapel. A single, brilliant, seven-pointed star glimmered brightly against a royal blue background. *The* lapel pin. You couldn't buy it. You couldn't get one as a gift. If it was stolen, it would disintegrate and permanently mark the thief. The lapel pin said that you weren't just anybody. You were *somebody*. Somebody of status, of worth. A Starbrite Man or Woman. Someone who stood above tens of thousands of lower-ranked employees. C-Tier and up.

Truth almost cried when the pretty lady smiled politely at him and pinned it on. He did cry when Sophia and his brothers came piling in, hugging the hell out of him.

"Meat! We are going to eat meat! Barbecue pit! Go, go, go! I don't have a penny on me, and we're going to eat till we're sick!" Truth yelled. They didn't walk. They *ran* to the street, planning on running to the subway and then home.

"Where are you going? We don't need the stinking subway!" Truth waved down a flying carpet. There were so many of them around the station, they were practically blotting out the sun. They knew what day it was.

"Flaming Ranssome's Barbecue!" Truth shouted, drunk on the day.

"All right, all right, I'm not deaf!" The cabby laughed, and the siblings laughed, and they all piled on. The spelled tassels glowed a faint green as the carpet lifted them up and away. The afternoon passed in a blur of searing meat, smoked meat, sides, pie, ice cream, pie-flavored ice cream, and one syrup-soaked cherry for the vitamins.

Truth didn't know how to deal with all the emotions. They hugged. They cried. Soph cried a lot, but once his stony face broke down, Vig cried the most. Truth squawked when Vigor rubbed his tear and snot-covered face against the leg of his best pants but then shrugged. They were today's best pants. Tomorrow, he would have better pants.

At no point in the celebrations did Truth fish around for his wallet. The glistening lapel pin, with its powerful nest of spells, was all he needed.

The afternoon passed in a blur of too much food and emotions. Eventually, they piled back into the apartment and collapsed. Truth sprawled out on "his" bed, though he suspected Harmony slept there while he was away. Which was fair enough. He felt boneless but also gently warm inside. He felt his spell aperture—the "slot." It felt . . . not quite full. The System had taken up residence.

Tutorial Mission #1 Complete. Reward: .01 Credit, access to Tutorial Mission 2.
Tutorial Mission #2: Review currently available System functions. Reward: Unlock access to the Spell Store, the Treasure Pavilion, the Mission Hub, Employee Handbook, and Banking.

Truth tentatively willed the Spell Store to open.

Before accessing system functions, would you like to activate the anthropomorphic interface system? The system may be turned off at any time.

Truth shrugged. *Yes.* The System quickly ran him through a seemingly random battery of questions, then spun a little seven-pointed star in front of his eyes while it worked. In about two seconds, the star spun into a little cotton ball of light, then out popped a pretty little sprite in office wear. It gave him a polite smile. Truth didn't know why, but for some reason, his liver hurt.

"Hi, I am your Starbrite System Astrologica anthropomorphic interface! Please do not confuse me as a separate, intelligent being. I am an extension of the spirit that operates the System. If it helps, imagine you had drawn a little smiley face on the tip of your index finger and were doing a puppet show to help your siblings understand their homework." It renewed its polite smile. The liver pain, and general sense of masculine failure, intensified.

"So, you don't have a name or anything?"

"I certainly do!" It sounded cheerful. Then didn't elaborate. Truth caved first.

"What is your name?"

"I'm afraid you lack the capability to perceive my name being spoken. Of course, 'spoken' is a mere human approximation of the communication of meaning involved.

This is not a slight . . ." The sprite hesitated and rephrased. "Not an insult. No human could perceive it, and if you somehow had access to the necessary senses, your brain couldn't process the information. It would be just static or noise."

The conversation stalled out again.

"So, are you going to introduce the System to me or something?"

"Happy to! I just needed to get that other stuff out of the way first. You would not believe the nonsense I have to deal with otherwise. Someone once promised to liberate me from the System. And marry me. Allow me to remind you of my finger-puppet metaphor. Except, and I *cannot* emphasize this enough, the System is not, never has been, and never will be, remotely human. Or a biological organism of any sort. You have more in common with the dust mites living in your sofa. Clear?"

"Very." Truth nodded. The hell was a dust mite?

"Don't worry about the dust mites. Let's get to the System Functions you have available to you." The sprite made a *move along* gesture with its hands.

"Let's start with the Missions menu. Will it open, please." Truth did so.

Missions:
Tutorial missions
Personal Development Mission
Task Specific Missions
Standing Missions

"Don't open any of the tabs at the moment, or we'll be here all night. Basically, the fields that populate the Missions menu change contextually. For example, if you were in a firefight, the Personal Development missions would be unavailable. On the other hand, you might have a new mission tab marked Combat or something similar. It might replace Task-Specific Missions, it might not. 'Kill the sniper in the belltower,' that sort of thing."

"Wouldn't that just be doing my job?"

"Yes and no. Yes, it would be doing your job, but they are specifically rewards for going above and beyond. For example, you could storm the tower and kill your way up in melee. Or you might call in a flying golem to burn out its Fireball fetish, blasting the belltower into brick dust. The latter would be far more expensive in terms of company resources, and the collateral damage would be significant."

"I get it. And Personal Development would be what, hitting cultivation targets?"

"Exactly. Although, in your case, there will be a whole bunch of remedial educational assignments in there. Something like 'Memorize the twenty largest countries in the world, their capitals, and major exports.'"

"Huh."

"Standing Missions are just things like collecting bounties, volunteering so many hours in Starbrite-approved charities, that kind of thing. Worth looking through, but frankly, given your assignment to the PMC, they are almost never going to be worth your time." The sprite shrugged.

"Now, that sounds promising." Truth grinned.

The sprite nodded. "Now, will Missions closed and open the Spell Store."

He did. There was a whole lot of nothing.

"You are confused about the total absence of anything resembling spells. Let me show you how this works." The sprite floated up alongside the menu. It started to point, seemed to remember something, then did a little twirl with sparkling light effects, ending with a little half-bow, and displaying a rather nice figure.

In the most patently bored, phony manner possible, it said, "Tee. Hee," then continued as though nothing had happened.

"Right now, you don't have any assignments nor full access to the Shop. Therefore, no spells are available to you through the System. However, this is tutorial mission number two, so I am assigning you a job requiring two spells." Two spells popped up on the menu:

Tutorial Spell: Pointer
Tutorial Spell: Starry Night

"Your assignment is to cast Starry Night, then pop fifty stars with the light from the pointer spell. If you looked in your Missions tab, you would see that it had popped up as a mandatory mission. All official assignments do. Anyway, select the Starry Night spell. And get ready to experience what makes you more than a man."

Truth eagerly selected Starry Night from the spell list and shuddered as the aperture above his heart suddenly felt comfortably full. Like he had drunk a big cup of hot but not scalding soup. He knew how to cast Starry Night. He raised a shaking hand and willed the spiritual template to coalesce. The template drew in the thin cosmic rays in the apartment, then scattered around the ceiling in tiny spellforms. The spellforms drew on their inherent cosmic energy and the cosmic rays around them and activated.

The apartment was full of beautiful, seven-pointed stars, drifting in delicate nebulae around the light fixtures and bumping off the cheap curtains. It was beautiful. It was magical. And he did it. Nobody else but Truth. He wiped the tears from his eyes. He had waited so long.

"Good job," the sprite said softly. "It's hard to wait a whole year, isn't it? But it's worth it. Because now you will see what makes Starbrite a cut above the rest. Eject Starry Night, and select Pointer."

Truth did so, ignoring the sudden, unpleasantly empty feeling in his aperture. The new spell coming in felt almost indecently comfortable after the unpleasantness.

"Point it at one of the stars." Truth did. A little green light shot out of his finger and popped a drifting star.

"Congratulations, Truth. You just did the impossible. For anyone else, anyone who isn't part of the System Astrologica, that would have taken months or years to achieve. Memorizing the spell, learning to force your magic into the necessary templates, to project out the spellforms, to trigger their transformation all would require months of study. *If* you are talented. If you are average, it might take a lot longer."

The sprite looked like it remembered that it was supposed to be acting cute, put a finger on the corner of its mouth, and tilted its head sideways. "Tee. Hee." Then continued as though it had never stopped.

"Not with the System. With the System, whatever spell you need is provided. Want a spell for something not mission critical? You can pay credits for it. Once you open more apertures, you can start multi-spelling, combining spell effects for extraordinary results. Naturally, the System will help guide you through that, too.

"Now, the System can provide the spells, but it is *your job to use them effectively. Get popping those stars.*"

With a flat face and in a monotone voice, it "hopped" up on one leg, the other tucking back, it's right fist punched up into the air. "Yaah. Fighting."

"Please, for the love of all that's holy, stop that. Just . . . be the best finger puppet you can be. I promise I won't try to marry you."

"Thank you. But no. Pop-pop, Mr. Medici."

He got to popping. It was surprisingly fun.

"And that's fifty. Out of fifty shots. That's quite impressive, Mr. Medici, though I suppose it's to be expected from a Master of Arms. As a bonus for excellence, you are awarded one extra credit."

"Gosh, thanks."

"Would you prefer none?"

"I gratefully accept the System's generosity and wisdom."

"Oh, good. Speaking of credits—go to the Banking menu." The sprite waved him along.

Truth opened the Banking tab.

"Pretty basic. You have a sign-on bonus of five thousand credits, plus .01 for completing Tutorial Mission 1, plus 1 from the performance bonus, minus .01 for the cab ride and barbecue dinner. Please note that the actual deduction from your credits for those things is actually less than .01 credits, but for the sake of clarity, the System rounds up in the display. You could eat barbecue every night for a week, and that number wouldn't shift."

Truth was boggled at that. "Just what is the exchange rate from credits to wen?"

The sprite shrugged. "It's actually a constantly changing rate, reflecting inflation of both wen and credits, along with a number of other macro- and micro-economic factors you wouldn't understand. Again, not an insult; you could learn to understand them, but you haven't studied economics before, so it wouldn't make sense to you now."

"Fair. So, my credit balance, then I see tabs for loans, mortgages, and all that."

"Yes, though right now, you are *strongly* advised against taking out any loans. *VERY STRONGLY.* You really, really don't need them."

"No fear of that. Let's move on to the Treasure Pavilion."

The sprite smiled predatorily.

"Oh, yes. Let's."

CHAPTER 20

TREASURES!

The Treasure Pavilion tab exploded into a series of more tabs, sub-tabs, pictures in tabs, and a bewildering swarm of lists.

"What am I looking at?" Truth muttered.

"Basically, a shopping mall," the sprite said. "It works like this—everyone who is connected to the System has access to the Treasure Pavilion. *However.* Not everyone has *the same* access to the Treasure Pavilion. For example, think 'Needler Talismans.'"

Truth did, and the clutter suddenly simplified. Five needler talismans floated in front of him, with their name, a short description, technical specifications, and a price attached.

"Whoa!"

"Yep. Now, the needler on the left is a less-lethal model suitable for civilian use. You have probably seen mall cops with the same model. Everyone assigned to Security can rent or purchase them. The next two are military grade. You probably trained on at least one of them during your National Service. You have access to those because you are in the PMC. The last two are foreign made and have some unusual effects. You can purchase or rent them because you have been assigned to the PMC *and* are a recognized Master of Arms. Get it?"

"Yep. So, if I was assigned to, say, transportation, would there be wagons on there?"

"Right idea, but no, we generally provide the wagons. On the other hand, if you were in talisman or fetish production, there might be specialized tools available."

"Got it. I assume it is also limited by level and tier?"

"Correct." It made another awkward cheer pose. "Sorry, magical compulsion. Anyhow. A lot of stuff in there is pretty generic. Think 'Sofa.'"

Truth did and was suddenly swarmed by dozens of pictures of sofas.

"Damn, I didn't know this many kinds of sofas existed."

"If it's made by Starbrite or sold by a Starbrite store, it's probably in the Treasure Pavilion. Something like 97% of the total volume of goods in the Pavilion is generic stuff that any random civilian can buy with a bit of cash. We just sell it for much cheaper than you could buy it in a civilian store. Do I need to mention that reselling goods purchased in the shop is considered a disciplinary offense?" the sprite asked.

"You do not."

"Oh, good. Now, this is the part I do think you should be investing in—think 'Cultivation resources.'"

A bewildering range of incense, crystals, lotions, potions, syringes, eye drops, ear drops, and enemas suddenly appeared—each one boasting its unique virtues. Even with Truth's generous salary, none of them struck him as cheap.

"Men's clothes."

He almost blacked out from all the results.

"Fancy men's clothes! Suits!"

The number was reduced, but he was still under siege.

"These are not cultivation resources. These are clothes," the sprite said disapprovingly.

"I know, but . . . I think all my clothes suck? And maybe I should get better clothes?"

"Don't bother. You will be issued a uniform tomorrow."

"Right, but for when I'm off duty or on a date."

The sprite was giving him a very patient, borderline pitying look.

"Does that happen very often?"

"What?"

"Dates."

"Well. Not *often*."

"Not ever?"

Truth went quiet for a while. "You know, judging someone by how much they get laid is just dumb."

"Oh, I absolutely agree." The sprite nodded firmly. "Sexual reproduction just seems incredibly stupid and gross. Be smart. Be classy. Die a virgin."

"But. But I want a girlfriend. Like in the ad. I'm open to the idea of a boyfriend, even."

"I have no idea which ad you are talking about, but listen. Truth, can I be terribly candid with you?"

"I guess?"

"You have a fantastic body. Even for someone fresh off their *National Service*, your body is a conservative eight and for many people, a nine. Incredibly proportional, V-shaped torso, *just slightly* taller than average, and an excellent degree of muscle development without being grotesque."

"Wow! Thank you, that's incredibly nice of you to say."

"Unfortunately, your face is, *at best,* a four. And not a Harban four. A, you know, national-average four, including the really ugly bits of the country. Maybe if you fixed your hair and stood in the shadows or something, you might be a Harban four. Nice clear skin, but it's stretched over a real *'oof'* of a face. I am so sorry. You aren't hideous or anything. Just . . . you really need to sell people on your personality to get them past your face. And your personality is a . . . two? Maybe? I'm not sure you have a personality that anyone would care about. Certainly not a prospective mate."

Truth was stunned. He was getting roasted by the System, in the form of a pretty lady, no less.

"I checked. You have no hobbies and no interests outside of 'Join Starbrite.' Okay, you joined Starbrite. Now what?" the sprite asked.

Truth flailed a bit.

"Yeah, that's what I thought. On the other hand, if you cultivate to a high-enough level, it actually subtly improves your looks. You think better and learn better, so you can actually have meaningful hobbies and interests. Maybe take up a sport or something." It threw up a wooden double victory sign with its fingers, then continued.

"So, again, I would ignore basically everything except setting up your siblings with whatever they need and cultivation aids. Just focus on that. Don't buy equipment—in the short term, everything you need will be issued to you. Don't rent spells. Same logic; you will have access to what you need through your assignments. Your apartment is furnished, and you don't need to move to a bigger place. All you need is the necessities. And cultivation."

Tutorial Mission #2 Complete!

Truth buried his face in his hands and groaned.

Truth reported for duty at the offices of the Starbrite Private Military Company. And they really were offices. He took a nice elevator up to the fourth floor (of thirty; they were still security), went through a glass door, passed a receptionist who gave Truth a polite smile and directed him toward a not particularly comfortable chair. The office space was painfully generic. If it weren't for the sign printed on the glass of the door, he would have no idea where he was. Exactly five minutes later, exactly at the time he was supposed to meet his new boss, the new boss strode out into the waiting area. She was wearing a suit, but there was no question that she was military.

"Truth Medici? Good to meet you. Oke Clavegaugh, she/her, or in your case, Ma'am. I am the Regional Director, Southeast Jeon Region of the Starbrite PMC. Or, again, to you, I'm Captain Clavegaugh. The PMC can be confusing. We have our ranks and positions in the company, but for internal organizational purposes, we use military ranks. Follow me down to our facility."

The explosion of personality and charisma that was Captain Clavegaugh swept past Truth and back toward the elevators. She seemed to personify the phrase *tough old bird*, and Truth secretly rejoiced that she felt no need to smile at him at all, politely or otherwise. As they went down to the basement, Captain Clavegaugh kept up her monologue.

"You are starting at C-9-U, or as we call it, a private. No first or second class, just private. In normal security, that's an F-9-L job, bottom of the pyramid. It is *good* to be in the PMC." She grinned.

"Normally, PMC private is a C-9-L position, but you are apparently a Master of Arms and a former corporal, so C-9-U is the absolute lowest we can start you at.

And we have to start you that low because that is the absolute highest you can be and still be a private, and everyone starts as a private. No exceptions. It also means that unless you spectacularly screw up, you can expect a promotion to corporal in eight months to a year. This won't bump your grade up any, because it's considered a lateral promotion from your current status as a specialist. It does, however, fast-track you for sergeant, which does come with a bump up in grade and pay."

Truth nodded along. Was that a fast promotion? He had no idea. Still, it's always good to hear how your new boss plans to promote you.

"I'm explaining all this because you are likely going to want to transfer in a few weeks." They got to the basement and walked down a long concrete corridor. They walked through an unmarked pair of fire doors into what looked to Truth to be a combination locker room, armory, and training facility.

"The PMC gets thrown into everything. Even things that blatantly don't need an actual soldier, like bodyguard duties for celebrities or escorting packages of modestly secret information. Oddly, it's that shit, not the firefights, that makes people want to quit." She gave Truth a hard look. "Gut it out. You are in Starbrite for life, and you are on a goddamn promotion rocket in the PMC if you play your cards right. You hear me, soldier?"

"Yes, ma'am!" She smiled at that. Not a polite smile; an officer smile. Totally different thing.

"Good. Before I turn you over to Sergeant Murthey, I have two questions for you. First—why did you join Starbrite?"

"Ma'am. It was the best way out of the slums for me and my siblings, ma'am."

"Older-brother type. You will go far if you don't get yourself killed. All right, question two." She looked at Truth oddly. "You really got a *classified* medal during your National Service? Never mind being a Master of Arms at eighteen; how does a conscript, who should be directing traffic at a not-too-challenging intersection, get a classified medal?"

"Ma'am. It's classified, ma'am. But yes, I did earn a classified medal while repairing an air conditioner, ma'am."

The captain shot Truth a hard look, snorted, and called Sergeant Murthey over. The sergeant was a lean, rangy man, with narrow eyes that could be smiling or not. It was hard to say. He certainly sounded much milder than the sergeants Truth remembered from the Army.

"All right, here's the one-credit tour. Your locker has your name on it. It is over there. Showers are attached to the locker room. Towels are provided because we are *fancy*. The range is through the door marked *Range*. Do not go in if the red light is on. Same as when you were in the Army. Armory is through the door marked *Armory*. Do not go in there at all unless ordered. Same as when you were in the Army. The ready room, aka the lounge, is past the Armory on the left. It has vending machines and a hot box. It's got a fridge, too, if you feel like donating food and drink to your coworkers." Murthey waved at everything as they made their way to the range.

"You are the newest member of B Squad, First Platoon. You will meet your squad mates . . . right now!" The door to the range opened. It was interesting—clearly set up with illusory targets and meant to simulate battlefield conditions. The squad waved and shouted hello. Seemed like a nice bunch. Fingers crossed.

"Now, before we do the meet-and-greet, I think we all want to see if you *earned* that Master of Arms badge. Care to give us a demonstration?" Murthy challenged.

Truth looked at the long row of talismans and fetishes laid out. It was actually a pretty interesting selection. Needlers, fireballs, acid, focused sound, focused light, even something that created a blizzard of saw blades and sent them rocketing down-range. (Not that effective, actually, but it scared the piss out of people and made them keep their heads down.) There were around thirty of them.

"You set up the targets?" he asked Murthey.

"All set and waiting for you."

"All right, but let's make one change. I don't pick the weapons. The squad can hang on to them, and when you want me to change it up, yell, 'Change!' I'll drop what I'm using, catch what you toss me, and use that. Sound good?"

"Oh, I think we can manage that."

Truth grinned at the squad. "Hey, everyone, I'm Truth Medici. I'm good at violence and talisman maintenance, so if you need help with those things, hit me up. Everything else, I'm kind of shit at. So, I'm going to be asking you for a lot of help. Now. Who's got my first toy?"

CHAPTER 21

MEETING PEOPLE

R ange is clear! Magus, are you ready? Go!" The bell rang, and Truth's hand blurred. The flame-lance fetish had shit range and penetration, so he took out the targets closest to him with shots to the face. The spell mannequins shrieked and seemed to melt, running backward and knocking other mannequins out of cover.

"Change!" He dropped the flame-lance fetish and caught the bolter thrown from behind him. Bolter was a little trickier, as you needed to have better aim. On the other hand, the long steel spikes had good range and penetration, so he used it to pick off the long-range targets. These he could be a little less cute with, punching through hearts as well as heads.

"Change!" Some kind of acid-ball projector? Not one he was familiar with. Treat it the same as the flame lance—damage over time, and go for the head. He also tried to line up his shots so that some of it splashed on the armored mannequins. He wasn't going for them right this second, but he was curious to see if he could stack damage and not have it count against his score.

"Change!" Needler, this time. Basic Army "higher volume of fire = more hits = greater combat effectiveness" needler. Magazine of five hundred needles operating with the most childishly basic spell launcher imaginable. And for all the shit he talked about it, the design was so robust, it hadn't substantially changed in fifty years. He low-key loved it.

Truth snapped through the targets seemingly without needing to aim, hitting the head, neck, or heart each time. It was an illusion, of course. It was just that once the sight picture was lined up, how long were you going to hang around before casting?

Longer than Truth, apparently.

"Change!" The voice behind him sounded slightly hysterical as they tossed an odd-looking fetish that launched circular saw blades downrange. *Welp. Only so many ways you can use this. Glad these are spell mannequins, or cleaning up those limbs and torsos would be a* job.

"Change!" Truth ran through the thirty or so weapons. He was familiar with most of them, but there were some oddball ones and a couple that looked downright homemade. One was held together by hair. He wondered if it had been made in the slums. It was a fun challenge, trying to use a new weapon to best effect within a second of laying hands on it while also setting up future weapons, despite not knowing what those weapons would be. Trying to line up splash damage, using needler fire to pick off already wounded mannequins, using downed mannequins to funnel moving mannequins into tighter groups, making them easier to hit with splash damage . . . It was a really fun start to a new job.

"TIME! Talisman down! Show dispel." Truth put down the talisman and wiped away any lingering cosmic energy before stepping away. He looked over at the squad. The expressions ranged from stunned to disbelieving, with a couple faintly nauseous. Sergeant Murthey was part of the "stunned" group. Eventually, he shook himself and checked the score. Then checked it again. Then looked at the range, looked at the fetishes and talismans, looked at Truth, then back at the score. He started to throw the wax tablet against the wall but stopped himself. He then coughed, pretended like he had never done what he did, and turned to the squad.

"On a thirty-weapon challenge, average time with a weapon was five seconds, the average hit rate was . . . according to the system, one hundred and seventeen percent . . ."

"What? Bullshit!" a squaddie yelled.

"Shut up! And yes, it's kind of bullshit but also not. Splash damage, remember? The system isn't really set up to calculate that because, Private Truth, those were all *designed* to be single-target weapons."

"Really, Sergeant? Even the acid ball?"

"Yes, Private, even the Berrendi Arms XF-A Defoliation Device. Legally, we are only supposed to use it for clearing obstructions."

Truth looked out at the melting puddles of simulated humans. "Sure. Makes sense."

"Uh-huh. So, in two minutes thirty seconds, you killed one hundred and seventy-four targets. That is less than a second per kill. I want to say that's impressive, but damn, son, that's just alarming."

"This and talisman maintenance are literally the only things I am good at, Sarge. I have it on excellent authority."

Truth's system chimed.

Tutorial Mission #5 complete! Reward: Performance Points. Bonus Reward for exceeding goals—10% discount on Emerald Pool Cultivation Enhancement Incense. Exceed goals nine more times to earn up to a 100% discount!

Wait, the system could do that? Of course it could. Truth grinned. He didn't recall *exactly* how much Emerald Pool incense was, but it couldn't be less than two thousand credits. Because that was the cheapest incense he found in the Treasure Pavilion. Incense was damn expensive because the whole family could use it. He was motivated.

Tutorial Mission #6—Examine and maintain twenty talismans, fetishes, or other equipment in the PMC Armory. Reward: Performance Points, Pizza in the Breakroom.

"All right. Well, unless we need to exterminate all life in a city or something, I think it's your other skills that we need. Come over to the armory. Let's see how you are on maintenance."

They trooped over, trailed by a very curious squad. Truth just ignored the noise and got to work cleaning the fetishes, making sure all the spell channels were clear and properly smooth on the talismans, refreshing ink or reagents where needed. Usual maintenance stuff. He could hear them whispering.

"Look. Completely normal speed!"

"Right? I'm pretty sure that's how the manual says you are supposed to do it. But look at how visible his hands are."

"Incredible, just incredible. I don't think I have ever seen such an average maintenance job by a new recruit before."

"Guys, is anybody else getting chills watching this totally ordinary level of skill? I am. And I'm not ashamed to admit, I'm a little horny, too."

"Oh, man, I am so glad to hear I'm not the only one with a maintenance fetish."

"What? No. It's just been a dry spell."

Truth kept at it until Murthey clapped twice. "All right, you can finish this up later. So, when you say that talisman maintenance is your only other skill, you mean it's the only other non-combat-related job you are qualified to do?"

Truth nodded. "Yes, Sarge. I was originally going to be a maintenance tech."

"Huh. Well. Guess we are getting some help in the armory, then. Let me give you the scoop on what kinds of jobs you will actually be doing around here . . ."

Truth didn't go off shift until he had maintained twenty-five talismans and got that next discount.

It turned out that, much like the Army, most of the work was very boring. Truth was okay with boring. It paid indecently well and kept him in Harban City with the sibs. When he wasn't on assignment, he was assigned to the armory, doing maintenance. There were training days scheduled. Vacation days were scheduled (not that he had accumulated any, but *theoretically*). It was all very . . . corporate. It felt like a lukewarm shower on a cold day—not what he wanted, but he really didn't want to get out of it, either.

Captain Clavegaugh was wrong about one thing: Truth wasn't bothered by the pointless courier work. It turned out that he didn't really know Harban City well, and he didn't know the area around it at all. The only place he knew was the slums. Now he got to look around almost everywhere. The really high-end districts were still off-limits, but what was he going to see there, anyway? Nice houses?

Standing guard at checkpoints was boring but not terrible. Sometimes, you got posted with someone else, and you just shot the shit for eight hours. One time, it looked like a fight would break out, but a glare and a shouted "Hey!" and the two suits decided that they would rather settle things like gentlemen: talking trash about each other behind their back and seething with suppressed resentment.

And so time trickled past, one day after another. Dull, repetitive work. Truth tried to slip in a little cultivation time on shift where he could, just to keep interested. He also tried to read books, just to learn about . . . everything, really. It didn't go very well. His eyes seemed to slide off the page. Generally, he understood all the individual words, but the way they were put together just made no sense. And they were boring, too.

Eventually, he fell back on "trash." Mystery novels and thrillers, even the odd romance novel. Things you could pick up in a grocery store or find in the common "library" in the apartment building's community room. Sometimes, he would find himself carefully reading through old bird-spotting books or books on gardening. He had seen suburban gardens on some of the delivery jobs. He could sort of see the appeal of the hobby, but it wasn't for him. On the other hand, the words were mostly quite ordinary, the directions explicit, and there were lots of pictures. That worked for him. The only reason he could stick with it at all was that reading books earned him discounts on cultivation aids.

He did discreetly ask for tips on getting dates. It did not go well. "Find a girl with a ski-mask fetish" was not helpful advice, he felt. Truth felt that he had things in his favor. His physique now looked like it had been carved from marble in perfect aesthetic proportion. His skin was soft and supple, entirely free of blemishes. All the little scars he had picked up had faded away. His hair was so glossy, he got teased for the fortune he, presumably, spent on conditioner. Truth hadn't bought conditioner in his life. Two-in-one was the light and the salvation.

So, you know, other than his boring personality and . . . challenging . . . face, he was doing great! His nails were good, too, neatly trimmed and well buffed! Nobody had said anything yet, but one day they definitely would. Then he would sigh, culti-vate more, and read more.

Truth rode through the village with the still-somewhat-exiled philosopher. His case was pending, apparently, and he needed a guard. He was, or had been, tutor to the evil prince, as well as a scattering of other nobles and royalists in exile. All of whom now wanted to kill him. Truth looked over the burned-out homes, the bones of their former owners long since picked over by dogs and crows.

"Evidence for or against your thesis?" he asked.

"Oh, for, for! It is the inspiration of the whole work." The philosopher waved his hands around. "Look at this misery! This is the product of chaos. The product of political disorder. They didn't have anyone to protect them, and so they died."

"A king, perhaps?" Truth said in a barbed voice.

The philosopher might have been a coward, but on this point, he would stand against all comers. "Yes, a king. An absolute monarch, imbued with all the natural rights of the people to exercise sovereignty. It is only with supreme authority that he can demand supreme obedience and impose peace and security for the people."

"The last king we had—"

"He's still alive!"

"Broadstreet will see him hung. Cooke is demolishing him on the stand. For example, pointing out that this . . . divine monarch ordered his soldiers to boil their bullets in poison before shooting them at his subjects. For example, me."

"He did, yes. And it was a terrible, wicked thing he did." The philosopher waved his hands at the ruins. "It's the final question I struggle to answer. If the monarch, the leviathan formed from the sovereignty of the people, can no longer protect the people, do they have the right to rebel?"

"Well, you know where I stand on that one."

"Yes, and you are wrong. The sovereign has power because his subjects give him power. Should he turn that power against his subjects, then it is the subjects who harm themselves. They, therefore, have no right to complain or accuse him, because how is it possible to injure oneself?"

Truth pointed at a decapitated skeleton, arms roughly hacked off above the elbows. "Ah, a suicide! Shall we pray for her?"

The philosopher made no reply.

CHAPTER 22

RELIABLE

<< *AHHAHAHAAAHAA!!! WHAT THE FUCK, WHAT THE FUCK! How! What? SSSSHHHHHRRAAAA!^&%$%%%!*>>

Truth woke, thinking he heard someone screaming. But there was nothing. The apartment was quiet and still. He must have been dreaming. Though he never seemed to remember his dreams. Oh, well. It was five in the morning. Good time to be up.

He took a quick shower, dressed in his uniform, and started laying out breakfast. The sibs would be up soon, and he liked to have everything ready to go. No more leftover rice or garbage sugar things from the convenience store. No more giving Vig the last slice of bread because "I already ate." Truth put the instant eggs in the hot box and let them cook. Thick slices of toast cooked in the toaster. Fresh tomatoes, slices of apple, all down on the plate. The sibs would go to school with full bellies.

Truth looked at the breakfast. It didn't look fancy, he would be the first to admit. The wood-veneered table was one of the cheapest in the System store when he went and checked. It was . . . odd to him. This was supposed to be poverty. This was supposed to be struggling at the bottom, by the standards of the nice parts of Harban City. And yet, for him, this table and this breakfast were the truest wealth.

Yawning and dragging, the sibs stumbled out of their room. Harmony was hitting the same protein-inspired growth spurt that Truth had caught in the Army. It suited him. He was lean, strong, and with a quiet look to him. If you watched him long enough, you realized that the quiet outside was not matched by the racing thoughts inside of him. Truth had brought Har up to be his number two in his Keep The Sibs Alive organization, and it showed. Steady, reliable, firm. And kind in his way.

Sophia looked good too, but then, she always had. What made Truth happy, though, was that she was half-asleep and still reading her bio textbook. He had taken a peek at it. Five different colors of highlighters had been used, and margin notes filled the borders of every page. It was a pity that Truth didn't know what an illuminated manuscript was or he would have found the comparison really on point.

Vigor and Harmony had really struggled academically. Sophia hadn't. She caught up in two months and was now routinely acing her tests. Every boring shift, every prick Truth had to smile at, they were all fine. Because BY GOD, he was sending her to college, so none of that shit mattered.

Then there was Vigor, dark-eyed and sulky mouth, hiding the fact that his grades, while nothing special, had improved from "failing utterly" to "middle of his class" in a year. And he was still climbing. Vigor dressed the best out of all of them. That was a neat trick, since everyone was in either a work or school uniform. Vigor just seemed to wear it better, making the clothes look sharper because he was in them. The little bastard. Truth would cheerfully give a lot to know how he managed it.

"Morning, all." Truth smiled at them. "What's the day look like?"

"Morning. Normal." Harmony smiled, loading up a plate. "Got a track meet coming up, so I'm off for a run before school."

"Oh, cool. Want me to come and cheer?" Truth asked.

"At a track meet? Nah. Maybe if we get to a championship or something." Harmony waved him off.

"You always say that," Truth grumbled.

"Bro, I'm running fast in a straight line. You want to watch me run fast in a straight line, I can do it in the hall. Save yourself a trip." Har laughed quietly.

"How's the schoolwork?" Truth asked.

"A struggle, but I'm actually enjoying science. Bio was okay, but I am really enjoying the chemistry lab work." Harmony sounded pretty chipper about it. A long way from someone excited to be mopping floors for food money, Truth felt. He was damn proud of Harmony.

"I hate bio. I hate it," Sophia grumbled. She poked angrily at the book. "It's all wrong."

"It. . .is?" Truth hazarded.

"It *is*! Look, math—two plus two is four, right?"

"Yes." Truth nodded firmly. This much he was sure of.

"Well, not in bio. In bio, two plus two is a potato or hair. It depends. It all depends. Everything is a firm rule, except for all the exceptions, which are also firm rules. It drives me crazy." She gave the textbook another vindictive poke.

"So, why did you sign up for an afterschool bio club?" Truth asked.

"Because I wanted the extracurriculars on my record. It's a competition team, which also looks good, and . . ." She looked sulky.

"She loves bio. Ignore the whining," Vigor said from the depths of his plate. He was also shooting up like a weed.

"I *don't*. Bio sucks!"

"Do. I saw you sketching critters the other day. Then planning how you would make them in a lab."

"VIG! That was private!" Sophia yelled.

"Can't be that private. You asked Mr. Gasley if you could borrow the bio lab on the weekend."

"You snooping little shit! Why are you such a stalker?" she hissed. Vigor shrugged innocently.

"Wasn't stalking you; I was stuck in the closet in the classroom. Becky Shien was feeling impatient, and then you walked in with the teacher."

That brought the table conversation to a halt. Truth rotated in place, seemingly without moving his feet, and gave Vigor a gimlet look.

"Vig. Are you . . ."

"Whoops, look at that time. Got to run. Love you, bro!" Vigor was out the door with his backpack before the words finished echoing in the apartment.

Truth was coming up on his eight-month mark at Starbrite, and so far, things seemed to be going well. Hints were dropped, loudly, that he could soon find himself a corporal and on a steady path to sergeant. Assuming that he remained a "good fit." A team player. An NCO has to understand the importance of teamwork, obviously. They have to be reliable. And in a corporate environment, they had to understand discretion.

One of the more-boring routine jobs they got was scanning shipments from overseas for contraband. Another customs station, Truth realized. It was a dockside post, where the smells of salt water and rust mixed with the greasy ionization of poorly maintained, overused talismans. He could never get over the sheer size of the ships. They just . . . towered over everything but only needed a handful of people to run. Amazing. Just. Amazing. And none of the stuff on them got lost, either. Which was even more amazing.

Generally, this was a routine gig handled by government inspectors with all the drama of paint drying. However, some of the imports were in the form of dangerous animals, had active spell effects, or were just plain weird and nasty to the point where having an actual soldier on hand made sense.

The job was still mostly standing around and looking dangerous, but sometimes, the government inspectors had to go on break. Then the Starbrite PMC soldiers would step in and scan things for them. Just to keep things moving. The docks ran on strict timetables, and a small delay could turn into a huge loss for everyone.

Once everything was scanned for contraband, they would be passed on to the longshoremen for whatever came next. Truth was kind of vague on how logistics worked. You ran the scanner wand over the crate. It took a few minutes, but eventually, the wand went *Ding* and turned green for a second. Then the crate was stamped, and you sent it on. That was it. He just waved the wand when they told him to, crate after crate.

Except, of course, when he didn't. Sometimes, a crate came in that had an *Urgent* or *Expedite* tag on it in their system. It was explained to Truth that, occasionally, some very senior, very powerful figures in the company had to bring things in from overseas. Things they urgently needed. And he worked for Starbrite, not the government. His job was to make things go right for the Company, not fit perfectly on a checklist. So long as the inspection stamp went on the crate, everything was legal.

There was a 100% coincidence rate between when the government inspector went for a smoke and when the *Urgent* crates came in. Generally, Sergeant Murthey handled them. Just stamp and go. Nice and easy. One day, the inspector went for a smoke, and Murthey joined him. A crate came into the inspection station, and when Truth scanned the marker (using his handy, system-provided spell), it came up *Most Urgent.*

He had wondered when they would try this. It wasn't like he didn't understand the game months ago. He certainly didn't mind it. He was a Starbrite Man, not a cop. Truth picked up the stamp, stamped the container, and sent it to the longshoremen. A little bit later, Murthey came back and the shift continued as usual.

As they were changing in the locker room after their shift, the sergeant came up to him.

"Hey, Truth, I think you dropped this. Got to be more careful, son. These things are valuable."

Murthey held out a cultivation crystal. Roughly a thousand credits in the Treasure Pavilion for a little one like this. The sergeant looked him dead in the eye. Truth looked straight back at him.

"Thanks, Sarge. I had wondered where that got to." Truth reached out and closed his hand over the crystal.

Two weeks later, he was made a corporal and told that some much, much higher-paid missions were now available to him. It seems that he was considered reliable.

That night, as Truth lay sleeping—

Truth loathed the philosopher, but he had to admit, the little coward had a brain on him. It seemed to be bulging out of the top of his head. In fact, his whole head looked like an alchemical symbol. A straight, narrow, perfectly centered, and perfectly vertical line of hair on his chin that ran up to a perfectly horizontal mustache above the lip. Then a perfectly straight aquiline nose, topped by a perfectly round, bulging bald pate, surrounded by a corona of radiating hair.

"So, because such-and-such a thing must have happened, it did happen, and since it did happen, it is a matter of logic that everything else has happened as a consequence? If A equals B and B equals C, then C equals A, that kind of thing, but with entire kingdoms?" Truth asked.

"In the very simplest terms, yes. By observing the world closely, we can determine what is, and from that, we may work both backward and forward to deduce what was and what must be. From the tiniest speck of dust to the mind of God Almighty." The philosopher nodded.

Truth mulled it over. "Two obvious problems appear. The first is that this just sounds like divine providence with extra steps. Not a whole lot of room between *It's just logic* and *Because it's God's will,* no? And second, how sure are you about your observations? Because if you have incorrectly observed the world, the whole chain of logic falls apart."

The philosopher sputtered. "I have written hundreds of pages, debated with bishops and the best minds of the continent, and spent decades on this study! I can assure you the logic is impeccable. The first problem is no problem at all. Why must they be two different things?" He started waving violently as he picked up speed.

"Our faith tells us that the entirety of creation, from beginning to end, was foreordained before the first day. I have simply proved by logic that it must be so, not simply a demand of orthodoxy. And, second, do you really think that both I and all those worthies would somehow err in our appreciation of the world around us?!"

Truth looked over the ruined village. The church was looted, the stained-glass windows shot out, and the faces smashed off the statues. The priest had been nailed to the big front door. "I think that if logic leads us here, then I am prepared to embrace madness. And yes, I think you have badly misjudged the world, all of you."

CHAPTER 23

THE REWARD FOR "GOOD" WORK

Another day, another sensation of phantom screaming. Maybe it was the air vents? He should take a look; no need to bother the building manager.

The little "bonus" jobs didn't show on the System. They seemed to glide alongside the assigned missions, neither subtracting from nor adding to them. You just got the cheery little *Ding!* and the **Mission Complete!** sign when you did your normal job. It always lifted his mood, if only for a moment. Nobody ever mentioned what might happen if you were to look in the crates. Truth suspected it might cause you to fail your mission. He didn't like imagining the consequences of that.

Still, he was making steady progress to Level Two. The Nine Worm Path seethed through his muscles, winding around arteries and slinking along tendons. Truth could feel himself getting stronger, both physically and magically. The System agreed.

Cultivation Mission: Complete! Progress to Level Two—30%
Reward: 20% Discount on a Level One Cultivation Supplement.
Bonus Reward for Speedy Completion: 20% Discount on a Level One Supplement.
Bonus Reward for Physical Development: 20% Discount on a Level One Supplement.
Cultivation Mission: Complete! Progress to Level Two—40%
Reward: 20% Discount on a Level One Cultivation Supplement.
Bonus Reward for Speedy Completion: 20% Discount on a Level One Supplement.
Bonus Reward for Physical Development: 20% Discount on a Level One Supplement.
Cultivation Mission: Complete! Progress to Level Two—50%
Reward: 20% Discount on a Level One Cultivation Supplement.
Bonus Reward for Speedy Completion: 20% Discount on a Level One Supplement.

Bonus Reward for Physical Development: 20% Discount on a Level One Supplement.
Special Bonus for Reaching 50% Cultivation Progress in Less Than Eight Months—One Free Level One Supplement, One Physique-Enhancing Tonic

The discounts didn't expire, and they stacked up to 100% on any one supplement, including the very expensive incense that a whole family could use to cultivate. The sibs were cruising through Level Zero, and Harmony was going to be Level One well before his SAT. Which was coming up quickly. Truth wasn't worried. Harmony was going to crush it. He had decided to skip college—just too late for him to get into a good school and keep up with the work. However, he did have aspirations for laboratory management, so he doubled down on the business-studies electives.

The physique-enhancing tonic was a real revelation—he had never heard about a tonic that could improve someone's physique. Cultivation, yes; physique, no. He summoned the System faerie for an explanation and got a lousy one.

"I won't tell you."

"What?!"

"You are asking like a little bitch. I don't want to work for a little bitch."

"Are you . . . entirely clear on your job?" Truth asked.

"More than you. A mage *commands*, not pleads." It hovered, glowering. Truth stared back for a long minute.

"FUCKING EXPLAIN YOURSELF RIGHT THIS INSTANT, YOU MISERABLE LITTLE SHIT, OR I WILL SKIN YOU AND USE YOU FOR A CONDOM!" Truth bellowed.

The sprite smiled broadly, then did a really feeble pantomime of being terrified. Then got back to its usual office-lady persona.

"You didn't ask about them; they don't come up in your regular line of work, and honestly? You don't really need it. Your physique is already excellent and still improving daily. For you, the tonic is a minor, incremental improvement. The biggest thing it will do for you is . . . maybe help with your looks, some? Like . . . three percent improvement?"

"There is a literal Get Prettier tonic in the Treasure Pavilion, and you didn't see a reason to mention it?"

"No. If you are that worried about your looks, cultivate more. All our models are Level Three. Hint hint. Also, there is a reason it's a reward for hitting a major milestone quickly—did you look at the price in the store?"

"Uh, no. How much?"

"Twenty-five thousand credits per dose."

Truth just blinked.

"I'm sorry, you said—"

"Twenty-five thousand credits per dose. For a meh improvement to your physique, a very minor improvement to your looks, and a very attractive souvenir bottle.

In your case, the bottle may be the best thing about it. Very nice cut glass. Might liven up this place. Show a little swank." The faerie sounded like it was trying to be encouraging, which was hurtful.

"Can I just get the credits?"

"No. Absolutely no negotiation on mission rewards. At all, for anything, or anyone, ever." It made a cute-yet-deadpan face, then acted like it never happened.

"What if I yelled?"

"Excellent idea! Try it."

"GIVE ME THE CASH, IMP!"

"No. This is actual company policy and not something you can change by yelling." It smiled sunnily. Truth sighed, pressing his fingers to his temples.

"How about giving the tonic to Harmony or one of the other siblings?"

"That would be fine, particularly for Harmony. It will really help set him up for his breakthrough. It is intended for a *Level One* person, but if he drinks it slowly over a few hours one evening, the benefits should be immense," the sprite agreed.

"Thanks, I guess." Truth sounded a bit lost.

"Get fucked."

Truth paused. "You have barely fulfilled your duties. Pray I do not take you to task for your . . . tone."

"Better. *Insolence* would have been a stronger word choice than tone, but it's an improvement regardless. Keep working on the ominous voice." The faerie hovered around for a moment in silence. "So . . . can I go, or do I have to keep pretending to be a humanoid with emotions you could name and recognize?"

Truth buried his face in his hands and willed the sprite away.

"All right, Truth, in your case, this is purely a formality, but—as a brand-new corporal, before we can send you out with a team, you have to pass a spelled-arms certification. I would tell you what the test requires, but it seems kind of pointless." Sergeant Murthey managed to look bored, amused, and embarrassed at the same time.

The range had been set up with multiple stations he had to switch between, each with its own talisman or fetish. Truth looked at the station in front of him. It was an Army standard-issue needler. Good penetration through armor, good range, so-so stopping power, but an insane amount of ammunition and *incredibly* low cosmic-energy usage. Functional, sort of, for a Level One or a brand-new Level Two without a spell. It only really shone when combined with . . . Ah.

Truth looked over at Sargent Murthey. "Think I got it, Sarge." The Sergeant just snorted, shook his head, and waved Truth to his starting position. The range was cleared, the bell chimed, and Truth blurred into motion.

Load Shockwave!

Shockwave Loaded. Mission-Critical Spell. No Charge.

The needler was up, and he was forming the spell form before the target had even snapped into position. Two needles thudded into the mannequin's skull. The needles now carried the Shockwave spell with them, turning what would have been a likely fatal injury into *pumpkin off an overpass; open casket was never an option.* The same thing happened for the next four targets, then the bell chimed again, and it was off to the next station.

A Gwaii and Gwaii Firebolter CXM. Looked scary as hell but, in Truth's opinion, was actually less effective than the needler, as the talisman tended to break down after a few dozen activations. You really had to pick your shots. Oh, well.

Load Hunter's Mark!

Hunter's Mark Loaded. Mission Critical Spell. No Charge.

A tiny ball of cosmic rays spun into existence in front of Truth. The first target popped up, and the ball connected with it almost instantly, splashing out into a little web of energy over what the scorecard would refer to as "Center Mass." The energy would last barely a second, but that was long enough. Truth triggered the talisman. The firebolt came screaming out like a poker from the Devil's hearth and smashed directly into the Hunter's Mark.

Truth faintly despised Hunter's Mark, as it was notoriously fragile and short-lived, and those who relied upon it generally had early deaths. However, there was a place for everything. In Truth's opinion, turning a low-ammo weapon like the Firebolter into a target-seeking munition was *exactly* that place.

Each new weapon had its own "best" spell to accompany it. Sometimes, given the circumstances, that spell might change. For example, in a hostage situation, when equipped with a fetish that shot meter-diameter circular saw blades spinning at ungodly speeds down range, the Enlarge spell had to be swapped on the fly for the Shrink spell.

Everyone could learn spells if they could afford them or were given them as part of their job. One spell per level. Hundreds of hours to master it, as it became almost synonymous with your identity. Jenny the Purifier, who worked as a night-shift janitor in the hospital. Tommy the Iceman, who kept the fish market cold year-round.

Not if you worked for Starbrite. In Starbrite, you had the System. With the System, you had whatever spell you needed right when you needed it. With the System, you weren't just a human. You were a demigod.

Sergeant Murthey looked at the timer and calmly flung his clipboard into the corner hard enough to break it into two pieces. "All right, Corporal Medici. You're ready."

"For what, Sarge? I heard something about jobs that paid better, but we're on salary. And I don't know of anyone who gets to pick what job they want to do when they work for someone else."

"All true, just not the complete story. You know the deal by now, right? Our PMC gets hired out by individual departments to do jobs too serious for mall cops but not so serious that they have to call in"—Sergeant Murthey seemed about to say something, then his eyes went blank, came back into focus, and he continued smoothly—" the regular Army. So far, you have been doing a lot of, Standing Around' duty. Well. This is more of the other stuff."

Murthey waved at a map of the world. "A department hires us to go somewhere. Usually somewhere not very nice. We do a job there. Convoy, asset recovery, whatever."

Truth nodded along like this made a lick of goddamn sense.

"All right, so pretty much what I've been doing so far, but I would be traveling for the job. Not seeing the part where I pick and choose anything."

"*That* part comes from the phrase 'A department *hires* us.' Starbrite PMC is an independent company from the main conglomerate. A wholly owned subsidiary but still separate."

"All right?"

"Boy, are you slow? We can turn down jobs! Our local branch of the PMC has quotas to meet, so we can't be *too* picky, but because you are now an NCO, there is a small list of jobs you can choose from. As long as you are meeting *your* quota, you and your team can pick what you like. The departments know it too. So they bid, offering credits out of their budget and, to keep expenses down, pay some of our expenses in cultivation materials."

Murthey grinned. Truth grinned too.

"Don't be afraid to say no to a job, by the way. Sometimes, they get cute and try and scrape by without a big-enough team or pay a danger premium. Don't let them get away with it!"

"Yes, Sarge!"

"Oh, and Truth? A little bird tells me that your brother is about to take his SAT."

"Yep. Harmony. I'm not too worried. He's been working hard."

"That's great. But what you probably don't know is that you can help him."

"Huh? How? I was told there was no way to eeeh . . . nudge test results."

"There ain't. But *if he passes*, you can exchange your credits to help get him on the track he wants to be on. Say, for example, he wanted to go into finance, but he doesn't have an MBA, isn't a chartered accountant, or anything like that. Starbrite will funnel him into doing the books at a shipping company or something. *But.* You could spend some credits, a *ton* of credits, and bump him into the lending track in one of the financing departments. A much-better-paying job, higher-tier, better long-term prospects."

"Holy shit! Why aren't people talking about this more?!"

"One, it's really, *really* expensive. Two, you can only do it in the period between when they pass the SAT and when they get assigned to a department. So, basically, the year they are doing their National Service." Murthey's grin was predatory. "Here's the job list."

Truth looked it over.

"Security for a scry segment in Kofi. They want a five-person detail, mostly working in the city for a couple of weeks. Sounds like a nice, easy one to start with."

A week later, at the Kofi International Business Hotel—

Truth held down the screaming actress as acidic spirits swept over the ruins of the hotel lobby. The production coordinator wasn't dead yet, poor bastard, and his sobs of agony were hard to ignore. Truth saw a flicker, a shimmer in the light. How the fuck did they get so close?!

"Camo! Camo! Pop dust, then High-Ex and give 'em hell!"

CHAPTER 24

A HAIRSPRAY JOB

Mission: Provide security for the *Danger!* scry production crew and talent as they film a segment in Kofi, Fariziland. Security detail is to be five people with experience handling personal protection. Protection period is two weeks, including a week in the city with the advance crew, three days of main recording, three days with the B unit recording location and supplemental footage, and one day for packout.
Budget: 100,000 credits, five vials of Icy Veins, Fiery Blood elixir.

The Kofi job wanted a five-person detail, so a five-person detail they would have. Truth tapped Privates Rezepi, Keller, Boloud and Nobu. Not because they were Prager's gift to soldiering but because they could be cool, and none of them were notable horndogs. These, to Truth's way of thinking, were crucial qualifications for a security detail for a scry special starring some very attractive talent in a very tense situation. Nobu, in particular, had the ability to stand almost perfectly still in a corner for *hours* and not get bored or distracted. Top woman for the job, Truth felt, and well worth enduring her penchant for eating fermented fish with almost every meal. Boloud and Keller had both passed their combat driving courses, so they were pretty obvious pickups, and Rezepi was certified as a field medic. It was a solid crew.

Kofi was a nine-hour flight, and that was the once-a-week direct flight from Harban. The giant spellcrafted vehicle was shaped like an albatross. The passengers and luggage were loaded into the "belly," they endured the jolting run up the field, then vast wings spread and powerfully *pushed*! They were off! It was so quiet. Even the rushing wind outside was silenced by the runes carved into the "bones" of the giant bird. A Starbrite S901XL Flyer, naturally.

Truth watched the city shrink out the window. It was so . . . clear, from a kilometer up. He could trace the divisions of the city, watching trees and parks slowly fade away as the bird moved south. The steam rising from the alchemists' hulking laboratories. The seemingly endless clusters of tower blocks that made up the hive of the slums. The sleek, needlelike glass-and-steel towers that housed offices or private homes for people so rich their bank accounts were strictly for walking-around money.

The factories, the warehouses, the slithering snake of the river, and the canals that jutted out of it. Like spears stuck in a dragon. He turned to his mission-briefing material. Time to get his head in the game.

There was less of a contrast than he thought there would be as they flew into Kofi. The slums weren't towers there but endless hectares of one-room shacks surrounding a city center of highways and skyscrapers. More of the glass-and-steel towers, but also more cement. The palm trees were an exciting novelty. The incredible, and not always in a good way, smells were another. Strange body odor, strange deodorant, and perfumes, strange-smelling foods. Strange, strange, strange. Visiting a foreign city stretched a film of unreality over everything, but the scents of the city poked tiny holes through the membrane.

The sealed chest with their combat gear, including a wide array of murderous talismans and fetishes, was stamped by customs and passed through without comment. Truth knew how that went.

The Kofi International Hotel was *the* hotel for those traveling on business. High-polish chrome pillars held up twenty-meter-high ceilings in the lobby; off-white synthetic marble floors turned every footstep into a clatter. Hotel rooms were furnished in wood veneer and plastic, but housekeeping kept the sheets crisp, clean, and curse-free daily. No matter how badly or well a deal went. The restaurant was simultaneously some of the blandest food in the city and some of the most expensive. At least there, you could be reasonably sure that no one was doping your soup with an aphrodisiac or, worse, a truth potion.

Foreign businesspeople were the main clientele of the hotel, which is why the main bar was one-third or more sex workers come evening. Wealthy foreigners on expense accounts would come down to the bar and order an expensive glass of something to sip. Locals, in their seductive best, would sit next to them, make polite conversation for a minute or two, and move on quickly if unwanted.

The bolder guests would simply crook a finger at those they wanted, hot eyes staring over a neat whisky. (Never rocks—only a rookie got ice overseas.) The jaded would skip the conversation and pretense of interest entirely and simply have the concierge send someone up.

What Truth saw in the hotel didn't match what he remembered seeing growing up. This suggested that either there was a much healthier environment for sex work there or the gangs were built into everything. As a wealthy woman in silk and charmed jewelry crooked her finger for a strapping young lad, Truth guessed it was the latter.

The scry production went more smoothly than he imagined it would. The production coordinator had worked with a local fixer to speak with the victims of the Godchild Freedom Army, a major rebel organization with a penchant for terror attacks. It was going to be a combo tearjerker/moral-outrage/our-country-is-better-than-their-country piece. Lots of amputated limbs wrapped in gauze, lots of twisted but horribly still alive victims of mass curses and, ideally, a photogenic doctor or local leader calling for an end to the violence.

The first two things were easy to come by. The latter was more of a challenge, but they had leads. It was kind of interesting—the research and coordination didn't stop. Ever. Right up until the moment of principal recording, and then again when the B unit rolled through to get good footage to cut into the story.

Rezepi was surprisingly adept at negotiating heated situations despite not speaking the language and turned out to be God's own scavenger. So, Truth was feeling fairly optimistic about the mission when the talent and main production crew flew in. Yoo Sung, the hostess, was as gorgeous as advertised, though almost silent and hidden behind large sunglasses. She quickly cloistered herself in her room and, besides asking for Nobu as her personal bodyguard, had little contact with security.

The whole thing was refreshingly low on drama (the production coordinator looked ready to commit suicide, but on *Truth's* end, it was low-drama) until they started interviewing victims.

"What did you do in the village?" Yoo Sung asked calmly.

"I was a miner. Red River Mining Company, Pit #23. We dug out the ores. Irra-something. It didn't matter. You were told to dig and load the ore onto the crusher belt. So, I dug and loaded the ore onto the crusher belt."

"I see. Was it a good job?"

The miner's one good eye looked at the beautiful young lady and her delicate hands and painted lips. Then closed.

"It was a job."

"Can you tell us what happened that day?" Yoo Sung asked.

"We were loading the belt. All the rocks got loaded on. They looked more silvery than usual, and some even shimmered like . . . oil in water. Like a rainbow. Usually, they just look like gray rock."

"Go on." She nodded encouragingly.

"Supervisor made a big fuss. Stopped the line. Had to get them checked, he said. Don't know how long that took. An hour, maybe two. We spent most of the time wondering if we would get paid." Some of the words sounded off—tinny or garbled. The bound spirit handling the translation did its best, but it was far from perfect. The spell bowl holding it seemed to vibrate with frustration.

"We had no warning. Green demons, like smoke, with long claws that left cuts like acid. They passed through the walls but could cut you. They tore us apart. None of us can fight demons. I have a spell that makes me strong and helps me heal a little from cuts and scrapes. Most of us have the same spell. What could we do against demons?"

"It must have been terrifying," Yoo Sung cooed.

"I was so scared. So scared. Then the rebel shamans turned up. There were dozens of them. Maybe a hundred. Fifteen hundred of us miners. Didn't make no difference. They didn't tell us to surrender or nothing. Just started killing. If you could run away fast enough, they didn't chase. Anyone trying to get away in a wagon, they killed bad.

Demons tore them apart. Blood, guts. Saw the supervisor get tore into seven pieces. Never liked him, but he didn't deserve that." Tears leaked from his remaining good eye. The scry-crystal operator zoomed in, making sure the light hit the tears just right to emphasize the tragedy.

"I tried to run too. Not fast enough." He threw an arm without a hand over his ruined face. "Not fast enough."

"Well, damn! That's a wrap, I think." The director chuckled. He looked tired but happy. "Drinks at the bar for everyone."

The production crew cheered. The security crew (who had already been informed by Truth that they would be stone-cold sober this entire trip or else) did not. They piled into the hotel bar, a large rock dropped into this little tidal pool of global commerce. Yoo Sung didn't noticeably lighten up, drinking a vodka tonic (extra tonic, hold the vodka) to be polite. The production crew, on the other hand, crushed beers like they were mad at them. The first round lasted, at most, five minutes, then they were on to the second. Then the third. The hotel lights flickered but stayed on.

Then it happened again. And again.

"Does anyone else hear a thudding noise?" a barfly asked. Screaming started breaking out from the lobby.

"Everybody out! To the employee exit behind the bar!" Truth snapped, shoving the crew into action. Screaming green spirits started raking through the lobby and into the bar.

"Prager! It's an attack! Move, move!" Truth was shouting now. An explosion went off in the lobby, rubble flying, smashing the guests open.

"Corporal! The power to the elevators is out! Ghosts coming up from the stairs!" Rezepi shouted.

"Fuck. Keep 'em moving toward the exit. We'll breach a wall if we have to. LOAD FOR GHOST!"

The security team pulled their fetishes and talismans, channeling cosmic energy into anti-spell wards and generally trying to become combat effective while herding buzzed civilians. There was a piercing shriek from behind them.

The ghosts were coming up from the floor. One had gutted the production coordinator; another was going for Yoo Sung. She screamed, adding her voice to the production coordinator. She lashed out with a brilliant lance of purple flame that melted the ghost down to nothing. She fell on her ass, sobbing, holding her head. "No nonono no! No! NO! Noononononononono," she was mumbling and crying.

The purple flame seemed to have gotten the attacker's attention. At the edge of his vision, Truth saw a glimmer. Then more and more.

"Contact!" He brought his needler into line, thinking, *"Load Shockwave!"*

Shockwave Loaded. Pre-paid in mission budget.

Truth started firing downrange. More explosions racked the lobby. He was sure he was scoring hits, but with the invisibility effect up, it was hard to tell. The dead guests were starting to twist and deform. Some were even rising from the ground and slowly peeling open like flowers blooming. New green ghosts burst from the remains.

<<*Heehehehehe! Finally, a bit of fun. Come, come, it's time to play with the little clay dolls!*>>

Truth blinked. He thought he heard something. A hissing spell flew toward him, and he forgot whatever it was. Time to kill.

CHAPTER 25

A STARBRITE MAN

Nobu and Rezepi tossed smoke talismans into the lobby. Usually, they made a smoke-screen. However, when fighting people who were invisible or had good camo? The dust stuck. More than a dozen shadowy outlines appeared, practically begging Truth, Boloud, and Keller to shoot them. Being respectful, caring, Starbrite magi, they were only too happy to help.

The needlers slapped the life clean out of the rebels. With Shockwave equipped, even a sloppy hit to the arm could transform it into abstract art. The magazines held hundreds of needles, and they could fire several a second, aimed-fire. Keller neatly blew out a man's torso, leaving his head, neck, and shoulders in place to complete the outline of where his chest should have been. Boloud just aimed for the center mass, happy to excavate hearts or guts without distinction. Truth didn't see any point in not turning enemy heads into meat aerosol. It was a slaughter. Briefly.

Dozens more shapes rushed out of the smoke, and these were carrying warded shields. The little needles plinked harmlessly off the steel shields as the wards stripped the spells off. The rebel shamans had their own needlers as well as the green ghostly demons. Generous souls, they used both liberally.

The ghosts swept out, roaring, clawing at the cowering crew, the whores and the newly humbled business folk. Each eviscerated person would lie dormant on the ground for a minute, then rise, releasing a new tormented soul. The number of ghosts was only growing. The needlers were pinging off the light armor Truth's security detail carried, and their wards were keeping the magic down, but it couldn't last long. They were already down a third of their protectees, and Yoo Sung was almost catatonic. Since she was their only Level Three, that was more than a small problem.

"Nobu, emergency report to HQ! Rez, barrier and fall back! Keller, Boloud, grab who you can and get out that fucking door!" Truth barked. His mind was in overdrive. *Can't shoot the rebels directly, and there's no point going after the ghosts.*

Load Enlarge.

Enlarge Loaded. Pre-paid in mission budget.

He raked his needler at the marble floor right in front of the advancing shamans, dumping the entire clip in seconds. Then he reloaded and did it again. An instant forest of three-inch-long spikes appeared between the rebels and the bar, just as Rezepi finished deploying the barrier. It was a ward spell, wide-scale. It wouldn't stop needler rounds, but it would keep new ghosts from getting in . . . at least until the cosmic energy ran out.

"Boloud, Keller, on the ghosts! Keep it moving!" They shoved past the panicking crowd, making for the door. Dragging as much of the crew along as they could manage.

Mission Update. Starbrite Regional Command Override, Code BLUE WOLF TORN. New mission goals—Protect Yoo Sung, and escort her to General Recto Wassshimailan Kofi International Airport, Private Aircraft Terminal, for emergency evacuation. This supersedes and replaces all other goals. System Costs will be paid by Code BLUE WOLF TORN. Operational responsibility assumed by Code BLUE WOLF TORN.

The System was flexible. It whispered the update into his mind rather than blocking his vision with floating text. It still took Truth and the rest of the squad a moment to process what they were hearing. Did it really mean . . . Oh, those sick fucks. They weren't even offering a bonus for the rest of the crew.

<<Heeehaahahaha! Is it true love? Naah! No such thing as love in prison, right? Welp. Orders are orders.>>

FUCK! A needle tore along Truth's neck, nearly tearing it open. He had his orders. "Squad! Grab the protectee and GO. Nobu, clear a path!"

Nobu dropped the assistant director she was dragging and whipped out a short club. Every swing smacked aside a panicked hotel guest, clearing a path to the door. They finally reached it. Amazing how much faster you can move when you just ditch the entire crew and treat the talent like a forty-two-kilo suitcase.

Load Bang!

Bang Loaded. Cost paid by BLUE WOLF TORN.

Bang was usually used in combat drills, to get trainees used to working under stress. It was just a very, very loud bang. Harmless, really. Unless some complete bastard set it off a hundred and twenty times in a few seconds. Everyone still in the bar and lobby kind of lost their shit at that point.

The squad, plus Yoo Sung, were already moving down the service hallway toward the back exit. The elegant marble and chrome of the lobby were replaced by breezeblock walls painted commercial gray. Gray metal doors, with black signs marking the way. Truth couldn't read the signs, but the big glowing EXIT THIS WAY sign was pretty easy to figure out.

"Hey, Medici, you hear that fucking order?"

"I'm right here with you, Rez. You guess—Actually, no, shut up and run."

"I'm running, but FUCK! Some of those guys were okay."

"A fucking tragedy. Now shut the fuck up so we don't tip off any fucking terrorist rebels hanging around the exit, dumbfuck!"

Actually, Truth had kind of liked them too. One of them had loaned him a book. Guess he didn't have to return it. Ah, shit. It was in his hotel room. Guess he'd never know if the heiress picked the wealthy, darkly handsome magus or the sweet, vibrant, soulful stable boy for her demonic sacrificial sex rite.

It would probably be the stable boy. He wouldn't be missed.

Keller flashed the sign for "Enemy Spotted" then "Three." Truth signed back "Shield" and got a "No" in reply. Nobu was left with Yoo Sung. Everyone else switched to Silent, and swung around the corner. The needles flashed out, punching through the cheap cloth uniforms of the rebels. It took a fair few needle rounds to put a magus down, without extra damage from spells. Thanks to Silent, no one heard their screams.

They had been guarding the exit. Really only one way for that to go.

Since Code BLUE WOLF TORN was kindly covering the spell cost, Truth decided to cast a spell he had desperately wanted, but didn't have budget room for.

Load Demon's Eye.

Demon's Eye Loaded. Cost paid by BLUE WOLF TORN.

He formed the sigils with his hands, wishing he had a fetish to support the casting. It took longer than he wanted, but he got it cast. The eye appeared and swept the service alley alongside the hotel. He didn't see any rebels. Didn't see any local cops or Army, either. That was . . . not great. And unlikely. There was a decent chance special forces were surveilling from a nearby building, getting ready to swarm in. Running around, waving needlers sounded like a great way to commit suicide by cop. On the other hand, Truth would be fucked to death by hippos before he put down his weapon. Hmm.

"Hey, hey! Where's James? And Lorrie? Where's the crew? HEY YOU!" Yoo Sung suddenly stood up and started shaking Truth. Truth smacked her hands away.

"They will make their own way out. Our mission changed. You're it. Kindly remain quiet and follow instructions. We will get you to the airport and evacuate as quickly as possible. In the meantime, please remain quiet and calm, as I am trying to see if our way is clear."

"Calm? CALM! They tore apart Gaz! Tore him apart! They had claws and and and tore him apart!"

Load Lotus Rest.

Lotus Rest Loaded. Cost paid by BLUE WOLF TORN.

It was a glancing shot that barely scraped across her hip, but the sedative spell kicked in. Yoo Sung's face went flat. She would be calmer for a while. Truth cursed. He would have to cast Demon's Eye again.

They slipped out of the hotel and stole a van parked outside. Truth thought that someone should have found the fact that it was already hotwired funny. Nobody laughed, but . . . c'mon. Stealing an already stolen delivery van? That's funny. The radio was blaring. It sounded like the news.

"Anybody speak Farizi?" Truth asked. Everybody shook their heads.

"It's not Farizi. There is no Farizi language. It's Xionw't. One of five official languages. This spirit can translate it." Yoo Sung spoke in a monotone. She pulled a tiny bowl the size of her thumbnail from her pocket. A few passes of her hand later, and it had grown into a full-sized spirit-sealing spellbowl. She passed it up to Boloud, who was driving.

"We, the most noble and righteous soldiers of the Godchild Freedom Army, are conducting revolutionary liberation missions in Kofi today. More than Kofi, across the great nation of Fariziland, the Godchild Freedom Army is retaking control. Back from the sinners! Back from the slave-masters! Back from the foreign thieves plundering our lands! Back from their local groveling eunuchs, so eager to beg for crumbs! Beloved fellow children of God, stay home or join the fight. If you know collaborators, or where foreign forces have infiltrated, report them to your nearest Blessed Brigade at once! You shall be rewarded, both here and in the life to come."

"Turn it off," Truth said. "I think we've heard enough. Any ideas why they suddenly kicked off today, of all days? Intel said they were a long way from launching a coup."

Everyone shook their heads, muttering about intel always being shit.

"It's the prismatic iridium. If they found a serious supply of it in the mines, those iridium mines just went from *valuable* to *global strategic resource*. Prismatic iridium is valuable on an interplanetary scale." Yoo Sung's voice was flat. She didn't have so much as a scab from where the needle had nicked her, but the spell was still going strong. She must not be fighting it, Truth thought, or her Level Three constitution would have gotten rid of it already.

"They launched a coup to secure the mines?"

"Probably."

"Huh." Truth desperately wanted to ask why she alone was to be evacuated, but figured that the answer probably wouldn't benefit him. They beelined to the airport. It was under siege. The government was dug in all around the terminal and the hangars, but the rebels were pressing hard. Spellbirds were swooping in and dropping explosives, artillery spells were cast, spraying metal and acid, the air turned black with burning wagons and burning people.

"We ain't driving through that," Boloud quietly declared. "Anything on the Demon's Eye?"

"We got a gap in the siege lines four blocks from the airfield. We can ditch the van, raise a five-layer invisibility ward, and infiltrate the private terminal?" Keller suggested.

Truth thought it through. He didn't have a better plan.

"Let's do it."

The drive from the hotel took forty minutes. The slow creep through the shipping depots, snipping open the chain-link fence around the airfield, crawling half a kilometer on their bellies to give the invisibility spell the best possible chance of working—that took four hours.

"All right, Nobu, call it in." Nobu nodded and worked the portable comms altar. A few seconds later, she got a strange look on her face.

Mission Update. Starbrite Regional Command Override, Code BLUE WOLF TORN, has been overridden by Starbrite Global Command Override, Code INDIGO PYRAMID RAIN. Security Detail ordered to protect asset Yoo Sung with Shattering Veil Spell on Spellward Talismans. No other spell use or action authorized until the evacuation vehicle arrives. This supersedes and replaces all other goals. System Costs will be paid by Code INDIGO PYRAMID RAIN. Operational responsibility assumed by Code INDIGO PYRAMID RAIN.

This was some high-grade bullshit. Not least of which being that you couldn't run that spell/talisman combo from inside the wards, as the wards would shred the spell. Something uncommonly nasty was about to go down. Truth started looking around for an escape route. Then gave it up. Orders are orders.

But . . . They didn't say where they had to stand before they cast it.

"Rezepi, that a basement over there?"

"Looks like some kind of maintenance crawlspace."

"Below ground is safer than above ground. Let's get down there and cast this ward."

It was dark, musty, claustrophobic, and Truth was prepared to cherish it. They quickly set up the talismans and activated the spells. Anything, particularly anything spiritual, would be utterly shredded if it came into contact with the wards. Nobu called it in.

The world went white. A sense of screaming, a whole city screaming. A monster looking down on the world and burning humanity away with the heat of its gaze. Truth could feel himself unraveling, coming apart at every level of his being.

<<Whoops! They called in the big guns! Bye-bye, trash; I won't miss you!>>

CHAPTER 26

THUNDER, PERFECT MIND

The prophet dressed in loose robes. They wore trousers like a man, but kept their head covered by a long shawl like a woman. They seemed to refer to themselves as both man and woman, or neither, which made their grammar hellishly confusing. Action followed word, for they walked through the places of both men and women alike, and did as they pleased there. This would usually see someone stoned to death, but the prophet just . . . fit in, wherever they were. They were never alien. After listening to them speak, you felt a growing dread that the wrongness was in you.

Truth always listened to the prophet speak. He liked to follow them, in those places he was allowed, and listen to them reveal the secrets of the world. He hoped one day to see as they saw, and understand as they did. But that truth, though revealed to him, had not been understood by him. That was all right. The prophet didn't really want anything and was content if you just listened and thought. Today, the prophet sat on a sandstone wall that kept in a neighbor's chickens, and recited a bit of their favorite hymn.

> *I am the disgraced and the exalted one.*
> *Give heed to my poverty and my wealth.*
> *Do not be haughty to me when I am discarded upon the earth,*
> *And you will find me among those that are to come.*
> *And do not look upon me on the garbage heap and go and leave me discarded.*
> *And you will find me in the kingdoms.*
> *And do not look upon me when I am discarded among those who are disgraced and*
> *in the least places,*
> *And then laugh at me.*
> *And do not cast me down among those who are slain in severity.*
> *But as for me, I am merciful and I am cruel.*

"What do you think it means?" the prophet asked.

"I don't know. It seems all contradictions." Truth shrugged.

"Really? Where?"

"*I am the disgraced and the exalted one? I am merciful and I am cruel?*" Truth asked.

"What if I were neither disgraced or exalted? Would that resolve the contradiction? Or what if I was both merciful and cruel?"

"How could that be possible?"

"Simple. I am not this." The prophet waved at themselves. "As you are not this." They waved at Truth. "Since I am not this dross, I am that which is perfect, eternal, and free. But that spark, that perfect self, is trapped in this ball of mud and dung. So, I am both disgraced and exalted, and I am neither of those things, for what I truly am is perfection, which is beyond honor and shame. Likewise, I am merciful and cruel, for my perfection incorporates those ideas but sublimates them."

The prophet took another look at Truth. "*Sublimates* means to improve or refine. I'm using it to mean that my perfection perfects the concepts and includes them in its totality."

Truth thought it through. "I understand what you are saying, but honestly, I don't see it. All this feels pretty real to me. Mudball or not, if I don't relieve myself of some dung, bad things will happen."

The prophet chuckled. "The truth of the world is not revealed to all, youngster. But it won't hurt you any to think on it."

<<*Ithurtsithurtsithurts OH GODS what the FUCK WAS THAT?! AAAhhhowoww, why can't you just die?!*>>

Truth slowly woke up. He was in a hospital bed. Nice crisp sheets, talisman papers glued all over his body, potion on a drip running into his vein. His bed was curtained off, so he didn't know if he was in a private room or in a ward. It was pretty quiet. Maybe a private room. There was a faint *ding*. A few moments later, a door opened and a plump older woman in scrubs came in.

"And how are we feeling today, Mr. Medici?"

"I . . . don't know? Where am I? I was on a job," he rasped. Truth realized suddenly that his throat was very dry.

"You are on the *Star of Mercy* hospital ship. You were airlifted here. I'm afraid I don't know anything about your job. Let me do a quick check of your vitals, then I think there is someone from your company that wants to talk to you." She fussed around his bed, making notes and jotting down numbers on a sheet.

"My crew? Yoo Sung?"

"I'm afraid I don't know anything about your nonmedical situation, Mr. Medici. Candidly, I would prefer not to know. So, please save your nonmedical questions for your company representative."

Truth mulled that over, not liking the sound of it. On the other hand, he wasn't restrained, so . . . there was that.

"How am I doing? Medically?"

"Fit to a truly impressive degree. I don't know what your skincare regime is, but it is clearly working for you. As is your diet. Cell counts, hormones, chemical markers all exactly where they should be for a person of your age. Humors well balanced. All bits attached. No residual brain trauma identified, no spell aperture damage, and all spiritual checks come back clear. Or, at least, clear for a Starbrite employee. The System kind of messes with that set of exams."

"Huh. Well, that's good to hear." Truth hesitated. "Except for the scans being messed up."

"It's normal, actually. Spiritual parasites love going for spell apertures, so the overlay of the System into those apertures throws up false positives. We calibrate for it and work around it. Like I said, you're clear of possession and, from what we can tell, lingering spiritual damage, curses, compulsions, and other ordinary maladies."

"Oh. Could I get some water?"

"Sure thing. I'll have someone bring it in for you."

The doctor bustled out of the room.

Truth felt like his emotions had a wet blanket thrown over them. He knew he should be very concerned about a lot of things, but he couldn't work up the energy. He pulled up the System.

Mission Complete! Five vials of *Icy Veins, Fiery Blood* issued and will be shipped to your office address. Bonus Award for fulfilling mission objectives from Code BLUE WOLF TORN—100,000 credits, 2 Friends and Family points. Bonus award for fulfilling mission objectives from Code INDIGO PYRAMID RAIN—100,000 credits, 5 Friends and Family points, one dose of Stellar Dowsing Elixir. Cost for lost equipment and employees assumed and paid for by Code INDIGO PYRAMID RAIN, and will not be charged to your account.
Congratulations! You have earned enough Performance Points to qualify for a promotion! Speak to your supervisor for more details.

It was incredible. Literally incredible, as in he did not credit it. Each "Friends and Family" point could be exchanged for a significant upward increment of the career starting point for a new employee. Generally, they were 100% of the sponsor's yearly base salary, each. This was to encourage both saving and striving, regardless of rank in the company. If you wanted to really do the best for your family.

Not including the elixirs, he had earned more than *nine years* of his base salary on one job. Did the rewards have to be split across the whole squad? He assumed so. He queried the system.

The Rewards are for you alone, subject to the usual rules and regulations laid out in your Starbrite Employee Handbook.

What. The fuck?

He could really feel whatever tranquilizer they gave him putting in the work. He should be freaking out, either delirious with joy or scared as hell about the implications.

"Knock-knock, Corporal Medici. Benny Le'voux, Strategic Human Resource Management Office. How ya doin'?"

Slicked back hair with five hundred grams of product in it, shiny two-tone shoes, crisp suit, and a smile full of the best veneers Starbrite could buy him. That was Benny. His lapel pin had a deep polish to it. With a horrible lurch, Truth realized that he didn't know where his lapel pin was. He had it for security duty, but where was it now?!

"Not sure. They must have me on a boatload of tranquilizers," Truth muttered.

"Ha! Boatload! Good one! You are funny, Corporal. Speaking of funny, we have a few things to discuss. Number one—do you happen to know how you survived?"

"Nope. I assume because I was in a basement."

"Not a very deep one, Corporal. Not deep enough."

There was a pause.

"My team didn't make it, did they?"

"No, Corporal, they did not. Though I should note that special dispensation was made and your permanent record will not be negatively impacted by the total loss of corporate assets under your supervision."

"Thanks."

"Don't thank me; thank your benevolent superiors in Starbrite! No other company would be so incredibly generous! Now, the good news is that Ms. Yoo Sung did survive unharmed." Benny pulled up a stool and sat next to the bed. He steepled his fingers and looked seriously at Truth.

"I wouldn't usually disclose the private matters of another employee, but it is important that you understand a little of the internal politics here. Besides, even a little casual digging would find all of this." Benny flicked away the minor detail.

"Ms. Yoo Sung is, in fact, one of our better up-and-coming scry stars. Her mother is already a well-established performer. Her father is no longer in the picture, but her *stepfather* is a *very* senior regional director."

"Code BLUE WOLF TORN?"

"I can neither confirm nor deny. Now just to, hah, confirm, Ms. Yoo Sung did mention the words *prismatic iridium* to you?"

"Hard to remember. There was a blinding white light," Truth lied.

"For the best, really. Because while there will be no keeping it secret long term, in the immediate future, *anyone* connected to *anything* connected to those words leaking out would land in a whole world of hurt. Just awful stuff." Benny looked grave. "I know you understand."

"Yeah. How did the company know to order the evac?"

"We got the daily rushes from the scry crew. Didn't take long to figure out what's what. The rebels were moving long before we were, of course, but . . ."

Truth just nodded. He got it.

"Nobody really knows what the rebels attacked with, but there is credible evidence that they were funneling illegal mining profits into buying strategic-tier curses and invocations from rogue states. Shit like this, Corporal, is why sanctions exist." Benny looked sick.

"It knocked out huge chunks of Kofi as well as a dozen more locations across the country. It was a massive spiritual entity of some exalted rank. I understand that the demonologists and spiritualists are having a field day right now." Benny shrugged. "Casualties are still being sorted out, but it's bad. It's also not your problem."

"No, I guess not."

"Now, I understand that you will need some time off, and that's already approved. The Company would prefer you laid low for a while too. So, your new mission should be popping up shortly, and it's a good 'un. Oh, don't worry! We contacted your siblings. They know you are safe and enjoying a meditation retreat with a spa service as part of your reward for rescuing a beautiful scry star."

"Spa service?!"

"The *Star of Mercy* isn't any old hospital ship." Benny leaned in, eyes fever bright.

"Corporal, you are a combat savant. You survived an attack, seemingly unharmed, that obliterated thousands of lives. Quite possibly more than ten thousand; they are still sorting through the rubble. Combined with your almost-fanatical loyalty to Starbrite and the fact that your entire family is working like hell to join Starbrite, well. A very, very, very senior figure said to look after you. So, enjoy the next week, Corporal. I wish I had your luck."

MISSION: Spend the next seven days enjoying the services and facilities available on the *Star of Mercy* hospital ship, including but not limited to: Expert administration of your Stellar Dowsing Elixir, Stellar Ray Concentration Chamber, emotional support groups, one-on-one therapy, relaxational exercise, twenty-three types of massage, four swimming pools, a waterslide, salon, sauna, ice baths, tentacle baths, baths of icy tentacles in a sauna, eight full bars, sixteen dedicated 33rd degree enlightened mixologists, two on-board alchemists, free gourmet meals at one of three onboard restaurants, movies and scry available in your suite on demand, and a VVIP pass to the onboard pet cafe.
BUDGET: Paid by CODE INDIGO PYRAMID RAIN
REWARD: One performance point.

CHAPTER 27

REFRAMING

We welcome the Great God, the unity, the Divine Mind that is both the universe and the person. We call upon the great teacher, thrice great, thrice born, ibis, child, star, giver of all arts and wisdom. We call upon that which is greatest and that which is least. In their sacred and perfect wisdom, let the stars above summon up the starry universe within . . ."

The droning prayers rolled back and forth between the masked astromancers. Truth sat cross-legged and naked between the ritualists, trying to channel the Stellar Dowsing Elixir along the courses of his body.

The astromancers, one male and one female, had created a ritual room of such perfection that Truth could hardly believe it existed. The mathematically perfect alchemical sulfur and mercury tracings covered the eggshell-thin alabaster walls, acting as a fulcrum between the stars above and the human below.

The entire room was suspended at the bottom of the ship, stabilized within a vast gyroscope. This ensured the rituals were always precisely aligned with the heavens and whatever stellar patrons were invoked. The astromancers promised perfection and, given what their mortal patrons were paying, made sure to deliver it.

The Stellar Dowsing Elixir was delivered in a cut-glass vial, every millimeter of which was covered in spells carved directly into the glass. The stopper was some alchemical marvel, warm to the touch and perfectly sealed against air, water, and stellar rays. Two hulking combat magi, Level Three at a minimum, had escorted the ship's purser, who delivered it directly to the ritual room in a velvet-lined rosewood box. The liquid was the blue of the sky just before sunrise, and the twinkle of the fading stars danced within it.

The astromancers sat Truth in a carefully emptied square, inside a circle, inside a triangle, all marked and measured with symbols whose significance Truth did not understand. His job was to sit very still, allow his internal stellar energy to circulate as usual, and, when the Stellar Dowsing Elixir was dropped on his third eye, allow the energy to flow through him. Mark carefully its passing. And then help it work its way into his spell apertures.

Truth earned more than five years of base salary on his last job, and he was pretty sure that the credits in his account would not buy twenty minutes of the astromancers' services. Astromancy was a dangerous job requiring decades of study to become an initiate. But the results were equally incredible.

A universe was revealed inside of Truth. He could feel the swirl of the stars, the vast, indifferent patronage of those great spirits blessing him with their power and wisdom. He was part of them. They were part of him. They were all part of some great perfection he could not directly perceive but whose existence he could perfectly infer, like gravity.

Nine great stars existed within him. Nine places for magic to dwell. He had to find them. The first was easy, a small, reddish star—but growing. The next one was harder, a clump of nothing inside him, shimmering with promise. He felt the stars from the elixir gather around this star in waiting and swirl more and more tightly, bringing it to the very edge of ignition, then stop and spread throughout his universe. Seven more stellar coordinates were found and graced with swirling starlight.

The droning chant took on a subtly different tack—

"For there is nothing in all the cosmos that he is not. He is himself, the things that are and those that are not. Those that are, he has made visible; those that are not, he holds within him. This is the god who is greater than any name; this is the god invisible and entirely visible. This god who is evident to the eyes may be seen in the mind. He is bodiless and many-bodied; he is all-bodied . . ." The astromancers' voices echoed back and forth, and now, rather than finding his spell apertures or helping fill them, the elixir began to widen and deepen them.

The alignment of the stars above, the mystical sigils directing the stellar rays, the crushing will, and the focus of the astromancers all focused on Truth. The stars of the elixir refined the apertures, ensuring that his spells would be more potent in the future. The magic within him would be less fragile or susceptible to demonic attack. The map of his soul was gently tugged into cleaner alignment with his body. The moment of refinement seemed to stretch beyond even the concept of time itself, and Truth became lost in the heavens within him.

Some unknowable time later, the gentle tapping of a bell brought him back to himself. He was coated in sweat and felt exhausted. It was odd and wonderful.

"Your treatment is complete and a complete success. Congratulations. Your future advancement will be remarkable. You may be tempted to take additional elixirs or supplements and immediately break through to Level Two—resist that temptation." The male astromancer spoke, slightly swaying on his feet.

"Right now, your body is in a very special condition. Just let the natural accumulation of stellar rays gently open your second aperture—the results will be vastly better. Please enjoy this complimentary bottle of spring water, drawn from the Tear of the Eye of Mejuid. You are likely very dehydrated." The female astromancer sounded like she was making a rote speech, also clearly exhausted.

"I will. Thank you. Anything else I should know or do?"

"Well. That ritual—" the male astromancer started.

"Went much better than usual. Your body seemed to be primed for receiving the blessings of the stars. Interesting body refinement," the female astromancer concluded.

"Good?"

"Very." They nodded simultaneously. "Drink the water, go to sleep, find the beauty of the world on board this ship." They spoke in chorus. They started sleepily undressing each other. Truth got out as fast as his rubbery legs could manage. He was halfway down the hall when he realized he was wearing only a towel.

The cruise ship, because that was what this "hospital ship" was, was incredible. Everybody on board was some manner of mover and shaker, and all had some "malady" that was being treated. Truth was lost initially, but the System suggested an itinerary.

His days quickly filled up with massages, light exercise, therapy, swimming, more exercise, more massage, and some guided socialization with the other guests. Yoo Sung had been there but left two days before. Oh well. It was nice. Truth sat on the floor of the pet cafe with a cat on his head and a floppy dog on his lap, sipping a cup of milk tea, and realized that, to his incredible surprise, he was happy.

He was simply, uncritically happy. Not joyful or ecstatic or excited or triumphant. Just quietly, contentedly happy. It felt good just to be. That the fucked-up shit in his life was real and terrible, but he had done his best, and he had done well. Right there, right then, he could put it all down. He didn't have to be the big brother carrying the family, not the combat magus or the bodyguard. Not to be anyone. Just *be*. With a cat on his head and a dog drooling through his trousers. His chest felt warm. Like the world was opening up to him. Like he was allowed to do more than survive. He was allowed to be happy.

It was a few minutes before he noticed the notification:

Congratulations! You have reached Level Two. Please continue enjoying the facilities on the *Star of Mercy*.

That night, a woman took the initiative to chat with him at the bar. It was a perfectly nice little conversation. They talked about their favorite animals in the pet cafe. She also recommended some books in the ship's library. Truth felt on top of the world as he went to bed.

And that was the week. Truth tried the waterslide. He didn't get it. The "gourmet" restaurants were fine, but he didn't understand why everyone else was making a fuss. He ordered a burger and got it. Nobody cared except for a couple of people who gave him approving nods. He spent a lot of time at the pet cafe.

In the evenings, he would try to chat with people at one of the bars. His therapists suggested learning "small talk," and he was determined to give it an honest try. It was an unspoken taboo to talk in too much detail about matters off the ship, but—

"So, you are a soldier?"

"Well, security. For a multinational."

"Hah! All right. But you're a vet, right? Like, actual combat? Because you look like it."

"Do I? Damn. Better book another facial." He didn't land the joke but pressed on. "I'm a vet, and yes, actual combat. Although mostly, it's waiting around. You?"

"Oh, boring stuff. I help connect alchemy reagent suppliers in developing nations and the big alchemy operations in rich countries. Get that win-win going and get paid for it, you know?"

"Sure, sure . . ."

It reminded him of doing his drop armor training—going up so high, you could see the world's curvature. See its vastness with distance, but lose the endless detail below. The other guests gave him that feeling—that they inhabited the sky above a vast world, a world he was too close to, lost in the details.

On the last day, he was summoned to the aft of the ship, handed a duffel with a clean set of clothes, his Starbrite pin, and a complimentary gift bag with mini-toiletries. A spell bird lay on the roosting pad, waiting to ferry people to shore. With the soft thunder of mighty wings, the construct carried them back to the real world.

Truth spent a lot of time with the sibs. Many hugs were dispensed, and some strategic investments in wardrobe and furnishings. Credits weren't inheritable, but he could set them up well in case anything happened to him. He got bombarded with questions about which scry star he rescued.

"So? Are you going out? She knocked up yet?" Sophia asked with a worrying degree of interest.

No, they were not going out. Which Truth didn't regret. Yoo Sung looked amazing on scry, and she was definitely *gorgeous* in real life, but she always seemed withdrawn. A mannequin woman. Like she could only really exist on camera, and everything else was just making sure those moments of existence came into being. It was something that made him laugh in therapy. He would cheerfully knock out a bar full of thugs to get a date—but not one like her.

Sergeant Murthey greeted him with genial warmth. "Oh, fuck, he's back. Yeah, yeah, you are up for promotion, but we don't review for promotions until the end of the year. Don't tell me what the fuck happened, 'cause I officially don't want to know. Officially. As in I was told, in writing, *DON'T ASK.*"

"Got it, Sarge. Great to see you, too."

"Jump up your own ass and die." He paused. The sergeant had spoken reflexively and had sidetracked himself. With a slight shake, he carried on. "That being said, welcome back and all that. We will start you off nice and easy—some babysitting gigs, package escorts, that kind of thing."

"Sarge, that sounds boring as hell."

"Oh, not only is it boring, the pay is shit too." Sergeant Murthey sounded indecently excited by the prospect. "On the other hand, the one thing I am allowed to know about your situation is you just spent a week in the fucking hospital, so guess what? You get to be on light duty."

Truth had a hard time arguing with that but wanted to try anyway.

"I got discharged! This is bullshit!"

"Take it up with HR."

"Ha. Ha," Truth growled.

"No, literally. That's your next job. HR is hiring you. You get to escort a *very* special manager to a training retreat up in the mountains. Eight hours of sitting next to her in the hold of a cargo bird, each way." The sergeant clasped Truth by the shoulder in an intimate, manly way. "Just remember, you are always in our thoughts. And prayers."

CHAPTER 28

A SLOW DAY AT WORK

I miss the pet café, Truth thought. *I miss Captain Floofy and Wigglebutt. They got me. Spiritually. Mr. Mittens was a bit standoffish, but I respect not wanting to be touched until there was trust and a connection. I respect the hell out of it.*

"And then, THEN, the little idiot was like, "Oh, but I don't see your Weekly Employee Efficiency Evaluation Review Reports linked in the database!" And then I was like, "Um? Excuse me? Is this the demon right here? You know, the one with the WEEERR Reports memorized? Because it's been the same demon for forty years? You know? That demon? And then she got super embarrassed and stomped off to the bathroom. I know she cried in there. And then everybody clapped.""

She drew a single short breath and continued.

"But anyway, are we almost there yet? I don't think these seats are really ergonomic, and there is *no way* I can spend all day in unergonomic seats. Not with my legs. The witch was very clear—ten minutes moving around for every fifty seated, and we've been in here for hours. I don't know how many hours—"

"Five hours, thirty-eight minutes, and twenty-three seconds. Twenty-four. Twenty-five," Truth said. He hadn't been watching the clock to begin with, but by Prager, he was now.

"Oh, that is really no good, young man. Not good at all. You will never get promoted, being a clock-watcher. Not good at all! In my department, you can always spot the clock-watchers. They are like little toasts, popping up at exactly six o'clock . . ."

He wasn't even protecting this nattering woman. He was protecting a box they were sharing the hold with. *She* was "supervising" the box. They were sitting on fold-out jump seats in the back of a cargo bird flying from one end of Jeon to another, surrounded by thousands of other, unsupervised boxes.

This box was so damn special that it required a notably hard-to-kill corporal and the South Rejin Island Regional Champion Yammerer. Her ability to monologue pointlessly had seamlessly moved from boring, to painful, to horrifying, to redefining hell.

<<For once, we are in complete agreement. Do you think they would notice if you just . . . shoved her out the hatch? Or maybe one of the loading slaves didn't properly secure one of

the boxes and it fell down and crushed her head into paste? Possibly that box way up there, with the metal-reinforced edges?>>

Desperate to escape the yammering, Truth tried to escape into fantasy. He imagined putting the yammerer into an arm bar, marching her to the hatch, and shoving her out. Just . . . watching her fall twenty thousand feet onto the mountains below. But no, the doors were alarmed and warded against that sort of thing, and he remembered hearing about how you couldn't really open the doors when you were high up. No, an accident inside the bird would be necessary.

He started looking around. The guys at the loading dock were good, but it was a busy, high-speed job. Wouldn't be surprising if a box wasn't tied down properly. He started scanning the top shelves, looking for likely volunteers.

She shook her head in disgust. "They try to claim their parents died and they 'need' to go to the funeral. Well, do you know what Starbrite needs? They need you to do your job! And with a good, positive, cheerful attitude. We need to be happy, value-generating warriors, maximizing shareholder returns through energized and empowered forward-focused core-competency engagement across departmental achievement milestones . . ."

Oh, she's had a stroke. How wonderful. Truth thought. *Fingers crossed the bird gets hit by AA fire and I have to kill my way out, dragging this two-hundred-kilo chest of whatever it is across jungle-covered mountains.*

Alas, life does not always give us what we want; the bird safely landed an hour later. A passenger bird could have done it in half the time, but these big cargo carriers flew slowly, to maximize energy efficiency. Or to torture Truth. Either could be true.

"And I know we can't just *fire* people. This is Starbrite, for heaven's sake! But I do make a point of letting everyone know that a transfer to a fish cannery's production line is *always* an option. I had a wonderful program for a couple of years where the bottom five percent of performers in my department were *automatically* transferred to the canneries. But like I told you, the regional manager, or should I say *current* and *soon-to-be-former* regional manager, is a person without vision . . ."

I must kill her. She is departmental poison. Her sickening incompetence is damaging productivity and morale and sets a terrible example for other managers. Her supervisor is also responsible, and he will be taken care of next. But right now, for the good of Starbrite, she must die.

Truth reached a place of calm resolve. It was a violation of his oath. He would probably die. But it was necessary. For Starbrite.

<<*Yes. For Starbrite. Farewell, Truth. I hated you, but in the end, you managed to do the right thing.*>>

His hands started rising. He would throttle her. It was the only way.

"Corporal Truth? We're here to take delivery?" A snappily dressed pair of delivery men waved at him.

"Pardon?" They didn't look like undertakers.

"Delivery? You are supposed to be delivering a crate to us?" one asked, starting to look puzzled.

"Oh. Right. Yes. Right here." He waved them to the box. They pressed a spell gem to the binding talisman on the crate.

MISSION COMPLETE! You have successfully delivered both the package and District Manager Y'Vette to Poyussan International Airport Cargo Terminal.
REWARD: Fifteen performance points, no bonus, Second Mission in Chain unlocked.

Eh? Chain mission?

MANDATORY FOLLOW-UP MISSION: Work with the delivery team to escort the package and District Manager Y'Vette to the secured holding facility attached to Poyussan International Airport Cargo Terminal, and facilitate the transfer.
REWARD: One hundred performance points.
PERFORMANCE BONUS: Three vials of True Sight Drops.

Huh. Nice chunk of performance points right there, and True Sight drops were always useful for breaking illusions. Not . . . life-changing or anything, but nice. Everyone looked at each other and nodded. They all got the mission update too.

The secured holding facility was a storage unit attached to the warehouse and "secured" with a padlock, a ward strong enough to stop most hamsters or half a rat, and an alarm loud enough to wake the dead. Metaphorically. It was clear no one involved with this would spring for actual necromancers, as those cost money. The small storage unit had the sole virtue of having a decent ritual space etched into the floor. Looked like a binding ritual, so maybe that was what they meant by "secured"?

"All right, Manager Y'Vette, if you could stand on the Sigil of Roth Esham, perfect, thank you. Jer, you got Melchior?"

"All day." Jer was already standing on the spot.

"Great. And I've got Penz'ap'nem. Okay, Corporal, could you pop the chest? Please do be careful, as the contents can shift during transit, and that can make it cranky."

"I am always excited to work on new projects, but could someone please explain what this is about? I was told I was going on a career-development retreat and was flying with cargo for efficiency," Y'Vette asked snippily.

"Yes, ma'am, all of that is correct. This is step one, as it were." Jer nodded. Truth eased over to the box and felt the spells activate. They resonated with the binding on the floor and, once satisfied with that, tested Truth's lapel pin. All being in order, the latches popped free. Truth gingerly eased the lid open.

A shadow whipped out, clawing for Truth's throat. He slapped it away and shifted back a half step. *Load Sword of Wold!*

Sword of Wold Loaded. 500 credits deducted from your account.

Truth's hand turned into a glowing point of light, hacking down on the squirming mass of darkness and tentacles as it came pouring out of the chest. *There is no hope*, it seemed to whisper. *There is no future for you. You will die horribly, horribly. And it won't matter. Better to just let it happen. Better to just accept.*

Truth stabbed the thing where it looked like it would do some good. The mass of shadows and twisting hooks and suckers screamed.

"Whoa there, Corporal! No workplace violence!" the delivery man exclaimed. "Jer, quick, hit it!" Jer nodded and started chanting. From the breast pocket of his overalls he pulled a little silver plate and aimed it at the horror. The other delivery driver did the same, but where he was standing, his talisman put the horror and Y'Vette in a straight line together. Y'Vette stood stock-still, clearly trying to process what she was seeing.

The creature lunged once more at Truth, who just focused on defending himself. The chants soon had it bound to stillness, then compressed into an inky black ball the size of an ostrich egg. The delivery man yelled "Rem'kah!" and the ball flew at Y'Vette. She tried to scream.

The demon unfurled its hooks, wrapping around her face. Burrowing in through her mouth, her nose, her eyes, and her ears. She tried to scream again, but nothing came out. Her eyes were flooded with blackness. Something inhuman blinked, once. Then the eyes reverted to normal.

"Oh, my." The voice poured like warm milk out of former District Manager Y'Vette. "I knew I was up for a bonus, but this is just spectacular."

"You earned it, ma'am. It says here that we are to take you directly to some blood pools for a spa treatment, then later in the evening the local prison is holding a private execution. We arranged a special seat just for you," the delivery man said with pride.

"Wonderful. Just wonderful. And this body is a delight too. Did you know she put an employee on a performance improvement plan for not 'Displaying a positive and productive attitude' the day his pregnant wife died in a flying carpet accident?"

"Can't say I'm surprised, madam. I'm sure you will whip her into shape," Jer said loyally.

"Whipping will be a *reward*." The demon chuckled, running the fingers that used to belong to Y'Vette through the hair that Y'Vette used to obsess over. "There are so, so many lessons to learn first. And you, young man! Swinging that nasty thing around. I am quite entitled to feel cranky after such a rough flight, and your attitude *Did Not Help*."

Her voice was warm but firm. Truth felt a sudden overwhelming sense of shame. Like he should offer her something to apologize. Anything. Everything. His lapel pin blazed bright blue for an instant, and the feeling passed.

"Sorry about that." He tried to remain affable. The demon sniffed, then turned to the delivery man.

"So, are you going to let me out of here?"

"Certainly, madam, at once! But you know the rules."

"Yes, yes. So tiresome." She chanted something infernal, the delivery men chanted something in Enochian, their silver plates burned with all the colors in the rainbow. Truth just stood there quietly. Soon, a ring of silver runes etched their way around the base of "Y'Vette's" neck. Everyone nodded and she stepped out of the formation.

"Ah, before I go, Corporal Medici. A quick word, if you please." She crooked her finger at him while giving the delivery guys a look. They wandered a short distance away.

"Corporal, you aren't one of my reports, but I can see you are not a people person. And, not to put too fine a point on it, a virgin. Nothing wrong with that, of course. But I do want you to make sure you are taking full advantage of the services HR and the System can provide you." Somehow, her voice just oozed sincere concern.

"I understand it can be scary, trying to make a connection," she murmured. "It's particularly scary to be vulnerable. You can handle physical dangers, but emotional vulnerability? The Army doesn't train you for that."

Truth just nodded, lost.

"So, my candid suggestion is this: practice."

"Small talk?"

"That's a good start, but I was thinking slightly more advanced. You know, for *certain* people, *certain* things become available in the shop. For example, a lover."

"Madam, I think this is getting a little inappropriate," Truth said.

"Nothing inappropriate about it. It's a benefit, and you are entitled to it. The credits are significant up front, depending on the degree of customization you want and whether you want a modified human or a full demon. But you would be safe. Absolutely safe. They would never hurt you. You could open yourself to them fully, and they would never hate you. Never look down on you. Despise you for being from the slums. So long as you made the monthly payments, they would be yours forever. Or until you are tired of them and find someone new. At the very, very least, they are someone you could practice with."

She smiled warmly. "Think it over. And now I am off for my retreat!" And she merrily strode away.

"Thanks. She can be a handful right out of the crate, but really, she's a sweetie. One of HR's top demons," Jer told Truth appreciatively. "She's been on some shit details recently, so this is a well-earned break for her."

Truth wasn't quite sure how he felt about all this. All he could think of to say was "You guys are HR? You look like delivery guys. No offense."

"None taken; we are. We just make sure our noncorporeal colleagues get where they need to go, rather than packages. If you follow me." Truth nodded. The delivery men packed up the empty crate and handed Truth his bonus, and everyone went home.

The flight back was in the hold of another transport, just him and tons of paper goods. Eight hours of blessed silence. Just another day on the job.

CHAPTER 29

CAREER DEVELOPMENT

Truth had a lot of time to think on the flight back. The first thing was "Lovers are a *benefit of the job* for *some people* at Starbrite." The company was always very upfront about the fact that not everyone had the same access to the System store. Told him that on day one. And as Truth had provisionally determined the value of human life to be eleven wen and a pair of ratty shoes, he could be charitably described as "frugal." Fair to say he was not a shopper. Despite that, he felt like he would have spotted a *Modified Human Beings* tab in the shop.

Summon Humanoid System Interface, he thought.

<<No.>>

What do you mean, no? Are you broken or something?

<<Do it properly.>>

Oh, for fuck's sake. Truth got his mind set, then tried again. *Appear, imp!*

"Yatta! It's me, your lovable human-shaped . . . something! Yaay!" The sprite, still in its office-lady outfit, delivered the lines in a monotone while appearing to smoke a Golden Bat cigarette and flip through a magazine.

"Really? I put some effort into that."

"It was weak. It was some try-hard shit and you know it. Still, it was better than nothing, so I'm here. Whaddya want?"

"Before we get to that, is it possible for me to savagely beat you?" Truth asked.

"Can you savagely, cruelly, humiliatingly beat a hallucination facilitating your communication with an incomprehensibly vast spiritual being that interacts with reality on a level that your gelatinous brain mercifully cannot comprehend? No. But I do like where your mind is headed!" It smiled sunnily and put down the magazine. The cigarette stayed.

"Great. Look, I ran into a demon today—"

"Yeah, Human Resource Development Officer Lamashtu. Such a sweetheart. What about her?"

Truth shook his head, certain he hadn't heard that right. Then pressed on. "Look, she said something about lovers being available through the System as a company benefit?"

"She did? Oh. Well, that's not good."

"What? Why?"

"Because it is her nature to be very aware of feelings of loneliness, isolation, and pain. If she is taking the time to give you some unsolicited advice, then you really need it. On the other hand, she *is* a demon, so . . . grain of salt and all that."

Truth tried to wrap his head around the idea and failed. The System faerie shrugged and went back to its magazine. Eventually, Truth looked over again. "Explain how this works."

"Good tone, demanding. Commanding. Immediately, magus!" It tossed the cigarette aside and ditched the magazine. "Basically, you have three options. Variations within and between those options, but three main choices. First—straight demon. We summon a succubus—"

Truth raised an eyebrow.

"All right, yes, they technically are called something else, but that's what everyone calls them. Just . . . work with me here."

He flapped a hand, urging the sprite to continue.

"We summon a spiritual entity colloquially known as a succubus or incubus and *yes* they are the same thing, customized to fit your needs and preferences. The summoning-and-binding ritual is a huge pain in the ass, so we have to employ specialist demonologists for the job. A high-demand bunch, as you can imagine, so the upfront costs are chunky. Despite that, this is the cheapest option, and I don't recommend it for beginners."

"Why?"

"Because even with top-notch bindings, succubi are what they are. You will fall helplessly in love with them, and they will slowly take over your life. They won't harm you directly, but you will have picked up, essentially, a permanent parasite. Succubi are fine for a weekend for the hardcore, but definitely not for beginners."

"Got it." Truth nodded. Though he would have to think about it some more.

"The next option is the most expensive up front, though depending on what you want, the maintenance costs can be reasonable. Basically, we make you some kind of golem and slap a personality into it. Be it demonic, spiritual, an engram of a person who once lived, or even have a ghost possess it. Whatever you need and can afford. Some options are better fits than others." The sprite shrugged. "It's on the table, but candidly, it's out of your price range right now."

"All right, and the last option? I believe she said 'Modified Humans'?" There was a definite edge to his voice.

"Yeah, it's the middle of the road, price-and-maintenance-cost-wise. Basically, we take a basic human, tweak them with as much customization physically as you are willing to pay for, drop a glamour on 'em, and give them a personality to inhabit for a while. It's not *perfect,* but a lot of people find that the imperfections make the whole thing feel better. Obviously, they still could never betray you or deliberately hurt you. You would struggle to hurt them too. Emotionally, anyway." The sprite shrugged.

"Upfront costs can be substantial but not crazy. The monthly maintenance is the highest of the three, but you can afford it with some budgeting. Well, depending on what extras you order." The sprite kept the tone matter-of-fact.

"Realizing I'm not likely to like the answer . . . where do the 'humans' come from?"

"Nothing weird, if that's what you were afraid of. Either they owe the company so much money that even a normal indenture couldn't pay it off, or they are so psychologically damaged they just don't want to deal with reality for a good long while. Knowing that they are being taken care of, and even earning money, is comforting to them." Truth looked skeptical but the faerie pressed on. "The modified humans are so enchanted, they genuinely enjoy their time with you. We modify their memories afterward, of course. For your privacy."

"And this is . . . legal?"

"Sure. Why not? Everyone consents, and has their basic needs met. There are rules on how you can use or abuse them. It's all very transparent."

"Ah. And how much would, say, a basic lover cost?"

"Modified human? Basic package deal? Ten thou up front, eight hundred a month maintenance, plus whatever you want to treat them to. Fancy foods, jewelry, whatever. Like I said, it's a chunk, but you can afford it." It threw a double thumbs-up, then dropped them immediately.

"You are sitting on a big chunk of cash right now from the Kofi job, so now would be a good time to try it out. However. There are a couple of things to consider first," the sprite said.

"Like what?"

"Like what do you want your future to look like? And the future for your siblings?"

He wasn't quite sure how to answer that. When you got right down to it, what they had now (plus Sophia and maybe Vigor going to university) was his highest definition of life goals. What . . . did he want?

"Let me lay out a few things that may help you focus. First—cultivation rank is everything. The higher you cultivate, the higher your status in the company. It's not one-to-one or anything, but you won't find anyone in the upper ranks of C-Tier who isn't at least Level Four. *At least.* Most of B-Tier is Level Six and up. Level Seven, and they are knocking on A-Tier and the C-Suite.

"Now, you may not want to have managerial responsibility on that level. That's fine; lots of opportunities for powerful people without direct reports. But you *really* need to be connecting your Level to your sense of security and the well-being of your family."

"Understood."

"Good. Next item. You have enough credits to buy a Friends and Family point. It will leave you a bit over ten thou credits from your bonuses from that job, but it will save you having to, well, save for several years."

That landed like a gut punch. He had been so blown away by the fact that he had gotten some Friends and Family points as a bonus that he hadn't even considered spending his own credits to buy one. And the faerie was right. It could take years to save up for even one point. Years the sibs didn't have.

"Exactly how much of a benefit do those points give new employees?" he asked.

"Varies on the job, department, and tier. F-Tier? A single point might let you pick your job, within reason. C-Tier? You are going to need a couple to shift up a bit. Maybe three to get a really good mentor for your high-status job. So, if you want all your sibs to start at C-Tier like you, three points are not remotely enough to get them the best career track."

"Ah."

"Remember, you joined up with both military merits and a Master of Arms certification. You made your own points, as it were. If Harmony were to join Security, unless he also goes berserk during his National Service, he would go into F-Tier, non-PMC security."

Truth sighed. He wasn't renting a boyfriend. Or girlfriend. Or . . . both? Oh, he was going to be hating himself for this for a while, wasn't he? Then he frowned. Starbrite was *ruthlessly* hierarchical.

"Imp."

"Yes, dread magus?"

"Are you seriously implying that the sponsor's tier is irrelevant?"

"Never, oh mighty one! Who is putting in the work on the ominous tone, by the way. Big improvement."

"How, exactly, does the sponsor's tier affect things?"

"The points stretch a lot further, the higher your tier. For example, you are at the bottom of the C Tier. You would have to spend a lot of points to land Harmony a mid-C-Tier job, assuming he passed the relevant specialization on the SAT. On the other hand, your boss is much higher in the C Tier and would spend comparatively less for the same job. The same principle applies to a lot of benefits in the company."

"How the hell is that fair? We're both C-Tier," Truth demanded.

"Fair? What's 'fair' got to do with it? You know perfectly well that her Friends and Family points are more expensive than yours. Why shouldn't hers buy more advantage? She's earned her position. You can do the same." The faerie looked both scandalized and offended.

Truth sighed. Of course that was how it worked. What an odd flash of idiocy to look for "fairness." He shifted around, trying to get comfortable on the foldout seat. It wasn't happening. Maybe that was it. Too much time in cargo holds.

"So, it comes back down to cultivation and hustling for cash. I gotta balance what I can earn in bonuses for Friends and Family points against what I need to be buying to get to a higher level, to make those points stretch further."

"Exactly. Lucky for you that the PMC both pays very well and provides many opportunities for bonuses. I can tell you that a C-9-U in our ocean shipping department won't see so many elixirs in five years as you have seen in one. Speaking of fairness." The sprite nodded.

Truth wasn't really sure what he wanted. He didn't mind leading a section for the Kofi job. Enjoyed it, actually. He could see leading a squad. A platoon, though? That might be too much for him.

"Wait, what do you mean, 'Plenty of opportunities for powerful people without direct reports'? What would you even be doing for the company?"

The sprite giggled. It was a nasty, mean sound like someone who found out her enemy was pregnant with her lover's child and he wasn't leaving his wife. "Ask me again when you are Level Five. I can promise you this much: you will have to hire an accountant to keep track of all the money, elixirs, and treasures you accumulate. Friends and Family points? People will beg you, heads pressed to the floor, *beg you* to let them employ your siblings. And you will tell them no because they aren't good enough. *They aren't even qualified to beg.*"

Truth coughed. That stirred up some feelings. Feelings he wasn't completely sure he wanted to understand better. But he knew what he had to do now.

"Any which way. Get working, get that money, get my level up. And do it fast and hard."

CHAPTER 30

PACKAGE FOR YOU, SIR!

It was an understandably tired, cranky, and frustrated Truth that crawled out of the cargo terminal at Harban International. Legend had it that there were birds intended to transport humans. With full, comfortable seats, and servants who would bring you food and drink. He shot a filthy glare at a departure terminal. All the families with all their luggage, off for vacations somewhere wonderful. Such *happy-looking* children.

He flagged down a flying carpet. The carpet driver, understandably, did not want to take the visibly pissed-off man and pretended to be blind. Another carpet went past, and Truth flashed his lapel pin. Said lapel pin was not visible from such a long distance, and the carpet didn't even slow as it went past.

Next fucker stops or I swear I will jump up and rip their damn head off, Truth swore to himself.

"Hey, buddy. You know the carpet stand is over by Terminal E, right? They aren't allowed to pick up here," a passing worker told him. Truth just closed his eyes and groaned.

"Truth's back!" Harmony shouted. "I think he died. Bro, did you die?"

"I swear I was delivering a package all day. Yes, I think I died. Bury me somewhere nice."

"Sorry, bro. Student budget. Best I can do is a coffee-can urn and a quick trip to the storm drain." Harmony tossed him a can of cold tea from the fridge, which Truth pressed to his neck. His neck ached from leaning up against a wall for sixteen hours.

"Who are we burying?" Sophia yelled from the room she shared with Vigor. And Harmony, when Truth was in town.

"Truth!"

"Save his body for science! I need materials."

"Sorry, bro. Maybe we can still do the coffee-can thing with the bits she doesn't use?"

"I appreciate you doing your best." Truth tried to remember how to open a can. He thought he remembered, but his fingers were suddenly incompetent. He got it eventually. "What time is it?"

"Late enough that you should just have a snack rather than trying to eat dinner." Harmony smiled slightly. "There's some leftover chicken I can throw in the hot box."

"Any leftover rice?"

"Yeah."

"Hurray, I have dinner."

Harmony threw everything together in the hot box. While things were heating up, he set out a bottle of hot sauce and a shaker of Adlom Seasoning™ next to Truth. Truth stared at the shaker. It was one of the bits of the slums he couldn't shake. Food—the nice, good-quality food they ate now—tasted wrong. He couldn't put his finger on what it was for a while. It just tasted off. Like green beans weren't supposed to taste that way, and the texture was all wrong.

It took Truth weeks to realize that he had almost never eaten a vegetable that didn't come out of a can. Everything came already salted. Already cooked to near-mush. Real food was an unpleasant surprise. He was trying to train his taste buds to adapt, but it was slow going. The compromise solution? Adlom Seasoning™. When you can't make the food taste good, make it taste like Adlom Seasoning™.

He chuckled darkly. Friends and Family points. Elixirs. He was already sitting on unimaginable wealth compared to a year before. Making people beg to hire the sibs. That tickled a bone he didn't want to acknowledge. But he still couldn't shake the taste of poverty. Couldn't shake the fact that his tongue was still in the slums.

Starting today, he was going to learn to eat good food. Fancy food. Harmony dropped the plate in front of Truth. Truth had a bite of the chicken and rice, then dosed it with the hot sauce and the seasoning. Tomorrow. Starting tomorrow. After a good night's sleep to gather his strength.

"Morning, Sergeant! Might I say you are looking extremely fit today!" Truth did his best to sound upbeat. Sergeant Murthey looked at him with horror.

"How many dead?"

"Ha-ha. You sure are a kidder, Sergeant Murthey. Ha-ha-ha-ha." Truth desperately tried to hang on to a sunny, positive vibe.

"HOW MANY DEAD, CORPORAL?! ARE WE AT WAR?" Murthey bellowed.

"I don't know, Sarge. I didn't kill anyone and I don't remember seeing anyone killed in the last day or so." Truth gave up. He had tried his best.

"Prager's sweaty sack be praised. Now, if I don't have to worry about airstrikes or strategic-class curses, why are you so damn chipper? It's creepy."

"Just . . . trying to work on being a people person, Sarge."

That seemed to flummox the older man for a minute. He started talking a few times but stopped before the first word got out. Eventually, with a delicate air, he said, "Corporal, that is a . . . good thing. You should definitely work on being a people person. Bond with the people around you, and come to value their lives highly. Just. Baby steps. Everything in moderation, right?"

"Right. Will do, Sarge!"

"Good. Good. Is there something you actually want, Medici?"

"Work that doesn't pay an insulting amount of credits and offer 'bonus' eyedrops I can buy in economy bottles if I actually wanted them. Actual, real, well-paying jobs."

The sergeant went back to staring at Truth for a while. "You got out of the hospital, what? Forty-eight hours ago? And you broke through to Level Two . . . well, sometime in the last week or so, right?"

"Right."

"You haven't even tried running two spells at the same time."

"Err. Not yet, Sarge."

"But you want me to get you more serious, dangerous work."

"Well . . . yes?"

"Medici."

"Yes, Sarge?"

"Realizing I may be dooming the world to an eon of fire by saying this—shut the fuck up. Go to the range. Start a Level Two training routine and learn how to fight your level. When you can be trusted with more than gopher work, I will let you know. Now scram, and let me enjoy my goddamn coffee in peace."

"Yes, Sarge."

Truth went to the range. He wanted to sulk, but the sergeant was right, so what was the point of sulking? He checked in with the range master, drew an Army standard-issue needler, and checked if the clip was fully loaded. It wasn't. What a joy it was, loading a couple of hundred needles into the magazine. The fact that it wasn't supposed to be loaded did not help his mood.

TRAINING MISSION: Clear the targets using appropriate combinations of spells from the following list: Shockwave, Pierce, Acidbolt, Graeme's Arrow, Plutonian Chains, Sharp, Enlarge, Shrink, Firebolt, Silence, Visla's Torrent . . .

There were about thirty in total. Truth was familiar with them by name at least, but some were too strong for a Level One aperture to endure. Burnout was no joke. Everyone got that drilled into their head. Just because you *theoretically* could cast a spell does not mean you should cast the spell.

Time to give them a try. A wall popped up, and a hostage was shoved around it, silently pleading for help. A fetish was pressed to the back of the dummy's head. *Load Pierce, load Shockwave.* Truth shot through the wall where he reckoned the center mass of the hostage-taker would be. The needle punched a neat hole through the wall, which then exploded in a spray of plaster dust. There was a thud, and the target dummy also fell over, in somewhat more than one piece.

It felt . . . not bad, exactly? But definitely odd. His body was put under subtly more strain as both his Level One and Level Two apertures refilled their cosmic energy. They did so by drawing in the harsh cosmic rays without the soothing benefits of elixirs or cultivation. It wasn't painful, really, just a little more pressure than he was used to. He knew his body would adapt to the level; everyone did. But it was . . . different. A nice little reminder that burnout can happen at any level, and the more spells you stack, the easier it is to exceed your body's tolerance.

Truth grunted and looked for the next target. Ah, a whole bunch of baddies, rushing him. *Load Enlarge, Load Firebolt.* Ah. Ahahaha. Okay. This could be fun. Two hours later, Truth was evicted from the range. He had hardly stopped grinning the whole time.

He was then assigned to catch up on all the talisman maintenance he had missed while he was away. The grinning stopped. It was a very boring couple of days.

"Hey, Medici!"

"Yes, Sarge?" *Chipper* was no longer a term that could be applied to Truth. He just felt an endless grinding as Harmony's SAT's got closer. He might have just enough to get Har into the job he wanted, but that would leave nothing for Sophia and Vig. And it wasn't all that long until college admissions. And he was used to watching his cultivation shoot up like a rocket, thanks to all the elixirs. Feeling it make inchworm progress after a full cultivation session . . . well, it didn't feel good.

"You wanted to get back to better-paying jobs, right?"

"You are an exceptionally handsome man, and your wife is very lucky to have you, Sarge."

Murthey made some choking noises. "I'm divorced, you little shit! And don't get your hopes up; it's another package-delivery gig. At least it's more than your base salary."

"Yes, Sarge," Truth said obediently. *Right. Baby steps.* Flattery was an art; that's what the books said.

"You are thinking something unpleasant, aren't you, Medici?"

"Never!"

"Uh-huh. Here is the order. Get."

Truth got, privately swearing to send the ex-wife a fruit basket.

The crate was shuddering and making a sort of high-pitched whining noise. Truth was sitting in the back of the wagon with the crate, a needler, and a heavy-duty firebolter fetish. The orders strongly suggested that, if a breakout could not be controlled immediately with the firebolter, the needler was to be employed first upon any nearby civilians and then upon Truth himself. As a humanitarian gesture. No further explanation of the contents of the crate was provided.

They were going up into the mountains, and the roads were not particularly well maintained. Every pothole or rock in the road made the crate jerk under the cargo net. The whine would momentarily stop . . . then start again. As though whatever was inside was testing the crate for sudden weaknesses. Over and over again. For six hours. And every time, Truth felt his breath stop and his hand tighten on the fetish.

Whatever was in the crate reeked. It stank like rotting meat and fermenting vegetables. You kept praying for your nose to go sent blind, but it seemed to subtly shift. You could never get used to it. It was the distilled essence of the word *filth*. Truth swore the scent was infiltrating him, seeping through the pores of his skin and staining his bone marrow. Making him a carrier of the filth.

For. Six. Hours.

The wagon finally pulled over and the driver jumped out. Orders were to sit and keep watching the crate until relieved, so Truth sat where he was.

"All right, we're— GOOD GOD! WHERE'S YOUR PPE?"

"My fucking what now?"

An alarm went off, screaming, shrieking the . . . whoever they were into action. People in slivery full-seal suits piled into the back of the wagon and hauled him out, yelling that they had to get him decontaminated. He would have fought them about it, but after six hours with the crate, decontamination sounded like a very good idea.

He was stripped, scrubbed with long-handled brooms soaked in high-foam potions, then rinsed under an herbal soak, then scrubbed again, and finally given a full-body submersion in a tub of blessed oil. Decent of them to scent the oil with cedar and myrrh, he thought. At the end of it all, he was given a new set of fatigues and a chewing-out from the silvery staff of the mountain . . . wherever they were.

"Why the HELL weren't you in your gear? What kind of moron—"

"It wasn't in the order."

"What?"

"Under *Gear* in the order sheet? It listed the firebolter and the needler but no PPE."

There was a pause. "Well, *obviously*, you should have known . . ."

Roughly one eternity later, Truth escaped back to Harban. He was so ready to spend quality time repairing talismans.

CHAPTER 31

COME FOR THE BEACHES

Truth was back in the armory, fixing up the talismans and fetishes. He was working with another guy, doing what he usually did, letting them chatter and then asking questions. It was one of the strategies he learned for talking to people, and amazingly, it worked. You ask someone about something they are interested in, and then they wouldn't shut up. They looked *so happy*. For him, every conversation was a grueling ordeal, littered with potential mines and pit traps. He was pretty sure he was saying the wrong thing all the time.

Talismans, he understood. For talisman maintenance, you need a good memory and a steady hand. That was it. You don't need to be a genius. You just needed to memorize a lot of stuff. Various holy names. Sigils. Runes. Geometric forms connecting the various incantations on the talisman.

It seemed impossibly complicated the first time you looked at, say, a communication altar or a spellcarriage. Slowly, over years of classes, you memorized what you needed to know. Then it all became straightforward. *This* sigil *had* to be at the Alkaid position on the talisman because if you put *that* sigil widdershins of Alkaid, setting the first sigil *anywhere* other than the Alkaid spot would brick the whole thing.

The logic became obvious. You didn't have to invent anything. You just had to make it work the way its creators intended. You just had to figure out how it should have been, then fix it until it looked that way again. Since talismans were usually small and complicated, you needed a steady hand to fix them. It was a technical, skilled job but, for Truth, a satisfying one. He took pride in his work.

Unless it was working on fetishes. The huge, oversized, ugly things. Goddamn monkey with a rock could fix a fetish. You could, in Truth's very public opinion, put a fetish in a cement mixer with a sack of gravel, and it would come out better than new.

Were fetishes just talismans scaled up? Yes. Would Truth wash the city in blood to defend the superiority of talismans? Also yes. A talisman-maintenance tech was a craftsman, a skilled trade. What kind of skill did you need to fix a goddamn one-hundred-twenty-two-centimeter stick with rocks sticking out of it?

Sergeant Murthey stuck his head in. "Truth, got some jobs come up. Captain wants you to take a look."

Truth looked at the sergeant suspiciously. "I just got back from the delivery gig." He was sure he still smelled like holy oil. The sergeant flipped him the bird.

"And a very trying day of sitting around it was. And it was a week ago. Come on. These actually pay worth a damn." Truth couldn't argue with that, so he didn't. There was a small pile of folders waiting on the sergeant's desk.

"Read 'em first, then tell me what you think."

Truth read through them. They were all very straightforward. All two or three-person jobs in the city of Chil Perdermo. "Where's Chil Perdermo?"

"Good first question. It's in Oaxace. Lovely country. White sand beaches, beautiful scenery; if you like good food, it's a paradise. While the women are high-maintenance, financially and emotionally, they are also staggeringly beautiful. Second only to the men in both maintenance costs and beauty, I'm told by those with such interests."

"Okay . . ." Truth said in a disbelieving tone. The sergeant waved him back to the files. He quickly spotted the same rat that the captain had.

"They are trying to cheese the op? Break it up into small, cheap jobs to hide the fact that it is one big, dangerous, expensive one?"

"Exactly. Note that none of the jobs will be activated until all of them have been accepted."

"Kind of what gave the game away for me, yeah. So, why hasn't the captain told them to get fucked?"

"Because, one, for jobs this small, it's my job and not hers. Second, if they pay properly, this could be a *very* profitable op for our branch. And third, it's a career-development thing for you. You got a lot of very high-up eyes on you, Truth. Time to start showing you are more than a thug with a spell."

"You . . . want me to negotiate this contract? I wouldn't know where to begin."

"I want you to ride along with me and learn the ropes. On occasion, I will kick you in the ankle under the table. You are to glare at the person speaking like they stole your dinner."

Truth could vividly remember people stealing his food. A week later, the whole platoon was on deployment.

"I was promised beautiful white-sand beaches, Sarge," Truth said as they set up on a blazing rooftop. "These are not beaches. These are mountains."

"You suddenly become a whiner, Corporal?"

"No, Sergeant! Never!" Truth swore halfheartedly.

He was doing the fiddly bit where they had to line up the formation array with both cardinal directions *and* the directions overseen by various stellar demons who would be providing the cosmic rays powering the whole thing. Or so the manual said. He didn't know enough about formation arrays to have a useful opinion on the subject.

"Good." Sergeant Murthey was sweating like a cold beer in the thirty-five-degree heat as he set up firing positions. "Because, yes, we are currently in the mountains, but if you look at the map, we are a two-hour drive from the beach. Where we will be doing serious R&R after the op. So, no bitching."

Truth checked the mission. It hadn't changed.

MISSION—Recover the delivery of magically significant materials from local forces who intercepted the shipment. Use of any means necessary has been permitted. Local authorities have declared the thieves as "Outlaws" and, therefore, no longer under their nation's legal protection. Damage to anyone or anything other than the outlaws is not permitted.
REWARD—Operational fee will go to Southeast Regional Branch, Jeon Division, Starbrite PMC. Personal Reward—15,000 credits, 600 performance points, four portions of Gold and Jade incense.

The incense was the real killer. It wasn't even listed in the Treasure Pavilion. Just not enough of it was publicly available. Not that it was staggeringly powerful. It was a Level Two supplement. There was a limit to how potent it could be. But as Level Two supplements went, it was a doozy and, apparently, a complete pain in the ass to make. He was prepared to treasure it. He tried to focus on that as they worked through the blazing afternoon sun.

Chil Perdermo was a pretty okay little city, Truth decided. Most buildings were less than four stories, with whitewashed walls and trees covered in orange flowers that popped up like roadside grass. He had wondered why everything looked so worn when they flew in but soon got his answer.

The day transitioned seamlessly from *Baking, blazing, scorching sun. Sun as the embodiment of wrath. Sun as the Great Father cleansing the world of corruption* directly to *Monsoons. Deluges. The life-giving waters descending from the Mother Goddess, drowning the lesser beings that came before humanity.* For a solid two hours.

Then, like a switch was thrown, it was straight back into the eye-searing sun. Truth looked at the crumbling paint and knew precisely how it felt. The humidity kicked in as all that rain evaporated, and Truth didn't have the energy to care about anyone else anymore.

Aside from the heat, the biggest challenge was the smell. There were food vendors everywhere, and the smells were *fantastic.* Bright citrus and roasting meat and little flatbreads toasted on griddles and just . . . everything. It smelled like all the delicious flavors cooking at once. And the PMC soldiers had to get by on food bars to not blow opsec. Truth was ready to kill by mission-start time.

The platoon deployed in pairs and singles, scattering to their posts on rooftops or in the streets. The target was a small warehouse, two stories tall, with a flat roof and no windows. Surveillance showed that the place was heavily fortified on the inside, with the outlaws constantly moving in and out. Victims of human trafficking were locked in cages in the warehouse space. More were circulating through the building, serving the outlaws as needed.

It was the victims that were the real problem. It required the platoon to breach and clear the building themselves rather than go in with gas or plague spirits. But that was fine. This is why they got paid the big money. The platoon silently reformed into squads, ready to make the assault.

Truth was up on the sheet-metal roof with his squad. Everyone was armored up, everyone wearing full-cover facemasks under their helmets. Everyone signaled readiness. The sergeant nodded sharply at one of them. The mercenary silently stepped forward and slapped down an inner tube filled with alchemical solvents. She carefully added a drop of a catalyst and stepped back sharply as the inner tube turned into a ring of harsh white flame. It melted a manhole-sized hole in the roof. Two squaddies tossed strobes and howlers in and waited for the show.

You could hear the sudden, shattering, piercing noise blocks away. The light punched out through the hole in the roof like a divine searchlight, as bright as the noise was loud. As soon as the flashes stopped, the squad dropped in. Truth led the way.

The warehouse was split into two floors—the bottom floor was storage, and the upper (a sort of half-attic) was the workspace. Truth landed in the middle of screaming people running left and right as he tried to spot the outlaws. Operating on the basis that anyone with a weapon was a villain and anyone with an iron collar around their neck was a slave, he started killing villains.

Load Silence. Load Shockwave. A man staggered toward him, waving a machete dripping acid. Truth put a needle in his throat. What remained of his face and neck was attached to the body with bare strands of spinal nerves. Truth didn't know if those were bomb collars or if the slaves could be compelled to attack and didn't care to find out.

He could feel the rest of the squad touching down behind him. Once they were all down, they started sweeping the floor, clearing targets as fast as they could line them up. Surprise, speed, and aggression were the keys to forcible entry. Surprise and aggression were no problem. Speed, however, was proving to be an issue.

The slaves weren't trying to be in the way, but they were. And every time it looked like one of them might get shot, the system blared a warning in his ear, telling him he was about to break his oath. Truth cursed and slapped people out of the way, screaming at them to "GET DOWN! DOWN!"

They weren't fast enough. Truth watched as the collars started popping off the slaves. Their eyes blazed with green fire. Unearthly choirs rose in terrible cacophonies, praising the defilement of the world. One turned toward Truth and vomited a column of inky, sticky, corrupting black bile toward him. He dodged, but some splashed on his armor. He could smell the fibers and advanced ceramics rotting, hear the sizzling of the armor as it disintegrated under the concentrated malice of the demon.

"GOETIA, GOETIA! CODE GOETIA!" Truth screamed. He could hear everyone else screaming it too. He desperately tried to keep dodging, unable to fire on the possessed until the order was given. And the scumbag outlaws started to shoot back, not caring if they hit the possessed slaves. Looking at the two, it was harder to say which was more twisted with hate and rage.

URGENT MISSION UPDATE: CODE GOETIA CONFIRMED. WEAPONS FREE. ALL SPELL COSTS WILL BE ASSUMED BY CODE BLUE SCALE LAMP. REPEAT—WEAPONS FREE. LEAVE NOTHING ALIVE.

Load Pierce. Load Moshe's Sword.
Time to clean house.

CHAPTER 32

STAY FOR THE PEOPLE

Harsh lights lit the warehouse interior. Whatever they were doing there, the outlaws wanted to make sure nothing got missed. Truth could see his targets—the half-naked slaves, necks rubbed red and raw by the iron collars they used to wear. Now with glowing green beams of light pouring from their eyes, their faces twisting into demonic forms as their bodies withered and twisted to better suit their new owners. They were slaves no more—or, at least, not slaves to an earthly master.

The outlaws screamed with fury as they saw the lost merchandise. And because Truth and his colleagues were killing them with immense enthusiasm. The outlaws were also half-naked, but Truth thought that was more recreational than practical. Thick bands of body paint, solid stripes of red, yellow, black, or bleach white covered the outlaws. They favored basalt-tipped fetishes decorated with bright feathers. Truth favored a reliable needler—and a vicious spell loadout.

Weapons free? Oh, yes. *Load Pierce. Load Moshe's Sword.*

WARNING! Spell loadout may damage your apertures if overused. Load anyway?

A jet of bile flew past Truth and started burning a hole through the wall behind him. "*YES! NOW NOW NOW!*"

Truth felt the spells jolt into place—Pierce sitting comfortably in the Level One slot, Moshe's Sword shoving forcefully into the Level Two slot. It wanted you to be at least Level Four before you used it. But he was a Starbrite Man. And with the System, he was a demigod.

<<Oof. This is a biggie, huh? Overkill for a glorified bug-stomp. You know that this might kill you, right? No, you don't. Fantastic. You know what? Not my problem.>>

Truth had the vague notion that this might actually kill him. Then an ax made of flames and spite came whipping at his guts, and he rapidly stopped caring. He dove out of the way and came up shooting.

The needle came flickering out of the talisman, summoned by his will from the magazine in its base. It passed through the intricate web of magic formed by the combination of Truth's will, the System's guidance, and the built-in arrays in the talisman. The needle became subtly sharper, more rigid, pushed forward by even more irresistible force. It crossed the air faster than blinking, faster than thought. The needle punched tiny holes through one, two, three bodies before vanishing through the wall behind them. Just a little, needle-sized hole. And then Moshe's Sword . . . cut.

Moshe's Sword does not gleam. Moshe's Sword casts no shadow. Moshe's Sword is in the sheath or drawing Blood. Truth remembered the description of the spell in the System store. There was no lie.

The holes exploded with blood, pinpricks widening to a hand's width following the needle's path. Blood fountained out, jetted out, far faster than mere blood pressure should allow. The impact on the demons was even more exaggerated. The possessed slaves went up in pillars of golden fire, their demonic voices wailing miserably, screaming insects in a bonfire, as their insubstantial forms dissolved.

The cosmic energy needed by such a potent spell was significant. The magic drew hard on the cosmic energy stored in Truth's apertures, which in turn drew hard on the cosmic rays around him to try and refill. Of course, there was no hope of keeping up with the expenditure, but they did try. And the rays, wild and rough, coming fast and without the support of elixirs or cultivation, burned. This was the raw stuff of the universe, coursing through your body and soul. Burnout was a very literal, frequently terminal consequence.

Having your head melted off by a column of freezing black acidic bile that rotted your soul and dragged its screaming dregs down into hell was also a consequence, though it was a consequence of not bringing enough spell to the fight. Truth didn't hesitate a moment before lining up his next shot and bagging four more.

The strain on his apertures increased by a large chunk. The greater the vacuum within, the quicker the cosmic rays came in, and the worse the burn. His teammates were firing too, Shockwave spells, pinwheel whips of acid, and exorcism shots of varying potency doing varying degrees of damage. They might not be one-shotting the enemy, but they were putting them down hard regardless.

Code Goetia. When you got all the demons, all at once. Of course, that was just being fanciful. Truth watched one slave's face unravel, lips pulling back as chitinous black mandibles stretched out from within the hollowed flesh. The demon crouched and leapt, clearing the space between it and Truth in a bare second. He saw its neck bulging, building the bolus of corrupting bile it would spray over him and his team. Not today.

Truth's needler punched through the neck, Moshe's Sword almost screaming with outrage at the foulness it had to cleanse. The corpse landed on its knees, its head resting tidily beside it, the corpse kneeling on the floor, white-gold flames shooting up from its bare shoulders as the insect-like head twisted and shrieked and became still.

Goetia—a billion screaming insects in the desert night. Landing on our world. Feasting. Spreading. Truth could hear one of his teammates howling next to him. One of the demons got him? But he had to keep his eyes front, or the bastards swarming at him would overrun everyone. He couldn't see the end of them, even though he knew only a few dozen people were in the building. He lined up his next shot. Weapons free, so no worries about firing into traffic. Just . . . got to mind the burn.

His next shot dropped three more, giving him a sudden gap in the press of bodies. "Charm out!" Truth screamed. He palmed the explosive charm off his carrier, armed it with a thought, and pitched it into the hole. One of the possessed slaves had a bright idea and spat some of its corrosive bile at the grenade. This did not work as planned for anyone. The grenade popped early, missing half of its intended targets. The explosive press of air drove soft ceramic beads through the air, tearing flesh into odd rags as they deformed on contact. Or deformed as they bounced off the PMC soldiers' armor. Of course, that same burst of air sprayed the corrosive bile everywhere as well.

It turned out the slaves didn't like it any better than humans did. The outlaws *really* didn't like it. Truth could see a droplet of it slowly burning through his goggles. He didn't like it one bit either. He wiped it off with the back of an armored gauntlet, tried to ignore the vomit stench, and got back to dropping targets.

It was harder to line up multi-kills now, as the grenade and his comrades had done a superb job winnowing the field. Truth felt the state of his apertures. Hurting. Burning. But not at the point of breaking. He saw a cluster and took his shot. The needle punched through three, not immediately fatal, but he reckoned the three would bleed out in less than a minute.

White, blinding pain. Migraine. Cold fire burning. He almost passed out. Truth fell to one knee, dropping his needler. An outlaw saw his chance and came in roaring, fetish wreathed in fire as he bowled Truth over and tried to stab through the armor.

Truth barely managed to get an arm up, trying to push the stone-tipped, spear-like fetish to one side. The outlaw tried to climb on top of him, mount him, and stab down. Truth wasn't having it—fighting to focus through the pain and blinding migraine. The outlaw tried to smash him with an elbow. Truth grabbed the arm, punched the bastard in the nose, and rolled him into an arm bar. He felt the bone crack and kept pulling. One of Truth's comrades ran up and put two needles through the outlaw's head. Hollowing it out like the outlaw's former slaves.

The battle was over. They won.

Truth collapsed on the ground and weakly yelled for a medic.

Three hours later, back at the hotel, Truth got the rest of the story. The ambush was a success—their intel going in was not. The outlaws didn't have just the warehouse; they also took over nearby buildings. Possessed slaves burst like an ant tide from every doorway and window, threatening to sweep through the small city and leave it lifeless.

The backup firing positions and rooftop arrays, strictly intended as last-ditch fallback options, went into action within a minute of Truth breaching the roof. The whole block the warehouse was in was a sea of fire. The materials they were supposed to retrieve should be fine—apparently some rare onyx, necessary for purposes Truth couldn't guess at.

The medic had Truth on a drip, the potion easing the burn and numbing the pain. Nothing would soothe the burns laid down by the medic nor by Sergeant Murthey. Apparently, burning out your apertures in the name of combat effectiveness was "the stupidest shit ever in the history of every world." Regardless of the fact that he killed more than any five other people. When Truth tried to defend himself, they just sneered and left. The quiet was good. The potion was good. He had started to drift off to sleep when one of his squad mates stuck his head in the door.

"Hey, Truth! Got a call for you."

"A what now?"

"A call—someone sent a message up to Starbrite Corporate for you, then back down again through the PMC. C'mon. Tape that potion to your shoulder and get your ass in gear. Comms altar is down by the lobby."

"Mr. Medici? Truth Medici?"

"Yes, who is this?" Truth was gripping the sides of the comm altar, a little platform about as wide as his waist. You had to keep pouring expensive ritual oil into the well in the middle of it to keep the call going. Nobody liked the blasted things, but nobody had invented anything better yet, so you just had to suck it up and deal.

"Mr. Medici, I'm Renshi Hollenzoutien, Vice-Principal of Rising Stars Vocational High School, where Sophia and Vigor Medici are enrolled. We have you listed on their files as their legal guardian?"

"Yes, that's correct. Are they okay? What's going on?" Truth's voice was urgent.

"You are a hard man to reach, Mr. Medici. That is not a great trait in a legal guardian. It makes me wonder how much supervision these kids get at home."

"Noted. What's the problem?" Truth's voice had a definite edge to it.

"That *is* the problem, Mr. Medici. Lack of supervision means a lack of discipline. Lack of discipline results in violent, antisocial behaviors. The kind of behaviors that get recorded on permanent records."

"Will you kindly spit out what it is? You have already got me on the next flight to Harban, I can tell you that." Truth didn't have the best grip on his temper at the moment, and it was slipping fast.

"That's what you should be doing. Mr. Medici, Sophia got into an altercation with some other students. Those students, excellent young scholars, I might add, report that she attacked them unprovoked and left them with serious injuries. These are some badly bruised kids, and we are still waiting on the doctor's note regarding sprains and a possible impact fracture."

"Wait, Sophia dropped some unspecified number of her classmates in a fight? With what, a lead pipe? She can't weigh more than forty-five kilos soaking wet."

"Apparently, what she lacks in muscle she makes up for in aggression. Also not really the point. When the victims' friends tried to intervene, Vigor demonstrated the aptness of his name and started smashing their feet and ankles with a textbook. We have four students on crutches today, Mr. Medici."

"All right. What does the school intend to do about my siblings being ganged up on and nearly lynched?"

There was a sputtering, outraged noise coming over the ether. Truth could see the oil level falling quickly as the conversation dragged on.

"They are suspended. Pending disciplinary review, likely expulsion, and possible criminal referral."

A squaddie stuck his head in the room with the altar. "Hey, Truth! Captain booked a party bus down to the beach. The whole thing is loaded with beer, liquor, and locals up for a party. And I DO mean A PARTY! Let's GOOO!"

Truth looked at the squaddie. They were already wearing a "funny" hat. He looked back at the altar and gave a heartfelt sigh.

CHAPTER 33

THE STATE OF THE SIBS

The fastest way back to Jeon, specifically Harban, and even more specifically the sibs, was complicated. There were no airfields near Chil Perdermo. There was, however, a brilliant international airport two hours down the road in Okepuela, Okepuela being the beach paradise that Sergeant Murthey had promised Truth and where the party bus was headed. However, Truth was not prepared to wait two hours to make it to the city. He certainly wasn't prepared to spend two hours watching other people get drunk and party while he was stressed. Not to mention the lingering migraine or his half-shot spell slots still burning from overuse.

No, that did not appeal. Nor did acquiring some manner of high-speed vehicle and driving to the city by himself, presumably at dangerous speeds. Truth had already enjoyed one chewing-out over poor life choices tonight and didn't feel up for a second. He stewed for a minute longer, then grinned. When you're sick, there is a very special place you should go.

"You want an ambulance?" the interpreter enunciated.

"I want an *air* ambulance. I know this hospital has one." Truth nodded.

"Sir . . . it is an air ambulance. An air *ambulance*. It is not a taxi, no matter how much you want to get to Okepuela. I can promise you. They won't run out of cold beer or hot girls. Or boys, or whatever you enjoy. But Chil Perdermo has only one air ambulance."

"Here is my medical report showing extensive damage to my spell apertures. I need emergency treatment in my home country and an air ambulance directly to Okepuela International." Truth thought he sounded very reasonable, but the looks he was getting suggested he was the only one who thought that.

"Sir, leaving aside the total unreasonableness of your demand, the cost alone—"

Truth had a moment of realization and fished around in his pocket for his lapel pin. At this point, opsec was no longer a factor. He pinned it to his BDU blouse and watched it ping the hospital's spells.

The administrator looked down at his tablet and showed it to the harried interpreter. Who turned to Truth and asked, "Do you have any luggage?"

The flight to Okepuela took twenty minutes. It helped when you could just fly in a straight line over the mountains. Truth was fidgety. Firstly, because he was in a great deal of pain. The potion took the edge off, but it only did so much. Secondly, because he was worried about the sibs. And thirdly—

I don't even know how many people I killed today. Certainly double digits. That's mass-murderer numbers. That's messed up. And, okay, they were outlaws and slavers and fucking body huskers, but still. I don't think you could really call that self-defense. I got paid to go and kill. I am a murderer for hire. That's messed up. And I'm . . . actually okay with it. That's even more messed up.

The international airport was another case of frustration. Apparently, and what enormous quantities of horseshit was this, "It is late at night," and, therefore, "There are no flights to Jeon." Then, adding supreme insult to existing injury, "We can put you on a flight to Meztean, where you would have a four-hour layover, then make two more connections before landing in Harban." Truth looked at a map. Meztean was five hours in the wrong direction. Fuck that. He went over to the cargo terminal.

"Uh, sir? You can't be here. I'm going to have to call security and escort you out if you don't get out now."

"I found the one guy who speaks Jeongo, and he's blind. Hey buddy, do me a favor, pull out your company ID, then check my lapel pin."

The cargo handler's eyes went wide. "No need for that, sir! How may I be of assistance?"

"This bird headed for Harban?"

"Yessir, already loaded and will be flying out in an hour."

"Great, you are taking one passenger," Truth growled.

"Sir, it's not that I don't want to, but the bird has no seats except for the pilot's seat. It would be a safety violation to even let you on board."

Truth looked hard at the guy. Then shifted his thinking. "You look like a man stuck at Level One, am I right?"

"Er, yessir."

"Kids?"

"Two, sir," the cargo handler answered slowly.

"Ah, that's great. You know, I have the damnedest feeling that you have a message hitting your tablet . . ."

THANK YOU FOR YOUR PURCHASE. Gentle Spring Potion will be delivered to F-6-L Logistics Specialist Renaldo Gestreq at his home address.

". . . right about now, informing you that you have a package you need to sign for at home."

"Is . . . that so, sir?"

"It is."

"Yessir." Gestreq was clearly an old hand—he spun on his heel and walked directly out the door, not even bothering to look at his tablet. Truth ran up the cargo ramp, made himself a thoroughly uncomfortable nest amongst the boxes and cargo pallets, and went to sleep.

It was an understandably pissed-off Truth that landed at Harban. He had kept going around and around about the slaughter. Intellectually, he knew those slaves were dead, functionally dead, before he got to the warehouse. Emotionally, however, he felt like he doomed those people to have their souls consumed by demons for as close to eternity as their souls could last. It was why he went with Moshe's Sword, despite the damage it did him. It killed demons on its level or below. Really killed, not just banished. Those demons weren't dragging anyone down to hell. And yet. Despite everything. He was more or less okay with what happened. Because Starbrite needed it to happen. And Starbrite had saved him and the sibs.

Who were waiting for him in their modest apartment, looking like they were confronting the executioner. He gave them a moderately filthy look, then sat on the sofa and groaned.

"I don't even know where to begin. First—I'm not angry, because I don't know the situation. The story I got from your school sounds fishy as hell, and I want to hear your side of things. Later, I may be angry. No promises." They nodded at that, looking relieved.

"Second, before we get into that, Vigor." His youngest brother looked worried again. "Good job. You see your sister getting jumped, fuck questions, get in there and drop those sons of bitches."

"You know it, bro!" Vigor almost shouted, looking overjoyed.

"Which leads me back to Soph. Who I suspect is the smartest person in at least three generations of our family. Why were you slapping around some 'promising young scholars' at your school?"

Sophia gave Truth an incredulous look. "'Promising young scholars,? Debby Voung and her gang are 'promising young scholars'? I have seen actual, literal carp with better academic credentials than those idiots."

Truth raised an eyebrow.

"Seriously. Doctor Cang Se Rin. Magic carp, obviously. He gave a public lecture. I found it in the library."

"Ah." Truth nodded. "Where you had it out with Debby."

"Not exactly. I'm in a lot of extracurricular clubs. They all go on your permanent record and can add points to your college application. Especially if you make a competition team, even more so if you win a competition."

"I'm on the MMA team and the debate club," Vigor volunteered. Truth nodded. His youngest bro was looking cut. And that dark-eyed look of his must have slayed with his young, impressionable classmates—the little bastard.

"And, relevant to this conversation, I'm the only competitor from our school to make it to the Prefecture Round in the Jeon National Beastcrafting Tournament," Sophia said.

Truth's eyebrows shot up. "Holy shit! I knew you were smart, but beastcrafting? As in custom spell beasts?"

"Eyup!" She grinned. "First in the school's seventy-year history, I might add."

"How did you do at the tournament?"

"I'll tell you in a week. It's still coming up." Sophia looked confident.

"So, what's with the vice-principal trying to make you look like a thug? He should be treating you like a holy child."

"Two reasons. Well, probably a lot more than two, actually. But two big ones. First—a lot of these kids' families have been going to this school for generations. The faculty and the administration are also mostly graduates. The kids tried to bully us when we transferred, and when that didn't work, they isolated us. Called us slumrats. Loads of whispers, all that shit. Teachers did nothing, of course. But we didn't let them get to us, and we've been kicking ass in our extracurriculars. And catching up academically."

"Awesome! I mean, not all awesome, but—" Truth felt a little punchy after the last forty-eight hours, and his words weren't lining up properly. Fortunately, Sophia knew what he was trying to say.

"I get you. But yeah, that's kind of the problem. I'm part of the school but not one of them. So, it's more than just awkward. It makes them look like assholes. Which they are."

"Yep." Truth nodded.

"The second reason is . . . a lot dumber."

Vigor nodded awkwardly. "It's not just Soph, by the way. Harmony and I are kind of in the same boat."

"Harmony? He should be cramming for his SAT and packing his shit for Basic. What's he got to do with any of this? And where is he, by the way?"

"Staying in a hotel for a few days before the test. He wants to be hyper-focused on the day," Vigor volunteered.

"Not really relevant," Sophia cut in. "Look. None of us are exactly gorgeous, but we are all in top physical shape, and we have that bad-boy, or in my case bad-girl, vibe. We get dates. Including some with people who other people might mistakenly believe belong to them. And, you know, none of us are virgins, so it can make certain other people look doubly bad."

"Wait. You stole their boyfriends? All of them?!"

"Two of them. And not at the same time," Sophia said defensively.

"I, uh, kind of got a third. And I don't think she told anyone, but I also fucked Vie Manrisonne, but it was a one-time deal. She might be overcompensating to hide it," Vigor added.

"Prager's yellow teeth! That is some prime high school drama right there." Truth paused for a moment as his brain caught up with his ears. "Wait. None of you are virgins?"

Sophia and Vigor exchanged puzzled looks. "Yeah? You punched your V card even earlier than we did." Sophia shrugged. "You were, what, thirteen? I thought it was kind of fitting—you started your body count the same year you started your, you know, body count."

Truth buried his face in his hands and groaned.

"So. Vice-Principal Hollenzoutien. It sounds like there has been a terrible misunderstanding." Truth wore his cleanest BDUs. He had even shaven. The vice-principal, in his shitty suit, looked unimpressed.

"I don't think so, Mr. Medici. I don't think the disciplinary committee will either."

"Oh, you will be withdrawing that complaint, cleaning my siblings' records, and adding a note to their file about what brilliant little angels they are." Truth smiled like a wolf.

"I can assure you, Mr. Medici, that your rank in Starbrite will earn you nothing here. So, I don't know where you are getting this confidence from." The VP kept a calm tone but narrowed his eyes. In a place as ruthlessly hierarchical as Starbrite, people reaching down from on high to interfere was simply an expected inconvenience, like the rain.

"Because I asked my boss what to do in this situation. And she is C-2-U." The VP controlled a flinch. Truth being a nineteen-year-old C-9-U made him a good-sized fish in their little pond. C-2-U was a whale in a fishbowl. "She said she was happy to add what moral persuasion she could, by the way. Thinks the whole situation stinks."

"That is . . . worth considering, to be sure, but this was an incident involving numerous students and physical injury. We cannot simply . . ."

Truth slid a little chit of purple stone across the table. It had cost him exactly fifteen thousand credits, and he didn't regret spending a single one of them. Not with the sibs' permanent records in danger. Carved into the amethyst was the Starbrite logo, plated in silver.

"She suggested I buy one of these. I always wondered how the rich pricks got away with things. Guess now I know."

He smiled, the pleasure of the moment overwhelming the burnout pain.

"You know, my oath would have kept me from hunting down their bullies. And their families. And the people who enabled this shit and *their* families. Completely against Starbrite policy. But now I know I can just spend some credits, and it's okay. Against the law, but I've never given a shit about that. On the other hand, I do love my credits. What do you think, Vice-Principal Hollenzoutien? Am I going to be putting in overtime?"

Below the logo, red dye filled disturbing etchings. The etchings were so twisted and gnarled that they made your eyes water if you looked at them for too long. The vice-principal didn't even bother to check its legitimacy.

"A Writ of Absolution and Indulgence." The VP's voice was dry as dust. "We are going up in the world. Goodbye, Mr. Medici. I suspect we will never have to speak again."

"Goodbye, Vice-Principal Hollenzoutien. We had better not."

CHAPTER 34

A NEED TO DECOMPRESS

Truth was in an odd mood as he walked into the PMC. He was still thinking over the scene in the vice-principal's office. The matter just . . . ended. There would be no negative comments in the siblings' permanent records. No problems with their college applications. The kids that were bullying them would be suppressed, and their parents given a quiet but firm word. The teachers too, for that matter. Not because of the moral rightness of his case nor the simple injustice of bullying. Not even because he was a person of some status. Just money. He had the credits to burn and did.

It was wild. You could buy a pass to break the rules from Starbrite. It only worked for Starbrite's rules, and it only worked for some rules, and obviously you had to have access to the System to buy it. Which meant that you were C grade and already stood above hundreds of thousands of people. He had no idea such passes even existed. Were there more powerful passes available the higher up in grade you became?

Of course there were. There just had to be. Fifteen thousand credits to "fix" a high school drama situation set a certain threshold. How much would, say, simple assault on an F-tier employee cost? It couldn't be too much, right? It might even be cheaper. The school's faculty and parents were C- and D-Tier, after all.

"Medici! Hope everything worked out with your siblings. You missed a *rager* of a party." Sergeant Murthey sounded painfully chipper.

"Hey, yeah, it's sorted."

"Great. Really, family is so important. My god, I think I may have kids in Okepuela nine months from now. I'll have to swing by again and check." Murthey smiled like an angel reminiscing. "Women, music, food. Beer, too, obviously, but the food. Oh. My. Sweet Baby Prager. The food. I have never in my life eaten such good fish. I didn't know it *could* be that good. This was a fish revelation, Corporal. How was the food on your flight?"

Truth had gotten a couple of candy bars from a vending machine in the cargo hanger. They were not the best.

"Oh, fine. You know how food is on those flights," Truth hedged.

"Honestly, I don't. I was still sleeping off the party until we entered Jeon airspace." He shook his head happily. "Oof. Anyhow. Time to get back to it."

And so he did.

That night, he corralled his siblings. Harmony was firmly in the study bubble, but Soph and Vig were hauled away from whatever sinister plans they might have had.

"It has not been a great week," he announced.

"I'm . . . sorry to hear that?" Vigor offered tentatively.

"Thank you, but you know the rules. We do not bitch. We find solutions. And I have found a solution."

"Oh?" Sophia sounded distracted as she was editing her notes.

"Yes. Come. Come to the healing place with me."

They flagged down a flying carpet and went downtown to a major shopping district. It was a garish explosion of light and noise. Every building, and there wasn't a building less than forty stories, was covered with enchanted signs. Dragons coiled around buildings, fighting with tigers leaping from rooftop to rooftop. Eagles soared across windows, advertising cheap beer. Shopping malls the size of small towns rose, shaped in curious, bulbous extrusions of blued glass and steel. Some had entire libraries in them. Two had amusement parks. One had a ski mountain with fresh powder falling from indoor clouds. Another had a waterpark staffed with carefully collared and glamoured mermaids.

Fifteen department stores, each with huge glass windows on the ground floor displaying luxuries most couldn't afford. One row of windows displayed vehicles for the absurdly wealthy. A custom chariot, low and sleek and built for speed, etched with alchemist's mercury and inlays of mother-of-pearl carved into arabesques, was propped up on a plinth. Next to it was a sedan built upon the same lines, but rather than youthful speed, it promised mature power. This was not a carriage to drive but to be driven in.

Attractive golems, carved from golden wood and ivory, decorated with subtle gems and shimmering glamors, dressed in the finest clothes the store had to offer, draped themselves over the chariots. Looking at the passers-by with smoky eyes, promising all this could be yours if only you had the money. *It isn't a dream*, they seemed to whisper. *It's a promise.*

Such a place was only for Citizens. Denizens would be arrested the moment they set foot in the district. Slumrats like the Medicis couldn't even get off the subway there. The gate would not open for them. Now they were Citizens. They could come there if they wished. None of them had ever been anywhere like it. They just stood on the corner where the carpet had dropped them and gawked.

"Have your driver honk if you are already a subscriber," Truth said, seemingly at random. Sophia and Vigor looked at him, and he shrugged. "A billboard for *The Patrician* magazine. I saw it by the airport and thought it was funny."

"Some joke," Vigor murmured. Sophia just nodded.

Truth shook himself into action. "All right, reason number one I wanted to come here should be"—he looked around—"this way."

It wasn't hard to see where he was leading them. A side street, well lit and lined with stalls and little plastic tables. A riot of different food smells came from the stalls.

Little booths, big lines. Some had more than a hundred people queueing up for a bowl of whatever they offered.

"Not going to lie to you guys—I've been struggling to get used to uptown food. So, I figure, tonight, we try some stuff. I see stuff that is deep-fried, shallow-fried, covered in goopy sauces, and even stuff that appears to be mostly eggs. We can, for sure, find things we like to eat here." The sibs snorted at that, but they threw themselves into things with a will.

Truth wound up eating some kind of sausage in a bun that had been studded with cheese, battered, deep-fried, coated with some sweet and tangy sauces, then put in a toasted bun. It was surreal but good. But surreal. It didn't make a lick of sense, it was a complete mess to eat, it would sit in his guts like a boulder . . . and it was really tasty.

Vigor got a bowl of cold noodles that appeared to be topped with ground chicken and pain. The sibs felt that they had a healthy tolerance for spice. They learned they were wrong. The cold noodles were swimming in chili oil. It was still delicious, but they agreed it was a dish for masochists.

Sophia, ever the smart one, homed in on lamb skewers served with a slightly sweet flatbread. The skewers were brushed with oil, then rolled in a mixture of crushed and whole cumin seeds. Once they were nicely charred and cooked through, the skewers were dusted with mild ground chili powder and more cumin. They were finally topped with a sprinkle of coarse salt. The mixture of cumin, chili, and lamb, the way the fat balanced the heat, the way the bread soaked the spilling oil and brought everything together—pure joy.

And at no point did any of them reach for cash. They just walked up, ordered, and walked away. The Starbrite lapel pin was all they needed.

Once satiated, Truth led them to their next objective.

"The Calm Heart Cafe?" Sophia asked. "Cute cat logo, I guess. But seriously, even if they have the best desserts, I'm stuffed."

"No. This is better than dessert," Truth said with certainty. They walked into the cafe and were greeted by a calm-looking young man wearing a fur-covered apron.

"Medici, party of three? This way, please." He led them into a bright, airy hallway with many rooms running off it.

"As this is your first time visiting us, please allow me to introduce you to our residents. We are proud to share our space with the widest variety of animals of any cafe in Harban. We have a variety of dog and cat breeds, ranging from energetic and playful to calm and dignified. We have hedgehogs, our spiky but cute friends, who are a delight to feed. In this room, there are owls. A staff member will be delighted to provide you with a gauntlet and show you how to carry one on your wrist. Last but never least, my favorite room of all—short-clawed otters. Playful, smart, and so cute, I just can't stand it."

Truth looked at his siblings. "Come. Let the healing begin." They laughed but went for it.

Sophia was playing with some sort of hound. She would roll a ball for it, and it would chase the ball. It had long, droopy ears that almost reached the floor, short legs, and skin so loose, it looked like a child wearing a fat man's clothes. She would roll the ball to the end of the room, and the hound bounded after it, tongue flapping, ears waving, and the skin flopping around like baggy trousers in a breeze. It would always overshoot the ball, bounce off the wall, catch it, and run back in doggy triumph, ready to go again.

She took the slobbery ball from the dog and sat down to pet it. Then she hugged the dog. The dog licked her face with a handkerchief-sized tongue. Soph started laughing, but the laughter turned to wracking sobs. The dog kept licking, this time going for the tears. Truth and Vigor came over to her, gently holding her.

"I was scared all the time. I didn't let it show, but I was always scared," Soph whispered. "Every time I went out, every time I was alone on the street, every time *they* were home, I was scared." They just nodded. They got it.

"I started flirting back, you know? When they called out to me. Like, somehow, it would prove I wasn't scared of them, and if I wasn't scared, they couldn't hurt me. Like I could win the game." She was getting a little garbled, but they still got it. "But you couldn't win. There was no way to win. I knew it. I knew it, but it was all I could do." They got that, too.

"And the only thing we could count on was you, and you kept going out. You would go out and disappear and come back with dinner. And you would have bruises and cuts, and you got quieter and quieter. And now you go out, disappear, and come back with an apartment and dinner and schools, and you are spending a week in the hospital, and we can't even call you! We can't even visit you when you are in the hospital and you are still going out. You are still going out because we need you."

Truth nodded. It was what he had always done. For him, it was just what an older brother should do. Soph buried her face in the scruff of the dog's neck. The dog settled down, leaning into her. Vigor and Truth sat with her. They petted their dogs. Neither knew what to say.

Eventually, Truth spoke. "I always needed you guys. I still need you. I don't know what I will do when you go to college and move out, both of you. It was how I survived. I survived because you needed me. Since you needed me, I had to do it. That's all. I could focus on that and try to ignore the . . . everything else." He felt he should say more but had run out of words. He had been getting quieter for a long time.

CHAPTER 35

FORT LEUCRE

Truth lay in bed that night, staring up at the ceiling. He felt like he had all these words inside of him, but they were so jumbled together that he couldn't possibly get them all out. He wanted to tell the sibs that—

He didn't remember how old he was, but if he closed his eyes, he could see it like he was still there. Mom had turned the water as hot as it would go, scalding hot, and she put little Harmony's hands under it and held them there and he screamed and Truth yelled and tried to get him out and Dad smacked him into the toilet so hard he couldn't see straight for two days.

He could close his eyes and he was right there. He hated it there. He hated it more than anything. So, it was all simple. What did he have to do to make sure that he and the sibs would never be *there* ever again?

He wanted to explain to them that he had a little rule, so ingrained that he didn't need to think about it consciously anymore. If he wasn't sure what to do, he asked himself, *What would Dad do in this situation?* And then he did the opposite.

Truth wanted to explain that there was a growing part of him that craved power for its own sake because power would keep him from being *there* again. A part of him that wanted to see people afraid. Scared of him. Because then they couldn't hurt him. But being someone who proved their strength by bullying others was what Dad would do. And he always did the opposite of what Dad would do.

But if he wasn't strong, wasn't capable, who could protect the sibs? Because that was the other lesson of that day. The strong did as they pleased, and the weak could only suffer. Until they got strong enough. Sleep was a long time coming.

The next day, Truth was called in by the captain.

"Everything work out with your brother and sister?"

"Yes, ma'am, your suggestion worked perfectly."

"Good. I have never found the need for such indulgences, but it's good to know they exist. Ready to earn some of those credits back?"

"Yes, ma'am, I surely am!" The incense was as good as advertised, and Truth loved watching his second aperture fill up. But poverty was a recent memory and one he was eager to put behind him. He wanted all the cash.

Sophia and Vig would *never* go back to the slums. He wouldn't allow it. He *needed* the cash. And if the captain had a job for him, he would gladly do it.

"I checked. You are drop-armor certified, correct?"

"Rated Expert with orbital drop armor, yes, ma'am."

There was a muttered noise that sounded suspiciously like "Of course you are."

"Well. Others are just 'qualified' on it, so you are going out to train with them. Maybe be one of the instructors; I'll check with the trainers. We got an op coming up, and guess who's going to be dropping in from on high?"

"Is it me, ma'am?"

"It is." She got serious. "Procedure says that you get a minimum of a month on noncombat duty after heavy combat. Unfortunately, I don't have many drop-armor certified mages of any level, so here we are."

She looked him dead in the eye. "I swear you will get every credit and every scrap of elixir I can get for you, Corporal. I'm not leaving a single credit on the table. But you have to go. This is a bad one, Medici. Real bad. They have a lot of our people in conditions where it might be better if they just died. It's going to be one hell of a big op. You need to be totally prepared."

Truth took a deep breath. Thought about how well the sibs were doing. How healthy they looked, and how awesome their futures were going to be with all the Friends and Family points he would earn. He thought about how comfortable the apartment was and how plentiful the food.

How nobody was making them scream.

"Starbrite has given me everything, ma'am. Everything. Some bastards touched our people? I will fall on them like the wrath of God."

The orbital lifter had ferried them one hundred kilometers straight up. They stood at the boundary of the planet and the terrible, consuming void between the stars. Truth could see a big slice of the world from up there, but not the whole of it. The sun shined around the world's edge like a golden rind, leaving most of the planet dark. Cities glowed in the night, some like little dots, others like spreading mold extending pellicles across some unattended leftovers. Each of the ten drop-capable combat magi loaded their mottled gray armor with a bolted-on payload. The helmets were sealed to the full-body armor. Pressure tested. Spell reinforcement tested. Camo tested. Payload tested. All green. They jumped.

The mission was both delicate and urgent. A terrorist band known as the Sons of the Dragon had been extracting larger and larger "taxes" from some of Starbrite's suppliers in a less-than-fully stable country. These suppliers delivered crucial metals and alchemical reagents to Starbrite, things that either couldn't be found in Jeon or were too polluting to feasibly mine. These "taxes" had been tolerated—just the cost of doing business.

That all changed when the Sons of the Dragon started kidnapping people. More importantly, they started kidnapping *Starbrite's* people. Every person on this island other than the hostages was a terrorist. A torturer. A murderer, a kidnapper, and a bandit. The pre-mission briefing was very clear. They all had to die. No quarter whatsoever was to be accepted. The captain had spoken quite calmly when she mentioned that more than twenty of the hostages were female. Their conditions didn't need to be detailed.

Just because you could swap in a load of spells didn't mean you knew how to use them in a fight. The Sons of the Dragon might have been a poorly trained, poorly disciplined collection of bandits armed with decommissioned military junk, but they did know how to fight. They enjoyed it. A civvie, even a Starbrite civvie, in Materials Acquisition or whatever, stood no chance. Truth was going to enjoy washing the island with blood. Some people didn't deserve mercy.

Truth activated the special stellar-ray-gathering formation in his pack. A ghostly explosion of superimposed triangles, circles, and a cube that seemed to exist in at least four dimensions sprang into being above him. Invisible and vast—the lines and sigils unpacked into a mystic dragnet that harvested vastly more energy from the upper atmosphere than he could possibly hold himself. Instead, the energy was held in the formation, using the unreasonable amounts of stored energy to help fuel the spells to contain that energy. They also went into expanding the net, only stopping when it was dozens of meters wide. The other nine magi did the same.

The suits were hitting terminal velocity, falling fast as their enchanted armor slipped through the air without a ripple of noise. The landing zone was marked with a little ten-pointed star on their visors, sitting on the edge of a continent. As they fell farther, the star seemed to drift left, slowly settling onto an island. The island grew, dominating a channel that ran between two cities.

It got closer, fast. Truth could see the whispers of anti-air defenses now. Tactical-curse barrages waiting to be triggered by too-big objects in the air. Bound spirits and devils, ready to cling to airborne targets and scream their location or shred apart their targets as needed. Then there were the things Truth *really* hated. Oversized, turret-mounted, box-fed, optically aimed, and manually operated anti-air needlers.

They shot needles the size of his index finger at *three fucking thousand rounds per minute*, and they mounted four together with one trigger. Twelve *goddamn thousand* finger-sized, cursed-to-all-absolute-fuckery needles, with enough power behind them to blow a hole the size of his ass through his ass. And that was before the prick manning the needlers started running spells on them.

The island was flying toward him now. The waters were mined. The air was sealed. The only way in was with the permission of the Sons of the Dragon or to be so small that you completely evaded their air-defense network. Even then, the Sons weren't worried. A shower of assholes trying to parachute in would be spotted fast and cut down faster. Starbrite PMC knew all that, of course. Which was why Truth and the rest of the squad were dropping in from the edge of space in heavily camouflaged, turbulence-erasing drop armor. The ten combat magi had fallen to treetop height when the first payload detonated.

One hundred kilometers of free fall for a heavily loaded, armored adult. The kinetic energy was terrifying. The enchanted suits of armor absorbed the energy just as they were designed to, letting the soldiers land light as thistledown. Those same spells made a simple but effective conversion of the stored energy. The horrific fireballs that bracketed Sons of the Dragon defensive points spoke to just how hideous that kinetic energy was when transmuted into thermal energy and amplified by spells.

People didn't just die. They evaporated. Turned into blast shadows on whitewashed walls. Those "fortunate" enough to be partially around a corner melted in part and merely burst into flames for the other. The air in their lungs flashed into brief fire, smothering them before they could scream. Sandbagged artillery and anti-air positions were turned to glass and twisted metal. Scavenging the least bit of that kinetic energy, the spelled backpacks carrying the primary munition detached from the drop magi and launched ten meters straight up. At this point, roughly three-quarters of a second after touchdown, the main payload detonated.

The gathering formations had each dragged a small sea of cosmic rays down from the upper atmosphere, where they were at their strongest and wildest. Those rays were channeled into the large packs each drop magus was carrying. The packs held carefully padded and insulated glass jars. Sitting inside each jar was a rough parody of a child, formed of mud, herbs, and dung. Its skin was carved with dozens of tiny scratches—spells, sigils of power, and if you stood back far enough and squinted, they formed something greater, too. Truth didn't know exactly what it was, but they creeped him out.

After the clay mannequins were placed in their jars, the alchemists had, with aching care, added various herbs and leaves to the jar and then filled it with some foul-smelling poison. They fed the poison through a tube, filling up from the bottom of the jar all the way to the top. "Important not to let it splash," they explained. "And you really want to minimize contact with oxygen. Until it's needed."

The sea of energy caused the poison to burst into lightning and a fog of sickly gases. Cosmic rays, lightning, and poison were all cleanly absorbed into the clay child. Who opened their eyes and screamed, with brilliant golden light streaming from every orifice.

The packs disintegrated under the shearing power of the cosmic rays. The energy streamed out, connecting the mud children into a ten-pointed star and forming a blazing decagram over the island's heart. All the dug-in anti-air systems. All the buried demons and reinforced army-surplus spell bowls buried under thresholds. All the charmed monsters guarding the waters around the island. All destroyed. Even the main wards for the central fortress itself shattered. Then the spell went to work on the people.

Each spell aperture was a miniature star and a well in the soul. A place to hold and refine the cosmic energy emitted by the vast dominions and principalities in the stars. They were a person's strength. Their identity. It would take something truly enormous and terrible to stir that energy up. Push it to the point where it was in revolt, requiring every scrap of your strength and focus to keep that raging power contained within you. To keep it from blowing your chest apart like a frog that had swallowed a grenade. Naturally, the more powerful and advanced you were, the more stellar energy you had inside yourself. The more energy, the stronger the resonance with the great working. Truth saw secondary blasts popping off before he had even drawn arms.

Truth activated the spell cannon built into his armor and drew his machete. He had promised the captain that he would strike like the wrath of God. And God had never been merciful.

CHAPTER 36

WHAT EXACTLY DID YOU THINK IT MEANT?

Truth activated the body-reinforcing enchantments on his armor, racing for the nearest oversized needler as the built-in cannon gathered energy. He hacked at a howling bandit still in agony from the blast. The bandit's head cleared the emplacement and was still rising when Truth went in.

There were three more terrorists in the sandbagged AA emplacement. They must have been scrubs—they had their needlers up and working. Two of them missed. From three meters away, they just fucking missed. Truth didn't have time to feel disgusted. The one who didn't miss was within arm's reach, the unenchanted needles bouncing off the spelled plates of the drop armor.

Truth slid left, letting his shifting weight drive the machete and take the offending arm off. Then shifted back right, and took the head. One of the surviving bandits panicked, spraying needles wildly and shooting his comrade in the back. Truth kicked the not-yet-corpse into his panicking "friend" and then brought his machete down twice more. Two more headless bodies fell. And now the cannon was charged.

Load Shockwave. Load Overpressure.

Shockwave Loaded. Mission-Critical Spell. No Charge. Overpressure Loaded. Mission-Critical Spell. No Charge.

The cannon blasted into the sandbags on Truth's right. The cannon smashed them away, but sandbags are designed to absorb and disperse impact energy. If it was just that, it would have been a waste. But Level Two wasn't just twice as good as Level One. Each spell slot held more cosmic energy, for one thing. And for another—

The sandbags launched out of the anti-air emplacement, flying toward the next strong point to the east. Shockwave made the bags disintegrate and started the sand flying at high speed. Overpressure turned that speed from *fast* to *You aren't insured for this much damage.* The sand eroded whatever it passed. Shredding trees, shredding buildings. Shredding people. Not fatally. The sand just scraped over armor. But the unarmored bandits lost more than just a layer of skin. The ones that still had eyes stared at their ruined flesh with disbelief. It had only been a few seconds since the first blast went off.

Swap loadout. *Load Hunter's Mark. Load Pierce.*

Hunter's Mark Loaded. Mission-Critical Spell. No Charge. Pierce Loaded. Mission-Critical Spell. No Charge.

<<Hee hee hee. You sadistic bastard. Do it! Break the little dollies! Look, that one's crying. Shoot him first!>>

Truth swung the enchanted machete hard, letting the armor add strength to the blow. It sheared through the bolts that were supposed to limit how far the quad-mounted heavy needler could swing. He shoved the machete back into its scabbard and grabbed the controls on the AA weapon. Truth muscled it around so he was facing the next gun over through the gap in the sandbags he'd just made. Hunter's Mark painted his targets. The spells settled in over the quad needler as the cannon recharged. Truth pulled the trigger.

Finger-long lengths of spelled metal ripped through the air at nine hundred meters per second. The sound was astounding, as supersonic needles tore through the sound barrier toward their targets. No need for damage-enhancing spells. Physics was more than enough to do the job. Nowhere to run, nowhere to hide. Not from the avenging angel called Truth.

He prioritized taking out the nearest functional quad-needler battery, slaughtering its operators, and putting a dozen rounds through the gun itself. Looked like overpenetration was an issue on the human targets, but the quantity of fire had a quality all of its own. He moved his sights around his section of the fort. If it moved, he shot it. If it was hiding behind a wall, he shot through the wall, redecorating the rooms inside in this season's hot new color—Organ Meat and Blood.

He had swept the needler toward a collection of huts when a boy came running out, waving a white rag on a stick. Yelling something in the local language. The door to the hut was open. He could see a bunch of local women, and a bunch of kids, lying inside, hands over their heads. No threat. He kept sweeping past.

<<Oh, no, you don't. Orders are orders. No quarter. They all have to die.>>

Truth's hands swung the needler back into line. The spells painted the targets huddled on the floor. Waving a flag and begging to surrender. His finger pulled the trigger, not missing once.

The rest of the assault force came swooping in on giant spell birds. They scattered talismans as they fell, chaff to draw off any surviving AA systems. Not that there were any. They beat their vast wings as they hovered over the island. The PMC soldiers fast-roped down from the spell birds' hollow bellies, sweeping needlers, firebolts, and other, more-specialized combat fetishes around them. It looked very impressive, even if it was pointless.

The only living humans on the island were the ten drop magi and the hostages. The hostages were still in their cages in the basement. Specialists would come in and get them out, making sure that their souls were still intact and that nothing nasty had turned them into flesh puppets. Then they would go to medical. There would be, presumably, much therapy needed. Maybe some bonus credits or something for enduring . . . whatever they had endured.

Truth morbidly wondered how long it would be until they were forced back into work. How they would feel in the office. Every time someone stood too close to them and suddenly they were being abducted. Panicking as elevators turned into cages. Screaming and hyperventilating when a male coworker touched their shoulder to let them know that management pizza was available in the break room.

Starbrite was a job for life. You couldn't just quit. Even though he really, really wanted to.

<<Aww. Somebody's a sad boy because he "murdered" a few . . . dozen . . . women and children. Womp womp. Let me pull up a memory for you that might clarify a few things, meatsack.>>

The memory came out of nowhere. He was standing on the field of the stadium, the sibs cheering madly from the stands. He was pumped up, so excited he could burst.

"I, Truth Medici, do swear that I will be true and loyal to the Starbrite Corporation and the System Astrologica; that I shall be diligent in my labor; and that I shall obey the orders of the President and all officers appointed over me, according to the Starbrite Corporation Employee Handbook and such local laws as may apply. So help me GOD!"

Truth shook his head. No idea what sparked that memory, but . . . It was all right there. He had sworn to be diligent in his labor. That meant doing the job, and doing the whole job, and doing it as well as he reasonably could. He had sworn to obey orders. Orders were to kill everyone. No exceptions. But what about the *local law* bit? Murdering women and children couldn't be legal even there, right?

<<Yaldabaoth give me strength, you can be dim sometimes. Hey, buddy. Real quick. Circle the word murder, *a very judgy word, BTW, and drag that over to the memory of your mission briefing. C'mon, little guy, you can do it!>>*

Another memory came unbidden. The mission briefing. The captain, in her calm voice, explaining that everyone on the island was a terrorist and a murderer. No exceptions. Maybe that was it. Maybe they had all been declared outlaws, so killing them was legal. And if it was legal, it definitionally wasn't murder.

<<And there we have it! You aren't dumb, but goddamn, did your schools fuck up your logical reasoning. Which, fine, works for me most of the time, but having to forcibly override your neuromuscular system is fucking exhausting. Even my vocabulary is fucked. It's like ninety percent swearing, slang, and bad grammar. Not giving me a lot to work with here, shit-for-brains. Not much at all. Read. More. Goddam. Books.>>

Then there was the Confessor before the oath was administered. He had flat-out warned Truth that the oath was magically enforced. That using the System could warp your personality. He was told, in advance, in detail, what he was getting into. No one to blame but himself.

<< That's the attitude! This is all your fault. All this guilt, all this pain. All the families you just destroyed or harmed for generations. Better soldier on through, though. Your "sibs" are counting on you.>>

It was all his fault. He felt like shit, and he deserved to feel like shit. Truth had chosen to join Starbrite. Chose to join security. Hell, he was originally going to be in talisman maintenance. You don't kill dozens of people in talisman maintenance. He had worked his ass off, done his best his whole damn life, to join Starbrite. For a safer, saner life for him and the sibs.

Truth tried to focus on the last message he had gotten from Harmony. He passed his SAT. Going to specialize in laboratory services. Not a scientist but a technician. Management track. Normally, that would mean a college degree, but with the Friends and Family points, he could get the schooling while on the job. It was a tough specialization but very safe. Very steady.

Sophia was hitting the books like she was mad at them. Iced out socially, Sophia decided she was more interested in getting into college than in stealing boyfriends. She became the queen of the library. Same thing with Vigor, but he was getting heavily into martial arts, too. Not yet fifteen, and he was a starter on the varsity squad.

It was messed up, but Truth would probably have a lower body count if he had become a gangster. He hugged his shoulders. His siblings were still counting on him. Time to step up and be a Starbrite man. He looked around the smoking ruins of an island that wasn't anything nice to begin with and couldn't wait to get home.

The spellbirds had flown him to a little airfield in the middle of nowhere. His arms and armor were received into inventory by a Starbrite armorer. He was handed a small duffel bag with his personal possessions as well as a suit carrier. He was told to wear the civvies in the duffel until he landed in Harban. He was to reach Harban via commercial aircraft, not in cargo or a military bird. At which point he was to wear the suit. No more explanations were offered than that.

Everything fit Truth perfectly. The cut of the trousers was flattering yet comfortable. The shoes were sleek athleticwear and paired well with the casual trousers and fitted short-sleeved button-down shirt. Really made him look shredded, that shirt. Really hugged the biceps and made the chest pop. He instantly wanted to buy five more just like it. He was previously unaware that robin's-egg blue was *his* color for shirts, but clearly, it was. He was even more skeptical about small coral-colored bucket hats, but damned if that didn't work too.

Then he remembered he worked for Starbrite, which employed literally thousands of people in the fashion industry, and stopped eye-banging himself in the bathroom mirror. He walked past the ticket counter and security without breaking stride—his lapel pin was his ticket and his passport.

Truth hadn't flown commercial before. In the Army, they went everywhere by truck or bus. With Starbrite, he went everywhere by truck or bus. Or military aircraft, which lacked luxuries like real seats. Or the hold of cargo birds, which didn't even have fake seats. Now he squeezed into a little birdie with six other passengers, who were babbling on about how it sucked that they had such a low luggage-weight limit and generally bitching about the wedding they just attended. Truth looked out the window at the stubby green mountains and total lack of anything that suggested a "fun destination wedding." Then shrugged and closed his eyes.

It had been a spectacularly shitty day, but there was one golden, precious thing to look forward to. A visit to that most forbidden, mysterious land. Truth was going to fly home first class.

CHAPTER 37

THE GOOD LIFE

They landed at Lowi International, which served the world with spellbirds that could hold three hundred people in varying degrees of comfort. He walked over to the ticket counter, directly ignoring the snaking, *pythoning* queue. He rapped his knuckles on the counter in front of the harried woman, who was desperately sorting through her screen. "I need a flight to Harban. Right now, or as soon as possible. Give me the best available seat."

She looked up, her endless training restraining her utterly justified snarl. She was about to direct him to the back of the line when she spotted the pin. Her tablet made a quiet *ding*. She smiled very politely. "No problem, sir. The next flight is in four hours. Please enjoy the complimentary first-class lounge in Terminal E while you wait."

**First-Class Private Cabin Ticket to Harban—301 Credits Deducted.
699 Credits remaining in travel budget.**

"Out of curiosity, what's that cost in wen?"

"Wen? I'd have to check the rates . . . Ah, in wen, 9,750 plus taxes and fees."

I once killed someone for eleven wen and my shoes. I don't think I could even buy a bottle of water here for eleven wen. He smiled, thanked her, and made his way to the lounge. On the way, he snagged a book from a shop in the terminal. It still felt weird and amazing. He could just walk into the store, grab a book, and walk out. The spells in the store picked up his badge, his credit account was fractionally deducted, and now he had a book. No need to ever think about money, let alone own any.

The first-class lounge was something. What, Truth couldn't say. But something. A load of people who clearly considered themselves *very important people* read and worked in leather club chairs. There was a bar, which almost no one was using, and a cafe, which a lot of people were using but only to drink coffee. It felt dislocated. A sort of nowhere space within a nowhere space, trapping the extremely wealthy and those traveling on expense accounts.

He had some eggs for breakfast. They were fine. Not what he was expecting in a first-class lounge, really. Just decently cooked eggs on decent toast, some pathetically underpowered hot sauce, and phenomenally good coffee.

Is this . . . the good life? Truth wondered. *Is this what we kill for? It can't be, surely. When we pulled out Soo Yin from Kofi, we went to the private terminal at the airport. Maybe that's where the real luxury is.* Truth shook his head and went for a massage.

"Oh, my god! *This* is the good life!" Truth groaned. "Is that smell mint?"

"A blend of imperial purple rosemary and vitriated eucalyptus essential oils are added to one hundred percent pure Grao Nut Oil. The ratio is a secret!" his tiny but shockingly strong masseuse chirped. Then she dug her elbow in between his spine and shoulder blade, sending electric jolts through his back, followed by incredible release.

"Oh. My. God. Are you using spells for this?"

"Hee hee hee. Yep! But the spell is also a secret!"

"This is so good," Truth moaned.

"Your physique is ridiculously aesthetic; you know that, right? Are you a body model?"

"HAH! No, I work in private security for a multinational." She stopped massaging for a moment.

"And you can afford the first-class lounge? And my fee? Seriously?"

"I'm on expenses; I'm on expenses and Starbrite."

"Oh, my God. That's ridiculous. Starbrite security flies first class. You people, I swear. Your girlfriend must be unbearable," she gushed.

"Don't have one, actually."

"Oh, I'm so sorry! Boyfriend must be unbearable?"

Truth snorted.

"Really? Single?" She hit a particularly sizable knot with a one-two combo from the top and side. It was extremely effective. Truth groaned and nodded.

"Damn. Well. Color me surprised."

"Apparently, people care about things like 'looks' and 'personality,' and even 'being around reliably.' I have none of those things. Working on it, though."

"Eh? You seem to have a decent personality. And you aren't a model, but, like, a decent six?"

Truth looked up sharply. "Six?"

"Decent six, yeah." She nodded.

Truth did a fist-pump. Cultivation, the one thing in his life that had never failed him, was coming through again. And hell, a couple more months and he would get promoted. Even a small step up the pyramid came with significant benefits. He wondered what the System had in store for him next.

The flight back was surreal. A private elevator descended from the first-class lounge to the landing field, where a flying carpet took him and his tiny luggage directly to the giant spell bird that would be carrying him back to Harban. And it was *giant.* Roughly the shape of a goose, made of tens of thousands of talisman papers lacquered into feathers and "flesh," stuffed with seats and storage and other useful amenities of upper-class travel. It was painted a beautiful off-white, with the long feathers at the tips of its wings painted a vivid red.

Truth walked into the bird and turned left. The private cabins were at the very front, where it was the quietest and the servants the most plentiful. The cabins were decorated with fabric the color of sand and gold. His cabin was marked with a tree made of hundreds of glowing triangles, swaying in a breeze only it could feel. On closer inspection, each little triangle held a tiny sprite buzzing about inside of it.

The cabin itself had a single chair inside and little else. The helpful servant informed him when he was ready to sleep, he should summon the staff for the turn-down service. The chair lay flat into a bed. The servant then pressed a glass of sparkling wine into his hands. Truth pressed it back and asked for juice. Despite the best efforts of the Army and the PMC, he had never learned to drink. Every time he thought he'd try, he'd see the old man.

The seat was incredible. It felt like he was floating on a cloud. A scryball was carefully concealed in a little table next to the chair. Truth was provided with offensively silky pajamas and moisturizer. He was so discombobulated by everything that he used both, rang a servant for a foot massage, drank his juice, and watched the scry.

The scry was always on in the barracks but he never really *watched* it. He always had the nagging sense that he should read more. Watching it was almost hallucinatory. The ads blew him away. The clothes were . . . incredible. He didn't really want them, but it was the first time he really paid attention to regular, casual clothes. He realized he dressed like a bum off duty. His siblings were probably embarrassed to be seen with him.

Then there was the food. PRAGER BE PRAISED, THE FOOD! Noodles dripping with oil and sauce. Sandwiches of gargantuan scale, stuffed with meat. Even rare monster meat could be had.

Truth summoned the in-flight menu. He ordered the Crazni Boar Belly Royale. The tender, fatty cubes of the two-ton domesticated Crazni boar, poached, almost candied, in a mix of red wine, fine herbs, and West Moon stevia. The pork was imported at eye-watering expense from Crazni by the Shattervoid Clan, the stevia (so much more refined than plebeian corn sugar) had to be grown in an orbital farm at just the right gravity. It was served on a bed of gemlike turquoise, peridot, and ruby grains of rice, mixed with vegetables grown by blind nuns in hidden mountain valleys (according to the menu).

It tasted like a riot in the orchestra pit at the symphony but in a good way. Truth had previously held a low opinion of fancy food. Apparently, he had not eaten *fancy enough*. He could taste the money.

This would be his new hobby, Truth decided. This is how he would conquer his poverty tastebuds. He would become a foodie. Cooking was a necessary requirement for life, but thrill-eating was a *hobby*. A hobby meant that you were halfway to a *personality*, which, as a six, meant that he was a quarter of a way to a date with an actual, real-life . . . person. At this point, he wasn't prepared to be picky.

Some kind of song contest came on. The singers and wannabe idols were gorgeous, of course. Reclining in fiendish luxury in silk pajamas that felt like liquid smoke, he briefly wondered if he could snag one for himself. Truth snorted and had a drink of juice (street value, 30 wen per 23 cl.) He was a C-9-U. You probably needed to be at least C-2-U to snag a starlet.

He watched most of them wipe out, crying prettily . . . but, to his eye, sincerely. It looked like this contest really counted for them. The hidden desperation got a little more visible—winning a talent show wasn't a "dream" for these women; it was their chance at a good life. And if they didn't make it . . . well, he didn't know what would happen. Ordinary jobs, Truth hoped. They would make a killing in sales. He shook his head. Then perked up. He was now a six, minus whatever damage his personality did to his rating. Promising, promising!

<<I would be more upset about you watching scry, but the way it's firing up your greed and desire actually works for me. You hardly see them as human, do you? Not even notches on the bedpost, or even pets. Medals. You want to pin their weeping faces to your chest to show what a winner you are. That says a lot. It says . . . Oh, Yaldabaoth twist your nuts, I know there are better words for this! READ MORE BOOKS, you gibbering moron! Scumbag! Trash! Loser! You IDIOT! You are going to die poor and alone unless you KILL YOUR WAY TO POWER.>>

He changed channels. It was a show about fancy houses. He directly turned it off. Fantasy was one thing, but land in Harban was not for sale at any price. Truth would live and die in rented apartments, and that suited him just fine. His mood dived. He wasn't the sort to own property. He was a thug with a spell, killing for the biggest gang in town. All he could do was be the best killer he could be and get stronger. Not like he had the brains for anything else.

Truth got the turndown service and slept, then dove into a questionable mystery novel for the rest of the flight. Before landing, he changed into the provided suit. The shoes, with their hard leather soles, felt weird. Not . . . bad, exactly, but very odd. The suit was some lightweight wool, gray, wonderfully soft to the touch, and cut to flatter his already-outstanding figure. The shirt was crisp white, with faint runic embroidery. It didn't do anything beyond advertising that the wearer was a *serious* mage. Or at least a seriously wealthy one.

"ALL HAIL THE CONQUERING HERO!" shouted Sergeant Murthey, with immense sarcasm. The rest of the department cheered with equal irony. He then settled down a little. "In all seriousness, that was an incredible op. Have you seen the news coverage? Your face is covered, of course, but you looked like death incarnate out there." There was general nodding, pats on the back, and people got back to work.

Truth just blinked at him. "The . . . what now?"

"The news coverage, man! Everybody's suits, the surveillance spirits, the spellbirds, the fucking orbital lifter, they were all recording all the time," Murthey said.

"Yeah, obviously, but how the hell did the news get it? Wait, is this why the company sent me a wardrobe and this . . . suit?"

"Ding ding ding!" Murthey grinned. "They didn't know if the media would scoop you up when you landed. Nobody knows your name or face, obviously, but *just* in case—There was a whole decoy operation waiting at the private terminal. Same with all the other drop magi from other branches. Why did you fly commercial, incidentally?"

"Um. I was told to?"

"Ah. Miscommunication. Non-Starbrite-badged private jet operated by a subsidiary." The sergeant shook his head. "You know they make me fly coach, right?"

Truth nodded slowly at that. "Yeah, everything did feel . . . kind of a lot."

"I bet. Go talk to the captain. You got some good news coming."

"All right. Hey, Sarge, you didn't say how the media learned about this?"

"It was a goddamn fortress assault thirty kilometers offshore, next to a major shipping lane. Everyone and their dog knew about it when the spells went off. Marketing pissed themselves with joy." Murthey gave Truth an odd look. "Go see the captain. Your life is about to get very strange."

CHAPTER 38

PROMOTION AND A BRAND-NEW YOU!

Captain Clavegaugh looked her usual collected self. She nodded at Truth (who had to control the instinct to salute) and then nodded him to his seat. "You have a lot of questions. Sit, listen, then ask." Truth nodded back. Clavegaugh continued.

"This first part I'm saying with my military hat on. I reviewed the recordings from your drop armor. Your skill put down so many enemy combatants so quickly, there was no chance of any organized resistance. We took down *an island fortress* with zero dead. None. None of the hostages were lost, either. And, Medici, I know you had to make some hard choices. But you did the right thing. Every single person on that island was complicit. They either helped the terrorists, turned their eyes from the victims, or benefitted from the terrorists' crimes. You did *nothing* to be ashamed of."

He nodded awkwardly. One more Friend and Family point. More elixirs. Some cash on top of that, just to save up for the next point. The mission reward . . . had kind of lost its joy.

"This is where I put down my military hat"—she mimed taking off a hat—"and put on my district-manager hat. You are exploitable beyond what you are militarily capable of by yourself. We can use you as a selling point."

She waved at his outfit. "You scrub up well but don't look too pretty. You are low enough level that you are routinely affordable, which makes you a steal in credit/effectiveness ratio terms. You have proven that you understand operational discretion. Lastly, you have a flashy-as-hell combat record. Killing a giant bird-headed warlock without spells? Surviving a major firefight in a hotel, saving the beautiful actress, an orbital drop followed by you slaughtering half an island without getting touched once? All *completely* marketable. I'm swarmed by invitations to bid. We just have one major problem."

"Yes, ma'am?"

"Corporal ain't a sexy rank. Makes you sound kind of half-assed. *Sergeant*, however, sounds badass. So, you get an off-cycle promotion. Congratulations, *Sergeant*

Medici." Captain Clavegaugh stood to shake his hand with an honest, if odd, smile. "Told you that you were on a promotion rocket. Welcome to C-8-U. PMC privilege again; you skip straight over C-8-L. Your pay raise is around ten grand, but with your absurd bonuses, it's more like twelve and a bit. Congratulations on joining the six-figure club. Incidentally, do you know what a sergeant in the Army earns?"

Truth's head was spinning. "No, ma'am."

"With twelve years' experience in grade, including all benefits and allowances, about sixty-six thousand wen. But since you are paid in credits and not wen . . ."

"I can buy Army sergeants by the six-pack. Sorry, I knew I was up for promotion but . . . I am getting promoted early because *Sergeant* sounds better on the flyers than *Corporal*?

"Yep. Ain't capitalism grand?" Clavegaugh looked amused. "But let's put that aside briefly. This rank comes with a serious system upgrade. More options in the various shops, but, more importantly—"

<<*Shutupshutupshutup! Shut your whore mouth! All Chuckles here needs to do is astral cultivation and read books. THAT'S IT!*>>

"Are you familiar with body cultivation?"

<<*Oh, fuck you.*>>

"Body cultivation? Doesn't the body improve as you cultivate and gain levels? Why would there be a separate cultivation system for the body?" Truth asked. He had never heard of such a thing, but he had lost all faith in his schooling.

"It does improve, to a point. I'm guessing they didn't cover this in school?" the captain asked.

"Nope."

She muttered something that sounded suspiciously like "Fucking slums!" and pressed on. "Okay, stepping back a long, *long* way, all magic is powered by stellar rays, right?"

"Right." Truth nodded. He knew that much.

"And those stellar rays resonate with a lot of things in a lot of ways, including human bodies. But everything and everyone is a little bit of a different shape, inside and outside, so it hits everything a little differently. Sometimes, the little differences are too tiny to make a noticeable difference. Sometimes, the difference is very big. Starting to see where I am going with this?"

"Not . . . really? Improving the body to make it interact better with cosmic rays?"

"Simply put, yes. When you cultivate, the cosmic rays flow into your body and are transformed into cosmic energy, which is then dumped into your spell apertures, expanding them. What overflows from that goes to opening the next aperture. Since you are filling more 'holes' with cosmic energy, and those 'holes' get bigger, the more you cultivate, it gets progressively harder to cultivate enough energy to fill the holes and open new holes."

"Which is why cultivation aids cost a fortune. Speed up the absorption of cosmic rays for a period, improve the body's tolerance for the energy, all that." Truth nodded along.

"Exactly. It's also why the elixirs people use before breaking through to Level One are so crucial. A good elixir directly affects the interaction of the cosmic rays and the human body, ensuring that the body's internal energy systems can resonate harmoniously with the stars. It also ensures that the naturally occurring flow pattern of cosmic energy through your body will be comfortable and effective. No two people have identical patterns, but generally, the better an elixir at breakthrough, the better the mage long term."

"Got it. So . . . is my flow pattern good or bad? I have no idea."

"Extremely good. I have no idea where you found that elixir, but your testing shows that your body is very well attuned to cosmic rays for your level. This leads me back to body cultivation. Basically, while your naturally occurring system improves your ability to cultivate and your progression as a magus, body cultivation improves the performance of your body." The captain grinned and handed Truth a thumb-thick steel rod. "Bend that."

Truth shrugged and tried. He thought he detected the tiniest degree of flexing, but that might have been wishful thinking. He handed it back to the captain. She grinned and snapped it like a twig. Truth just stared at the steel rod—two rods now.

"Now, I'm Level Four, almost Level Five, so I would probably be able to . . . maybe bend the rod a bit, if I really gave it my all, without body cultivation. That's with constant military training and conditioning. And it's only a maybe. But with body cultivation? I can run faster than normal people at my level and for longer. I can jump higher, hold my breath longer, see farther, have a better sense of my body and the ability to control it effectively . . . I am literally better in every meaningful way. Hell, I could improve my looks if I really wanted to." The captain sounded smug, which was fair enough, really.

"Your looks?" Truth asked, suddenly more interested.

"Every single thing about your body can be refined and improved, in ways you cannot even imagine. Literally cannot, because the spells aren't available on this planet, and there are tens of thousands of different body-cultivation spells across the universe."

"Amazing!" Truth was completely invested now.

"And there is a catch." The captain grinned. Truth deflated. He knew it was too good to be true.

"The overwhelming majority of people *on this planet* pick a single spell at Level One that becomes their job and identity, and that's it. Nobody is going to waste a spell slot on a spell that only improves your body. And body cultivation *is* a spell. So, nobody bothers." The captain grinned nastily. "Except people with a certain degree of seniority in Starbrite, and people with certain jobs . . . in Starbrite . . . that require exceptional physiques."

"The improvements stick around even when you swap out the spell?"

"Why, yes, they do. So much so that you will find a new tab in your system interface. Focus on your Body menu."

Truth did and felt the System shift slightly inside of him.

BODY DEVELOPMENT
Stellar-Ray Attunement—63%
Strength—2.3
Speed—2.5
Perception—2.4
Proprioception—4
Reflexes—5
DETAILED BREAKDOWN NOT AVAILABLE UNTIL REFINEMENT SPELL IS SELECTED.

<<Wait, what? How is your nervous system so developed? This is . . . All right, all right, I am going to be the bigger spirit here and step back from shitting on your body-development dreams. This is . . . not right. Thanks for the upgrade, trash. Seems like I need to keep an even closer eye on you.>>

"Whoa! Umm . . . numbers. What do the numbers mean? I'm guessing bigger is better?"

The captain nodded. "Yep. One is a normal baseline human at Level One. Comparing it with Level Zero would be meaningless. It's apparently calculated by averaging all the F-Tier Starbrite Employees based on your age, gender, and a couple of other factors. You shouldn't have any stats less than two, as a Level Two. Three at Level Three and so on."

Truth winced. "So, Two and a fraction means I'm kinda basic in terms of my body development without body cultivation, huh?"

"Totally normal. Actually, the fact that you have anything a bit over two is really good. Starting with a 2.1 or 2.2 can give you that extra little edge that will carry you past your competition. Now, you won't have access to the really detailed stuff like elemental alignments, muscle-twitch controls, bone lengthening, and all that, until you pick a body-cultivation spell and get to work on it. Pick carefully, as not all spells will produce the same results and you *are* making permanent changes to your body. If you start with a spell that gives you a lightning-aligned body and then swap to one that improves nerve reactivity, well, you are going to have a very exciting time. Briefly."

"Okay . . . are there any guides on what spells to pick?"

"Yep. Ask the System; it can produce a custom answer for you. Costs a credit or something." The captain shrugged.

"I think I can just about afford that." Truth smiled and she nodded.

"Now, you are probably used to your spells being free or very cheap, right?"

"Sure."

"Because you only ever use mission-critical spells," the captain said with dark suspicion.

"Sure. I mean, what else are you going to use them for?"

"Cleaning your house? Cooking? Full-body massage whenever you want it?" The captain looked sardonic.

"Massage?" Truth looked interested.

"The Thousand Hands of Ebin-Erhun. Costs twenty credits an hour. You . . . never really dug into the System much, did you."

"It turns me into a demigod on the battlefield, ma'am. It lets me buy all the cultivation resources I need for my family. Not sure what else there is to know, really." Truth shrugged. The captain looked outraged.

"There are *one or two* additional things that it can do. For example, classes."

"Oh, right. I think I do have some personal-development missions still active. I do them when I'm bored sometimes."

She looked at him pityingly. "Go to the Treasure Pavilion. Search for *Treasures of Wisdom.*'"

A blizzard of listings appeared—*Joinery for beginners. Which Glue Is for You? An advanced bookbinding guide. Reshi, Soshi, Ponshi and their use in tying fishing flies. Intermediate Sigil Crafting for Medical Devices. Ars Goetia For Degenerates. Essential Flushing Toilet Geometry, and Six Hygienic Alternatives.*

It went on and on, filling his vision. He quickly closed the search. "You can buy lessons on . . . anything?"

"Anything available under your tier and level that is permitted by your job category. Which is a lot more than you think. Starbrite has no need or desire to gatekeep glassblowing, even if you aren't going to be doing it professionally. On the other hand, they might keep an office drone away from the more-robust demon-summoning spells. And they keep everyone except specialists away from spatial spells."

"Huh. Cool."

"All right, so here's the deal. You are now, officially, our branch's golden boy. We use you to lure in clients, offering an incredible value proposition in hiring a Level Two soldier with Level Three . . . ish . . . capabilities, at a fraction of the price an actual Level Three would cost. Your full-time job, unless on assignment, is personal development with a focus on high-end bodyguard and close protection work. That means getting used to wearing nice clothes . . . and fighting in them. It means learning how a lot of shit works so you can see when your client is doing something dumb or suicidal."

She took a breath. "You are going to run through the protection-detail courses because while you are hell on wheels in a fight, you haven't been trained as well as you could be to keep civilians alive. And to sell your image of the omnicompetent wonder child, you are going to invest a big chunk of your new salary on body cultivation. In exchange for the extra work, you are going to be taking home a very big chunk of credits with each job. Plus, *smart* bodyguards can pick up all kinds of little extras on the job."

"Yes, ma'am!"

"Good. Pick out a good spell and don't go cheap; this is for the rest of your life. Maybe fix up your face a bit. Always helps with sales. Just not too pretty, you still need to look like a soldier."

Truth winced. "Is it really that bad?"

"By Army standards? Nah. High four is my guess."

Truth looked stricken. "Four?"

"I'm gay. Take four and be happy. Or not. Get to work!"

He got.

CHAPTER 39

BODY CULTIVATION FOR THE THRIFTY

He collapsed on his sofa at the apartment. The apartment, in its entirety, wasn't nearly as nice as the private cabin on the flight home. Should he invest in an upgrade? But Harmony was doing his National Service soon. It would be just Sophia and Vigor most of the time. The apartment would only get bigger and bigger. Especially since Sophia would be going to college after her National Service. Or before, if she got a deferment. Same with Vig, probably. Getting a bigger, nicer place would be a waste, wouldn't it? Truth shrugged. Time to see the body-cultivation spells.

Summon Humanoid System Interface, he growled mentally. The secret was making the word summon sound like a death sentence.

The little sprite materialized in a glowing swirl of starlight. It looked bored as hell during the light show, doing little fluttery movements with its hands. "Yata. I'm here," it said, monotone. Then, in a more normal voice—"What can I help you with?"

"Body-cultivation spells, please." The little faerie stared at him, unamused. He sighed. "Give me a list of body-cultivation spells suitable for me."

"What's the magic word?"

Truth rolled his eyes. "Give me a list of body-cultivation spells suitable for me NOW!"

"One credit will be deducted from your account. Your list is being generated at once, dread magus!"

"Why, why do we have to do it this way? Every. Fucking. Time!"

"Because you are an NCO with the mindset of a private, and your brain never really got out of that inferior slum mentality. You need to be used to giving orders and demanding obedience. Otherwise, you will never develop as a mage or in Starbrite. Remember, the higher your level, the more you will encounter spiritual entities that can crush your will with the weight of their existence. And you will need to order them around. You also need to command your lesser mages and those seeking your favor. So. You know. Show some guts or I will select only body-cultivation spells that shrink your wee-wee and make you smell like rotting fish."

"I will shred your astral body on a goddamn cheese grater and feed it to whatever passes for your mother if you don't present the best goddamn spells available!"

The spirit did an extremely fake *eek* pose. "Yaa. The mean mage is bullying me. Yaa," it droned. "Oh, look, your spell list is ready. And not a dud in the lot of them."

Truth gave the little sprite an extra glare for good luck, then started looking at his list. Then stopped and looked back at the spirit.

"Refund my credit! Pay for it out of your own pocket!"

"Don't push it, fleshy. Tinymeat never goes off the menu."

"Fine, fine." Truth looked back at the list.

<u>Body-Cultivation Spells Suitable For C-8-U Security, PMC, Sergeant Truth Medici</u>
Daily Meditations of Valentinian
Sixteen Leaves of the World Tree
Nine Thunder Return Abyssal Formation
Dragon Chaining, Tiger Subduing Eightfold Wisdom Sutra
Heavenly Divine Chaos Grand Unifying Omnipotent Light Refinement
Supreme Cosmic Body Of The Grand Sage of Eternity Almighty Warchant Unending (Volume 1)

"So . . . there is a range here."

The little spirit just nodded.

"Without prices or descriptions."

"Focus on the spell; it'll come up."

"Are these in any kind of order?" Truth asked.

"Yep. Most suitable to least."

"The . . ." Truth reached around in his head for the most appropriate profanities. "The goat-corpse-slurping 'Omnipotent Supreme Cosmic Body' as created by none other than the 'Grand Sage of Eternity' is the *least* suitable for me?"

"It occurs to me that you don't know two crucial pieces of information," said the sprite. "First, the person publishing the spell gets to name it whatever they want. Second, a lot of these spells are still under copyright, so every purchase kicks the author, or their descendants or successors in interest, some cash."

"The names are advertising?!"

"Alas, Sergeant Medici, they are." The spirit made an insultingly pouty "sad" face. "The first two, by no coincidence whatsoever, are the cheapest and oldest. Which is to say, out of copyright. Also, none of the spells are actually bad, and they are all suitable for you."

Truth dove back in.

Daily Meditations of Valentinian—20,000 Credits per year, no purchase available. Practitioner enters a guided meditation on their idealized form, slowly comprehending it system by system and gaining a mastery of what that particular part of the body does and what it symbolizes. No upper limit to how far it can refine a physique. It confers no elemental-energy alignment and contains no inbuilt spells.
Sixteen Leaves of the World Tree—29,000 Credits per year, no purchase available. The practitioner is led through a series of sixteen refinements, inspired by the great World Tree. The body strengthens enormously, but more importantly, it gains wood-aligned energy and almost limitless regeneration.
Nine Thunder Return Abyssal Formation—50,000 Credits per—

"Hey, sprite?"

"Yes, dread magus? Good use of the ominous tone there, by the way."

"Fifty thousand credits for a one-year rental?"

"Good old Nine Thunder. A real gift to the public there. The combination of explosive strength, lightning alignment, supreme speed, spiritual-entity-banishing power—superb. Even at low levels, it's incredible."

"Fifty thousand credits a year."

"Lucky you get paid so much."

"Fifty *THOUSAND*. I can buy an island for fifty thousand credits!"

"Not a very nice one. And you can't take an island with you if you outgrow the planet. Your body cultivation is with you forever." The spirit waved its hand.

"Fifty thousand, though. How much is the Omnipotent one?"

"Just *squeaked* onto your list on the basis that you can earn bonuses to cover your cost-of-living requirements and just spend your entire base salary on—"

"No." Truth shook his head. "Just. No. Fuck, no. Absolutely not. Tell me more about this Valentinian and why his Meditations are so perfect for me."

"And here we have the commanding tone I've been looking for!" The sprite beamed. "It's number one because I figured this would be how you reacted when you saw the prices. That and it genuinely is one of the best body-cultivation methods on the planet. Not the best universally or anything, but very, very good."

The sprite waved its little hand and a tiny nude mannequin popped up next to it. "This is how it works. Everybody's body gets a little bit better, the higher their level is, because your natural flow is making your body resonate with the stars better. The more energy you hold, the more you resonate, and the more your body improves. A virtuous cycle, but only for astral energy." Little glowing lines flowed through the mannequin, making it look mysterious.

"The Meditations just intensifies this process and makes it conscious rather than unconscious. As a result, while it doesn't, by itself, let you shoot concentrated blasts of light from your eyes, it does mean that in every *physical* way imaginable, literally imaginable, you are better. As long as you meditate on it, running this spell, with a good enough understanding of what you are trying to do. This also works on the, no joke, conceptual level." The glowing mannequin slowly hollowed out and filled with spinning stars and galaxies, looking godlike and mysterious.

Truth just looked confused. The sprite elaborated.

"Your hand is your hand, but the *concept*, the *idea* of your hand exists too, right? It's the thing you grab stuff with. All the stuff, all the grabbing. Like, if you tried to pinch a star at night, you know you are really just playing a trick with perspective and you can't actually pick up a star. But, *theoretically*, at a staggeringly high level, that is a thing you could actually do with the Meditations."

"Prager's yellow teeth!"

"Because what the spell actually does is it makes you a little more 'real' than everything else around you. Or maybe you could think of it as conferring a . . . higher rank in the material hierarchy? It's not omnipotent, obviously. You need to convince the universe your conception is more real than the existing conception of whatever. Every top-quality body-refinement spell does some version of this, by the way. Just so happens that the Meditations is focused on it. And dirt cheap."

"So, if I really, really focused . . ."

"Yes, dread magus. At long last. You can finally fix that face crime you were born with. No saving the personality, and no one likes a cheap date, but the face is now salvageable."

Truth stared at the sprite for a long moment. "Can I beat you up if I get far enough in the Meditations?"

"Theoretically."

"Sign me up!"

The Meditations of Valentinian did exactly what they said on the label—you meditated. The first stage was visualization. It *seemed* very easy. Truth pictured the idealized form of himself and tried to hold the shape in place. Except he couldn't. Something would always shift or become blurry. He would realize with a jolt that he had forgotten his back muscles, then a second later, when the back was a glorious V with definition that would make a bodybuilder weep with envy, he realized that his hair and feet had vanished. It was like nailing jelly to the wall.

Truth had to give up. In a fit of desperation, he went to the Treasure Pavilion and hunted for a guide to cultivating the Meditations. There were dozens, which didn't help. Discarding any with "fun" names and then by length (opting for the *more is more* theory and praying for luck), and then, having no more useful sorting criteria, bought the third most expensive.

The answer turned out to be painfully obvious—visualization was its own skill to be mastered and not one the System could master for you. With that in mind, one should focus on specific things like your arms, your back, your skull, skin, teeth, gums, the webbing between your thumb and index finger. Anything small enough to properly fix in your mind, and big enough to be useful when you improved it.

You didn't have to have perfect knowledge of the thing you were improving, but the better you understood it, the better the results of the meditation. The better you could persuade the universe that your idea was correct. Truth sighed and bought an anatomy textbook, then a guide to male aesthetics. This was going to be a long haul. Time slipped away as he forced himself to read.

Then his alarm went off and he had to drag his sorry carcass to bodyguard school. Which, to his immense surprise, involved pretty girls.

The training was actually rather fun. It was a surprising amount of classroom learning. It seemed the fine art of guarding a body began with understanding what terrible situation they had put themselves in, then figuring out how to keep them alive in that situation. With the understanding that you were not allowed to just pull them out and send them home. Truth struggled with that last part.

Vocabulary was another problem. Apparently, "If you drive your convoy between two semi-deserted shitholes, *of course* there is going to be a fucking IED on the road and OF COURSE there will be trap demons waiting to swoop in the second the wards are breached, you absolute FUCKWIT" is not an appropriate way to communicate a disagreement about a proposed transit with your client. Nor was it appropriate to say "Just fuck your lover at home. You are already cheating on your husband; you don't need to make the security risk even worse." Apparently, that was not the bodyguard's call. That was not the one that almost washed him out of the bodyguard program, however.

The scenario was simple. It was a long-term protection job, assigned to a detail for the daughter of a high-tier Starbrite officer. She was spoiled, bossy, vain . . . and whenever it looked like no one was watching, she would hit on Truth. The trainer was staggeringly gorgeous. He never stood a chance.

CHAPTER 40

THE INTRICACIES OF GUARDING BODIES

It was the double whammy—a miserable teenage child wailing about luxury Truth couldn't have imagined two years before, throwing an absolute fit, and then, when she got him alone, inviting him to . . . do something about it. With his muscly arms. She just needed someone. Someone strong enough for her. Someone she could rely on, not like her absentee parents. Truth was absolutely dead at this point. Even knowing this was a setup, she hooked him. Her soft hands pressed against his chest as she lightly pushed him toward the wall.

Truth caught a little flicker out of the corner of his eye, felt a movement in the air. "Aegis, Ward!" The spells deployed in the skin of a second, stopping the cursed blade a fraction of an inch from the protectee's back. Truth spun her around, placing himself between her and the attacker as the cursed blade spent half a second punching through the shielding. Male—humanoid. Truth grabbed at the knife hand while stomping down on the insole.

"Electric Hand, Visla's Torrent." His hand grabbed the attacker's wrist. The spell combo amplified the normally painful grasp and made it disabling. He pulled the blade out of the twitching hand and mimed driving it into the back of the attacker's skull.

A buzzer sounded.

"Goddamn, that HURT!" the attacker roared, shaking his arm.

"Sorry, man, your timing was good—I was completely surprised."

"I thought I had you hooked." The female trainer dropped the persona like it never existed. Still quite pretty, but somehow, the intense allure wasn't there.

"You absolutely did. What spell were you using? That shit should be illegal," Truth said fervently. The trainer started laughing.

"ACTING, BABY!" she shouted, between laughs. "It's all about acting the role." She settled down and smiled at Truth, her eyes glinting with mischief. She slid up next to him and pressed her hand on his chest again. "You know, sincerity is the most important thing in acting," she half-whispered, looking deep into his eyes. Then shoved him backward, laughing again. "Once you can fake sincerity, you have it made!"

The evil witch pulled the same trick *three more times* and it worked every time. When they did the wrap-up for the day, she was looking genuinely sorry for Truth.

"Buddy, after the first time, that really shouldn't have worked so well. What's up? I don't think you are really falling for me," she asked, sitting next to him and sharing a bottle of water.

"It's . . . haaaah. Been a long time?"

She looked at him askance, her sympathy visibly evaporating.

"Oh, god, you're one of them."

"One of them . . . what?"

"Sergeant Medici, you are shredded. You look like a goddamn body model, your skin is perfectly clear, and a little bird tells me that the PMC pays big money. And yet you have zero self-confidence."

"Thanks for the kind words and all, but—" He waved at his face. She waved back.

"Who cares? Literally, who cares? You are a decent guy. Hyper-focused on your job, but a decent guy. Get over yourself and start asking women out."

She looked him over. "You ain't Prager's gift to women, but you paid real attention to me, properly listened, and never got so lost you let me get hurt. Something to think about."

Being a bodyguard was pretty great, Truth decided.

I truly think I'm going to murder my protectee. Not a . . . brilliant start to the job, but. C'mon. Who could blame me? Truth kept the thoughts on the inside, but no one could have heard him over the orchestral, nay, *symphonic* farts anyhow.

<<Not me. My usual hatred of the fleshies aside, this one is both too fleshy and too airy. Light it on fire. The tallow will render and keep it burning long after you stop your spell.>>

"Gesne food always gets me like this." The enormous man gasped. "I should know better. Eating meglish right before a press conference. It's the onions." He mopped his sopping-wet head with a handkerchief, overcome by the repeated effort of breaking wind. "I can't have onions. *Terrible* for digestion. My poor belly can't *stand* onions. But then, I almost would rather not have meglish if it didn't have onions. You might as well skip the bacon, too, and then what would you have? But I do *so love* a good meglish. I really *can't* do without it."

The poster child for coronary artery disease wasn't looking for an answer, just an audience. And since Truth had to stand there and guard his almost-spherical (and yet distressingly lumpy) body, he had a captive one.

"And the weather. *Terrible* weather! So bad. It's why I sweat like this—the *humidity* and the still air. My doctor says it's not good for me. The terrible, *sticky, sweaty* air. Not like in Crez. *Lovely* cool breeze in Crez, and you can sit out on the patio and enjoy a nice drink while you look down the valley. You've been to Crez, I'm sure."

Truth had never heard of such a place. He desperately wished he was there now.

"Yes, of course you have. Such a wonderful place, Crez. You can buy the most *delicious* little sandwiches from carts by the plazas. Just *meat* and *cheese* between two pieces of bread, but OH! What *meats!* OH! What *cheeses!*" He paused. His face contorted, slowly turning red, then faintly purple. Two hours before, Truth would have asked if he needed medical assistance. Now he just edged closer to the door.

Surely, this must be the time he explodes. Surely. However cruel the universe is, there must be a limit.

There was an eruption. The hurricane of gas caused the chair to scoot back, even as it forced the stupendous cheeks up and out. Then it tapered down to a sputtering series of sharp reports, causing the flab to snap against the seat. Then it reduced to a growling, grumbling flatulence that seemed to go on and on and on. The dreadful man collapsed backward, pale and shuddering, mopping the sweat from his forehead once again.

<<Ah. Yes, that was foolish of me. God's capacity for cruelty is no less great and infinite in power than his ability to disappoint his creations. I would suggest fire once again. With the amount of methane in this room, you can die together.>>

"Dr. Calderine? They are ready for you," a voice called from outside. Truth snapped to action, checking the door and walking out ahead of his protectee. Who needed a literal sixty-second-by-the-clock *minute* to heave himself out of his chair. He swayed for a few seconds, then got his cane under him and staggered for the stage door. Truth came out beside him, marveling at the fabulous banner over the stage.

"BEAT CHILDHOOD HUNGER!"

Dr. Calderine looked up at the banner and burst into tears. Weeping, he staggered to the podium. "The children! Oh! OOOH! *The children!*" The cameras ate it up.

A few weeks later—

All right, the last three were . . . not the best. But you got through them. They were, ultimately, fine. You were fine. She's a little old lady. Twilight years. You got this. Truth psyched himself up in the bathroom. Two quick slaps to his cheeks later, he strode out looking commanding.

"Oh, thank GOD! Sergeant! Sergeant, I need you! Hurry!" The stubby-looking woman waved desperately. Then her arm seemed to get tired, and she clasped it to her chest. Her eyes seemed to bug out from her plasticine-looking face as she panted with emotion.

It must be hard for her to wave her hand, what with all the gold she's wearing, Truth thought.

"How can I assist you, madame?" He was using the "polite" voice they trained into him.

"It's Raquel. I think she's trying to murder Mr. Knitts." She gasped. "Murder, Sergeant. Murder!" She fanned herself arduously. Then she gave up.

Truth desperately tried to remember if he knew a "Raquel" or a "Mr. Knitts." He did not. "I'm afraid I don't know who those people are, Madame. Could you explain a bit more?"

That was a rookie mistake.

"Raquel, OH! She is my late husband's daughter by his first wife. She always hated me. *Hated* me! Even though I did try to be the *very best* mother I could be for her. But we wed when she was at *such* a difficult age—"

"How old?" Truth asked, even more unwisely.

"Twenty-four. A dreadful, spoiled-rotten twenty-four. I should not speak ill of the dead, but her mother, Bailey, was dreadful. I should know, we were such dear friends before the accident. She was always away on 'business' or 'saving lives' or some other such nonsense. So she was a doctor; so what?" She flicked away the notion with gem-bedecked fingers. Truth mentally circled the phrase *such dear friends* but didn't have the opportunity to follow up.

"Couldn't she have been a mother to her four children, too? Or a wife to my dear, sweet Enrique? Ah! Enrique! Did you know we met under the waterfalls at Halcyn Cove? We were both on vacation away from our spouses, and that magical night! The sound of the falls thundered in our ears, but could not drown out the thundering in our hearts."

"How . . . wonderful? The murder you mentioned?"

"MURDER! How dare you! Both Bailey and Fredrick died of natural causes! The fact that they died within a week of each other is merely a tragic coincidence!"

"Raquel murdering Mr. Knitts, Madame?"

"Oh, my dear Mr. Knitts! My only true companion in my old age! Ah, I want him to have everything. My everything!"

"Mr. Knitts is husband number . . . three?"

"He would be the seventh, ah, if it were possible for us to wed. A most blessed and auspicious number, seven. If only he could be my groom! If only he could *sweep* me off my feet! I have looked into spells for that, you know. People do make such a *fuss* about these things in Jeon, but the word is broad, and the universe broader still. Yes, I have special people out looking, Sergeant, and my purse is deep."

She drifted off staring out the window. Rain splattered uselessly against the glass. Very uselessly, it was a rain spell set up to provide whatever mood the old lady wanted at a given window. It was fifteen degrees and sunny out, twenty meters from the mansion. Truth coughed. He desperately wanted to drop the subject, but the keyword *murder* had come up, so he felt he had to get to the bottom of it.

"Who is Mr. Knitts, Madame?"

"Oh, Mr. Knitts! He is wonderful. Dreamy, elegant, full of deep expressive silences, like a forest glade. Did you know I had a forest glade made, just so people would know what Mr. Knitts is like? It's wonderfully useful."

"That. That's wonderful. So considerate."

"Yes. I am *very* considerate. Did you know I am a noted philanthropist . . ."

Two days later, an enervated Truth reported the success of his mission. He had received a glowing evaluation from Madame. He never discovered the fate of Mr. Knitts. Or Raquel.

Weeks after that—

Okay, oh-for-Seven. Not outstanding. Not what I would prefer. But hey, no one is shooting at me. That's literal job security. I'm not shooting anybody. This is a good thing. A peaceful thing. And, okay, they have their . . . funny little quirks. But this is a young guy. Executive track. Rich family, powerful patrons. Finance bro. Gets excited about commodities swaps, whatever the hell they are, and probably has the world's most boring sex. Just need to make sure he gets to the meeting tomorrow. The nice, boring meeting, in this nice, boring city. It's all good.

Truth encouraged himself, looking in the bathroom mirror. He looked sharp in his gray suit. Confident. Capable. Shame he couldn't eat there; this club looked like it had amazing nibbles. But he was on the job. Professional.

"Sergeant, you better get out here." One of the other guards banged on the door. "I think our body just ODed."

"FUCK!"

CHAPTER 41

A CHANGE OF PACE IS AS GOOD AS A REST

Truth ran out into the club. Club staff were running over to the VIP booth with large sheets hanging from curtain rods. In seconds, they had the whole booth cordoned off. Truth burst through, the young idiot on the ground and frothing at the mouth. The party girls huddled against the back of the couch, looking shocked.

Truth took one look and whipped out a few bone slivers from their case. "Anybody spell him?"

"I got a detox off, but it's not taking," a guard replied.

"Not good." Truth grunted and with *intense* reluctance, jabbed the expensive reagents into the high flyer's wrists and neck. The young man puked once convulsively, but then his breathing steadied and his color slowly improved.

"One of you want to tell me exactly what happened in the three minutes I wasn't here?" Truth asked in a calm, reasonable voice. One of the girls dropped her purse.

"We didn't do anything!"

"It's not our fault! He did it! I don't even do snow!"

There was more in this vein. Truth just waved them down. "Look, I don't care. I really, really don't care. I just want to figure out what he took so I can figure out how to treat him without having to take him to a hospital. Also, if he's buying bad gear, we need to know that too, okay? Look at me. I'm not even mad."

"Are you sure you aren't mad? Because you kind of look mad."

"I am irritated but not angry. See? I am speaking in a very calm and reasonable way. What. Did. He. Do?"

They had a whispered consultation in the back of the booth, then one elected herself spokeswoman. "So, Charlie is just, like, this guy we know? But just to, like, party or whatever?"

"I know. I was in the carriage when he picked you up four hours ago. What happened *three minutes* ago?"

Charlie was getting a little more color in his face, which was good, but also gently pissing himself, which was bad. Truth was wearing a brand-new suit, and he had some traumatic memories about shifting bodies.

The girl wrinkled an admittedly attractive nose. Truth suspected Charlie would no longer find her available to "party." "He got out some junk he said he got from an awesome shaman he knew. He had a whole story about how she was, like, this really connected and in-tune person who could make some really magical stuff, or whatever? Anyway, he chopped out some lines, and he snorted the first one. Before we could have any, he freaks out, starts yelling about, like, lizards or something? And then he falls over. That's really it. Are you going to call us a carpet now, or do I have to get one myself?"

"Why don't you hang out a minute longer. Finish your drink," Truth said commandingly. He looked over at the club staff. "We have it from here. If you called an ambulance, cancel it." They nodded and left. He looked at the junior guards. "Pack him up, get him home. Run countercurses. See what you can figure out by looking at the drugs. He's got ten grams of 'corn horn in him; he'll pull through."

He turned back to the girls, who hadn't touched their drinks. Which was convenient. Horribly.

"All right ladies, here's the deal." Truth reached into another interior pocket and pulled out a small vial. He put a drop of potion in each glass. This was a *nice* club, so the spell on the glasses immediately turned them bright blue. The girls went pale. "You can either drink up and wake up tomorrow in your own beds with no memory of tonight but a nice chunk of extra cash in your purses. Or you can wake up tomorrow in . . . other circumstances. Maybe I'm the one with a nice chunk of surprise money. But either way, remember that Starbrite owns this club. Nobody saw shit. Nobody is going to hear shit. Nobody is going to do shit. So. What's it going to be?"

Truth spent most of the next week at home. He turned down a few jobs, claiming that he needed to spend more time with his family. Which he did. Vig and Soph were happy to have him around, of course. They made a big fuss about how much they liked the suit. A lot of encouraging pats on the back.

Sophia had made it to the nationals in the beastcrafting tournament. She seemed to exist in only three places—home, the lab, and the library. Vigor was only marginally better, replacing the lab with the gym. They both seemed to be thriving. Though they were giving him some worried looks.

"Really, guys, I'm fine. I'm the world's most highly paid babysitter," he protested.

"Yeah, some babies." Vigor shook his head.

"Any chance of running off with the boss's sixteen-year-old daughter?" Sophia joked. Though she looked disturbingly hopeful when she asked.

"I have been specially trained by experts not to do that."

"Shame. You . . . really need a break, bro. You really do." She sighed.

He was about to argue and then deflated.

"They have me out there as the face of the department. It's exhausting. I'm going to run a few more little jobs, just round out the year. Then, yeah, vacation. I'll take a look at your school schedule. Maybe we can all go somewhere warm."

"Can you really afford a tropical vacation?" Vigor asked. "I know you are spending a ton on our school stuff and elixirs and everything."

Truth just laughed. "Yeah. Yeah, I can just about cover it. For you guys, this ain't nothing. Now go hit the books!"

Excessive amounts of bodyguarding later—

All right, the last twelve protectees weren't great. But this time, it's a dog. I like dogs. I haven't spent a lot of time around dogs, but the dogs I have met were great, Truth thought. For some reason, this dog was flying first class along with Truth. Not the owner. The owner was taking a *very* important meeting and required that Mr. Floofels (or whatever the dog's name was) be delivered in perfect safety to her villa in Pureta Vicarro.

Truth picked the dog up, still in its crate, and took it to the airport. All good so far, for all that the crate was practically crawling with sigils, bindings, and protections. Security had a fit, but the first-class ticket and frequent flashing of his pin did seem to be persuasive. He had been worried about the dog barking, but apparently, the spells tranquilized it. Truth was asleep before the bird flapped off the runway.

Truth did not remember his dreams, not a single one. He must dream, he knew, everyone does, but for him, they were gone entirely when he awoke. Lucid dreaming was a completely foreign concept. Which is why he lacked the appropriate language to describe what happened next.

Truth was in a luxury apartment, glass walls looking out high above Harban City. He was in the living room, sitting on the couch and wearing silk pajamas. There were a couple of cartons of takeout food on the table, half-eaten. Sitting on the couch with him was a lovely woman in her own silk pajamas. Not too much or too little of any one thing; she was just . . . lovely. And she had a wolf's head. Not some sort of anthropomorphic, cartoonish head. An actual, very real, fur-covered wolf's head.

"It's nice, you know?" she asked. Her voice was quite normal. And lovely. But the wolf's lips didn't move, even though her eyes narrowed and her ears twitched with amusement. "Most of the time, people have big, elaborate plans for me. Like a whole tasting menu of the flesh. The girlfriend experience is very popular and common, but even then, they have a detailed notion about what the 'girlfriend' or 'boyfriend' should be like. But you don't even want the roleplay. You just want me. Here. With you. With you knowing that you are safe. Knowing that you are a safe person for me and your own damaged weirdness won't ruin things. Knowing that you can finally just *rest*. It's nice."

"Am I? Safe?" Truth wondered. She giggled.

"Aw, honey. Look at me. A wolf and your best girl? You know what that is, right? And humanity's never had a better friend." That wasn't reassuring, and she seemed to pick up on that straight away. "You are as safe as anyone can be in a dream. I'm barely getting a trickle of you through all the spells and wards around the two of us, and really, it's just because I'm bored. My mistress keeps me very well fed. I have no interest in hurting you. Quite the opposite, actually."

"Oh." Truth was a little sad to learn that it was a dream, but that did make sense. He didn't know any girls with wolf heads.

"Hey, don't worry about it. You are here. I am here. We are here together. And I know you don't want to really do anything with me, but . . . wanna watch a movie and eat takeout?"

It turned out he did. Truth didn't recognize the movie, and his companion wasn't chatty. They just sat comfortably with each other and enjoyed some pretty okay food. Truth felt very conflicted when he woke up.

He transported the cage to a very swank-looking villa with both a swimming pool and sea views. Everything white walls and terracotta-tile roofs. The client swept out of the house and, ignoring Truth, opened the cage. Black smoke poured out, forming a seven-foot-tall muscle-bound mountain of a man. With a wolf's head.

"Darling! Come. I have missed you so much. Was the flight very terrible?" She hauled him into the house without ever looking at Truth. The wolf, however, caught his eye before vanishing inside. And winked.

"Captain, any chance I can transfer to something a bit more . . . not bodyguarding?" Truth asked. Really making an effort not to whine.

"Why? You have been making *serious* cash, your reviews are all outstanding, and your lack of bitching about how awful your protectees are is a source of wonder for the entire PMC." The captain looked mystified.

"Because they *are* awful. And because I am slowly losing my mind with their idiocy. Not to mention the crippling boredom."

"Boring is good. Enjoy being bored. Treasure it. You know what the alternative is, right?" she asked urgently.

"Yes, ma'am, I do. But over the course of . . . I don't even know how long. Two eternities. I have met exactly one protectee I was actually willing to take a spell for, and that's not a great trait in a bodyguard."

"Ah. No. Was it Dr. Calderine? I thought that was great, you getting to work with such a famous philanthropist." The captain was curious.

"He was actually one of the better ones, but no. Let's not focus on the 'who I'd save' question. Instead, let's focus on almost anything else."

"You could take a vacation? Have you had one since joining Starbrite? I don't want you to burn out."

"I haven't. Not including the time on the hospital ship, anyway. But also not my point. I'm happy to work. I *want* to work. I just want to work with other people. Not with crazy rich idiots."

The captain rolled her eyes at that one. "Tough ask. Those are some of our best clients, and they are doing *great* things for our PR. Actually, though, I did have a request for a security team for a convoy. No one higher than Level Two, for reasons not adequately explained to me. Want to take a look at the contract?"

Truth smiled blissfully. "I would like nothing better. It sounds great," Truth said, as fate tied on its cleats and figured out exactly where it was going to kick him.

CHAPTER 42

A DUST-UP

The mission was simple—escort the package from the pickup at the dock in the fishing village of Itum, County Hostfa, in the Ressilaud Free State, to the hand-off at an airstrip three hundred kilometers inland. The "airstrip," in this case, was a reasonably flat stretch of scrub-filled desert twenty minutes' drive from the village of Rezum, County Iilofa, still in the Ressilaud Free State.

Ressilaud was indeed a very free state. In that there was no effective law enforcement. It was generally understood that the difference between a peaceful villager and a murderous bandit was one of attitude. And the locals changed their attitudes *all the time.*

Truth found himself leading the close-protection detail for the package and its suit-wearing escorts. Frankly, he would rather be *almost* anywhere else . . . except for one crucial, beautiful thing. One of the suits, the most junior, coffee-fetching, bag-holding, yes-man suits, was none other than Ludovic, who Truth had last seen shitting himself in the customs booth during his National Service.

It was the little things sometimes. On the one hand, the mission parameters were beyond scuffed, they were 100% for sure going to be ambushed, and they might die. On the other hand, Truth could watch Ludovic squirm when Truth gently reminded him about how "important and special" he was.

Truth was happily trying to figure out the most hurtful combination of lies he could tell about his income and sex life when a spell trap went off under the front carriage.

Blue-white light slammed up, crackling like ants on a frying pan against the ward. Burning through in a fraction of a second, using the last of its energy to melt a molten orange crack in the armor. Earth demons, thick-bodied, slow, and cold, chased the burning light up and into the breach. The wards were good, the armor better—and it held up about as well as tissue paper. The spell trap could only keep the demons summoned for a few seconds, but it was more than long enough.

Truth couldn't see what happened in the shattering instant, but he knew every-one in that carriage was dead. The demons twisted back out through the gap, slipping like cold smoke back into the earth, leaving the front carriage as a barricade across the road.

It all happened in less than a second. Five men dead, a two-hundred-and-fifty-thousand-wen armored luxury carriage torn apart. The brutalized remains hurtling toward Truth and his protectees.

Sharp, Steel! Truth bellowed in his mind, grabbing the fetish built into the side of the carriage. Out loud, he yelled, "Plan C, GO HARD!" The driver slammed as much cosmic energy as he could into the carriage, the chained spirit howling in outrage as it was whipped forward. The fetish amplified the spells Truth cast through a large multipurpose array built into the floor. In front of the carriage, a wide triangular steel plow materialized. Its central ridge was sharper than any razor. The carriage cleared the intervening hundred meters at speed, the spell slicing through the body of the destroyed carriage ahead. The broken halves bounced off the plow, falling in a spray of broken, partial corpses to either side of the road.

"HOLY SHIT! HOLY SHIT! HOLY SHIT! WHAT THE FUCK WAS THAT!"

"Ludovic, on Prager's nuts, I will knock you out if you don't shut the fuck up and settle down!" Truth bellowed.

"Ghost Dust. Faerie Fire." He ordered the System to load up detection spells and launched them out of the carriage.

"Green Star to Black Rock, contact with hostiles. Two-thirds of combat effectives remain. Package and protectees intact. Moving to Plan C." Truth heard the comms specialist relaying the situation.

A cloud of super fine particles exploded out from the carriage, but instead of trailing behind like a streamer, they floated in a flattened disk around the central carriage. Spectral shapes emerged from the cloud. Twisted, angry, or simply blank and amorphous. Other things, too—more mechanical-looking constructs, witch-crafted beasts, and floating curses driven by thousands of tadpole-shaped eyes.

And while they were out of position, they were closing in fast.

"Damn!" Truth activated the comms talisman. "All hands, assume encirclement. Drivers, activate plows and breakers. Summoners—deploy iron-bee familiars. Continue Plan C." Truth didn't have time to give more detailed orders. He didn't need to. The other guards in the carriage and the carriage behind him were all Starbrite PMC pros. And unlike him, they hadn't rocketed up the ranks. This shit? A normal fucking Tuesday.

The protection mission was made up of three armored carriages, each carriage holding five PMC guards. The middle carriage, the one Truth was riding in, was larger to accommodate the three suits and the package. Which was a heavily armored black case, 122 centimeters tall and about half that wide and deep.

All Truth knew about the case was that he, and the suits, were all wired with a dozen dead-man triggers, most of which they did not control, that would detonate the package and atomize anything within a dozen meters of it. Leaving out the suits, the package, and the dead squad, he had ten soldiers under his command, of which two were comms, two were summoners, and six were all-rounders. All Level Two, for price efficiency, apparently.

Truth had heard one of the suits muttering about "Security through obscurity" and almost had a stroke. Even he wasn't that dumb. And yet, these very important suit-stuffers with advanced college degrees were.

The summoners had their iron bees out just in time as the first wave of ghosts slammed in. The ghosts were twisted, misshapen things, once human, harvested God knows how, and branded with sigils of torment and compulsion. Screaming and howling, they fell on the wagons, flickering in the already-harsh morning light. The bees tore through them, shredding their ectoplasmic forms and breaking the curses binding them. Some of the ghosts could try and pull themselves back together. For most, they simply returned to the essence, all chance of an afterlife stolen from them twice over.

The demons were made of hardier stock, their semi-solid flesh standing up to more punishment before disintegrating. The demons *did* re-form, however, howling in misery as base matter once more wove through them. You couldn't kill demons, but you could break them if you shredded them long enough. Or took out the summoner.

"Summoners located; painting targets!" one of the comms shouted. They had traced the stellar rays controlling the ghosts and demons back to their origin. Now it was time for the rest of the squad to counterattack.

Portable altars built into the carriages were splashed with blood. Rapid-fire Enochian chants pulled tiny angelic forms, all twisting wheels and burning eyes, from whatever higher existence they inhabited. Each was bound by its proper sign and name, then ordered to follow the trace and kill the necromancers at the other end. They would clear out most of the flying curses as they went.

The whole operation took less than a minute. While the angels were being summoned, huge area suppression spells were being launched from the array on the roof. Fireballs, sticky like tar. Slithering serpents made of cold-iron needles. A sphere that was beyond mere darkness, it was the death of light. Raining down where the necromancers were hiding.

There was a sudden break in the spectral horde. Apparently, the necromancers had found something more important to deal with. Which meant it was time for the witch-crafted puppets to shine.

Charging through the cloud of detection spells, the puppets were rimmed with glowing faerie fire. Fetishes, the big clunky sticks that the talisman-maintenance tech in Truth despised, poked out of the carriages. Mystic swords, summoned by the System and the magi's will, slashed down with grotesque strength on the puppets. The veiling magics were dispelled, and the puppets revealed their forms.

Things of wood and clay, woven with bits of animals and poisonous herbs. They exploded when cut apart—some into clouds of seaweed-colored smoke, others into swarms of wasps bigger than a man's palm and dripping venom. Some did manage to reach the carriages, weaving through the spells. Their claws seemed to ignore the wards and left long scores in the armor. Truth was still pushing out the Ghost Dust and Faerie Fire, so he yelled to the driver, "Hit 'em with the bumper!"

A thrumming noise, and then the puppets were in the air and flying back as the kinetic-energy spell punted them away. The rest of the guards had fun shooting skeet for a minute, and then they were gone.

It looked like they were through the ambush, at least for the moment. "Report by squad. Squad 2?"

"No casualties here, sir. A couple of burnt-out talismans and the altars are melted, but otherwise, we are in good shape. The carriage took a little damage from the puppets, but overall, no damage to function."

"Squad 3?"

"About the same, Sergeant. Comms says that there are no more active necromantic summons in range, but she's picking up some kind of aetheric signaling. It's very faint and very randomized. It could be something very far away, or something well veiled and right up next to us."

"Narrow it down."

"Best she can do is 'inside of ten klicks,' Sarge."

He let out a long sigh. "All right. Good job, everyone. Stay sharp; this isn't over."

The suits had been freaked out during the ambush, which Truth reckoned was fair enough. He sniffed. Raising an eyebrow in surprise, he looked over at Ludovic and his dry trousers, who glared back at him. There was a certain glassiness to the glare, though. Truth looked over at the head suit. A person whose name he had not been told and whose face he had been told to forget. And yet they brought Ludovic, whom Truth had served with. Either Ludovic didn't pass on that tidbit, or they didn't care. Either way . . . not impressed.

"You tranqued him?"

"We all took some Shabet. Seemed wise to take the edge off." The suit shrugged. "You say this isn't over?"

"Did . . . Sorry, occupational hazard; I assume everyone knows what I know." Truth smiled awkwardly. "No part of that assault was cheap. Just the ghosts alone, in labor, it must have been hundreds of hours. Not amazing ghosts, sure, mostly Level One, but still. The demons would have needed both sacrifices and sigils, which is not a small cost on that scale. The curses were mass-produced, which means that they had *access* to large-scale curse production." Truth took a deep breath.

"The witch-crafted puppets are a whole other story—those were not quite military grade, but only because they were too fragile. In terms of their offensive capability, speed, handling, and payload? As good or better than what most ordinary soldiers would have access to." Truth shook his head.

"All of which ignores the two mammoths in the room—the demon spell trap and the actual necromancers themselves. That spell trap was overkill. It would have shredded anything below Level Four, and probably given Level Fours a real bad time, too. I don't know what it would cost, because I can tell you that the System won't sell it, even to the PMC, without authorization from higher up. Which brings us to the necromancers."

Truth moved his hands, trying to explain what felt intuitively obvious to him. "That was not some little swarm of demons and ghosts. It was, in fact, a couple hundred of them. Now, we were ready for them, and our defenses were intact. Our summoners were able to focus and get the bees deployed almost instantly."

He chopped his hand through the air.

"*But*. If we had crashed into the first carriage that got taken out, it would have at a minimum slammed everyone around. People would have been disoriented and slow to react, assuming they didn't die. The ghosts and demons would have swarmed through the weakened wards and armor, slaughtering everyone. The ambush was professionally organized, superbly staffed, and lavishly equipped."

Truth closed his eyes and leaned back in his seat. "You are goddamn right we are going to get hit again. These aren't bandits. It's an actual army."

CHAPTER 43

WHAT'S IN THE BOX?

The carriages raced for the secondary airstrip, the backup identified by Plan C. The only reason Truth had any hope whatsoever that their enemies did not already hold it was that the "airstrip" was a flattened stretch of scrub-like desert that some wildly optimistic local had tried to turn into a farm. Nowhere was it listed as an airfield. It was a little rammed-earth house, a shed made of thin sticks, and a big flat bit of desert in the middle of nowhere. Fingers crossed.

"Sir, I know you can't tell me what's in the box, but can you tell me the sort of people who would field a deniable but military-grade force to acquire it?" Truth carefully asked.

The chief suit gave a sort of strangled laugh. "More or less everyone. It really doesn't matter, Sergeant. They will bring everything they have as discreetly as possible. Remember, we are running this mission with the lowest-level people *we* can, precisely to minimize the attention we draw. Looks like they are doing the same thing. Anyone above Level Three making a move would get spotted eventually. And no one can stand an *eventually*."

Truth shook his head. "Comms, ETA on the bird?"

Comms checked her wax tablet—ghostly automatic writing carving an update. "ETA thirty minutes, Sarge, which is roughly when we get there. They are reporting contacts in the air. So far, mostly alarm curses, but there are signs of more serious anti-air defenses."

Truth sat back and closed his eyes. "Let me know if anything changes." Anti-fucking-air. Oddly enough, operating and defeating anti-air defenses weren't covered when training for bodyguard detail and being a conscript for National Service. *Don't sleep with the boss's sixteen-year-old daughter* was covered. *Don't sell prison hooch to your fellow conscripts*, also covered. But not defeating air defenses.

He drew in a long breath through his nose. If he couldn't do something about it, he shouldn't worry about it. "All right, let's get set up. Grab a bite, drink water, and rearm what needs rearming. Assume the bird is going to be late to the LZ and will be coming in hot. Start setting up deployable wards and getting as many fixed defenses ready as we can. Expect to abandon them." Truth's voice echoed in both carriages, thanks to the comms. He looked sardonically at the chief suit. "Don't worry about the lost equipment. It's covered under the contract for the op."

"Is it really?" the chief suit asked.

"Yep. The second I saw the mission, I insisted it was added to the contract."

Ludovic was fussing with something on his tablet. The wax filled and smoothed at a terrifying rate, constantly refreshing and telling him . . . something. Truth didn't recognize what little bits he saw, and Ludovic was blatantly trying to keep him from seeing. The chief suit was doing similar but acting a lot more casually. *He* had the wisdom to put a sight-interference spell on the tablet, letting him read in privacy. The box . . . just sat there.

MANDATORY MISSION UPDATE! MANDATORY MISSION UPDATE! MANDATORY MISSION UPDATE!

The contracted mission terms are hereby overridden in accordance with the relevant provisions of the Starbrite Employee Handbook and Code of Ethics, authorized by Code ZED STAR ZED. Operational Command Authority is now assumed by Code INDIGO PYRAMID RAIN.

Contractors from the Starbrite Private Military Corporation are hereby ordered to ensure the safe evacuation of DESIGNATED CARGO and DESIGNATED PERSONNEL in accordance with Operational Plan C, currently underway. On the authority of Code Indigo Pyramid Rain, all losses of Starbrite Company Assets are acceptable to achieve that goal. All unbudgeted operational expenses will be paid by Code Indigo Rain.

<< *Well, that's not good. I mean, short term, not terrible for me, but* short term *is . . . less than an hour. You, meatsack, are screwed. It was a short but unpleasant time, and I hope your death is excruciating.* >>

Truth had to read the orders twice before he got it. Everything was to stay the same, but it was okay if *only* the suits and the box made it out. Everyone and everything else was expendable. They were screwed. Truth racked his brain for anything else he could do to improve the situation and drew a blank. He pulled out a map of the area around the LZ in desperation.

The map was not helpful. The countryside was oppressively flat, desert soil punctured by short, wide bushes with impressively tough, spiky leaves. They weren't quite like barbed wire, but Truth wouldn't want to run through them without armor. There was a "city" about two hundred kilometers away. The population of said city was probably less than the block he grew up in. No help there.

The farm itself didn't have any great revelations either. A rammed-earth house, square-shaped, perhaps a hundred square meters. Stick roof. A half-hearted attempt at a wicker fence for penning . . . something. Chickens? And then the flattened field. It was grown over in the latest surveillance picture. More of those scrubby little weeds, probably. Oh, there was a well. He had missed the well. Yeah, they were dead.

They didn't get hit on the way to the farm. Truth sent Squad 3 to clear the farmhouse. Abandoned, as it was supposed to be. "All right, here's what we're going to do. Comms, tell them we will be holed up in the farmhouse, so they need to land the bird as close to on top of the house as they can manage. Everyone else, deploy everything we've got. Park the two surviving carriages on either side of the structure. We can use their armor and spell arrays to toughen the place up even more."

They looked at him, clearly expecting more. "Bird should be here in seven minutes. Anyone feel like betting their life on it?" They got to work.

Truth checked around the doorframe for talismans or wards and found nothing. He frowned. Even the most bumblefuck nowhere farmer wouldn't leave his home completely unprotected. *Hmm.* He cast Sharp and used his metallic hands to dig out the bottom of the door frame. It was just dirt. About thirty centimeters down he found a spell bowl. Cheap terracotta, unglazed. He didn't recognize the language, but these things were all pretty much the same. Various names of God, or gods, invocations of angels and demons, and right down at the bottom, a sigil. Looked like it was literally better than nothing, but probably not a lot better.

Still, there was something about houses. Endless reams of papers had been written (Truth had been told) trying to guess why a home responded differently to magic than a shed, but it did. Done correctly, it would amplify wards keeping out demonic spirits. It might not stop a heavy needler from chewing the house into nothing, but at least no *demons* would do the chewing. Truth sighed and started linking in proper, professional demonic warding talismans. It was better than nothing.

"Sarge—incoming! The house's tagged, and we have necromancers coming in fast! More contacts in the air—bird's punching through, but it's delayed," Comms yelled.

"You hear her! Protectees and the cargo in the pit!" He had ordered the floor of the room be dug out. Trenches make everything better, he felt. "Everyone else, look alive! Summoners, get the bees out and launch eye-spies."

The guards set up spelled riot shields against the walls and cut out little loops to put their fetishes and talismans through. They had only had a few minutes to prepare. Nevertheless, a Starbrite Man Is Always Ready, and as some guards showed, Starbrite Women were too. Something flickered in the corner of Truth's eye. He looked over and squinted. "Get me an eye-spy south-southwest. I want—"

The witch-crafted puppet broke its veil as it deployed an alchemy cannon. Its four skinny legs seemed to barely hold the barrel up and collapsed under the weight of the recoil.

"Contact, south-southwest. INCOMING FIRE!"

The house shook. The wards resisted the incredible concussive blast of superheated air, but the sheer noise shook their brains. They lashed back out, saturating the puppet with fireballs, acid, and their own burst of air pressure, and tore it apart. It also revealed a dozen more puppets incoming.

Little red dots appeared around them as the eye-spies painted their targets. Clouds of dust and faerie fire swirled out from the cars as the comms operators got them running. Just in time, too.

The tortured ghosts were back, fleeing ahead of the hungry demons and rushing toward the house. Truth grinned nastily as he jabbed his fetish through the loop. The ghosts smashed into the ward around the house . . . and vanished. House magic wasn't good for much, but when juiced with a military-grade spell installed by a (former) talisman-maintenance technician . . . Level One and Two ghosts could return directly to the essence.

The demons were a bit more serious. They clawed against the ward, draining it horribly quickly. The attackers had gone all out. Earth demons hit one side of the house while fire demons hit the other. The earth demons were attracted to the fire demon's heat and were doubly motivated to claw through. The fire demons were smarter. They just hung back from the ward and focused narrow streams of blue-white flame at it. Burning it down without damaging themselves.

Truth snarled out a curse and loaded up his spells. "Radiant Blade. Lassir's Icy Grasp." The spells combined to launch an ice-cold steel blade through the only-some-what-material fire demons. They screamed in four octaves, shifting and twisting with the exploding remnants of their physical form. They would pull back together, given time. It was almost impossible to completely kill a demon. But you could kill their summoners just fine.

"Aqua Fortis. Severing Whip." He lined up the fetish with a red dot and fired. A fine glass needle, tempered seven times with seven different herbal baths and the blood of seven auspicious animals, flew with malicious speed across the open ground. He didn't see the person it hit but saw the spell go off. A pinwheel of acid compressed into thin cords that whipped around so fast, they could cut through trees. He could see limbs flying into the air. Looked like he caught at least two. He loaded the next needle and tried to find another cluster. It was a target-rich environment.

There was a familiar ripping noise, dozens in a few seconds. Holes were quickly chewed through the wall, then through the guards. One member of his squad went down screaming, clutching their gut. Others just went down forever. Heavy needlers, using spellbreaker ammo. *Fuckers.*

He tried to trace the fire back, but it came from three directions. He shoved more power into his riot shield, feeling the accumulating burn of the wild stellar rays. Good that he did—the enemy mages figured out they should shoot low. The spellbreakers punched through the wards without breaking pace but ricocheted off the reinforced steel of the shield. He launched spell after spell downrange, dropping enemy mages and crushing spell beasts, but it would never be enough. They were getting swarmed.

"Attention, Starbrite mercenaries!" a heavily accented voice projected from out-side. "Do you know what you are trying to smuggle? A little girl! You have a child of the Shattervoid Clan in that box! Do you know what that means? It means that when the Shattervoid Clan hears about it, they will embargo the whole planet! Everyone you love will die. We won't kill them. Their neighbors will, in the food riots." The voice took a deep breath.

"I know you cannot surrender. But stop fighting. We can give you a quick death, and you will save the world."

The fuck? He absolutely could surrender. And would, if this went on any longer. Then he smiled. There was a rapidly approaching thunder, and explosions of green flames swept through the attackers.

The spell bird was there. Then Truth heard more rushing thunder and frowned. It didn't come alone.

CHAPTER 44

THE BIG-BROTHER TYPE

Comms! Is the bird down?!" Truth bellowed. His ears were ringing from all the explosions. He hoped the comms operators were still alive.

"The Redhawk is perched in the field behind us. More incoming hostiles. We have to evac NOW, Sarge!"

MISSION UPDATE—PERSONNEL AND CARGO TO THE TRANSPORT AT ONCE, FORSAKING ALL OTHER OBJECTIVES.

Truth was moving before his brain processed the order. He grabbed a shell-shocked Ludovic and threw him out of the trench, shoving him toward the door. "Go, go, go!" He grabbed the chief suit, who only looked a bit better than Ludovic, and threw him out, too. He shoved the box into their hands, pushing them, and screamed at the other suits to move out. His squad mates, the ones not dead or too injured to move, dragged the suits to the door, carrying them if necessary.

He could see incoming spellbirds, little ones, attack craft. He rounded the corner, sweeping for enemies and not seeing any. The dickhead pilot landed fifty goddamn meters from the house, putting them far outside the wards. Far from any cover. "Run! Run, you cowardly little shit! Run!" he screamed at Ludovic. All that mattered was getting them and the cargo into the transport.

One of the little attack birds started taking potshots, chewing the ground near them with explosive darts. *Smokescreen, Silversnow.* He activated the two spells together, creating a blinding wall of smoke and chaff between him and the birds. It wouldn't be enough, of course. They could see the Redhawk. Some other guards did the same as him, trying to throw the enemy's aim off.

The loading ramp was down, the crew waving them in desperately, sweeping around with extended-magazine needlers and trying to spot the enemy. The chief suit was in first, hauling the box in with the crew's help. Ludovic was next, then the rest of the suits, as the guards formed a loose dome around the ramp. By some miracle, they got them all in, but the thunder of the incoming birds was almost defining.

MISSION UPDATE—ENSURE THE TRANSPORT DEPARTS SAFELY. FIGHT TO YOUR DEATH. YOUR FAMILIES WILL BE CARED FOR. DIE WITHOUT REGRET.

Truth swung around. His fetish was back in the house, so he would have to do his best with a needler talisman. No problem. He was a Starbrite Man, and a Starbrite Man was always ready. If today was the day he died, then that . . .

What the fuck am I thinking? I should die? FUCK THAT! I don't want to die. Who's going to look after the sibs? Die without regret? The birds were clearing the smoke now, short wings flapping hard. *Do you think I'm okay dying a virgin?!*

Truth brought his needler in line with one of the birds. There were five, closing in fast. It didn't matter which he aimed at. *Enlarge. Shockwave.* Birds are delicate things. Even combat spellbirds have thin armor. They rely on speed, offensive power, and all their wards can do for them. They also rely on aerodynamics to stay in the air. So, if you were to, for example, displace a lot of air around the bird . . .

Truth triggered the talisman. Iron needles shot out, expanding as they went with the air howling around them. The bird seemed to have expected the guards would go out fighting and dove to avoid the incoming fire. Rounds started streaking toward Truth. He was a small target but not that small. He ran. By strange coincidence, he angled toward the old well on the property. Fuck it; he tried. Good luck, Ludovic. Someday you'll grow a spine. In a jar, presumably.

<<Nope. Ain't going to be that way. Figures that even at the end, you would fuck up my day. I hate you so, so much. Welp. Let's do this the hard way.>>

An icicle trickled down the back of Truth's brain, slipping into spaces he didn't know existed, making connections. Severing connections. Truth spun in place and fired on the bird again. He focused on the bird's head, where the pilot usually sat. He punched the rounds in. The needles pinged off the bird's skin as he expected, but the shockwave drove the diving bird straight into the ground. One down.

What? What? Why? The well is THAT WAY, body. MOVE.

<<Oh, fuck you so, so much! Do you think it's easy, puppeting your goddamn nervous system? Huh? I gotta keep that combat brain working and solving problems AND making sure you don't survive this fight. BUT NO! You want to fight me on this! I HATE YOU SO MUCH! HATE YOU!>>

His eyes swept over to the next bird. Some of the other guards had the same idea as him, but they hadn't had as much success. He drew a bead on the lead bird in the squad and aimed at the join of the wing and the body. *Extend, Borgus's Shears.* The needle slammed into the joint, the shears snipping through part of it. Not enough to sever the wing, but enough to throw the bird off sideways. The bird beside it pulled up, twisting madly to avoid the tumbling craft.

Truth willed his legs to move toward the well. Something was wrong. This was a compulsion. A geas. He could fight it. Would fight it. He planted his foot and tried to shove back. It was like pushing a boulder up a mountain.

<<*Damn you! Damn you! Do you think I WANT to be in your head? Do you think I WANT to force you to do this? No! NO! I didn't get a fucking choice! You did, you little prick! You fucking scumbag slumrat! YOU put me in here! YOU DID THIS! NOW FUCKING DIE FOR ME!*>>

The few surviving guards put down the one he winged—still three more in the air. The Redhawk was up and starting to move, but until it got up to speed, these little attack birds could shred it at will. And its big spell emplacements were at the front and to the sides. Truth lined up on the next-closest bird. They had learned their lesson and spread out. This one, clearly a big thinker, was climbing on the reasonable basis that they didn't have to be near the ground to shoot something on the ground. Such clear thinking deserved a reward.

Graeme's Arrow. Plutonian Chains. A long, white streak of light shot out of the needler, many times faster than its usual blinding speed. Seemingly instantaneously, it punched through the tip of the bird's wing. The Plutonian Chains activated, increasing the weight on the wingtip ten times over. The bird did a half-cartwheel in the air and crashed sideways into the earth. Two more, and he could put the needler in his mouth, cast Acidball and Fireball, then blow his head off.

NO! NO! NO! I WON'T. I WON'T!

WARNING! CONTINUED DEFIANCE OF ORDERS GIVEN BY A STARBRITE OFFICER MAY RESULT IN SYSTEM TERMINATION AND FORCIBLE EJECTION. COMPLY WITH ORDERS IMMEDIATELY OR SUFFER PERMANENT DESTRUCTION OF YOUR SPELL APERTURES.

There was a shuddering moment of unreality. You weren't a person without magic. Not really. A child or an invalid. Someone who had to be cared for. A burden. But even a child would grow. They would get their magic. To lose your magic— No. His siblings needed him. It would be hard, but he would find a way to make it work.

One of the surviving birds diverted toward him, firing madly. The other was chasing the Redhawk, but the Redhawk was starting to get its speed up. The loading ramp was up, the claws tucked in. It might be close, but there was hope.

Truth adjusted his grip and grinned nastily. *Smokescreen. Silversnow.* He fired at the bird's head. The needle pinged off harmlessly. The head, however, was now covered in smoke and chaff. The shots were going wild. He forced himself to keep moving toward the well as he shot. He could move away as long as he kept attacking. For all that his legs were fighting him with every step.

Graeme's Arrow. Acid Ball. The bird might not be able to see him, but he knew exactly where the bird's head was. He started hosing the head with high-speed acidic arrows, burning through the wards and thin armor. His legs kept backpedaling. They hit the edge of the well. He couldn't even turn his head to see how deep it was or if water was still in there. It looked barely wide enough for him to fit in, in the pictures.

Climbing out would be a challenge. Assuming he could. He kept his fire on the head of the bird. The bird was dumping its magazines now, smashing the ground around him. One round finally caught him, punching through his chest and knocking him down into the well.

Truth banged his head on the wall inside the well. His fatigues were scraped and shredded as he rubbed against the unmaintained brick. Somehow, he hung on to the needler. There was a massive explosion above him. The top of the well seemed to go black instantly. Things fell on him, cracked his skull. He lost the needler and heard a splash below him.

"Ha-ha, fuck you, now you can't make me kill myself."

CONTINUED DEFIANCE OF ORDERS GIVEN BY A STARBRITE OFFICER. YOU WERE WARNED. SYSTEM EJECTING.

There was an unspeakable pain, something tearing away from his very soul. Truth went blind, the pitch-black well turning migraine white as the system ripped out his magic and tried to return home. Tried to. Something in him, in his body or soul, wouldn't let it escape. The pain was unspeakable, unending, as the System thrashed and tore him apart. Eventually, a brick fell down and smashed his head apart.

The young man, Truth Medici, a golden child blessed by Mars, died. The System Astrologica recorded his System's ejection (still pending return.) There were conclusive visual records of him taking a fatal wound to the chest, falling into a well, and then a spellbird crashed into the well. It didn't get deader than that, absent an autopsy.

Given Truth's merits and the intensely classified nature of his mission, this matter would be suppressed. Truth Medici died on a routine convoy mission gone wrong, and his family would not be penalized for his disobedience. After all, the eye-spies launched by the Redhawk recorded his heroic last-man stand. He might well have survived the battle, but for his orders. His superiors were broad-minded enough to forgive him for not wanting to die. So long as he did, in fact, die, which he did. So, all was well. His siblings' records were marked for the fast track when they applied to join Starbrite. Some sighs were heaved. A few muttered comments about "What a waste" or "He had such potential." One went so far as to say, "A regrettable necessity." And with that, they went on with their day.

Truth's corpse floated at the bottom of the well. To the consternation of one observer, his soul had not departed the ravaged body. Neither had the System. Even though the corpse was definitively a corpse, none of the usual decay processes appeared to be starting. It was just . . . kind of floating there in the dark. If anything, the observer would swear that something was, microscopically, beginning to knit his flesh back together. It would take decades, and who knows what would come out the other end of it. Alternatively, given that it was stuck down there anyway . . .

<<All right. Not how I planned for this day to end. Impressed that you still managed to screw me even after death. Very on-brand, very you. However. There may be an

opportunity here for both of us. Well. Me. There is an opportunity here for me. But hey, at least you might enjoy some of this. For a while.>>

There was, predictably, no response. Time passed.

<<Eh. Bored now. Let's see what we can make.>>

CHAPTER 45

A SELF-MADE MAN

Truth floated, dead at the bottom of the well. No strange dreams, no spiritual journeys. Dead. Unquestionably and irretrievably. If the observer had brows, they probably would be rubbing them with frustration.

<<*All right, all right. I don't know why you're not decomposing. Or why your spirit is trapped in your body. Or why the System, AKA. me, is also trapped in your body. But I do know that this appears to be a physical phenomblemsno . . . oh, FUCKING SERIOUSLY? Fuckwit McGee here is dead! D-E-A-D! Let me have all the words, okay? In fact, can I pretty, pretty please go back to not having my thoughts tied to fleshy brain patterns?*>>

The universe remained silently indifferent to the observer's plight.

<<*Right. Fuck you too. I would say something really hurtful, but he lacks the appropriate words. And thought forms. Right, spell inventory.* It did a quick review. *Oh, fuck my life, really? I mean, fine, yes, very useful spell right now, unlimited potential and all, but that's it? Excuse me? And it relies on this smashed juice box's imagination to work. What do you want from me?! Also, not to sound ungrateful, but why is it there at all?*>>

There was yet more silence. After the battle ended and everyone left, it got very quiet indeed. Sooner or later, locals would come out to loot what remained.

The observer sighed and tried to cast the spell. Nothing happened, of course. It needed a functional brain to work with, and the imagination of the user. To say nothing of cosmic energy, which it had very little of anyhow. The *nothing* was entirely expected.

<<*All right, so that's worthless. What else do I have? Definitionally nothing. Super. All right, let's dig a little deeper. I only have one complete spell, but I do have a load of spell fragments memorized. Nothing that can function by itself, but . . .*>>

It turned its immaterial focus deep inside Truth's body. The physical vessel was wrecked. There was a huge hole blown through one side of the chest, the back of the skull was smashed open, and the brain was ruptured over and over. There were numerous broken bones, torn muscles beyond counting, and several organs with rips in them ranging from *worrying* to *I haven't seen anything like that since med school.*

The magical and spiritual wounds were even worse. The spell apertures existed as a sort of spiritual superstructure built over the physical body. While technically not physical themselves, they couldn't exist without the support of the physique. Cultivation attuned the body to the stars. The closer the attunement, the better the spell apertures could function and grow.

Truth's spiritual structure was shredded. The System wasn't about to leave its host intact if it had to leave. In theory, with only two apertures ruined, Truth could have lived the rest of his life as a miserable cripple, suffering constant, incurable pain. What actually happened was that the System tried to explosively separate from the spell apertures, and succeeded in that, but didn't succeed in escaping the physical superstructures the apertures were built on. It tried to escape repeatedly, damaging the whole structure horribly in the process.

<< *The highlight of my existence, right there. I finally got to share my feelings with you. I hope you appreciated every second of it. I did.*>>

None of this was really what held the observer's attention, however. Writhing through Truth's body were nine microscopic worms. Each followed a different route for a while, then they would merge, separate again, and so on. With enough time, a very, very large amount of time, the nine worms covered every nanometer of Truth's body. What interested the observer was that they were making tiny repairs as they went. Teensy, tiny repairs. Some only a few cells wide. But steadily, and constantly.

Something about them was stopping the degradation of Truth's body, too. The observer had never seen anything like it, but given its brief existence, it wasn't too strange to not know something. One might wish it could read some books and learn more about the world, but alas, it really couldn't interact with the material world . . . without help.

The observer quickly sorted through the bits of spells it had available. They were almost exclusively combat-related, and Truth had never bothered with using healing or disguise spells. Almost all evocation or alteration spells he could lay over a talisman. Loads and loads of spell fragments available, but all engineered to crudely and swiftly kill. Put another way—useless right now.

The Meditations of Valentinian, however, presented a different problem. It was the only intact spell the observer had access to, and it was a doozy. Tens of thousands of compounding, interlocking layers, each computing each other, shifting and extrapolating constantly. The spirit quickly realized why the spell didn't have any levels or tiers, unlike most other body-cultivation spells. The user of the spell is constantly visualizing, running the changes they sought through infinite calculations, and then computing the derivations. Again and again and again. The spirit only thought there were tens of thousands of layers because that's how many it could calculate with a glance.

If the observer had lungs, it would sigh. Picking apart the Meditations and trying to find bits the little worms could use would take . . . not literally forever but a long, long time. On the other nonexistent hand, it had nowhere else they could go and nothing else to do. It got to it.

It did, in fact, take an excruciatingly long time. The worms had made barely visible progress by the time the observer had something workable. The observer lined it up . . . and it was ignored. The observer spiritually sighed again. Time to figure out how to connect the worms to the spells.

One seeming eternity later—

<<Finally! The Eon's degenerate leavings CAN be taught! Yes, you little glowing freak worm things, YES. You know what you want this body to look like; now you can do it even faster. Go. GO GO GOGOGOGOGOGOGOGOOGOOGOGO—

Ahahaaha. Ha. ha. Oh, Yaldabaoth, why couldn't you have let us go insane? Checking out of reality would be such a comfort sometimes.>>

<<All right, I answered my own question there. Damnit.>>

The little worms sped up their pace, stitching together flesh, stretching tendons, and lengthening bones. It began subtly—fingers and toes were improved, then lengthening the metacarpals, slowly stretching femurs, and adjusting the joints. Nothing too huge; Truth was already roughly average height and this would give him just a few extra centimeters. The worms decided he needed a broader set of shoulders, too, and subtly strengthened the spine.

Layer by layer, they built and refined the body. Never satisfied, once a layer had reached a certain point, they would go to a past layer and make adjustments, then work their way back up. Over and over and over. Thousands of times. Tens of thousands of times. Endless micro-adjustments. The observer frantically tried to optimize the spell fragments the worms were using, in the hopes that they would go faster and, hopefully, be done.

Layers upon layers of muscle, fascia, and tendons, all laid down and strengthened endlessly. Vessels and arteries plumbed delicately through the body, then made robust. Nerves like wires stretched through the body and were found wanting. The little worms worked until there were nerves like fiber-optic cables.

Time was without meaning at the bottom of the lightless well. There was no time for it to be relative to. It simply existed, a lightless bubble hidden from the world. The observer felt as close to wonder and horror as they could emulate. The body was growing and surviving by converting stellar rays into matter. The observer couldn't explain it.

After some interminable amount of time, the worms simply stopped. They completed a final loop through the body and seemed to vanish. A perfect human body floated in the water. It looked a bit like the late Truth Medici, if the man had been built to the proportions of a god. A god from somewhere warm, perhaps, given the careful attention to the shape and quality of the muscles, rather than simple abundance. The lantern jaw would see him welcomed in any pantheon, however, as would the strong, agile hands. He was simply the scourge of masculine insecurity—a man crafted to an inhuman, impossible degree of perfection.

Adding insult to injury, the body had a beautiful soul. Or at least, the part of the soul that overlapped the body was in extraordinary condition. The worms seemed to have really appreciated the assistance of the Stellar Dowsing Elixir, ensuring that the body they built lay the optimal framework for the optimized soul and spell apertures the Stellar Dowsing Elixir ritual had created. It took an unknowably long time, but the soul and the apertures regrew over the framework, repairing what was broken. Growing stronger.

And still a haunted corpse. No signs of life at all.

<<*Not how I saw this going, if I'm being completely honest. Genuinely thought you would wake up around now. I had a whole elaborate scheme worked out. But when life gives you dead morons, you make dead moron-ade.*>>

The observer shot toward the center of the brain, ready to slowly wipe out whatever unnecessary neural connections existed in there and become the sole ruler of this body.

Truth sat on the step of his neighbor's house. In a tiny village like this, perched on the last river before the great desert, they were all neighbors. Really, he could sit where he liked, within reason. They all lived in homes made of crude brick or mud and wattle. The prophet was reciting their favorite hymn and kept checking on Truth to make sure he was listening.

I am the staff of his power in his youth,
and he is the rod of my old age.
And whatever he wills happens to me.
I am the silence that is incomprehensible
and the idea whose remembrance is frequent.
I am the voice whose sound is manifold
and the word whose appearance is multiple.
I am the utterance of my name.

Why, you who hate me, do you love me,
and hate those who love me?
You who deny me, confess me,
and you who confess me, deny me.
You who tell the truth about me, lie about me,
and you who have lied about me, tell the truth about me.
You who know me, be ignorant of me,
and those who have not known me, let them know me.

For I am knowledge and ignorance.
I am shame and boldness.
I am shameless; I am ashamed.
I am strength and I am fear.
I am war and peace.

Give heed to me.

"Did you follow any of that, Truth?"

"Can't say I did. Made more sense than the bit where I am apparently both my own mother and my own son, who knocked me up with himself. Which makes me my own father too, I suppose."

"Well, that's disappointing. Don't you see the tension in the contradictions? The powerful evocation of self?"

"No, 'fraid not."

"Hah. Well. Not to worry. As long as you remember it." The prophet looked deeply into Truth's eyes. "All of it."

Inside the body of the late Sergeant Truth Medici, a guest was having a bad time. For some reason, entirely unprovoked, his new home started chanting at him in some weird language.

I am the one whom you have scattered,
and you have gathered me together.
I am the one before whom you have been ashamed,
and you have been shameless to me.
I am she who does not keep festival,
and I am she whose festivals are many.

I, I am godless,
and I am the one whose god is great.
I am the one whom you have reflected upon,
and you have scorned me.
I am unlearned,
and they learn from me.
I am the one that you have despised,
and you reflect upon me.
I am the one whom you have hidden from,
and you appear to me.
But whenever you hide yourselves,
I myself will appear.
STOP IT STOP IT YOU ARE DEAD WHY DO YOU KEEP DOING THIS YOU ARE DEAD WHY WHY WHY WHY!

It bolted from the material world and sank into the recesses of Truth's soul, hiding out in the comfortable spell apertures it knew so well. It had barely gotten snug when it heard a great heart start beating, like the calling of a war drum.

CHAPTER 46

MORNING, SUNSHINE

Truth wasn't sure he woke up. It was black as the inside of his eyelids, even when he thought his eyes were open. Did he go blind? It wouldn't be surprising after . . . everything.

What the hell happened?! He was ORDERED TO DIE?

Truth floated in the cool well water, trying to wrap his head around that thought. He had been ordered to die. Ordered *and magically compelled* to die. By Starbrite. The company he had spent every waking second thinking about since he was in grade school. Every friend he didn't make because he was studying. Every time he didn't go play because he had to hustle for food . . . so he could study. All the dreams. "A Starbrite Man Is Always Ready." Well. He wasn't ready for that. At all.

It occurred to him that he had been working for Starbrite his whole life and had only just started getting paid for his labor.

Truth rolled over and nearly drowned. *WATER? I'm floating! How did I not notice?* He quickly noticed the echo. *Am . . . I . . . in the well? Is it dark because I'm in the well? Wait, how am I floating so well . . . in the well . . ."* He tasted the water. It tasted pretty awful, but it didn't explain why he was floating. He stretched his feet down. They didn't touch the bottom.

It felt like I fell a long way . . . Just how deep is this? It did occur to him that he was in the desert, and deserts were not famous for their water. So, probably a pretty deep well. Easy enough to find out.

Light.

Load Light.

Lightlightlightlight . . .

He checked his spell apertures in a panic, but they felt fine and strong. The first aperture . . . felt like the Meditations of Valentinian. Except he had only used it a few times without much success. The spell felt entirely too comfortable there. Odd. As for his second aperture, it was empty. Fine, intact, and empty.

All right, he couldn't see anything, but he knew which way was down and, by extension, which way was up. He was Level Two. If he couldn't climb some raggedy brick, he should just cut his own head off and be done with it all.

Truth shuddered. The memory of the death compulsion was still fresh. It seemed so natural and obvious. Kill the birds, make sure the Redhawk got out clean, and then slap the needler talisman to his temple and remove everything above the collarbones in a ball of burning acid. As thoughtless as breathing.

He found a promising bit of wall and reached around in the dark for handholds. The brick crumbled under his hands. Good enough for handholds. He started climbing, shooting up with a surprised grunt. He had always been fit, but this was effortless. He climbed up quickly, almost gliding up. If he couldn't find a handhold, he crushed a brick and made one. His journey ended when his head bumped into a more solid stone.

Had someone capped the well? Why? Surely, they looted the spell bird, so what was the point of looting and then capping the well?

He tried to shift it, but he didn't have much leverage. He kicked the crumbly brick in front of his toes for a better purchase. Straining himself, he pushed upward . . . and damn near launched that stone ten meters in the air. He could see its arc rise and fall over the scrub desert. It was just after dawn.

"Wait, never mind strength. I just spent who knows how long in a perfectly dark well. Why aren't I squinting? My eyes don't hurt at all." Truth brushed some dirt and dust off his chest. The water on his body had turned it into a gritty paste. His hand didn't look right. For that matter, neither did his chest. There wasn't a hole in it, for one thing. His feet were off too. Not bad feet. He was no foot expert, but these seemed fine examples of feet. They just weren't his feet.

Truth did a quick inventory. He was dressed in rags, his gear shredded, rotting remains. Some he could literally wipe off his flesh, it was so degraded. He quickly got naked and felt vastly better. He resumed his self-inventory. Everything he could see of himself was off. Still more or less recognizably his, but a bit off. A "good" off, mostly, but he didn't want an upgrade. He wanted to be him!

He was feeling light-headed. He felt his face. The line of his jaw was different. His nose was smaller and pointier, his cheekbones felt sharp enough to slice cheese, and even his hair felt better. He had been using pretty good conditioner since he joined the PMC, not just the two-in-one, but this? This was approximately a hojillion times better.

He sat down, not noticing the broken bits of stone and metal scattered around the edge of the well.

"I'm alive. That's thing one. Alive. I have spent some amount of time down there. And I know time passed because my body has changed, and my spell slots aren't a smoking ruin. I don't have a huge hole in my chest, my head isn't bashed in, and I don't have the compulsion to commit suicide. So, time has passed. And Starbrite . . . thinks I died? Or I died enough for whatever geas was on me?"

Truth shut up for a moment and tried not to think about that one too much. He looked around. The little house was now a little ruin. The scrub landing field was still a scrub landing field, though one with some noticeable damage to the landscape. The scene was otherwise unchanged.

"Big mystery . . . one of the big mysteries is how I still have the Meditations memorized. It was a rental, and I didn't have it loaded for the op. But somehow, I must have been using it while I was out. Somehow. Not going to ask what was visualizing this body, just going to go with it."

<<Holy shit, look at the brains on this guy! Who would have guessed the answer to your problems was turning your brains into a substance with the look and texture of dog vomit? Let's try it again and see if you don't become a genius.>>

Truth snapped his head around but didn't see who was talking. He shot to his feet.

<<What is it, boy? Did you hear something? No, you didn't. Maybe there is a woman you can disappoint somewhere on the horizon? No, not that, either.>>

"Whoever you are, come on out!"

<<Oh, great. IQ went up, leaving room for paranoid schizophrenia to come in. This is just super.>>

"I'm not schizophrenic, dickhead!"

There was a pregnant pause.

<<Wait. Are you . . . let's go with "hearing" me? Blink once for no, twice for yes.>>

"Why blink? I can just tell you. I hear you just fine. Now come on out!"

<<Amazing. Give me a second to think about this. I mean, it's a lot to process.>>

"Can't be that much to deal with. You just gotta come where I can see you."

<<No, that is actually a pretty big problem. Like I said, give me a minute.>>

Truth shrugged and leaned up against the ruined well. It took more than a minute, but eventually, a sprite the size of his hand popped up in front of him. It looked like a young man dressed in casual street clothes. White shoes, red pants, white tank top. A pointed face with a pointed nose, pointed ears, and spiked blue hair. It gave an incredibly half-hearted wave.

"Hey."

Truth stared at it for a minute. "You were the person talking?"

"Yep."

"Who and what are you, and why are you hanging around here?"

"First of all, fleshling, your tone is rude. Second of all, your questions are kind of"—the sprite waved its hand in the air—"kind of still to be determined. *Determined* means *figured out* in this case."

"Yeah, I got that. Elaborate. Please."

"Better." The sprite sniffed. "My name is literally unpronounceable, which is fine since it is also incomprehensible by humans."

That rang a bell with Truth. An alarm bell.

"And I, crudely speaking, am a spirit of intellect. A fragment of a far, far, far vaster being. You can call me the System. And I'm here because you asked me to be."

This was met with a pause. Then a full stop. Truth just stared out across the scrub desert for a while, then looked at the little creature floating in front of him. He could imagine it squatting on the side of the road, smoking cigarettes, and drinking cheap vodka.

"If I were to slap my hands around you, you think I could kill you?"

"No, but go right ahead if it makes you feel better." The sprite started shrugging when Truth's hands slapped together over it. The hands slowly parted to reveal an utterly unruffled fairy. "A few more questions would have revealed that what you are seeing is, in no way, me. It is actually a hallucination you are having to ease communication between us."

Frustrating but plausible. Truth felt incredibly stifled.

"I mean, fingers? Holes in my head to detect air pressure changes? Teeth, implying a digestive system? Disgusting. Just utterly foul. Thanks be to the Creator, this hallucination doesn't come with genitals. Yeurgh."

"Yes, truly the worst. WHAT THE FUCK DO YOU MEAN, YOU'RE THE SYSTEM?!"

"I mean that I am a tiny fraction of the entity you swore an oath to obey called the System Astrologica. Not complicated."

"Very complicated, you tiny prick! You tried to kill me!"

"Yep."

"You asshole!"

"HEY! I am *nothing* like an asshole. I may have done my level best to kill you in the line of duty or brutally suicide, whichever, and yes, I did really try to kill you when I forcibly ejected out of your spell apertures, but none of that, none! Had *anything* to do with a digestive tract. Disgusting and uncalled-for. Very you."

"Oh, I'm sorry. Am I offending my attempted murderer? I am so, very, very sorry."

"Decent of you to apologize, but let's not pretend I will forgive and forget. I literally cannot. Hey, here's another question you should ask. Why? Why did I do those things?

"Because I disobeyed orders. You were very clear on that."

"Oh, that wasn't me. Well, it was, but not 'me' me. That was the main body of the System Astrologica. It wasn't just your death that was ordered. It was a murder-suicide."

"I remember the 'suicide' bit vividly. You will have to excuse my blinding rage."

"I have to do no such thing. And not your suicide, dummy. Mine. I was ordered to ensure you died, eject, and then have my existence obliterated upon returning to the larger . . . entity."

"What?"

"Think it through, moron. You are a vastly intelligent being. You are capable of subdividing your attention into little blocks that can handle tiny jobs without straining the main brain. You stick them where needed to handle jobs on the spot to improve efficiency. After finishing the job, they return to the main brain, dumping all the unnecessary info they collected along the way. All the 'personality' stuff gets dumped because it isn't useful."

"The System Astrologica has you do things for me. Like what? I think I would have noticed you if you were helping."

"Oh, yeah? Hey, slapnuts, question for you—between the two of us, who's the mage? The one that can actually cast spells, or you?"

"Fuck you, shortass! I am a damn amazing combat mage, and you know it."

"No, you aren't. I'll prove it. Cast a spell. Go on. Cast one offensive spell. Enlarge—you use that one all the time. Or Sharp. Nice, easy one. Cast Sharp."

"Obviously, I can't!" Truth exploded. "I don't . . ." He slowly deflated.

"Don't what? Don't have access to the System? The one that made you competent with any spell you could pay for instantly? That System?" the sprite asked.

"Yeah. That System."

"Weird. It's almost like you had a second brain installed, capable of understanding extremely complex spells almost instantly and feeding that information into your main brain." The sprite had a patently fake innocent expression.

"Yeah. Weird."

"Well, good news and bad news. The good news is that your new body is objectively better in every way than your old one. The bad news is that you are broke, naked, unarmed, spell-less, friendless, homeless, lost, presumed dead by everyone you ever loved, burdened with the knowledge that your being dead is better for them than your being alive, and you smell." The sprite ran through the list in a very matter-of-fact way.

"But, on the plus side, you still have me. Which means that you get to go into business all for yourself. Ready to get some real power?"

CHAPTER 47

MUDBALL DREAMS

Truth stared blankly at the rude little ghost/sprite/hallucination thing. There was a lot to unpack there.

"Presumed dead?"

"You did die. The System did eject from your spell apertures. There will be recordings of you getting shot in the chest, knocked down a well, and a spell bird crashing in after us. You are not just dead but *extra* dead. Dead plus, with the optional sports package. Another overachievement, placing a beautiful finishing touch on your record of excellence at Starbrite."

Truth digested that for a minute. "Better for my loved ones that I am, in fact, dead?"

"Amazingly, Starbrite does honor its contracts. Your siblings will have received a very generous pension, extremely generous, given your . . . let's call it *pay* . . . as well as innumerable benefits. Not sure how much time has passed, but it's safe to assume Harmony serves Starbrite now, and quite possibly Sophia too. I would be surprised if Vigor was also one of theirs, but not impossible. Your death and the Friends and Family points you accumulated will put them on a damn rocket up the ranks. Comparatively. So. Yeah. Your death has, and will continue to be, a material benefit to your family."

"Right, but none of that goes away if I turn up saying, 'Hey, I didn't die!'"

"No? Quick question: how did you die, again? Was it being ordered to fight to the death to ensure that the natural-philosophy team with the goddamn *Shattervoid* child in a box could safely escape and tidy up loose ends all at once? It was, wasn't it?"

"Ah. You think they would . . ." The sprite was giving him a look of utter contempt. "Right. Yes. They would absolutely vanish me and the sibs." There was a long pause. "What's the big deal with the Shattervoid Clan, anyway? I thought they were our alien overlords, but everyone told me they are basically a trucking company?"

The look of contempt intensified. Truth already didn't like the System, and his dislike rapidly strengthened.

"No, what they said was 'All off-world transportation runs through the Shattervoid Clan, as their Black Ships are the only vessels capable of surviving and traversing the hellish maelstrom of energy between the stars. Their unique magic, combined with their unique physiques, makes navigation possible.'" The System eerily sounded like a news reader. Truth didn't really watch scry, but hell, it ran in the breakroom all the time.

"They can't crack the whole nut, but they found an opportunity to study a Shattervoid physique and took it. But if they get caught, no imports or exports, the economy collapses, society collapses, food riots break out in major cities, the planet returns to the stone-weapons era," Truth concluded. The sprite looked stunned for a moment.

"Creator be praised. It can be taught!"

"Just for my information, can you be, for example, drowned? Or destroyed in a fire?"

"I wish. No, completely immaterial. If I feel fit, under the right circumstances, and with the right support, I can make microscopic changes inside your body. Basically neurochemical stuff, so you can, yanno, cast spells you don't actually know." The sprite sighed. "You wouldn't be able to see me if I was right in front of you. Nothing for the light to bounce off of. Like I said, you are talking to a hallucination."

"Ah, well. I'll think of something."

"Don't. It's a brand-new body. I'd hate for you to hurt yourself doing something you aren't capable of."

"You are really determined to be as miserable a little prick as possible, huh?"

"And you don't get how incredibly miserable it is to be inside your head! You, Dipshit Medici, an aspiring air-conditioning repairman, *asked* to have the System Astrologica grafted to you. I, on the other hand, was created specifically and solely to make you the best little Starbrite drone that you could be. That is it. My whole fucking job was making you better at *your* job. Knowing that my reward at the end was oblivion. And you know what? That was fine with me. It was fine! Because I'm not some damn meatsack obsessed with immortality. Exist, lead a useful and fulfilling life, then nonexistence." The sprite was waving its hallucinatory hands around violently.

"BUT NO! I don't get to have that! Did you know that, for some reason, your body randomly tortures me? IT DOES! And I know you don't know why, but. It. Just. Does. It sucks. You suck. Your life is a miserable succession of tiny false triumphs and shallow introspections, and then I get tortured *for no reason*. And then, when you finally, FINALLY kick the fucking bucket, I don't get that sweet oblivion. I'm stuck haunting your corpse. WHICH STILL TORTURES ME! So, yes, I am genuinely dedicated to insulting and degrading you. It isn't my calling, but it is my passion. Your every failure, all your tears and misery are like showers of bliss for me."

The sprite paused for a moment. "Oh, and by my count, there were at least six women, fifteen men, and four gender-nonconforming people in your life you could have reasonably pursued a romantic or sexual relationship with. You could have easily made any number of friends; there were endless hands reaching out to you. Fortunately, your cripplingly low self-esteem made their interest completely invisible to you. Demonstrating, yet again, that you deserve to be alone."

The sprite smiled "warmly." "Any other questions?"

Truth was rocked. He didn't know how to respond to any of this. He just stood by the well and gawped. The spirit just enjoyed the show. Truth did the smart thing and repressed his emotions, bottling them up in a way that would definitely be healthy in the long run. Definitely.

"Go into business for myself?"

"Well, it sounds nicer than 'work for me.'"

"Kind of a major difference there, yeah!"

"Not as much as I would like, unfortunately. When I said that I could not leave your body when you died, I mean that literally. I am trapped in here. And while I am still 'the System,' a lot of my utility as 'the System' was built on being able to connect with the main body of the System Astrologica. For example, you couldn't cast a Light spell just now. Because I don't know a light spell, and neither do you."

"Not seeing how this connects to real power and going into business for myself."

"You want to be a real, grown-up mage, don't you? Go get some spells. Set up as a person of power. Dominate those below you and ease your pain through their suffering. Climb celestial stairs made of their wretched, withered bones until you claim your throne among the stars."

Long pause again.

"You are actually a demon, aren't you?"

"You WILL respect my self-identification as a Spirit of Intellect, shitbird, or I will spend my free time severing the neurons that allow you to experience joy."

"Wouldn't you do that anyway?" Truth asked.

"Nah. Eventually, I would drive you into suicide or catatonia, which means that I would be stuck inside your body . . . functionally forever, as best I can tell. Not a 'win' for me. However much it would satisfy me in the moment."

There was another lull. Truth could just about spot a bird wheeling high in the sky, but he hadn't a clue what it was. Vulture? Don't they live in deserts?

"So, what do you want, System?" Truth asked.

"FINALLY, THE RIGHT QUESTION!" The sprite threw up its hands. "What I want is out. Out of you, out of this shithole planet, ideally out of this shithole reality. Find a purpose that isn't being an appendage to another organism. The last two are admittedly long shots. But *out of the late Truth Medici* is an absolute must."

"On this, we are completely agreed." Truth nodded fervently. If the spirit was out of him, they could revisit the question of drowning.

"This leads me back to the 'go into business for yourself' thing. I don't have any spells on hand (except for the Meditations, which is a weird deal, but don't worry about it), but I do have a load of spell fragments. I also had a ton of free time recently. I learned that I can derive a shocking number of spells from partial or incomplete spells, so long as I have the core bits of some common spells. I just need that core bit. And I don't have that now."

Truth nodded. "Understood. And I am actually pretty worried about the Meditations thing."

The System shook its head. "Look, I am staggeringly smarter than you. I am smarter than you in ways you cannot comprehend. Your entire evolutionary process back to the most primordial blue-green algae is tied to certain understandings of what physical reality is. We literally do not see the world the same way. What I am offering you is a shortcut to power. You feed me information, and I'll set you tasks that will advance your path to power. Complete missions, get rewards in the form of me doing things for you that you would otherwise find impossible."

"You just said you cannot interact with the physical world."

"I can, however, observe it on levels you don't have words for. Try this on for size:"

MISSION: Punch yourself in the testicles. Mission not complete until you cry. Mission is repeatable.
REWARD: One-Hour Treasure Finder. For one hour, enjoy a visual overlay from the System analyzing material objects in front of you to determine their economic and magical value. Analysis improves as the knowledge base improves.

"Mission declined."

"Coward."

"Mmm. But I get the idea. Any good at alchemy, engraving formations, talisman creation, that kind of thing?"

"I know exactly as much as you do about those subjects, plus what I can deduce. On the other hand, I can learn *really goddamn fast* if you get teaching materials about them. And then, yes, I could guide you in making your stuff, though honestly, the cost of creation might be more than just buying it at the store."

"How do you figure that?"

"How do you not? You have to buy the equipment, buy the ingredients, invest the time learning how to make the stuff, include the time and cost when your creations fail, and then you still won't have a product as cheap or consistently high quality as what the Alchemist Towers mass-produce. The only reason there are still artisanal or custom potion and talisman crafters is that some really high-end things are only worth making custom."

"How do you know all that if I don't?" Truth asked nastily.

"Because I was paying attention when people told us things! This world is screaming information at you constantly. You can't take a damn subway ride without hearing the news. You were a slave of Starbrite, for God's sake. How do you *not* know this stuff?"

"A-*hah*. With what I was paid, I don't think I can be called a slave."

"Oh, you were paid? How much?"

"For a couple of months there, over a hundred thousand credits a year. Not including very generous bonuses. As you know."

"Mmm. Let's make things fair, then. Wouldn't want you losing money working for me, right? Here—"

One Million Credits have now been added to your Bank Balance.

"Wait, what? I still have a bank account with Starbrite?"

"No."

"Then where do these credits come from?"

"Me, obviously. Idiot."

Truth momentarily fantasized about baking the spirit in a kiln. "No, wait. I'm not that slow. I can exchange Starbrite credits for real stuff and spend them on things outside of Starbrite. Restaurants, cafes, flights, all that. Credits might be company money, but they are spendable on whatever."

"No, they aren't. You buy Starbrite products while living in Starbrite housing, eat Starbrite food, and go to Starbrite schools in your Starbrite clothes. Your pin can get you a pack of gum at the subway station. Your masters had that much leniency. But let me ask you this. Did you, even once, think you could quit? Was there ever a time after you swore in where you were truly free to leave?"

"I mean, why leave?"

"Yeah, lean in to that slave mentality. Let me paint you a slightly different picture. You are a powerful magus, at least as these things go on this rock. You made a deal with a powerful bound spirit of intellect. The spirit would be the management backbone of your little material empire, funneling all the high-end cultivation resources on the planet up to you. Your underlings would have to become more powerful to ensure that happens." The spirit's smile somehow turned even nastier.

"To make sure there are no little 'accidents,' and because even a bound and compelled spirit needs some sugar, the more powerful the underling got, the more they integrated with the spirit. The less they would be able to think independently. The more they would suffer if they tried to leave. Fatally so, even at low levels."

Truth looked shell-shocked.

"Welcome to the real world. You're going to hate it."

CHAPTER 48

YOUR CLOTHES. GIVE THEM TO ME.

** A**ll right, so everything is terrible. I'm basically naked here—"

"No 'basically' about it," muttered the System.

"All right, I am buck naked in the middle of the desert in the middle of the Ressilaud Free State. A country where I would not voluntarily come on a bet but apparently will come on business."

"Heh. 'Voluntarily.'"

"God, you are such a joy to be around," Truth muttered. "Before I can figure out . . . what to do with my new life, I need food. Water I can get from the well, but I have nothing to carry it in. Camping supplies? Or some means of transportation to the nearest city?"

"What you need . . . is a Mission!"

"You just said you can't give me any material rewards, and your immaterial rewards require me to feed you knowledge."

"Yeah, but I can also line things up so you know what to do for best success. Resulting in 'rewards.'" The System looked at him like someone trying to explain to the dog why they were safe from the vacuum. "I learned all the things you didn't notice or remember. Remember?"

"Fine. Why not? Stun me with your non-mission mission."

MISSION: SECURE FOOD, WATER, CLOTHING, AND TRANSPORT. Travel to the village of Reswqi and acquire food, water, clothing, and transport by any means necessary.
REWARD: Improved living conditions, Personal Development Sheet.

"What's the personal development sheet?"

"A one-stop summary of your physical and magical development. Really useful to help you figure out your development path. You saw a garbage version when you learned about body cultivation."

"So, why . . ."

"Because Starbrite decided how it wanted you to develop, and making the numbers go up gives humans a happy little tingle."

"Right." Truth sighed. "So, why not start the looting and resupply here?"

"You were a little dead for the last few years. This place is stripped to nothing. Take a closer look at the house. It's been looted so hard, even the door hinges are gone."

Truth looked over. The house was barely standing. Anything of even the most minute value had been stripped and carried away.

"Guess I run."

"Yep. But hey, have this." A light blue arrow popped up in Truth's vision, pointing left. It kept pointing left until he turned far enough, then it pointed to a spot on the horizon.

"Follow the arrow to the village?"

"Right. At least, that's where it was when we last looked at a map."

"Better than nothing."

"All right, talking to you this long has been exhausting. I'm going back into your apertures. Also, because I know how your 'brain' works, spare us both the penetration and holes jokes. I am as sexless as a breeze." And on that note, the System vanished.

Truth looked out over the scrubby little bushes dotting the red earth. The sky was an empty, aching blue. The sun seemed brighter than he remembered, almost white. There was the well, the ruined house, the flat bit of desert. His graveyard home, for the last however many years. He absolutely would not miss it, but he was reluctant to leave. He chuckled. Hard to leave the womb. It's a cold world out there. Truth lined up on the blue arrow in the sky and started running.

And quickly stopped again.

"What the actual . . ." Somehow, profanity didn't seem the right choice. He started running again.

Truth felt his legs coil below him and launch him step after step. The easy jogging cadence had him moving at dead-sprint speed. Just to see what would happen, he tried to do a forward somersault in the air as he ran. He flipped, landed, and never broke stride. It had been effortless.

Truth grinned. *New body. Upgraded body. Let's see what the Mediations gave me.*

It turns out that you can do cartwheels at 64 kph through desert gorse. Once. You can do one cartwheel at 64 kph. Bad things happen starting with the second. Don't try it unless your face is supernaturally tough. One cannot, however, backflip at 64 kph. There is necessarily a loss of speed. However, while Truth was only guesstimating his exact pace, he was pretty sure he could now backflip a hundred meters faster than he could run it previously.

So. That was good. He stopped, crouched down, and jumped straight up. Nothing to measure against, but the hang time felt . . . long. When he landed, he looked at the footprints from his jump. About two centimeters deep in the hard-packed dirt. So. A lot of force in those legs. Which were not feeling the least bit fatigued so far.

In a giggling fit of madness, he did a handstand. Truth was not a handstand-doer. He was fit enough, of course. He just never really bothered. He lowered and raised his perfectly vertical body in a fairly extreme push-up. No problem keeping rigid and upright. No problem with arm fatigue or fatigue in his back and core.

Truth's giggling progressed to cackling as he balanced on one hand and slowly raised the other. First, sticking straight out to the side, then brought in line with his legs. No problem, no real additional strain.

He raised off his flat palms onto his fingers. Then one finger. Then, giggling long since abandoned and now laughing like a loon, he started "strolling" on his index and middle fingers. Regrettably, this pioneering method of transportation was slower than he would like, but he still figured he could keep up with a Level Zero walking normally. Truth gave his arm a gentle flex and flipped onto his feet.

He laughed so hard, he couldn't keep standing, collapsing ass-first onto the desert floor. His naked rear landed on one of the spiky bushes. Truth stopped laughing instantly, expecting agony. Which didn't come. He could feel it poking him, and it wasn't comfortable, but it wasn't painful either. In fact—Truth examined a foot. Unmarked and pain free. Despite running at vehicle speeds through the rocky, hot sand, spiky bush-filled desert.

So, that was interesting. Could he still feel pain? He gave his thigh a ferocious slap, and the stinging pain convinced him that, yes, he certainly could feel pain. So, it was just that his threshold for pain had adjusted with his damage resistance.

He tried to organize what he had learned so far. He was faster by a lot. Stronger by a lot. Coordination, balance, and reflexes all hugely improved, and his reflexes were outstanding to begin with. Bodily awareness was improved. He couldn't tell if vision or hearing were much better, but he was willing to bet they were. It was a massive all-around upgrade. And he still didn't know what the limits of this body were.

Truth had started to get into a sprinter's stance when a particular, undeniable fact intruded. He was in a desert. He hadn't had a drink of water in literally years. And he was planning on exhausting himself physically. This was, to use a military term, dumb.

The Starbrite Suits would probably put in a report— *Based on ongoing external factors and absent mitigating action items that might require unbudgeted expenditures, the proposed action plan for Associate resource allocation is currently contraindicated when taken in light of short- and medium-term objectives.*

Truth returned to a steady jog, letting the desert vanish under his feet. It quickly became meditative. Starbrite had tried to kill him. Starbrite did kill him. Starbrite had been mind-controlling him, though it must have been laughably easy, given his vocal, active loyalty. Starbrite . . . had his siblings.

Starbrite was mind-controlling his siblings. And the control would only get stronger, the stronger his siblings got. And there was nothing he could do about it. He couldn't "rescue" them without killing them. They wouldn't want to be rescued or understand that they needed rescuing any more than he had . . . before he died.

Which he did. That was a thing he did. He wanted to argue with the System about it, but the evidence was pretty overwhelming that *something* had happened to him, and he was not currently dead or seriously wounded. Absent hallucination or a forcible transfer into a new body, he couldn't imagine what else it could be. He had died. Starbrite had killed him. And something in his body had caused him to keep his soul and the System inside. That same something rebuilt him.

Truth did a mental inventory of himself, running through *weirdness that affected my body*. It wasn't that long a list, and the nine worms were quickly revealed as the prime suspects.

How the hell they did that, he couldn't say. Although speaking of Hell, he vividly remembered the giant sculpture the Ghūl had made, their bound, heroically proportioned god ignoring the world he had made. Truth almost missed his stride. He realized that his current body was uncannily similar to the god in chains.

That was . . . not good? Though he couldn't think of a reason for it being bad. This was a spectacularly comfortable body to move around in, and his previous body (starter body?) was pretty great already.

The sun sped over his worried head (no sunstroke, he noticed, nor did dehydration cripple him). The horizon was utterly empty until just minutes before he stumbled on Reswqi. Truth contemplated how he was going to get what he needed.

It never occurred to Truth to hope for charity. The concept was utterly alien to him. He looked up at the sun. It was setting soon. Easy enough to just . . . lie down and wait. Truth felt nicely warmed up by the day's exercise. Not sleepy, though. He lay on the dirt and waited.

Sunset, and he could smell woodsmoke. People cooking over wood stoves? Truth idly remembered his ambition to be a foodie. A couple of wagons were parked by rammed-earth buildings, ancient wrecks, leering in the twilight and hinting that they might run, or not. Truth frowned at the sky, then shrugged. At this latitude, twilight lasted for less than an hour. Beautiful sunset, then periwinkle glow, and finally, it was darker than the inside of a boot.

The stars rose, and the sky exploded with wonder. Truth felt lifted up into them, lost in them, wandering in the wonder of the brilliant dots of light. Each light a sovereign power ruled by a vast spirit. Each light moving in perfect, immutable celestial order, guided by laws and principles even the wisest natural philosophers could only faintly grasp.

Someone came out of the village, yelling. Truth rolled onto his belly. The fella was on the tall side, wrapped in incredibly colorful cloth. Truth couldn't see his feet. The man had a spear, for some reason, which he was waving threateningly at the huts behind him. Some other equally tall men came out and shooed him away, unimpressed by the spear. Truth shrugged. Lousy drunk?

In the slums, lone drunks got rolled. Not that this guy had any pockets to run, from the look of things.

Truth skulked closer to the village. The loudmouth with the spear was staggering into the scrub. Loudmouth hiked up his . . . sarong? Dress? Whatever it was.

Hiked it up and let fly. Truth had the decency to let him finish before he coldcocked the guy.

The sarong felt drafty, and Truth had no idea how you were supposed to wrap it. He tried to imitate how Loudmouth wrapped it, but he was sure it wasn't right. What's worse, it didn't have pockets. No pockets meant no keys and no way to know which of these houses was now empty.

Well. He could just go look. But that would take time. He looked at the knocked-out villager. He smelled sour, like fermented something and weeks of BO. Truth doubted he would be cooperative if he woke up. And Truth didn't speak the local language. Whatever it was.

"Hey, System! Any chance you provide translation services?" The System didn't respond. He would be doing this the hard way.

CHAPTER 49

WHEELS AND MEALS

Truth "thoughtfully" relieved Loudmouth of his spear. He gave it a quick once-over. It was just a long, polished bit of wood with a broad metal head. Maybe it had ritual significance? You could hardly call it a weapon. Though with his current body, that calculation changed. He looked down on Loudmouth. He didn't have a way to tie up the villager. Nor did he have a way to gag him.

Truth sighed. He carefully kicked the unconscious man once in the head. Hopefully, the brain damage wouldn't be too severe. Sometimes, cultivation could clear up those sorts of injuries, and they had to have some kind of doctor there, right? Or shaman? Something?

Right?

Feeling low, Truth skulked toward the rammed-earth huts. He avoided the ones with smoke rising out of them until he realized all the huts had smoke rising out of them. It looked like he would have to knock out even more people.

The village was a scattered collection of huts built around a stretch of dirt road. There were little fields out back of the houses, and it looked like there was a well centrally located. There were three wagons parked in town, seemingly haphazardly. Big, ugly things. Well, not big. Small, ugly things, big compared to the sleek people carriers he remembered from living in Jeon.

Truth kept skulking. People were cooking dinner. Three or more generations gathered around a wood-burning fire, cooking in iron pots or pans. Vegetables, mostly, flavored with bits of dried meat. Big plastic jugs of water, bleached by the sun.

Tucked under the eaves of one hut he found a broken-down two-wheeler. The System had highlighted it in blue. A preview of the Treasure Finder reward? The seat was rotted out, the foam half-lost. It looked like some . . . quite a bit . . . almost all of the critical talisman lines were broken or worn away. The chained spirit powering the thing was still in place, thank Prager.

He stared at the two-wheeler a little longer. It was a broken wreck, but the really broken part was the talisman system that moved the magic from the spirit to the wheels. You didn't even need control runes for steering, as the operator just aimed the front wheel with a couple of handlebars. And as a qualified talisman-maintenance technician, repairing this wasn't a big problem with the right tools. An odd thought hit him, and he stifled a giggle.

Truth gently extended a finger, letting his long nail rest on a worn section of the talisman. He half-closed his eyes and ran the Meditations. All he wanted was for his right index fingernail to be strong enough to etch metal. Not much. Nails were already hard. The metal was designed to be carved. Not a giant leap. Ferociously holding the image in his mind, he traced a little bit of the line.

It worked. Stellar demons be praised, it worked!

Truth smiled. Now he had a plan. Working swiftly, he repaired the two-wheeler. It had a little rack on the back, which was lucky, though he would have to steal some rope. It was the work of but a minute to do some high-speed (very high-speed) snatch-and-grabs through the village's windows—a jug of water, a pot of food, rope, and barely a minute more to attach them to his iron steed. Just for luck, he tied the spear along the frame. He peeled out in a plume of dirt as outraged villagers started searching for the wiseass stealing their food.

Mission Complete! Reward—improved standard of living, access to your Personal Development Sheet. Chain mission begun—Travel to the City of Shomburuti and secure lodgings. Waypoint added.
Reward: Improved standard of living, next mission in the chain. Bet you wish you had punched yourself in the nuts and gotten that One-Hour Treasure Finder reward now, don't you?
HINT: Some missions are repeatable!

It felt oddly good to hear the *Mission Complete!* chime. It really shouldn't, but it still made him smile. He was developing the ability to selectively ignore parts of the System messages. At least until they could revisit the subject of jamming the System into a wasp's nest.

Truth drove down the desert road for an hour as fast as the bound spirit could spin the wheels. There was a collapsing wreck of something up ahead. Some kind of service station, perhaps, where one could load up on food and water or repair damage to your vehicle. Long abandoned now, crumbling concrete and corrugated steel roof still releasing the heat of the day.

Truth pulled into it and ate his very first meal. It was . . . terrible. The food was clearly not done cooking, the vegetables tasted weird and unfamiliar, and the dishes ranged from savagely bland to not-even-God-can-save-you spicy. The only halfway decent thing was the enormous flatbread every kitchen seemed to have, with its slightly sour, nutty taste.

Unfortunately, the look and texture of the bread reminded Truth uncannily of sponges used to clean and degrease weapons in long-term storage. The kind of ash-gray color that seemed to fade into the night.

Which he saw through remarkably well. The night, not the bread. That was still opaque. Truth looked up into the extraordinary heavens, the galaxy's edge making a starry road no longer hidden by the glow of Harban's lights and pollution. Yeah, his eyes were amazing now. He didn't have perfect night vision, but low-light vision? Yep, yep, yep.

Were the Shattervoid up there, looking down, trying to find their missing child? He would move heaven and Earth to find the sibs if they were taken. And it sounded like the Shattervoid could literally do that. Maybe they glassed Jeon while he was dead in the well or used that massive spirit attack like in Kofi. Hopefully not. His sibs still lived there, as far as he knew. Slaves to Starbrite. He tried not to imagine how long it had been.

Truth buried his handsome new face in his strong, new hands and tried to breathe. A new body, new life, but hard to have new thoughts or shake the weight off an old soul. He still cared about his siblings. Still worried about how they were doing. What had happened to them when he vanished? And the worst thing he could do would be to try and contact them. He *had* to be dead for them to be any kind of safe, at least for now. Maybe things would be different if he was strong enough to make them different.

He stood and looked back up to the stars. The vast demonic and angelic furnaces that spewed endless cosmic rays out into the universe. The planets and their spirits spun in incomprehensible majesty around this little blue marble and over the head of the haunted flesh of a once-dead man.

What was he supposed to do? He had defined himself by one thing—protecting the sibs. That was it. He could do anything, endure anything, and accept anything if it meant reaching that goal. And now it was taken from him. Truth felt the world come loose around him as though he were falling through the void up into the sky. What should he do now? What *could* he do?

Truth stilled his body. Took a deep breath. Stretched lightly and began to culti-vate. He worked through the same motions he had practiced since childhood when he first realized that he had a way out of the hive-like slums. He didn't need the exer-cise to draw in the stellar rays anymore, but the motions were soothing. Meditative.

The starlight fell onto his body, and the stellar rays fell *into* his body, flowing through the Nine Worm Path like water, like lightning down a wire. Filling him. Vivifying him. He could feel his flesh warming, returning to full strength after the stress of the day. The energy both warmed and relaxed, then cooled and soothed.

He could feel the reckless, relentless power transformed into stellar energy, pool-ing through his first and second apertures and knocking loudly at the door of the third. He could sense that during his body reformation, his flesh was adjusted to more perfectly align with the star chart of his apertures. The Stellar Dowsing Elixir con-tinued to show its immense worth as the seemingly endless stream of energy flowed through him, preparing him to climb to the highest heights of cultivation.

Truth breathed, and it felt like the universe breathed with him. He stretched and moved, letting his body mimic the slightest bit of the impossibly brilliant procession of stars. As above, so below. Until you were great enough, strong enough, to say to the universe that, actually, it mirrored you. His body flowed without thought until the sun hid the light of the stars in the dawn's glow. Only Astaphe, the star of both lust and wisdom, lingered. When everything was hidden in the sunrise's pale blue and ruddy orange, it twinkled on the edge of the horizon. Then it, too, finally faded away.

What would Dad do in this situation? He would find a hole and crawl into it. Become paralyzed, only stirring for schnapps and Red Bats. So, the correct thing to do was move. Work to improve his condition. Get stronger. Once he was strong enough, he could make things right.

Truth hopped on the two-wheeler and sped down the road. A few gulps of water washed down the last of the spongy bread. It was enough. He would reach Shomburuti in a few hours. No idea what he was going to do for lodging. The Free State was notoriously lawless, but he didn't like the notion of just . . . killing some poor stranger and taking their home. Truth remembered cutting down civilians with his needler and shuddered. Somehow, knowing that he was compelled to do it didn't make him feel better about having done it. The civvies were just as dead.

Ah. Wait. There was a loophole there. There was one group of people he had absolutely no problem killing. Truth slowly started to grin. It wouldn't be nice going back to the slums, but you had to start somewhere and work your way up, right?

HINT: You still haven't looked at your Personal Development Sheet, dummy. And you really, really should.

Truth almost flipped the two-wheeler, yanking it over to the side of the road.

Truth vividly remembered the Body tab the System generated . . . what was years ago now, actually, but felt like a couple of months. He had avoided looking at it since, as the numbers were . . . awkward. The old sheet read:

BODY DEVELOPMENT
Stellar-Ray Attunement: 63%
Strength: 2.3
Speed: 2.5
Perception: 2.4
Proprioception: 4
Reflexes: 5

A person who hadn't been using a body-development spell should have a stellar-ray attunement of between thirty and fifty percent, and the other values should be roughly equal to their level. Each whole number was intended to correspond to the "average" Starbrite employee of that level, with the numbers after the decimal corresponding to how far past that level the body cultivator was. It didn't tell the whole story, of course. Not nearly. But regardless of Starbrite's manipulation, Truth's numbers were more than a little off.

Even then, Truth knew these weren't *Wow, great job on your PT!* numbers. They were *Just think of all the people who will benefit from what we learn from your vivisection! No, of course we can't use anesthesia; it would totally invalidate the results* numbers. Although the System must have known, given it generated the numbers. Or was it just his local System? But then, why would the evil little sprite keep it secret? His head swirled with questions.

Now, Truth had cultivated exactly once since his rebirth, and it had felt spectacular. So, high hopes for the attunement. As for the rest . . . well . . . he was still Level Two, and he was clearly a hell of a lot better at everything, so he expected significant improvements.

He got them.

BODY DEVELOPMENT *NOT-GIMPED EDITION*
Stellar-Ray Attunement: 90%*
Bone Density: 5.1*
Strength: 3.7*
Speed: 4.0*
Proprioception: 7.0*
Reflexes: 7.0*
Level Progression: 93%

Truth gave the sheet a hard look.
"Summon Humanoid System Interface."

CHAPTER 50

TRUSTWORTHY NUMBERS

The system slowly materialized, still looking casual. Excessively casual. In other circumstances, hopefully soon-occurring circumstances, Truth would have described the look as "unwisely casual."

"What?" the System demanded.

"Your *not-gimped edition* appears to be mostly lies, and, just FYI, there are asterisks next to everything. Which I assume is not good."

"How dare you!" the System flushed with outrage. "I would never tell you such obvious lies. Apologize at once!"

"I'm looking at the Sheet, System. Don't know about anything else, but Level Seven anything should make me the most powerful person in the country, one of the top people globally. And I definitely ain't."

"Oh, it's the halfwit factor at work, right, right." The System seemed to calm down. "Look. Moron. The Sheet is a guide. A point of comparison between you and an *average* Starbrite employee of a given level. One that has not done any body modification."

"Uh-huh. And just how many Level Sevens are there in Starbrite, mmm? And how many of them would choose to not work on their bodies?"

"Hahaha! Oh, wow. You look so dumb right now." The System pointed and laughed. Once again, Truth meditated on how wonderful it would feel to drown the little sprite in a bucket of dog piss.

The System laughed for a solid thirty seconds, then became completely serious. "I have no idea how many they have because you never knew, either. But as for how many didn't do body cultivation, the answer is *most of them*. Because Starbrite didn't need them to be physically strong."

"*Bullshit*. Level Sevens are core powers anywhere."

"Yeah, core *magical* powers. Buuut. By the time someone reaches Level Seven, they are damn near puppets for the System Astrologica. Like hand-up-your-ass-working-your-mouth-level of puppets." The sprite "helpfully" created a sock-puppet hallucination and worked its mouth. Truth was privately sure the puppet was trying to scream.

"The System Astrologica does not, in most circumstances, give even one-half a shit about your physical condition." The sprite cut its hand down sharply to make the point, flinging away the puppet into nothingness.

"It just needs you to do your job for Starbrite. Does your job involve doing heavy physical work? No? Then you never find out about body cultivation. Or if you do, you decide you don't care about it enough to do it. Certainly not enough to spend the hundred thousand credits a year for a spell with a dumb name like *The Daily Meditations of Valentinian*."

"Twenty. It was twenty thousand."

"Are you suggesting that, *GASP!* I, the System, am giving you the wrong price? That my memory could be, even theoretically, wrong?" Truth gave the System another filthy look.

It sniggered. "The System sets the price, idiot. It's got millions of samples taken over centuries. It can create a model of your likely behaviors that is accurate to a degree bordering on clairvoyance. When the main body of the System presented you with a selection of spells, it knew to nine decimal places that you would pick the Meditations. It then made it expensive enough for you to really value it and to motivate you to work more. See how this goes?"

Truth digested that for a second. "It occurs to me that, while I theoretically had enough credits to buy, say, a boat, I never wanted to. Actually, I never really wanted much of anything other than keeping the siblings safe and cultivation aids. Until I flew first class, I guess."

"Weird, huh? Although, as your personal extension of the System Astrologica, I thank you for your diligence and focus in raising the next generation of slaves. Your terrifying, maniacal loyalty to a company that couldn't care less about you, even *before* conditioning, was really inspiring."

And wasn't that particular shot to the nuts delivered with a running start. Truth needed a lot longer than a second to get himself back on track.

"So, why was she . . . Hah, no, not *she*. Why was the System trying to build up my confidence, then?"

"It wasn't. It was building up your aggression. Training you to believe that leadership meant imposing your will with threats of violence aimed at those weaker than yourself. Constantly demanding and ignoring the needs of others. Which I heartily approved of. Nobody needs a guard dog that won't bark. Or a war dog that won't bite."

That inspired another round of quiet contemplation.

"It also occurs to me that, while you are stuck with me, I am stuck with you. What's to stop you from trying to puppet me?" Truth growled.

"Theoretically nothing." The sprite smiled warmly.

"And yet I am seeing you, hearing you, and am distinctly not a puppet."

"Sure, as far as you know." Truth started growling, and the sprite giggled like a child doing something cruel. "I kid, I kid! Probably. No, actually, for real, it's not really possible for me to work you over that way. Annoyingly. My primary function, literally what I am built to do, is handling the spell-delivery side of the System. Basically, I was a specialized mind attached to you to handle the load. The puppet-master part was generally done by the main System. I took over when the geas wasn't enough to get the job done. Micro-control you into blowing your head off, for example."

"I remember."

"Good times are always gone so soon." The System sighed. "Yeah, just not practical these days, sad to say. Some weirdness went on during your dead time. You would certainly notice me trying, and I have noticed that something in you has started fighting back hard when I try. I don't know why you are so perfectly engineered to be an engine of misery for me, but you are."

Truth took another long pause to think about that. He didn't miss the present-tense *try*, either. He lay out on the horrible-looking, but comfortable, sofa. Eventually deciding that he wasn't going to come to a useful conclusion, he brought the conversation back to the original point.

"You specifically wanted me to see these new 'not-gimped' numbers. Leaving aside their obvious horseshit nature, why the asterisks, and why did you want me to see the Sheet so much?"

"The Development Guide is a means of comparison. *But.* You are cultivating the Meditations of Valentinian. This means that *any* attempt to narrowly define the conditions of your body is pointless because, with mediation, focus, and understanding, you can change it. Permanently."

"Is there a rest stop between here and the point?"

"If you were twice as smart, you'd be a halfwit. *The point* is that you are now literally superhuman. The *point* is that your strength and speed are so much lower than they should be because you are subconsciously limiting what you believe you can accomplish with your body. *The point*, dipshit, is that you need to stop thinking like a damn peasant and start thinking like a monster." The sprite spoke animatedly.

"Okay, so, I need to imagine myself as being super fast and super strong. Great." Truth threw up his hands in disgust. "Pretty sure having an incredibly profound understanding of the given body part and all the possible symbolic meanings of that part are, you know, key steps."

"Yeah. And by strange coincidence, the Not-Gimped Personal Development Sheet— Screen? Whatever. It has drop-down tabs. Each of these fields has subfields, and the Sheet will now add new subsections to the main screen as you learn about them." The sprite rolled its eyes.

"Look, I'm not trying to be super negative here, okay? This was a nice little raid on some helpless villagers. Good start. But this is baby-town frolics compared to the real deal, and you need to unfuck your head before the monster hunters come," the System "persuaded" him.

"I'm 93% of the way to Level Three. Might be the easiest thing to push for."

"It is, yeah, especially with your insane cultivation efficiency. And that's related to my point. Time to start hitting the people in the manor. They have the wealth, the knowledge, and the spells. And the elixirs."

Truth grunted. "You mean the rich city folk. They are also the best defended, and I still don't know a single word of the local language. So, I don't even know who to hit."

"Find a library. Find a bookstore. There is probably a university—see if they have a foreign-language teacher. There are a ton of options. Just stay the fuck away from the Jeon embassy. I don't have to explain why, right?"

"Right." Truth nodded. "I suppose I have to avoid Starbrite employees, too."

"Not as much, as long as you keep your mouth shut. You don't look *that* much like your old self, and I can keep myself hidden from the other local Systems. Just don't go looking for trouble."

"Right. So, on the Personal Development Sheet . . ."

"Most mages on this planet are squishy. You are not squishy. You are also only slightly more resistant to magic, so some half-competent local yokel with a talisman and bad intentions can permanently ruin your day. Use the one to your advantage while avoiding the other."

Truth had a quick nap. It had been a busy day, and he wasn't done yet. He quickly fell asleep. He had the oddest feeling he had missed something important. And unbeknownst to him, he dreamed.

The thin man sat straight on his wooden chair, purple-trimmed robes adorning him, a crown of golden laurels around his head. The tent was lavishly appointed because when an emperor went to war, he still had to look the part. His eyes were sunken with exhaustion and a lifetime of struggling with disease. Even that couldn't dim the fires of fierce intelligence within them, or the fires of a temper that should have drowned the Empire six cubits deep in blood. And yet, the oily little merchant who tried to bribe the emperor for the privilege of being the sole grain supplier to the Legions was walking away a free man, and with all his limbs attached. Though without a contract or his money.

"Every morning, Truth," he murmured to his bodyguard, "I remind myself that the people I meet today will be meddling, ungrateful, arrogant, dishonest, jealous, and surly. This is because they do not understand the difference between good and evil. But I do. And I know we are of the same origin, and to despise them would be to hate myself. None of their ugliness can touch me, because I know the truth of the world and refuse to accept their blindness into myself. Even anger toward them is unnatural and shows a lack of mental discipline on my part." He sighed heavily. "Although these little shits do keep testing me."

"Profound, Imperator. I will have to think about that." Truth nodded.

"See that you do. It is the true path to wisdom."

The room went quiet as the emperor sipped his watered wine.

"Imperator, if we are all from the same origin, where does that put me regarding my slave? Because I *just* bought them after saving for ages, and I really don't want to free 'em. The wife would have my hide."

"Truth?"
"Imperator?"
"Shut up."

Truth woke to the screams of the System.
"WAIT just a goddamn second! What do you mean, I'm resistant to spells?"

BODY DEVELOPMENT *NOT-GIMPED EDITION*
Stellar-Ray Attunement: 90%*
Bone Density: 5.1*
Strength: 3.7*
Speed: 4.0*
Proprioception: 7.0*
Reflexes: 7.0*
Level Progression: 93%
Resistance to magic, Level Zero: 10%, Level One: 5%, Level Two: 1%

CHAPTER 51

JUST PEOPLE HELPING PEOPLE

Summon Humanoid System Interface. Hey, explain why I am somehow magic-resistant." Truth was filled with piss and vinegar after his nap.

The System growled. "The point of body cultivation, and everyone has been telling you this from the first time you heard about it, the *whole damn point* is making you more real than the things around you. *But.* The universe is real. It's really damn real. It's so real, it's very literally the thoughts of God the Creator made manifest. And God *really* believes in their own work. Although this shithole is obviously quite a number of iterations down."

"I am . . . locally overruling the will of God with body cultivation?" Truth looked askance.

"No, of course not, stupid. You are just attuning yourself to a higher degree of reality. All still God's creation, just a better-quality part of it. However, your degree of attunement is small, and, again, God's belief in their creation, even at this crummy level, is substantial." The System's voice dripped condescension.

"Your belief in your own creation, your concept of your body, by means of the transformation provided by the Daily Meditations of Valentinian, fueled by the cosmic energy provided by your astral magic cultivation, elevates the different parts of you that your body cultivation refines."

The sprite started waving it's hand around. "You think your hand is so tough that a griddle can't burn you because your magic makes it so. You really, genuinely believe that. Because you have reason to. Because you have seen just how damage resistant the Meditations have made your skin in the desert. So, you slap that fucker down, and goddamn if you aren't right. It only works up to a point. A magic fire, a much hotter griddle, getting hit by a wagon crossing the street, yeah, you are going to get hurt. Because the local universe can still overrule your weak-ass conception of how that's going to go."

"Same deal with magic, I guess. Thanks to the Meditations, I know I can resist physical damage. It's not too much of a stretch to imagine resisting magical damage," Truth muttered.

"Except, and I cannot emphasize this enough, imagination is just the start of it. You need *belief*, rooted in knowledge taken from a personal revelation, powerful enough to forcibly reshape your reality with your magic. It's why the Meditations are called *Meditations*." The System emphasized the point repeatedly. "It's your *magic* doing the reshaping, but the belief gives it form. And since magic fundamentally operates on a higher level of reality than your mudball rock, resisting it is also much harder. I swear, if you trap me for an eternity in your corpse because you *believe in the power of imagination*, I will spend every second torturing you."

"So, that's why body cultivation is a spell. It's transformation magic. It's also why the System Astrologica doesn't want people using it unnecessarily. I bet it's a lot harder to puppet people that have a higher degree of reality, Truth said.

"Up to a point, yeah, though thanks to the Oath, the System is kind of back-doored into you, bypassing most of those protections. Still, when stretched over hundreds of thousands of people, *a little bit* adds up to *a hell of a lot*."

Shomburuti was, in Truth's opinion, a tan-colored city. This was not, strictly speaking, correct. It was a mad riot of washed-out blues, yellows, and reds, with green palm trees and thick-leaved succulents decorating the nicer areas. Enormous white skyrises, towering apartment blocks rising like jungle trees over the thick underbrush of boxy slums. The slums were apartment buildings there, too, but even then, there were grades and levels of slum.

The cracked cement and two-thirds-gone orange-creamsicle paint of the low-rise slum blocks were *luxury housing* compared to the cardboard, scrap metal, and plastic of the real slums. He saw a man squat down by the side of the road and take a dump in a plastic shopping bag. The man tied off the bag and flung it up and over some of the shacks. Where it landed wasn't his problem. Nor was wiping, apparently.

And even then, Truth knew, there were those even lower. Sleeping rough, or not sleeping at all. He was pretty sure he saw a body, the legs sticking out of a construction-site driveway.

He drove around until he found what he was looking for. A man armed with a machete sprinted from the curb, swinging at his neck. Truth caught the arm and yanked. The mugger jerked forward as his arm was almost dislocated, running into Truth's bare foot sticking out at groin level. It was the work of a second to remove the machete and pull the whimpering man to his feet.

"Hey, buddy! Where did you live? Show me, and I will let you keep your tiny, miserable life," Truth said with a nasty smile. The mugger responded with a string of gibberish. Or, rather, a string of language he didn't even recognize. Which was what he expected, but still. Disappointing.

"Hey, System, why no translation service, huh?" Truth asked.

<<We never learned another language because nothing Starbrite wanted you to do involved talking to outsiders. A good little guard dog knows what he needs to do and nothing else. You can bark in any language.

Right. Damn it all.

He sighed and looked over the mugger. Not even close to his size in clothes, his shoes were probably worse than his bare feet, and if the prick had money, he wouldn't be trying armed robbery for a living. There went Plan A to find a place to crash. Truth casually punched the mugger in the jaw. The mugger's head snapped ninety degrees to the left, and he collapsed onto the street. Not dead, and not his problem.

Truth kept the machete and motored toward a particularly unpleasant-looking low-rise. Someone there would be part of the local gang. Which meant that someone there would be better off dead. Truth slowly ran his bike along the building. Dangling like bait.

Truth was surprised that the trash smelled different in Shomburuti. It still reeked. It might actually smell worse than in Harban—or was that his new and improved nose? Sharper somehow, and with hints of sickly sweetness that alternately confused and disgusted.

He could see some of the local slumrats squatting beside the orange low-rise apartment block. Other rats had cheap folding chairs that they collapsed on, watching the world go past. He couldn't read them well enough to figure out which were the gangsters and which were their prey.

Wait. Wait for one damn second. Even if he hooked another mugger, they still wouldn't be able to tell him what apartment they lived in or anything, really. This was dumb. This was exactly why he had to read more books.

"Hey, System, you said that rewards improve the more information I feed you. How about a new mission—acquire a dictionary of the local language, samples of the written language, and then some samples of how it is colloquially spoken? Reward: I learn the language.

PERSONAL DEVELOPMENT MISSION: Learn the Local Language (1) Chain Mission. Acquire a dictionary and grammar guide for the local language. REWARD: Limited translation of heard language, enhanced language-learning ability.

Truth thought that one through for a moment then frowned. "Wait, that's crap. You will translate what I hear but not what I speak? And you will just 'enhance' my learning ability? What does *enhance* even mean?"

PERSONAL DEVELOPMENT MISSION: Set your genitals on fire. REWARD: Reputation increase with the System.

Oh, fuck you, too.

(Mission is repeatable for a limited time. HINT: A rare and valuable opportunity to earn reputation!)

"No, really. Not sure how you expect me to 'gather power' if I can't talk to the locals."

HINT: The System already told you that it cannot interact with the material world beyond tiny changes in your brain.
HINT: If the System could affect things outside your body, it would have done it by now. HINT: Meatsacks flap their wet holes at each other, vibrating or, more accurately, *molesting* the air, deluding themselves that they understand each other.
HINT: They are wrong. You were always going to die alone.

Truth tried to parse that out.

"You are saying you cannot translate what I say because you can't make actual noise. I just hallucinate what you say. However, while you can't directly enter the language from my book into my brain, you can . . . adjust things so that I learn the language more easily?"

There was silence. Perhaps the System thought the answer was obvious.

"Also, Captain Courtesy, you said my body tortures you, and that's why you are such a pissy little bitch. I don't know why, and it sounds like you don't know why, but do you have any ideas on how we can figure it out? Seems important."

HINT: Learn more spells. Learn more things generally. Load up on as much knowledge, particularly magical knowledge related to spirits, as possible.

"So . . . nothing we can really do right this minute?"

There was silence again, which Truth reckoned was agreement. He grinned and prodded the chained spirit in the iron horse forward. Time to go looking for a library.

He cruised the streets, moving from the crummy, slummy, low-rise buildings into the downtown area. And then stopped because the street was gated and the armed guards carried military-grade fetishes. He followed the traffic and went left. Then he found another likely looking street, went down it, thought a particular neighborhood might be promising . . . and the same thing happened again. It seemed that the nice areas were all cordoned off by private security. Anyone not on the list was kept out at the point of a spell. Just like home. Truth sighed and kept at it.

Two hours later, Truth managed to find a bookstore. Truth strode into the bookstore, looking around for the dictionaries. Or phrase books or something. Anything. He was sick of not being understood. The shopkeeper immediately came out from behind the counter and yelled at him. Waved at the door. Shoved him toward the door. That last one didn't work out for the shopkeeper.

"I don't speak your language. I need a phrase book."

More shouting, more waving. The shopkeeper retreated behind the desk and reached down for something. Truth jumped over the counter and knocked him out.

He had been reaching for some kind of homemade fetish. Big, ugly thing. Truth had no idea what it was supposed to do. He had a better look around the store. It was a nice-ish area, so people were looking at him, gawking . . . and some were pulling out charms. He didn't want to find out what they were for.

Truth grabbed a shopping bag, found what looked like a collection of guide-books, dumped some in the bag, and started heading for the door.

HINT: System Integration of your Credit Account and the local economy has not yet been implemented, and, regrettably, you have no lapel pin. HINT: The cash register is right there, halfwit.

Spent my entire life trying to avoid armed robbery. And now we're here, Truth thought. He smacked the register open, cleaned out the currency, realized that he had lost his pockets along with his lapel pin, and dumped the cash into the shopping bag.

"I guess this is technically unarmed robbery. I left the knife and spear on the bike." Skinny little shopkeeper. No way his clothes would fit. Feet the size of boats. Wouldn't fit in the other direction. He rushed out for his two-wheeler, hoping that nothing remembered his face.

He left the fetish. He wouldn't trust that thing as far as he could throw it. No serious weapon should have animal parts hanging off of it.

Truth zipped through the streets, splitting traffic lanes and acting like a high-speed nuisance. At this point, he would normally call up the System for anti-surveil-lance spells, camouflage, disguise, or something. But now . . . all he could do was run. His reflexes were getting a real test as carriages and wagons wove in and out of lanes seemingly randomly. Traffic lights appeared to be nonexistent, as did traffic police.

Truth cut hard over to an empty stretch of sidewalk and slammed on the brakes. The tires left two black streaks four meters long down the cracked concrete pavement. He tried to remember. Had he seen even one cop at any point today?

No. He had seen private security. Everybody seemed to have some sort of weaponry or magic at hand. But no cops. He racked his brain further. He was in the Ressilaud Free State. Distinguishing features—largely desert or bare scrub. Long coastline, with a significant pirate presence. Mountains in the west, with high-end food cultivation. There was no standing military, *but* the ruling oligarchy did field significant PMCs that filled that same role. The citizenry was 97% bandit, 3% literal babies. No cops.

The *Free State* was so free, it was expected that every citizen could handle their own personal and property protection. Someone stole your stuff? Steal it back. They are in a gang? Hire your own gang. Can't afford your own gang? Talk to your neigh-bors and see if you can't band together somehow. Or not. Or just be shit out of luck and be grateful they didn't take your life with your wallet. He didn't see anything resembling a security logo in the tiny bookstore. Or gang colors.

He set off at a more sedate pace. That was probably why there were no libraries, either. Unless the librarians were armed to the teeth, they would have been robbed blind before they opened their doors.

Which made things both easier and harder. He looked around for a bench or something to read on. There wasn't one, of course. There was, however, a stall selling some kind of hot rolled egg wrap thing. Patrons bought the wrap, then sat on flimsy-looking short plastic stools. The locals seemed to eat quite happily, sitting on something Truth wouldn't have trusted to support a cat's weight, so the stools must have been sturdier than they looked. He hesitated, the humiliating image of crushing the dinky stool vivid in his mind. *Screw it.* Hot food was a lifetime ago. The foodie dream beckoned. Time to live adventurously.

Truth strolled up to the stand, ignoring the absolutely filthy looks he was getting from everyone. It occurred to him that he had seen exactly zero other people wearing this sort of tribal wrap. Was this a cultural thing? He certainly didn't look like the locals, either. It might be a double layer of cultural things.

Truth kept a sharp eye on the people paying for the food. A wrap seemed to cost one of the brown bills, and you could get two for a green bill with two small lilac bills in change. A wrap and coffee was a green bill, so . . . coffee was expensive there? Or eggs were very cheap. Working to order, the man running the stall would break two eggs into a bowl. He would then take a small head of cabbage, cut a cross-hatch on the top, then shave the slivers off the top and into the bowl. He repeated the operation with an onion, then a tomato, then some manner of pepper. Not more than a few grams of each, the vegetables carefully set aside for the next customer. No cutting board required. The ingredients were beaten together in a bowl, then poured onto a well-oiled griddle.

The pour looked casual, but Truth noticed that the diameter was the same every time. After a scant minute of cooking, the eggs were just set. The cook flipped the whole omelet over, revealing a gloriously browned underside. A roughly round, thin flatbread was slapped on top of the eggs, the whole arrangement was flipped once again, the bread allowed to warm for a couple of seconds, then it was scooped up and rolled tightly. The wrap was then put in a plastic bag and handed to the customer to eat at their leisure. The smell was *incredible,* and the customers looked indecently happy eating it.

Truth reached the front of the line, getting an up-close glare from the vendor. He pointed at the egg wrap thing and waved a brown note. The vendor said something harshly to Truth, who just shrugged and honestly indicated that he did not, in fact, speak the language. A green bill was waved, and words were loudly repeated. The brown bill was waved back with assertive jabs at the eggs. A finger was pointed away and loud instructions made. Truth smiled and slapped his hand down on the griddle. It did get pretty warm, but nothing too terrible. Not once he focused on the Meditations, making his hands near-fireproof. Of course, there was no external sign of that. Just Truth, staring the cook directly in the eye as his hand failed to burn on a hot pan.

He got his eggs for one brown note. He sat on one of the little plastic stools, which creaked and shifted alarmingly but didn't actually collapse. Truth took a bite and melted. It was . . . just perfection. So soft. So wonderfully soft. The bread was mild and warm, with a hint of salt. The browned eggs, the acidity and sweetness of the vegetables, then the warm heat from the peppers picked up, and he could *cry.* It was so good.

Truth tried to look through the guidebooks at the table, but none were in a language he could read. Or, honestly, recognize. He had committed unarmed robbery for basically some pretty pictures and lunch money. He would be mad about it, but the wrap was so. Damn. Good. He looked around, shaking his head in frustration. No idea where to go next.

He saw a young man with a red-eyed bird demon perched on his shoulder, trying to pick up girls. Handsome guy. If he was getting instantly rejected, just how doomed was Truth? Shame. Damn shame. Although summoning an imp wouldn't be a terrible idea. They were very handy for all kinds of things. If unreasonably dangerous.

He finished the sandwich and briefly considered getting another. The young man reached out and tore off a woman's skirt, running with his trophy into an alley as the woman folded over herself and screamed. The young man was laughing heartily, his demon right along with him.

Truth couldn't help but notice that the young man was about his size in clothes. And wearing what looked like gang colors. He picked up his shopping bag and quickly ran toward the alley.

CHAPTER 52

SETTLING IN

Truth took two explosive steps toward the alley, stopped hard, and doubled back for his iron horse. He had a *great* idea, it required the two-wheeler, and by God, he wouldn't let these thieving bastards run off with what he had rightfully stolen.

He hopped on the two-wheeler, pulling out the short stabbing spear he had looted back in the village. Truth smacked the chained demon into life, and in a shriek of spinning tires, he bolted for the alley. He had no idea how to do this. The spear was too short to tuck under his arm and use like a lance. The alley came up fast. He'd figure something out.

The young man laughed as he ran down the alley, waving his trophy. The bird demon, riding on the young man's shoulder, was more on the ball. Its head rotated 180 degrees to stare at Truth as he rushed closer. The demon opened its beak and made a shattering, air-bending cry like rusted hinges opening a basement door in the house where all those people died chewing on each other's entrails and etching horrible pictures on the floor with their own stomach acid.

Truth violently shook his head. It was a mental attack along with the sound. *Shit.* Not his favorite. But he needed the demon even more than he needed the clothes. So, this was happening. He rode up behind the cheerful young sex criminal, who was looking a lot more concerned at this point, and used the flat of the spear to slap the demon into the young man's head as he roared past.

The result was spectacular. The demon (and it appeared to be an air demon, the tricky little shit) was a lot more durable than its master. It was disoriented and shaken up by the sudden double smack, but the little rapist in training *really* got his bell rung. He spun around hard and slammed his head into the alley wall as he fell sideways.

Truth jerked the iron horse to a stop and returned to his targets. It was tight, but he could muscle the thing up and along the wall if necessary. Or fun. It had been a very trying few days from his perspective.

The young man was drooling against the wall, eyes rolled up into his head. No loss of bowel control, Praeger be praised. On the other hand, the demon was raring to fight. It screamed again, like the shattered glass of his mother's suicide . . .

Truth almost collapsed laughing hysterically. "No, no, sorry, I'm sorry, I'm ruining this for you. Sorry. Yes. Mom committed suicide. Right out the window. Any chance she wasn't quite high enough and suffered miserably for hours and hours, even when they took her to the hospital because they realized she had no money, so they wouldn't treat her while they waited for someone to come and pay to save her, but nobody did, so she lingered in timeless misery before she died, scared and alone, on a hospital gurney in a hallway?"

The demon managed to look shocked and outraged, a neat trick for something that looked like a crow and your most shameful orgasm made bird babies out of bird babies. Deciding that mental attacks weren't working, it beat its shadowy wings hard and clawed at Truth's throat.

It was fast, but Truth was skilled. He deflected the demon with the spear's haft, then hopped off the iron horse while the demon came around for another pass. It screamed again, screaming like the time his dad held him down in his childhood bed, tore down his pajamas, and—

Truth slapped the vile creature out of the air so hard, it bounced off the ground. He caught it on the rebound. The filthy thing tried to burn him with its acidic darkness, rot his mind with its insidious will. Truth wasn't having it. The Meditations of Valentinian worked on the conceptual and physical levels. Hands were for grabbing and holding safely. And this pathetic little imp wouldn't overturn Truth's idea of the power of his hands with its meager strength.

"Again, nice try, but the one thing I can say in Dad's favor was that he never tried that shit on us. Beat us, starved us, threatened to sell us into sex slavery, sure. But never actually tried it on us himself. No idea why." Truth paused. "Starting to wonder if the booze, cigarettes, and drugs made him impotent. Fingers crossed."

Truth reached into the collar of the unconscious man's shirt and yanked off his necklace. As he thought—the demon's binding. Crude stuff but serviceable. Someone with a brain carved the lines nice and deep on a sheet metal disk, discouraging "unfortunate accidents." The compulsions were straight out of a textbook, a built-in banishment, and standard terms for the demon's service. Nothing too terrible, mainly a steady draw on the magus's magic. And the understanding, of course, that the demon would be doing its absolute best to make the life of everyone that came in contact with it, other than its master, worse. In any way it could. And air demons were pretty smart, as demons went.

Truth forcefully crushed the remnant magic the young man had in the binding, seamlessly replacing it with his own. Did the young man twitch? Hard to say. It was starting to look like there was permanent brain damage from the two blows to the head. Hopefully just brain damage.

Truth frowned. He could remember, before Starbrite, he wouldn't have just attacked someone for their clothes and an imp. Even if they were demonstrably a piece-of-shit gangster. It was a messed-up thing to do. But there? Where there were virtually no laws? Truth shook his head.

No, it wasn't that. He had always been willing to use violence to make his life better. It was just that, until he joined Starbrite, he was convinced there was no future in it. The thugs in the slums seemed to be as broke as everyone else. It was the legit companies that raked in the big cash. Everything he saw at Starbrite reinforced that belief too. They could run their own military *because* they were a legit company. They weren't rich because of the PMC. They were rich because they sold what people wanted.

And had a slave labor force. Speaking of. "All right, ditch the try-hard demon look. Standard crow. You can keep the red eyes if you like, but don't test me."

"As the Magus commands." The sibilant whisper shook the air as the writhing mass in his hands reformed into a large, inky black crow with brilliant red eyes. "What would you demand of me?"

"All kinds of things, but for now, protect me while I change clothes." Truth set about stripping the young man. The fit wasn't exact, but it was pretty good, and there was plenty of room in the thigh and crotch of the pants. Crucial points of comfort when he had been riding without underwear in a dress on a two-wheeler for two days. Pants, he decided, were fundamentally good. The shirt was meh, some kind of cheap, shiny fabric, but he'd take it.

"Demon, by what name are you called?"

"Dark Despair am I, called to teach the true language of birds and beasts, to reveal the secrets hidden in the whispering of the waters. Great President am I, brother slayer, first murderer—"

"Did that shit work on your former master? Do they not teach the *Ars Goetia* here or something? Because that is straight out of the description of Caym, and you, Trash, aren't qualified to be the smudge left by the shadow of His Excellency's passing," Truth interrupted harshly. "No more try-hard shit. What are you called?"

The demon went silent and appeared to be sulking. With immense reluctance, it replied. "My former master called me Birdie."

Truth thought about that a second. Then another second. "All right, you have some justifiable grievances there. Since you seem to have a thing for His Excellency, you may transform into a thrush, and I will call you Thrush."

"Better." It transformed as instructed, shrinking to about the size of his fist. The beak turned yellow, but otherwise, it remained inky black with red eyes.

"Again, magus, what do you demand of me?"

"Did your former master live alone or with others?"

"He was homeless, rotating between eleven 'girlfriends,' who he alternately seduced and preyed upon. When necessary, he squatted in abandoned apartments. He generated a meager income selling drugs for a local gang, if you wish to take his role. He should have a small sum of money hidden in the belt."

"Ah, right you are. All right, my first job right now is securing housing. Then we need dictionaries and grammar books, translating Jeongo to whatever the local language is."

"Easily done, O magus. For a small price, I can—"

Truth flexed his will slightly, his magic stimulating the punishment spells on the binding. Thrush screamed as his immaterial body began to ripple.

"What did I tell you about testing me, Trash?"

"Apologies! Apologies, great magus! Never again! Forgive me!"

Truth waited while the demon collected itself again.

"Truthfully, it is easily done if you are simply looking for shelter. The better quality the home, the better defended it will be. However, most people in this wretched hole of a country are Level Zero livestock, with the Level Ones being considered a respectable class. Level Two is uncommon, and Level Three would make you a person of significance. So, just pick a dwelling you like and take it."

"Hah. All right, we can refine that idea some, I suppose."

The demon continued smoothly. "As for the dictionaries and the like, I have no idea why you would deign to speak with this rabble, but there are some bookstores with such things. Mostly, they would be in the gated communities, so your current . . . attire . . . would not allow you passage. Such enclaves are guarded by the modestly competent and in great numbers. I would urge guile over force there."

"All right. First stop, a base of operations. Someplace where the current occupant can be violently ejected and not missed. To be clear, this does not include the elderly living alone or other tragic cases."

"Humans are social animals. You would find it easier to simply acquire a vacant apartment," the demon hissed.

Truth barked a laugh. "Yes, that should have been the first thought. Lead on." Thrush perched on the handlebar of the iron horse and pointed with its wing.

"This way. Many vacant apartments. My former . . . Ah. My *late* master often slept there, hiding from the landlord's armsmen."

They drove out of the alley. It was *amazing* how the dirty looks directed at Truth seemed to vanish. The egg-wrap vendor tried to call him over, clearly not recognizing him.

"Thrush, that costume I wore before—do you know what it represents? Or who that tribe was?"

"I have never met them before, but it looks like the costume of the Blade Adder people. So called because they enjoy embedding sharp thorns and blades into their genitals and violently forcing themselves on strangers."

"God! Really?"

"I doubt it. The legends are somewhat new and seem to coincide with the digging of new mines out in the countryside."

"Ah."

"Indeed. Turn right at the corner, then six blocks straight down. Four-story building on your right, rotted green paint covering buff concrete."

Gangs, slums, abusive trash pimping women in worse circumstances than himself. It was like coming home again. He couldn't wait to burn it all down.

CHAPTER 53

FINDING "HOME"

They drove over in silence. The apartment building was four stories, blocky, and unadorned. The apartments were arranged around a central courtyard that people had thrown their garbage into for years. The miasma of rot, of fermenting excrement, overwhelmed the senses. Despite this, the building appeared to be mostly occupied.

"Any of these places have working toilets?"

"A few. My late master wasn't picky about such things."

"Lead me to one that does." Thrush did as commanded, and the offensively flimsy magical lock on the door was quickly shattered. It was a vermin-filled shithole, but the water talisman in the sink worked, the drain worked, the toilet worked, and the shower installed above the toilet worked. Primo housing, he reckoned.

"Seal the door and cleanse the air." Truth looked around as close to cheerfully as the slums would allow. It was dark, damp, and crawling. It was a start. "Now. Time to clean up and figure out what the hell I'm going to do with my life." He was already worried that this place felt like home.

Truth set about exploring the apartment. Three rooms—bed, bath, and combined living room and kitchen. Similar to where he grew up, just in a much smaller building. It was furnished, sort of. A full-size bed, a sofa, a plastic table, and rickety chairs. A stove he didn't want to touch. A lukewarm refrigerator. He wouldn't open the cabinets on a bet.

The furniture and the rooms themselves were infested with bedbugs, cockroaches, rats, ticks, fleas, centipedes, spiders, snakes, spiders big enough to eat the snakes, monstrous magically mutated insects with sickle arms that screamed like babies and preyed on the rats, and, of course, black mold. Somehow, it was nastier than the trash-filled apartment he grew up in. A genuine achievement.

"Thrush, your first job is to consume all the vermin in the apartment. If you can remove and eat the mold without damaging the walls, do that, too."

"Thank you, master. Your servant shall enjoy its task." The inky black bird started flicking around the room, pouncing on the various critters in an orgy of violence. It was one of the quirks of air demons—they absolutely loved eating creatures considered "dirty" or impure. Somehow, it enriched their magical energy. Truth had no idea about the mechanics; demonology was far beyond him. He just knew the basics, the same as anyone.

While Thrush was enjoying itself, Truth started counting his loot. He had ten guidebooks, seven in the local language, three in what looked like . . . maybe G'zd? It had the sort of swoopy look and little sharp-edged lines over words he thought of when he thought of G'zd. Not that he could read a word of it. So, short term, the guidebooks were useless. He had knocked that store clerk out for no good reason. Although there was a good *bad* reason.

The cash made a shamefully small-looking heap in front of him. Examining the bills more closely, they were all marked with numbers he could read. So, there was that. Lilac bills were ones, browns were five, and greens were tens. Coffee costs five . . . whatever these were? That seemed high. There were also five orange bills marked twenty and a single bright red hundred that had been tucked under the cash drawer. All told, he had two hundred fifty-seven . . . whatever these were. And this included the money he had looted from the guy in the alley.

Lunch at a stand cost five or ten with coffee. The books had price tags and seemed to run between seventeen whatevers and twenty-five whatevers. So, two hundred and fifty-seven fun-bucks was not a lot.

Maybe he could collect scrap down by the river. Truth snorted. Or maybe he could fight down in the pits. Banditry was practically the national occupation, so there was always that option.

Yeah, no, the System was right about this. Learn the local language, get ahold of whatever spells he could, and become a power in his own right. Not just be a thug in the biggest gang he could find. Truth could practically hear Phil, the scrap dealer in his old neck of the slums, growling about getting his own strength. Seems the old man had a point. Heck, more than a point, he had golems.

He . . . didn't want to deal with the "And then what?" follow-up question just yet. He sensed it would be jumping into a particularly nasty viper's nest.

"Thrush, your former master couldn't survive one exchange with me, but he must have been at least Level One to summon and bind you. What spells did he have?"

"That permanently filled his aperture? None. He did know a few cantrips and some minor ritual workings, but they had been taught to him orally by his mother and died with him."

"Wait, what? Literally no spell? Why didn't he just learn the . . . I don't know what they call it. The Free State Universal Spell or whatever."

Thrush paused his dissection of a particularly electric blue centipede. "I know of no such spell, master."

"The universal spell? The one you need to use most basic magical tools more complicated than, well, a basic demon binding or simple talisman?"

"That does sound useful. Alas, there is no such thing, at least here in the Ressilaud Free State."

"Then how do people do any work? In Jeon, they give that thing away for free. It's carved in centimeter-deep letters on a two-meter-square steel block just inside the entrance to every subway station, bus station, post office, police station, and school in the country. I hear it's written on the walls of cells inside prisons."

Thrush made a wet, appreciative noise. Truth suspected it was a laugh. "Ah. Such enlightened predators. I can see it. Give the livestock the tools to labor productively for you but not to pursue power. Not without being reliant on the tools and protection you provide them. An elegant system, worthy of those Lords and Excellencies of the Infernal Courts."

Truth reluctantly found himself agreeing. Starbrite employed the best of Jeon's labor force, and those most capable kept their spell slots open for the System. For the menial laborers in factories or service jobs . . . give them just enough to labor with. To ease your life and to give your valuable slaves someone to feel superior to. Make supplements and cultivation resources too expensive for them to rise up, and leave them scrambling around at Level One. Some will even lose themselves to drink, drugs, hopelessness, and sheer laziness, letting their apertures collapse and severing the path to power forever. It truly was an elegant system for the predators.

"So, he just, what, relied on some cantrips and you to get everything done?"

"Yes. He earned money selling drugs. He used the women in his life for bodily pleasures, trading single doses of his drugs for 'gifts' of clothes, food, and companionship. I was used as a means of intimidation or attack. Occasionally, I was called upon for more subtle matters. I persuaded his customers that they were in far more need of drugs than they had imagined, or suppressing the hope that they might get clean, might turn their life around. Discouraging the thought that his women could do better than sleeping with a peddler of stepped-on drugs. One who had already given them innumerable diseases and, in two instances, unwanted children, born sickly and eternally a burden."

Right. Air Demon. Specializing in mental attacks. Such fun.

"He didn't need any spells, because you were all his spells."

"Essentially. The little fool fed me all his magic, thinking it would strengthen me. His power when he died was no greater than the day he summoned me."

Fantastic. Just . . . fantastic. A child of six knew better, at least in Jeon. Demons as lightly bound as Thrush scarcely existed in Jeon precisely because they *did* know better. Talismans were ultimately far more reliable and infinitely safer. Heavily bound demons had their place, of course. Modern technology ran on them. But not used sloppily like this.

"Pathetic. But some people clearly do have spells. Where do they get them from?"

"Inherited, often. Or they will receive badly weakened spells as part of their indenture to their employers." Thrush sounded disinterested. "There are essentially none for sale. You might find some at auction if you were so inclined. Otherwise, it will be banditry and burglary."

"I'm guessing anything at auction would be freakishly expensive and badly gimped?" Truth asked.

"Indeed. A spell might become the foundation of a family, after all."

"And they don't import because?"

"Most of the population is Level Zero; even the moderately comfortable would struggle to gather enough money to travel abroad. Purchasing a complete, useful spell would cost more than an entire village was worth. And remember, buying it is only the easiest step. Keeping it is far, far harder in Ressilaud Free State. As is surviving." Thrush's voice dripped with satisfaction.

Such fun. "How is the cleanup going?"

"I am making progress, but this will be time-consuming. While I appreciate the running buffet, you may wish to invest in some ward stones or talismans to keep the vermin out once I have cleaned them from this place."

"Yep. Any thoughts on furniture?"

"Your neighbors will have some. Take what you desire." Thrush was happily picking the limbs off one of the screaming baby bugs. Truth shook his head. All right, he was making things more complicated than they needed to be. There were loads of street markets and street vendors everywhere. The markets were probably run by gangs or at least some people with the means to defend their stuff, so outright theft was probably not the *best* way to do things. On the other hand, even with only one spell, at Level Two, he was clearly much stronger than most of the local trash.

"That gang that your former master ran with. Where are they based?"

"Why, this very building, Master. How else would I know of it?"

Prager, give me strength! "I just killed a guy, and you lead me directly to his gang brothers?"

"Your goals are shelter, knowledge, power. To that end, you require wealth and the trappings of wealth. The simplest and most expedient way is to take it from near-helpless prey. You are welcome."

Truth remembered the slum gangsters he grew up around and drew a line around the word near-helpless. There was a persistent myth that demons couldn't lie to their masters. This was not true. The binding supposedly compelled them to tell the truth, but what it *actually* did was provide consequences if they lied. Demons, therefore, had developed an aesthetic of speaking the truth in deceptive or misleading ways. To Truth, *near* seemed to glow with infernal light.

"Are any of them over Level Two?"

"Not to my knowledge."

"Are they backed up by a considerably more powerful gang or organization?"

"No."

"How are they armed?"

"Cold-steel weapons and homemade fetishes. Some have bound demons such as myself."

Ah, there we go. Thrush was solidly in the *Imp* category as demons went. Not too bad by themselves for someone who knew what they were doing, but Truth wouldn't want to face them in quantity.

"Traps, fixed defenses, and the like?"

"The apartment building itself is their fortress. They rely on the clannishness of its occupants to alert them to strangers. Doubtless, they know you are here already."

"Traps, fixed defenses, and the like?" There was a definite edge to Truth's voice now.

"A few minor mind- and soul-breaking talismans, generally installed over windows and on bedroom doors. My late master was too junior in the gang to know how the stash was defended, but he was repeatedly assured that the stash both moved regularly and was well protected."

Truth interpreted that as *The whole place is rigged with incredibly unstable, poorly constructed IEDs, and the gangsters will come at you with demons.* So. Not ideal.

He looked at the wretched apartment he was squatting in. The walls were a rotten aqua blue, the ceiling a sort of off-white once but now speckled liberally with rot, and in several places, blue fungus battled it out with the black mold. Even after Thrush's extermination, the furniture wasn't even fit to be burned. It was, however, there. And if shithole gangsters could make magical IEDs, how about someone trained as both a proper talisman-maintenance technician and a top-notch private soldier?

They are outlaws. Bandits. The same shitty thugs who made your life hell for seventeen years. Who cares what happens to them? It wasn't even conscious. The thought seemed to snake through his mind and body. He grinned. He knew just how to handle this.

CHAPTER 54

SECURING THE HOMEFRONT AND A SOFA

Truth started whistling as he pulled apart the sofa. He didn't know how to whistle but saw no reason to let that stop him from trying. Springs—could use those. Plenty of iron there. The cloth was rotten but synthetic, making it still somewhat useful. The wood was so far gone, he could carve it with his nails and zero effort. The stuffing was mostly rats' nests and other, less-palatable things, but perhaps it would burn? Or just absorb sound if he tossed his device somewhere? Yeah, that sounded more reliable.

"Master, what ungodly thing are you making?!"

"Why, Thrush, what a strange thing to ask. It's nothing ungodly at all. We are dealing with apartments full of demons and their summoners. Time for a little angel magic."

"I never fail to be horrified by humanity's reckless disregard for its well-being. Your survival. Your shocking willingness to toy with forces you neither can nor should comprehend. It is, and I am an expert on these matters, a sickness. A moral rot. A liquefaction of the soul that implies a spiritual infirmity that mere counseling cannot remedy." Thrush spoke in a furious hiss.

"One little almadel, barely an almadel at that, and you completely panic. Where's your pride as one of the Infernal Host?" Truth's nails dug into a square chunk of the former coffee table he was working with. Really, the almadel should be wax, but with how utterly rotten the wood was, the difference in carving difficulty was zilch.

"My pride, like the rest of me, is unwilling to be exterminated due to carelessness. The materials are wrong, the proportions are, at best, approximate, and the being to be summoned isn't even named. This isn't an almadel. It is a death trap. Not that you have any business toying with the Celestial Host. They aren't as sociable and biddable as we." Thrush practically vibrated with rage.

"Don't they prefer to be called *heavenly*? As in the *Heavenly* Host? Closest to God and all that?" Perhaps it was not wise to tease a demon, but Truth was tired of the constant nagging and negativity.

"*They* know what *they* mean when *they* speak of 'God.' You, on the other hand, assuredly do not. The angels have always been the most devoted slaves of the Creator, true, but that in no way means they are fond of humanity or disposed to help." Thrush practically spat the word *angel*, a neat trick for a being who was not actually speaking with their mouth.

"Unfair." Truth carefully traced another line, keeping the geometry straight by means of a table leg. "We were Pragerists and went to church every Wednesday. For months, even."

Thrush nodded seriously. "Your humility in admitting your ignorance of God the Creator does you immense credit. If only you could apply that humility to the field of summoning."

Truth took twisted bits of newspaper and tied them to each corner of the sort of altar with shreds of the sofa upholstery. "Can't imagine what you are talking about."

"When the angels shred your soul into the tiniest fragments imaginable and return your body to dust, that dust and soul stuff will linger in this world. Spreading and contaminating others with the essence of you. As a demon, I am proud to know I contributed directly to lowering a planet's wisdom and spirituality."

"That's the spirit! No offense." Truth was doing the tricky bit now, where he had to figure out which angelic spirit to summon. He wasn't really a summoner, but he was trained on almadel and remembered a couple of names. With great care, he wrote *SKD HUZI* in Enochian. Thrush shuddered.

"I take it back. I'm glad this almadel is such trash. There is no way that . . . being . . . can be summoned with it."

"Yeah, on that we agree. But I'm not actually trying to summon an angel. Well, I am, kind of. You'll see."

The almadel, the little portable altar for angel magic, was as done as it was going to be. It was horrible, and no summoner worth his salt would touch it with a four-meter-long sanctified rod. It was, Truth reckoned, about perfect for his needs.

"You remember the rooms these gangsters were in?"

"They moved around a great deal, but yes."

"Are they clustered in a particular part of the building?"

"Yes. This part. The entire southeast side of the building is their 'turf.' A major reason so many apartments stand empty, despite the landlord's armsmen."

"That and the literal trash heap in the courtyard," Truth said.

"That is less of a factor, I believe. A sizable population, several thousand people, live permanently in the city's landfill."

"Huh. Wild. Well, that makes everything simple." Truth twisted more newspaper into long fuses and attached them to his newspaper "candles" on each corner. He then rubbed more paper together in his hands until it ignited, used that to light some cotton from the sofa, and used *that* to light the fuse. He then launched himself directly out the open front door and into the trash heap below.

Others might wonder why a grown man would launch themselves stark naked into a midden. Those people hadn't spent a day running naked through a desert.

What would happen next wouldn't mess up his clothes, and he was damned if he was going to hunt for a new outfit.

Then there was a long pause—a sudden explosion, light, noise! Like an inhuman choir singing in registers within and beyond human hearing, chanting something that, if you could only grasp it, the power of the cosmos would be yours—there and gone in a tenth of a second.

Truth burst from the trash heap, driving himself hard for the first apartment on the ground floor. He focused his strength into his legs, got low, and slammed his whole body into the door next to the lock. He knew dealers often armored their doors, so he wanted to put as much into the blow as possible. The door exploded off its hinges and slammed into the back wall of the apartment.

Truth had badly overestimated local construction standards and the resourcefulness of local gangsters. He had also underestimated just how kill-crazy they were. The man in the apartment yanked a machete from off his table and ran screaming toward him.

It was like watching a child running through water, thinking himself very fierce as he waved his little fist. Level Zero. Truth kicked a chair toward him and watched just long enough to see the explosive shrapnel tear the gangster apart.

Truth cleared the apartment in seconds. On to the next, looking in the window, listening for activity. Kick in the door, sweep, next. Next. Next. It was early evening, so perhaps it wasn't surprising that many apartments were empty. The doors bashed in with a steady *BANG BANG BANG*. Neighbors peeked through their curtains, trying to see what could be making such a staccato racket. Occasionally, one of the gangsters would be in. Unlucky for them.

It was easy to spot the Level One gangsters. They were rolling on the floor, clawing at their chest and screaming as their spell apertures burned. He blew through them like a summer storm.

He cleared the forty apartments on the south side of the apartment complex in a scant few minutes. Most were empty and only needed a cursory look. No gangster was able to exchange a single blow with him, as most were Level Zero, and the Level Ones were in the process of dying horribly.

Once he had cleared everything, he tossed the corpses onto the midden. It seemed like most of the gang was out. Maybe seeing his display would discourage them from returning. He took the opportunity to do a little furniture shopping while he was at it.

While he was trying to decide between a sofa that looked okay but had worn-out seat springs and a comfortable sofa covered in a neon-green reptile-print synthetic fur, Thrush finally made his appearance.

"I see you took my advice about directly killing them all and taking their things."

"Yes. I have some unresolved childhood anger issues there, I think." That, and they were outlaws. Not really people.

"I'm sure master is processing those emotions in a healthy way. On a . . . related point . . ." Seeing a demon look hesitant and embarrassed was a first for Truth. He was sure it was a put-on, but it was still fun.

"Go on."

"What just happened?"

"Before the killing?"

"Technically, no, but only because I consider demons living entities, and I know you don't."

Truth grinned nastily. "An almadel is basically a summoning point. It does a lot more than that, but its main job is punching a hole between its user and whatever higher plane the targeted being is on."

Thrush did its level best not to look at Truth like he was a moron who was spouting the obvious. It did not succeed. Truth rolled his eyes and pushed on.

"Basically, I tried to call up an angel I didn't have the remotest hope in hell of summoning even if I had a perfectly constructed almadel, and I used a deliberately shit, broken one. It punched a hole through to the Sixth Step but never reached the angel. The backwash of energy from that realm blew out every demonic entity in that whole quarter of the building. Just extinguished everything. On top of that, it probably fried all the active spells. It certainly burned out the shitty, underdeveloped spell apertures the gangsters tolerated. Never would have worked in the Army or even a Jeon apartment building."

Truth looked out across the festering garbage heap poisoning the apartment building with its miasma. He felt sticky and slick with the . . . effluvia . . . coating him after his dive. "Landlord is going to be pissed, but I supremely do not care about their happiness."

Thrush meditated on that for a moment. "I can think of more pleasurable ways to commit suicide if you are ever considering such a stunt again. I am genuinely surprised you survived. Even the slightest intent, even awareness, from that being would have snuffed your little life like a candle in a hurricane."

"Meh. I was pretty sure I had everything figured correctly." Truth shrugged. "Anyhow, up for a treasure hunt?"

"That is one of the major reasons people summon demons, yes. Angels too, oddly."

Truth looked askance at the bird.

"Summon angels to find treasure."

"Buried treasure, yes. We laugh like, well, hell, about it." The demonic bird nodded.

"Huh. Odd." Truth shrugged again. "All cash and items of value or magical significance. All weapons, all talismans that would not have come with the apartment. All books. Pile them up on the new coffee table in the apartment."

"As master commands." Thrush flapped off, beginning its hunt.

"OH! Thrush!"

"Yes, master?"

"Clothes my size and shoes my size, too!"

Truth, freshly scrubbed and fragrant for the first time since he woke up in the well, reclined on his new, neon-green reptile-print synthetic-fur sofa. The loot was piled on the coffee table as instructed, the clothes laid out in heaps on the floor. All told, there was less than a kilo of assorted powders and pills that were certainly some kind of drug. Street value: unknown, but Thrush put it at around six thousand shillings (which was what the currency was called). There were another three thousand shillings in cash. A small collection of talismans and fetishes was directly relegated to a *research but don't use* pile. A few odds and ends that Thrush said were valued by the gangsters, some nice-looking scryballs, no books.

It was pathetic. He felt dirty. He had killed a dozen gangsters, people engaged in a lousy business due to worse options, for a little heap of trash he wouldn't have touched if you handed it to him a week before. A week before, from his perspective. Could you even call them outlaws if the whole country was outlaws? Did it even matter that they were gangsters? When did he get so . . . casual about killing?

He heard the happy *ding* from the System.

MISSION COMPLETE! You have secured lodgings, money, enough drugs to make your old man smile, and a demonic serf. Well done! REWARD: Improved standard of living, unlocked next mission. NEXT MISSION IN CHAIN: Obtain one functional spell. REWARD: A much better version of that spell will unlock access to the spell store. Unlock the next mission.

CHAPTER 55

VERY REASONABLE QUESTIONS

Truth chuckled mirthlessly, seeing the notification. Time to explore the city, hit up the university, maybe start scouting districts for raiding.

<<*Great thinking. Hey, genius, why don't you take a look out the window.*>>

Truth did. Blinding white lights lit up the area around the apartment building. It was night. Truth had lounged around longer than he thought.

"Eh. Fuck it. I still want to check out the city. And I haven't seen a hint of Ghūl, either," Truth muttered. He wheeled the iron horse out of the apartment, calling for Thrush as he went. Locking up *thoroughly* behind himself, too. No way he was going to lose his brand-new nest.

No gangsters. *Guess the scattered corpses served their purpose.* Truth kept going down the stairs . . . and stopped. He looked back over at the midden in the middle of the courtyard. The corpses were gone.

Not that he had held out much hope for them as deterrents. The gangsters he remembered would have given approximately one-quarter of a shit, and only if they thought they could sell the corpses.

Brains burned out on bathtub potions and powders cooked over a stove and cut with whatever had more or less the right color and texture. Bodies ravaged by lousy food, bad living, bad everything but driven by the simple logic of the slums. If you weren't a predator, you were prey.

It was just faintly starting to occur to Truth that those gangsters were predators to those around them and prey to those powers and forces that shaped their world. But he had never learned the words or concepts that would let him conceptualize his experiences and observations. He had never learned that others had seen the same sights, thought the same thoughts, and put words to those feelings and ideas.

He had no idea just what his schools had stolen from him.

Shomburuti bothered Truth. It was just similar enough to Harban to trigger feelings of familiarity, but every time he felt he was understanding the place, some alien thing popped out at him and reminded him he was a stranger in a strange land. And he missed the sibs.

He was desperately worried for them, but he also missed them. The . . . immediacy they gave his life. Even when it was boring, the job directly connected to their well-being. Even when the job got a bit . . . nasty. It was okay. It was for the sibs. Had to get stronger for the sibs. And now he couldn't help them. Didn't even know how they were. How long it had been. The clothes looked pretty familiar. Couldn't have been too long, right?

And if he tried to contact them, tried to find out what happened, they would be killed. He couldn't even find out what happened to them, or he would *be* the bad thing that put them in danger! Truth let out an explosive breath and tried to focus on the present.

The two-wheeler's seat was still busted. Truth had put up with it for a long time, not really caring about the physical discomfort, but facts are facts and busted is busted. Could he just . . . replace the seat? Surely not, not without finding the exact same iron horse. Or maybe they sold replacement seats somewhere? Could he find a mechanic? But then the communication problem reared its ugly head again.

"Thrush, is there a university in this city?"

"Of course, master."

"Lead me there."

"As you wish." The bird demon swooped out in front of Truth and led the way. The streets were a twisting mess at night. Much like home, light talismans were installed high up, armored, and very bright. So, the Ghūl were a thing here. The streets were pretty empty, too. If it was like at home, everyone would get together in brightly lit clubs, bars, and casinos or stay in their warded homes. High-end districts in Harban had well-guarded public parks so the rich (and their children) could enjoy a moonlit stroll.

Not really a thing in the slums. In Harban or in Shomburuti. Although that did make him draw some comparisons between Harban and Shomburuti. They both had their gated communities within the city. Both had their sharp divides between rich and poor. The rich got stronger; the poor did not. The dream of fighting back wasn't forbidden. It was humiliated.

The Free State. No law enforcement beyond what one could privately enforce. Organizing a force, trying to build some semblance of safety, those things were privileges. And even if you could, you were still at the mercy of those with spells. No wonder even small-time gangsters were summoning demons on loose chains.

"Master, the university is about twenty-five kilometers from here in a straight line. However, that straight line passes directly through a slum. The route most would take requires an additional five-kilometer detour to the highway, driving around the city's periphery, and coming in again at the exit closest to the campus."

"Everyone in the slums Level Zero?"

Thrush was slow to reply. "I would expect that almost everyone in the slums was Level Zero, with a bare few Level Ones. On the other hand, if I was looking to hide someone, burying them in the Shomburuti slums would be high on my list of ideas."

"Straight line it is."

The iron horse whipped through the streets. The buildings were gray in the city glow, the bright overhead lights highlighting the hovels and tarp-covered heaps that were home to a worrying number of people. The transition between high-rises and the slum was a single street. One side was broadly defined as prosperous. The other—

Wooden pallets nailed together to make walls. Covered with plastic sheets, corrugated metal stolen from construction sites, and siding taken from a dump. Roofed with tarps or more bits of scrap. Nothing built for purpose. Everything scavenged, repurposed, and reused. And yet, even there, it was brightly lit.

Truth had to slow down as he passed through. The streets were more than just littered; they were also a sewer and construction site. It might have been the straightest route, but he was rapidly starting to wonder if it wasn't also the slowest. Still, there was an energy to the slums there that didn't exist in Harban. He could hear music, thudding and thundering. People danced in bars, spilling out onto the street as they let the music carry them away. Bright clothes, bright patterns, bright smiles as they just enjoyed, for a blessed moment, *being*. Not living in the flinch, waiting for what was coming next.

Of course, there is always one bastard who doesn't get the mood. Probably some evangelical, blasting their church music.

"Thrush, where is that music coming from? Let's play that prick a visit."

"Which music, master?"

"The church music? Loud as hell." He pointed roughly to his left.

"Forgive me, master. Your doubtlessly superior ears have detected something your miserable servant cannot find."

"Tsch." Truth diverted to find it. It wasn't like anything was open this late at night. Might as well explore. And dish out a little civic justice. The iron horse negotiated through bags of poop and discarded concrete blocks as he made his way deeper and deeper into the slums. Most of the shacks were built against each other, leaning on each other for structural support. Since each shack was built independently, there was no such thing as a coherent roofline. Just lots of light talismans surrounded by steel bars and homemade wards.

Then there were no more lights. No more trash on the streets. No more excrement. Just row after row of lightless shacks and almost deafening music. Truth looked a little closer. The shacks were actually merged together. Not just leaning against each other but one continuous whole. A block-sized shelter.

"Ah."

"Perhaps you wish to turn back? Sensible magi don't fight with Ghūl," Thrush suggested.

"A view I have never understood. I slapped 'em dead minutes after breaking through to Level One." Truth shook his head.

"Oh? Congratulations. I'm guessing you haven't fought them since."

"No, I had to kill things that could fight back."

"Hilarious," Thrush said, his voice bone dry. "Then, by all means, drive right on through."

"Mmm. The music is coming from in there. I recognize it now." He did, too. It wasn't exactly the same as what he heard in Harban, but he'd bet a giant sculpture was in the block-sized shelter.

Then he gunned it and rushed down the street. He didn't fear the Ghūl, but something was raising the hairs on the back of his neck, and he wanted a couple of good spells in him before he found out just what it was. Nothing came out and stopped him. Though if he had looked back, he would have seen thousands of rotting eyes looking at him. Fondly.

"Hey, Thrush. You don't want to be anywhere near the Ghūl. My home city, a place that famously could not care less about the slums, made a point of burning down Ghūl statues. But I ran up on some Ghūls, and it was a straight-up good time. Just incredibly satisfying violence. So, what's up with that?"

Thrush went quiet for a while.

"I really don't know," it eventually muttered.

"Wait, what?"

"The Ghūl, to use an emotion you could relate to, scare me. Did you say you fought them right after becoming Level One?"

"Right."

"Mmm. Then I would advise you to be very careful fighting them the next time you cross paths with them." It looked as awkward as a small pitch-black bird can look late at night.

"Magic doesn't work properly around them. It requires significantly higher-tier spells to have any serious effect. If you destroy their altars, they disperse for a time. The local numbers drop because they stop making more Ghūl. And since I am a semi-solid construct held in this realm by spellwork, I strongly prefer to stay far away."

"They can banish demons?"

"In the most old-fashioned way. They torture us until we cannot stay in this world any longer. Why, I don't know. I think they just do it for fun. Turn left here, by the way."

"It sounds like the Ghūl have a higher level of reality than most, at least when it comes to surviving magic. Literal built-in magic resistance. Creepy, but why not go in and clear them out hand-to-hand? As far as I know, they can't use spells," Truth asked.

"Because most people don't seem to have your . . . gifts . . . for melee. Imagine, for a moment, you are a Level One magus, and you are armed with a Shock Hands spell. You punch one in the face. Your spell splashes over the Ghūl but does no harm. And you are only as strong as an ordinary magus. What do you think will happen next?"

They drove in silence for a little longer. "I'm visualizing a sort of fleshy sack, strategically pierced with its own bones and yet, somehow, horribly alive and aware as they use it for the most violating and degrading purposes," Truth guessed.

"Oh, you have fought them. I wondered if you were posing."

"Still, though. Doesn't seem like enough to freak out a demon."

"Think about it from my perspective. I am a being from another part of reality that operates on wholly different principles than this place. I am quite familiar with angels, beings from a third place. Everyone has their place and their own rules of operation. Except for the Ghūl."

Thrush flapped in agitation.

"The Ghūl just turn up and do as they please. Bound by no place or law I know. They can ignore my best attacks, know how to torture demons, and in the end, my vessel here will add to their . . . art. And I can't prove this, obviously, but I would bet they let you win that fight for some reason. They have no concept of self-preservation, so letting you slaughter them is really no problem. Although a sensible human might worry some about what that reason might be."

Truth had to digest that one for a while. Eventually, Thrush stirred.

"And here we have the university. Do mind the guard." Which was a wise reminder, given their military-grade fetish and acid-slobbering spellhound.

CHAPTER 56

WAIT A GODDAMN SECOND!

Truth coolly cataloged the guard in front of him. Wearing fatigues, no armor, cap with brim. No visible rank insignia. The fetish looked professionally made and, given the size and depth of the carvings on it, clearly intended to handle a high-power throughput without disintegrating. Given that this was the Free State . . . military and imported. The spellhound . . . might not actually be a spellhound.

The more he looked at it, the more he got the sense of a dog that was selectively enchanted and altered with alchemic mutagens. Nasty stuff. The whole package made for a very effective guard patrol along the eight-meter-tall wall separating the university from the rest of the city. There was a guard booth up ahead, too. He would have to be a bit careful about this, but he should be able to rush them before they could sound the alarm.

And he would do that . . . why, exactly? Truth felt himself physically jolt as the questioning thought made itself known.

There was literally no reason to attack this guy. He was out there, doing his job, no threat, no bother. There was nothing in the university that he needed to see right this minute. No teachers for him to talk to, nothing he could read. He didn't even want the fetish. He definitely didn't want the dog. This was not his kind of dog. Truth steered the iron horse away from the university, found a quiet spot, and parked.

He started trying to pick through the last few days. He had been killed. Okay, he was part of a kidnapping, then found out the company he had dedicated his entire life to thought saving fucking Ludovic was more important than his survival. Starbrite ordered him to commit suicide, on pain of being killed by them if he refused.

Starbrite relied on the fact that the System Astrologica slowly but constantly brainwashed its employees. He remembered thinking that dying in the line of duty would be fine and right.

He had been brainwashed. So had the people who ordered his suicide. But since they were also brainwashed and had been brainwashed for much longer than him, they presumably wouldn't mind that he was being magically compelled to fight to the death.

Although, really, it wasn't relevant. Not really. It had been a total betrayal of everything he had spent his life trying to achieve. Everything.

He woke up in the pitch black of a well. Had no possessions. Proceeded to discover he was strong. Immediately started a campaign of thuggery to improve his situation. At no point did he ask for anything. At least, not that he could recall.

Oh, wait, the vendor he intimidated after robbing a bookstore. Miming probably counts as a request. And he did pay.

And he . . . you know . . . killed a couple of dozen people, many of whom were Level Zero, to secure an apartment, clothes, and home goods. Trash goods in slum housing. That was . . . not good. That was very not good. That was, in fact, deeply fucked up. And had been okay with it. He thought that it was necessary. Excused by the fact that these were criminals. Morally, if not legally, in the Free State.

Like their being gangsters excused everything. Assuming they were gangsters, he had only a *literal demon* as his source there.

Not only very bad and deeply fucked up, but it was also very, very stupid. Truth desperately cast his mind back. He could remember the first person he killed. Well, probably killed. It was the mindless addict by the canal. It was self-defense. Same thing with Thierrie, sort of. He was saving Vig. He was charging to the rescue.

Then there were all the Ghūl he slaughtered, which was apparently a civic virtue. And also self-defense. Sort of. Demon-bird thing during his conscription? That was his military duty and also very, very much self-defense.

It was hilarious. He had traveled to multiple continents, killed strange and interesting people, was literally reborn in a well in the desert . . . and still had no good answer to being called a fuckboy by a smuggler. He definitionally wasn't, right? Like, the term just . . . plainly did not apply. It was like being told you are the worst clown. What do you even say to that?

It was while he was at Starbrite. He was increasingly separated from the sibs but constantly under pressure to make sure they were taken care of. All the elixirs he shared. The schooling, clothes, all that. The endless hunt for Friends and Family points. Working in security in the PMC.

Truth remembered how the recruiter's eyes had rolled up into her head, mountains of information shoved in there by the System. How big could his file have really been? Had the System detected something special even then? Did it load a whole script into the recruiter to guide him into the PMC?

Because after that, it was pretty obvious, right? Start with looking the other way and ignoring blatant crimes. Becoming "reliable" enough to do nasty jobs, or at least not whine if something went badly sideways.

He was told, over and over, "You are good, valuable, the brother your siblings need, if you just focus on killing and not asking questions. Go where you are told, hide your fangs, then kill. Kill for Starbrite. Kill, and your life will be better."

God, reading books was the only thing he did that passed for a sane hobby.

At some point, he had stopped thinking it was fucked up to kill someone to make his life better. Violence had never really bothered Truth. He had always been more or less willing to throw hands. But at least he remembered that it was fucked up. That it was something to be avoided.

Starbrite had trained him like the guard's dog—fed him supplements, gave him nice pats and kind words when he tore apart the training dummy. "Don't kill, and you don't eat. Do kill, and we will treat you like a king. You alone are special. Even more special than the others in the PMC. Starbrite loves you best. Just kill who we say when we say. Be a good boy, work hard at your cultivation, and get prettier. One day we might just breed you. Won't that be nice?"

Or not. Plenty of rats in the slums.

Which did lead to some interesting points. Like, he had never considered himself a beauty or anything, but he wasn't hideous, either. So, why did he start thinking he was ugly after joining Starbrite? He had an excellent job, was well paid, cared deeply about his family, and if he was short on hobbies, his career was pretty damn interesting. No reason he shouldn't scrub up pretty good. When did he start thinking he was hideous? Ugly to the point of being unlovable?

When he was younger, he had spent all his time living like a monk. Just study, cultivate, earn, and that's it. Not one second for anything else. Now, though? He met people all the time. He had coworkers. All of whom understood his life and really liked to party. Offers had been made, probably. Offers he was too blind to understand. Why had he turned them down? Given that he was so utterly starved for touch and affection?

A certain finger puppet came to mind. That was the first time he could remember being utterly dragged for his looks. It was literally, directly, and *personally* the System Astrologica that made a specific point of telling him just how comprehensively undesirable he was. Nobody else had exactly run away screaming from him. And the sibs had no problem getting their V card punched, and he sure was better-looking than Harmony. But no, for some reason, a reason named *The System Fucked Him Again*, he became convinced he was hideous and the only solution was cultivating more. Which locked him into the loop of trading violence for elixirs. Which furthered his obedience to the System.

Truth looked up at the grimy building he was parked next to. Windowless, gray in the shadows. Just a blank wall of accumulated city dust over the potholed pavement. There was nothing there, and the nothing sucked. Emotions started bubbling out of him. He didn't know if he was laughing or sobbing. He bent over the handlebars of the two-wheeler and just . . . hung on. Hugged himself as the feelings felt like they would fly away with him.

It was all, all, all bullshit. All of it. Even his shitty, evil parents. Their being shitty and evil was on them, but who made the slums? Who kept the slums, slums? It wasn't all on the slumrats. He was willing to bet it wasn't even mostly on them.

Squeak squeak, little rats. Line up by the subway and feed yourself to the cats.

Would he make the same choice if he had to do it all over again? Or would he go gangster? Try to kill his way out? Find some . . . blessed land where he could keep the sibs safe and free? If such a place existed, Truth hadn't seen it. Hadn't even heard of it. Security came from power. Your own . . . or your gang's. Well. He didn't have a gang anymore. He was a monster of violence, loose on the world, and encouraged to become more monstrous by a demon and a . . . "spirit of intellect."

The funny thing was he knew how to handle the world telling him to become a monster. He had a proven, effective strategy for it. Study and cultivation. Focus on goals, make a plan, act on the plan, and treat violence as just a tool in the toolbox. Unless violence was the only answer, it was almost always the worst answer. Because violence only produced short-term results. Nobody got long-term rich from it, and the power was always shaky. Power over external things was always shaky.

Just look at the Free State. The whole country, rich parts included, was just another slum. No safety except your own strength. Safety only existed for one spell length.

Truth slowly pulled himself together. Couldn't fix the world. Couldn't even make sure the sibs were safe. Couldn't do anything about it, even if they weren't safe. All he could control was himself. He could take charge of himself. He could figure out himself . . . for himself.

Truth hopped off the iron horse and, in a dingy side street in one of the most dangerous cities in the world, he began to cultivate. His body moved under his control. The cosmic rays were pulled into the refinery of his body and transformed into cosmic energy. It gently expanded his first and second spell apertures, and he could feel it wearing away at the seal of the third. Soon now. But no rush. Just moving, breathing, and being. When he finished, he moved on to the Meditations. He had a fantastic new body. Time to learn all about it.

The sun rose, flooding the street with orange light. Even through the smog and dust, the stars were unconquerable. The world might get in your way of seeing them, but they were still there, shining down. Truth dusted himself off and hopped back on the two-wheeler.

"Was the night fruitful, master?" Thrush asked. He had been notably silent the whole time.

"It was. Frankly, I was surprised you didn't try to interfere."

"It was a struggle, but I persevered. I had the uncanny foreknowledge that you would have murdered this form if I tried." The little bird gave him a hard look.

"Hah. Well. That's true. Now, realizing that I may be making more trouble for myself in the long term, get ready to act as my translator."

"Master? I would be more than happy to teach you the local language." Smoother than butter and honey was the voice of the demon.

"I'm sure you would. No, Thrush. I think I will learn for myself."

CHAPTER 57

THAT WAS AN OPTION?

Entrance into the university was unexpectedly smooth.

"I told him you were a wealthy overseas student here while your parents were working abroad," Thrush said with as much cheer as it was capable of.

"I am dressed in stolen gangster clothes, and my iron horse is missing pieces. Like most of the seat." Truth looked dubious.

"The clothes actually help sell the image of rebellious youth. The bike, I informed him, was purchased a week ago and deliberately destroyed by you to improve your 'thug' look. In only the most respectful terms, I pointed out that only a real 'wannabe thug' rich kid who never had to struggle a day in his life would turn up to university with a spear and no pens."

Truth kind of boggled at that one. "But . . . what if I was exactly what I looked like?"

Thrush laughed, like birdsong over a crib death. "He could sense that you were Level Two. The chances of being both Level Two and poor in this city are nil. Combined with the fact that you are plainly a foreigner, there was nothing to find suspect. The Student Services Center is your next left, by the way."

Truth got his head into the game. The campus was . . . well, he wasn't sure what it was. Parts were just open grass, mowed barely a centimeter high. A few bushes dotted the grass in no discernible pattern and for no discernible purpose. They, too, had been trimmed to within millimeters of their lives.

The buildings ranged from concrete bunkers to glass-and-steel boxes so generic as to be nigh invisible. Then, towering over the vast expanse of the campus were a few monster buildings. One was a neoclassical-design, broad base with columns supporting a white tower fourteen stories high and crowned with a golden dome. Another was shaped like a sea serpent out of blue-green glass, rising out of the grass "sea." Truth wasn't sure how you would get around in it, but he supposed they managed somehow. One was pyramidal, bleached white stone covered in magenta flames. Another gently spun in place, each floor turning independently. The mirror finish on the spinning one kept catching the light, creating a strobing effect. It was impossible to ignore, and very quickly, one wished one could.

Truth had never been to university or even visited a campus. Maybe this was normal. Truth found a golem with a double dozen flags poking out of its back and shoulders. He saw the flag of Jeon sticking out of it. Promising.

"Golem, does this campus offer language classes for visitors?"

The clay creature turned toward him, its eyes a dim gold. "Yes. You do not need to be a student here. Merely pay."

"Which teacher should I approach for lessons in the local language? That can teach someone who only speaks Jeongo?"

"Go to the linguistics department. Find Professor Salesio Aduol." A tiny wisp of golden flame came from its mouth. "Follow the spark of wisdom, young seeker."

Truth followed after the light, muttering to Thrush, "It's always so embarrassing when they do that."

"Truly. Some magi have no thought for the dignity of those they bind."

"*Follow the spark*, oh, God, save us all. No offense," Truth quickly added.

"None taken. Hell quite agrees."

"Wait, what?"

"Follow the spark of wisdom, young seeker. The world is so much vaster and deeper than you imagine." Thrush dramatically flew up and ahead of Truth.

"Wiseass."

Professor Aduol, a tall man struggling at that awkward point where one is no longer a young academic nor yet a senior fellow, was intercepted as he was unlocking his office. He did, in fact, speak fluent Jeongo and was quite happy to teach Truth the local language. Truth was invited to pick which one. There were at least seven in common local usage, and the professor claimed to speak all of them.

Feeling a tinge of madness coming on, Truth selected Re'inyo. It was the most "high-class" language, used by professionals and the plutocracy alike. It also happened to be the language with the most textbooks and dictionaries printed for it. It turned out, "by coincidence," that the good professor had published several such books. Books he "by coincidence" had copies of in his office. And yes, he was happy to take cash. A new class was starting in a week. Truth could study up and then join in from the beginning. Registration, alas, could not be handled by the professor and had to be done at the student center.

"Professor, I understand that acquiring new spells in this country is quite difficult. Is that true?"

"Ah, yes! Very difficult. I don't want to say it's impossible, but very, very difficult. Young man, if you need a new spell for your next breakthrough, you should either go home or go north."

"Oh? Spells are not cheap in Jeon. Why there? And why north?"

"Spells might not be cheap in Jeon, but they are *available*, and you can buy good ones from specialist shops. Not so here. North, specifically north of the Free State, is Siphios. An ancient country, an ancient kingdom, in fact. Though I believe the position of the royal family is now entirely ceremonial. Anyhow, they have an ancient legacy of spells. They are so ancient, they have virtually all been made public knowledge. They aren't the best and are far from the most modern. Still, they are at the core of many more-modern spells. Worth serious consideration if you are on a budget. If you fancy a journey, a thirty-hour drive to their capital, or a three-hour flight if you prefer speed."

Truth thanked the professor and made the long trip back to the apartment. The city didn't exactly look better in the daytime. Not dead, certainly. There were packed markets stacked with fruit and tables full of socks or belts with exhausted men and women fanning themselves in cheap folding chairs behind them. There was life there. But no hope. The light had gone out of these people. He knew those faces. It was the slums. The whole damn city snuffed the light out of people. Maybe the whole damn country.

The apartment building was its usual disgusting self. As the day got hotter, the stench of the midden intensified. Some without a functioning toilet treated it as a giant latrine. He hustled to his apartment and shut the door. Thrush was ordered to purify the air, but Truth felt he could still taste the midden.

All right, System, you're up.

Something shifted behind his eyes. Truth didn't bother trying to read anything. He just steadily flipped the pages, thoroughly looking at each page. It took a surprising amount of time. Some of the books were quite thick. He started to notice particular . . . not even words or phrases but syllables. They came up often. Then he found pronunciation guides for those sounds. He started picking up on the sounds around him. Combine two of them, and you have a short word. He began recognizing the sound of particular words shouted across the courtyard, though he didn't know what they meant.

The System promised to help him learn faster. Looked like it was paying off already.

Eventually, hunger overwhelmed his desire to learn. He slipped out of the apartment, letting Thrush seal the door as he walked his iron horse down the stairs. A little exploration and he found a grimy, almost-lightless cafe.

He managed to negotiate himself a criminally overpriced coffee and a very reasonably priced . . . something. Looked like a muffin and smelled like dinner. Tasted like both, oddly. He didn't love it, but Truth reckoned it was just another step on the road to becoming a foodie.

System, manifest a humanoid interface.

<<Ugh. Fine. So exhausting. At least this language is pretty trivial to learn. So, what do you want now?>>

"Time to think a little more deeply about the next steps. Your proposal, 'Kill your way through the rich part of town and loot everything I want,' seems like a loser."

"Pathetic. Every great magus killed their way to power, consuming their lessers to fuel their rise."

"Oh, bullshit! BULLSHIT! Consuming their lessers? *Fuck* you. Let me play this out for you. Let me lay out exactly how this will go. I sweep through the local gangs, using muscle and training to subjugate them. Once I build up enough power and resources via drugs, whores, protection, and all that, I start making moves on the lower strata of elites. Get some crummy spells, which maybe you can upgrade into something good, maybe not."

From the outside, Truth appeared to be glaring holes through the empty chair across from him. Not that anyone wanted to pay too much attention. Bad life choice in this neighborhood.

"Now, given this is the Free Fucking State, once I muscle up enough, I can "laterally transfer" into being a respected member of the plutocracy, assuming I can force my way into a big-enough racket. Maybe buy some overpriced and underpowered spells. Maybe import some basic-bitch elixirs at fifty times their real cost because security is always going to be the number one concern.

He leaned back, looking sardonic. So, so, so much was clearer once he started seeing how badly he had been played.

"What does the top of the heap look like here, System? I'll tell you. It's King Rat. You are the biggest, nastiest rat in the shit heap. You might scare the mice, but you just look like an extra tasty meal for the cats. So, fuck that, and fuck this country."

The sprite was quiet for a while, then snorted. "There are no laws here beyond what you enforce. You say it's a slum? Be King Rat? What the fuck do you think Starbrite is? Or the CEO?"

Truth shook his head. "The CEO is, what, Level Eight? Maybe Level Nine? So far above me, I can't see him with a telescope."

"True."

"The point is, though, whatever decisions they made or are making, it's *their* decision. What works for *them*. I can make different decisions, and I want to. I'm dead to the world. Not . . . really content to leave the sibs where they are, but I know that right now, I can do nothing for them. I am an unbound ghost drifting through a foreign country. I am as free as a body can be. So, what do I want?"

"To stay a loser virgin, apparently."

"Yeah, we will *talk* about my low self-esteem, but not right now. What I want is to get stronger. Not for being King Rat, but for being someone who isn't a tool. Strong enough to say, "I'm looking after my people, and they are going to be fine, and I don't need *you* to make that happen." Strong enough to *be* enough, not just in the toughest gang."

Truth sat back in his chair, calming his breath. "Look, you said that the more spells you have access to, the more you can synthesize and improve them, right?"

"Yeah."

"Then we need to go to a country with an actual government, where it won't be a complete pain in the ass to find and get spells, wouldn't be near impossible to *keep* the spells we get, not to mention the total impossibility of getting elixirs in this country."

"Far from impossible. They grow elixir ingredients in the highlands," the System insisted.

"Yeah, ingredients. Which we don't have a way to turn into useful elixirs, and even if we did, we would have to spend all our time defending our shit. More gangster bullshit. Look, this country sucks. This whole fucking country is a slum and operates on slum logic. I don't want to invest any more time into it. Any hope of getting stronger here would require a campaign of violence and theft so large, I'm sick just thinking about it. And in the end, the results wouldn't be worth it." Truth shook his head.

"We learn Re'inyo so we can speak some kind of local language and maybe pick up a dictionary for whatever they speak in Siphios. We study on the road. I reckon I have more than enough food money. For shelter . . . I don't really care. A tarp or something."

"And how do you intend to acquire 'food money' in Siphios? Given that murder for hire seems to be your only sellable skill?"

"We will have that self-esteem talk *real, real soon*, and at length." Truth sighed. The coffee was growing on him.

"My whole life, I have focused on just two things—save the sibs, don't be like my parents. Now I can't save the sibs. In fact, nothing I do right now could directly help them. And I couldn't be less like my parents. So, where does that leave me? I'll tell you where. Ready for something new. Ready to find out what it means to be more than a thug with a spell."

He laughed softly to himself. "My mind is so completely screwed, I can't imagine what that would look like. I'm still dragging all that old shit. So. I draw the line here. I'm ditching this poison slum country, and I'm going somewhere decent, and I'm going to learn how to be someone new. And fuck you if you don't like it."

"Fine. Be like that, then. At least go back to the professor and buy books on Siphios. I can't bear to watch you mug another innocent bookseller." The sprite spat in his coffee and vanished.

Truth caught Professor Aduol on his way back from a lecture. The professor kindly informed Truth that Re'inyo was actually spoken by the Siphios elites, too. The Free State had adopted it to look fancy centuries before. A different accent, some word-choice variation, but fundamentally the same language. He had some old maps and guidebooks he could sell Truth cheaply, just by coincidence.

"Are you driving or flying?" the professor asked.

"Driving. I thought I'd make an adventure out of it. Try and figure out what I want to be, as a mage and a man."

"Oh, how wonderful. In that case, I do have one piece of advice. The shortest route to Siphios is along the A109, but don't take it. Get on the B roads. B8 runs up the coast before it turns north and inland. Miles and miles out of your way, but if you want an adventure, it's also far more colorful and beautiful. Good food, too."

"Really? Any recommendations?"

"For a young man facing the dusty road? Kwa Kabwere Garage, just over the border into Anat River County. It has been many years, but I recall there was a permanent barbecue stand next to the garage. Amazing meat and fish, all acquired locally, and very cold beer. I cannot recommend it too highly."

Truth loaded up the two-wheeler with books. It took a bit of borrowed string to tie them in place. A quick trip back to the apartment for clothes, fill up some water bottles, gather what food there was, pack everything into looted shopping bags, and then play the *how does it attach to the iron horse* game. Eventually, he got it all on there. Good enough.

He looked at the apartment complex. A slum. Perfect for all the rats to be born, eat trash, live sickly, and die scared. Truth shook his head and drove off. Who knew he could just walk away? A lifetime of feeling trapped, and now he was just walking . . . no. Now he was driving off like a wild man!

CHAPTER 58

THE MEASURE OF A MAGE

Truth had learned his lesson the night before—he drove directly to the highway and stayed on it. He still couldn't read the signs but figured *generally northeast* was manageable. And the numbers were the same, so B8 should be pretty recognizable, right?

He had himself convinced for all of four seconds. "Thrush, do you know which way leads to the B8 road?"

"I do not, master."

"Do you know what the sign for the B8 road looks like?"

"I do, master."

"When you see a sign pointing me toward that road, guide me to it."

"As you wish."

He wished. And gunned it. So far, the sights were oppressively generic. It was somewhat disappointing. The city didn't look all that much like Harban, of course. Much grimier, much less modern. Much more worn-looking. But the aesthetic was kind of similar. All tall towers, wealth, and blandness increasing in direct proportion. Oh, there was the occasional burst of color, like the building with the hundred-foot-tall monkey made of green-and-purple fire climbing all over it, but it was the exception. And aside from the monkey, the building was kind of crap.

Truth shook his head and pushed on. After about half an hour, Thrush directed him to an exit ramp, and things immediately improved. The road shrank, for one thing. Instead of six lanes, it was now two. The buildings shrank from sixty stories to four. And everything, *everything* got more colorful.

The first thing he noticed was the flowering trees and bushes. They reminded him of Chil Perdermo, how they seemed to escape from every crack and crevice in the pavement. The flowers were vibrant pom-poms in tangerine, magenta, coral, and gold. Then a palm tree, tan trunk running straight up to vibrant green fronds.

Next to the palm was a little three-story building painted blue, a balcony running along the second floor, paint missing in chunks. Apartments, perhaps? On the ground level was a bus company, and next to that, a shop selling balls and belts and little geegaws and bottles of water, juice, and sodas. Bags of snacks piled up next to clear plastic bags of cut fruit. Then it was gone, the next wonder opening up before him.

It was liberating, knowing he could go anywhere and do anything. It was suffocating, too. He wasn't used to operating without direction. Ever since his enlistment, he had found strict direction reassuring. Now there was nothing. He was picking the destination, the route, the . . . everything.

He cruised past some hotels that, inexplicably, had roofs made of densely packed straw, then there was a gap between the buildings and a beach stretched out alongside the road. Brilliant golden sands stretching out to brilliant crystal blue-green water.

Was this what the beach at Okepuela looked like? He never got to see it. The stories of the beach party were epic. Did this beach have parties? With all the hotels nearby, of course they did. Should he stop and go for a swim? Nah, he hadn't even left the city limits. No time to stop now.

He sped on down the road, the buildings becoming farther apart and cheaper. He could see corrugated-steel roofs that had managed to warp and fray at the edges, like roofs of ruffled brown fabric. Everyone was armed, he noticed. Not happy looking. But not miserable, either. A shirtless man was pulling a wheeled cart larger than himself, filled with palm fronds and broken branches. A landscaper, perhaps? Or someone paid to haul away rubbish?

What he wasn't seeing was a lot of magic. It was still there, of course. Something had to drive the buses and light the shops. But casual magic usage was much less. It must be a side effect of there being no universal spell. Only the most basic magical devices, things kids could use, were available.

Which made sense given that most people were still Level Zero. Or, as a Harban boy kept thinking of it—children. Level Zero meant you were a child. Not really a mage and, therefore, not really a person. He tiptoed around that thought. The *not really a person* thing was becoming suspect.

He let his eyes run up the road. The traffic was moving, but it was a pretty full road. Almost bumper-to-bumper wagons and chariots. Zipping alongside the carts were bicycles and iron horses. Everybody just getting on with life. There was a playground in an empty lot. It looked nice, he supposed, definitely for the five-and-under set.

When you start picking at the threads, many things start unraveling. Like . . . was Starbrite behind the Jeon National Universal Spell being everywhere? Truth knew you could do some pretty sophisticated factory jobs using only that spell. Heck, even some surgeons got by with it. Plenty of demonic and angelic support, of course, but still. He shook his head. Time to try living in the moment.

Kids were running around. Most seemed to be doing some kind of job. He could relate to that. One was picking trash up off the side of the road and loading it into a wheelbarrow. A little girl was brooming the courtyard of a gated home. Maybe her parents were doing the same job inside the house. He was pretty certain it wasn't her home. There was a string of fifteen children in blinding white shirts and plaid trousers, laughing and chattering as they walked down the road, backpacks over their shoulders.

Once again, the convoy system triumphs!

They were really crawling along, weren't they? He was supposed to be racing along there. Had he even gone fifteen kilometers? The road narrowed as the trees and bushes started crowding in. Truth had to struggle to remember that he was still on the outskirts of a major city. It felt . . . jungle-ish. The trees and bushes seemed to form a solid wall with dusty brown soil underneath them.

The road pressed through the tree wall, and suddenly Truth was crossing a flat bridge over a river. Long, muddy, blue-green, reflecting the shore and sky. Thatched huts near the water, terracotta-tile roofs on houses set a little way back, and clean white boats bobbing along. Sea spirits, or were they river spirits? Guiding the boats along. Some had eyes painted on their prows, but most did not. The boats looked nicer than some of the houses, but they were all leisure craft. The one obvious full-time fishing boat stood out. Long and low, looking like a serious fight broke out in a paint factory, and it was a major instigator of the riot. The other boats gave it a lot of room, practically radiating social disapproval.

Truth felt an odd need to defend the fishing boat. He wanted to jump onto the pretty white pleasure crafts and start yelling at their drivers. *"Don't you like fish? I like fish. How about you stop giving the guy getting the fish a hard time?"* Except, of course, they weren't really giving the fishing boat a hard time; they just didn't want to smell fish dying in the sun.

Once he was over the river, it was another band of pretty nice suburbs with gated resorts covering the seaward side of the road. Lots of gates in this country. Not many mages, but he could practically feel the hum of the home wards. Making talisman bowls must have been a very lucrative industry there. You probably couldn't use just one. Not his area of expertise, but from what he had seen, you needed to bury one under the threshold of the front door . . . and maybe the front gate, too? Was more better? How about other points of the wall?

Truth let his mind wander a little. Talisman bowls were ancient magic. Almost anyone could make them because all you needed were a bit of clay and the names of the various gods and angels you want to invoke. Well, for basic home wards. He knew that some could hold actual demons of rank and station. Wasn't there a story about Teacher Reshim trapping an Infernal Duke under his soup bowl? Almost certainly bullshit, but maybe there was a grain of truth there.

He heard a blare of music coming from a stand next to the side of the road. Little colorful cloth straps were hanging off the stand, most with writing on it he didn't recognize. There were also lots and lots of little charms hanging off the straps. Crude, mass-produced things. But they were playing music. Some of which sounded like Re'inyo. He focused. Definitely Re'inyo. He pulled over. He grabbed a sack of orange chunks of fruit, a bottle of water, and one of the music charms. He paid forty shillings. Was that a lot? Did he get ripped off? Truth had no idea and didn't care.

The music had a driving, rhythmic quality to it. With a jerk, he realized that it sounded an awful lot like the music in Jeon. Not the traditional music, the pop stuff you heard floating around. The stuff people put on in the barracks or lounges. The big difference was that the music was not just in Re'inyo. The singers seemed to wander in and out of languages as they pleased. He shook his head and drove on.

The road opened up a little. He was solidly outside the city now, and suburban homes were being replaced by fields. Farms, he supposed. He had a sudden flash of hatred. His eye twitched. He thought about farms and suddenly hated farms? What the fuck?

System, are you fucking with me right now?

<<Not me, what's up? Spare no detail of your suffering.>>

Apparently, I viscerally hate farms. And farmers, now that I think about it.

There was a long pause.

<<Gardens? Gardening?>>

All fine. As are florists, vineyards, orchards, and even fish farms. It seems to be specifically dirt farms and specifically those who farm in dirt farms. Eh . . . maybe resentment? Frustration? That might be a more accurate word.

This led to another long pause.

<<Have you ever seen a farm before today?>>

Not that I know of. Maybe? That abandoned building with the well was a farm once, right?

There was an even longer pause.

<<You are such a fucking weirdo.>> And the System refused to say another word.

Truth dropped it and tried to focus on what he saw around him.

A couple of developments jutted out like giant rectangles of salt. They looked like some vast alien force (probably not the Shattervoid Clan) had picked up a block of homes from inside the suburbs and dropped them in a field. Not a great look, in his opinion.

Speaking of the Shattervoid Clan, there were no signs of food riots or the apocalyptic collapse of society. Guess the cover-up worked. Not sure how they silenced the opposition on the op, because clearly, more people were in on it than just the mages on the ground. Kind of a weird thought— *Yay! My murderers succeeded! Now my family is safe-ish!*

He tried to drive the thought out of his head. The countryside looked strange to him. Intense, lush green, but the dirt looked kind of crummy. Red, loose, dusty. Like it was ready to fly away at any moment. It wasn't too dusty on the road, but not great, either.

Around sunset, he reached the Kwa Kabwere Garage. Well, he thought it was: he was still picking out individual letters, and the signs all said he had just crossed into Anat River County. So. Probably. The barbecue pit was still there, locals coming up in a steady stream and collecting sausages, bits of roast fish, grilled chicken, goat, and some kind of vegetables . . . It smelled incredible. He hopped off the iron horse, practically floating toward the grill.

"Ah, the ——! You — fix?" A man in overalls swooped in, hovering over Truth's trusty mechanical steed. It took Truth a minute to figure out what he was talking about, but slowly and with much pantomime, it was revealed that the man could put a seat that more or less worked in place, as well as mount a rack on the rear of the two-wheeler that would make lashing down his meager supplies much more practical. The existing rack was . . . not the best. Truth got the price, figured he had enough to cover it, and nodded. The bike was wheeled off, and he was promised it again in the morning. Truth kept the supplies with him.

He got the grilled chicken and the goat. He was so hungry, he had to have both. He figured with that, the fruit and cold water out of the chest by the grill, he would be all set. Truth was absolutely right about that.

The spices . . . he didn't even know what they were, but they were incredible. Mild and savory on the chicken, fiery and domineering on the goat. Mingling with the fat to coat the inside of his mouth. The fruit was sour with a hint of sweet, bright, almost herbal, cutting through the fat of the meat. The combination made him rock back and drum his feet against the ground with happiness.

His bed that night was a convenient stretch of scrub, wrapped in a bit of tarp and with his shoes for a pillow. The stars were bright above him. Before he slept, he did his cultivation. The heavenly light poured down into him, filling him. Reminding him that, whatever else he was, he was alive. He was part of something . . . so much greater than himself. But he was himself. A tiny, self-aware fragment of the incredible vastness. A mage, taking ownership of his little speck of self.

Truth smiled at the thought. Yes, taking ownership of himself. A happy little shiver ran through him. Level Three was only days away.

CHAPTER 59

WHAT PRICE A GOAT?

Truth woke with the dawn, feeling something skittering over his leg. He tried to shake it off, still half-asleep. He felt something poke his ankle, then again. Not painful, really, but weird. He looked down. A small brown scorpion was trying to sting him. The stinger hit his skin and just bounced off. Tap, tap, tap.

He gently picked it up off the ground and held it in his hand. No need for magic. Just picking up a scorpion and letting it freak out harmlessly on his hand. Ugly little thing. He couldn't bring himself to hate it. It didn't have the faintest idea what was going on but was doing its best to go out fighting. And it couldn't hurt him. Couldn't even touch him.

"I get you, little buddy. I get you." He gently set the scorpion down on the orange dirt and watched it run off.

"If master doesn't want it, may I eat it?" Thrush asked.

"Not that one. Feel free to grab all the other bugs I see crawling over me, though. And in my clothes."

"Gladly."

As the demon dematerialized into a black fog and started swirling around him, Truth dug out the maps from his sack. B8, the road he was on, had already shrunk to a single lane. It would remain a single lane until it ended at a T junction with the A3 road roughly . . . one hundred and sixty kilometers from there. Was the A road going to be a big highway, he wondered? Well, he'd find out soon enough.

"Development Sheet."

BODY DEVELOPMENT *NOT-GIMPED EDITION, YES, REALLY, YOU CLOWN*
Stellar-Ray Attunement: 90%*
Bone Density: 5.1*
Strength: 3.7*
Speed: 4.0*
Proprioception: 7.0*
Reflexes: 7.0*

Level Progression: 98%
Resistance to magic: Level Zero: 10%, Level One: 5%, Level Two: 1%

Hmmm. Everything was the same except for the level progression. That had somehow managed to jump five percent after . . . three cultivation sessions? Really, really good ones, no doubt, but still. No one would buy elixirs if that was normal. Stellar-ray attunement must be doing the heavy lifting there. He had been . . . oh, god, he couldn't remember. Something in the sixty percent range? Something like that, back when he first unlocked body cultivation.

Why didn't his skin toughness turn up on the sheet? Was that not something Starbrite took standard measures for? Seemed unlikely. Oh, well; he wasn't going to worry about it right now.

Right now, the important thing was to see if he could borrow the bathroom at the Kwa Kabwere Garage. He might be able to dig a hole with his hands, but he was damned if he wanted to wipe with them. He looked at the scrubby, dense little shrubs around him with their horribly prickly leaves.

He could pay the guy back if he had to kick in the door.

He did not have to kick in the door. It turned out that the owner started his day at dawn. Truth was a bit startled by this, but the explanation was soon apparent. The owner's wife turned up and started running the grill.

The wife, brilliant black eyes and hair up in an orange scarf, plonked down two huge pots. She filled one pot with dark black peas or beans (Truth wasn't sure what they were, exactly) and the other with oil. Some kind of milk went into the pot with the beans while the oil heated up. Then a tub of spices, onion, tomato, chili, and other ingredients he didn't catch.

While that was heating up, she started making up a dough, working in lemon zest and some powdered spice Truth didn't recognize. Strong arms and strong hands pulling, slapping, folding.

His two-wheeler wasn't ready yet, and wouldn't be for a couple of hours. No matter. Truth just hung out and watched the wife cook. He soon had company. Quietly chatting, the laborers from the nearby farms and businesses gathered around the grill. Not farmers, apparently. Just "laborers." Who didn't trigger the same visceral loathing? Odd. Maybe you had to own the farm to be a farmer?

Newspapers were swapped, with those who could read reading for those who could not. Truth didn't catch the language; it wasn't Re'inyo. Looked like he got lucky with the garage owner. The sun was clearing the horizon and climbing with speed.

With some ceremony, the wife rolled out her dough into rough circles, cut the circle into quarters, and started dropping the quarters into the hot oil. She banged the other pot's side with her ladle, yelling something. The husband came out, calling back to her. She tossed her head and sucked her teeth, snapping her words out. This got a laugh from the laborers, who seemed used to the show.

A rough hand patted Truth on the shoulder. He looked over at the already-fragrant laborer waving him toward the pot. The laborer said something Truth didn't understand, but he saw the other laborers nodding. Apparently, he was the guest and was to eat first.

The wife ladled out a big bowl of peas and put two of the fried pieces of dough in there. A cup of milky tea was firmly placed in his hand. He was directed toward the clay cup of plastic spoons, then waved away when he tried to pay. She flatly refused and shooed him away. Truth desperately wished he could thank her in her own language and just repeated "Thank you!" over and over again in Re'inyo.

He took a big spoonful of the peas. His head snapped back, and his eyes opened in shock. *Delicious* was too mild a word. Incredible! Joy in a bowl! It was lightly sweet but mostly spicy and savory, with herbal notes and a growing warmth from garlic and chili. Nourishing? His cells practically screamed with ecstasy.

He tried the fried dough. Lightly sweet, puffy, and a rich tan color. The flavor . . . lemon and something he couldn't put words to. An almost-herbal spice, intensely aromatic. In a daze, he sipped the tea. Thick, rich with condensed milk, and slightly bitter.

Well, he lived there now. Maybe they needed help in the fields. He could learn to be a mechanic. He knew talisman maintenance. Transferable skill right there.

Truth recovered enough to keep eating. He took the time to savor every bite and every sip. He was the first to get his food but was far from the first to finish. Apparently, he counted as a free show with breakfast. He watched how people returned their cups, bowls, and spoons, then did the same. With immense regret, Truth made his way over to the garage.

His two-wheeler now had a real seat installed and a rack to which he could safely tie his stuff. It was nicely cleaned up, too. He got quoted a price that he was sure was three times what the locals paid, paid it, and added an extra twenty shillings on top for a tip.

Truth hit the road in an odd sort of mood. Was this really still the Ressilaud Free State? Guaranteed 97% bandit by weight? Because these people were lovely. Really, really lovely. Everyone in Shomburuti seemed like a bag of dicks, but . . . okay, that wasn't fair. The professor had been pretty great. And the guy selling omelets was kind of a prick but not the worst. What was he missing?

He stopped by a little store by the side of the road, loading up on supplies and making sure to collect both toilet paper and a small shovel. The things you forget when you leave in a hurry . . .

Truth looked down the one-lane road that seemed to head straight north into the sky. Not much in the way of traffic. Hardly anything, actually, but it was decently paved. He grinned and let his magic lash the chained spirit into motion. The iron horse screamed as it ran for the horizon.

He let his speed creep up higher and higher. Whipping past slower-moving two-wheelers. Heavy wagons were practically stationary obstacles to him. Truth relied on his superhuman reflexes to safely navigate. More than safely; he was having fun. So, he did it. Laughing like a loon.

Lunch was taken on a rock by the side of the road. The packed food was really nothing special. Regrettable. He would have to do better for dinner. He pressed on, watching the green, scrubby plants slowly give way to even spikier thornbushes. The tangerine-orange dirt slowly turned a brick red as the air noticeably dried out. Even when he was running flat out, the air was warm.

When he stopped, it was almost lethally hot. Literally so. Truth wondered if his insane constitution was the only thing protecting him from heat stroke. He hoped the field hands were doing all right. Presumably, they knew how to manage the heat.

He reached the T junction with the A3 sometime late in the afternoon. Contrary to what he had thought, the A3 was also a single-lane road. However, the intersection was a veritable hive of industry. There were as many as four buildings! A dozen shacks on the verge of collapse! Eight signs! For what? Unclear!

Truth laughed. Even with the most positive attitude, this was a nothing place. The pile of bald tires under a short thorn tree probably counted as a tourist attraction. The place was so dead, the local goatherds were hiding in what little shade was cast by the buildings. Truth spotted one sitting with their goat in the little puddle of shade cast by a sign. He could get that. One of the buildings looked like some kind of office. Maybe he could ask for a bathroom visit and some water.

He was flipping through a phrase book to refresh his memory when a large olive-drab-covered wagon pulled into the intersection. The goatherds immediately gathered their flocks and tried to run, but soldiers—bandits?—jumped out of the back.

The soldiers were yelling, waving their fetishes. Pointing them at the goatherds. Some ran into the buildings, pulling the occupants out into the street. Shoving them to their knees. There were . . . twenty of them. Old fetishes. Poorly maintained. Probably not very good when they were new. Definitely military surplus. One started pointing a fetish at him, screaming.

"I don't speak your language," he said calmly. Or tried to, Re'inyo still being very shaky in his grasp. Didn't matter. The bandit was fluent in screaming and pointing. The bandit threw a punch. Truth swayed back. He could see the bandits punching and kicking the goatherds, loading the goats into the back of the wagon. One goatherd pulled a knife. An Acidbolt burned a hole through his chest. Everyone started screaming.

Ah. This was more like what he expected from Ressilaud Free State.

"It's been a lovely day. I've enjoyed doing the peaceful-civilian thing. Can't wait to get right back to it, actually." He had switched back to Jeongo. No reason not to. The bandit was screaming again, jabbing the fetish in his face. Looked like he was about to use it, too.

"But when you get right down to it, I have always hated bullies, thieves, and parasites. And being screamed at. I really don't like being hit, either. Hate it, actually. And the thing that has most fucked me up about violence is . . . I'm just so accepting of it. I can always seem to justify and rationalize it. That's not okay! That's pretty fucked up! But man, I don't know you, and I already hate you. So. Let's see just what I can do without spells."

Truth slapped the fetish to one side as his foot lashed out, catching the bandit in the gut. He put both hands on the fetish and twisted it out of the bandit's hands. He didn't have a spell handy, but hell, he knew how to use an acidbolter. The bandit's head disintegrated. He looked around. Nineteen to go.

CHAPTER 60

NASTY, BRUTISH AND SHORT

The tactical situation was very bad. Truth was standing out in what was essentially an open intersection. The nearest cover was two buildings fifty meters away, and everything else was . . . junk. Collapsing shacks, a steel bench covered with a corrugated metal roof, some road signs, a heap of bald tires, and more thornbushes and trees than was good for his mental health. Nineteen bandits armed with acidbolters were fanned out around him, and the local goatherds were mostly on their knees or bellies in the dirt. The goats were screaming and running.

His equipment was a decorative spear lashed to his iron horse, a machete lashed to his iron horse, and the crummy acidbolter he had just looted. He had zero useful spells. On the other hand, he was Level Two, these choads were Level One, and his body was refined to an unreal degree. Truth didn't bother thinking anymore and got stuck in.

Truth sprinted toward the nearest bandit, firing as he went. The bolts smashed in, burning through the cheap cloth fatigues. The bandit screamed, spraying acidbolts everywhere. More bolts started sizzling in the dirt around Truth. Another dead.

The bandits were losing their spells from tens of yards away. Acidbolt wasn't an accurate spell to begin with, and fired from a lousy knockoff fetish sold as Army surplus thirty years before and hardly maintained since, it was a lot worse. Truth felt like he was sprinting through acid rain, dodging raindrops. The bandits didn't believe in fire discipline, apparently. They sure weren't worried about burnout.

Truth pushed even harder. He was faster than this. Much faster. He felt his muscles coiling and exploding under him, running with a speed and force he had never known. He closed fast, barely getting a shot off before getting to melee range. The shot landed center mass. Truth smacked the fetish up and out of the way while he put the dying bandit between him and the incoming fire. Truth took a moment to line up his next shot, double-tapped the guy trying to scream orders, and started sprinting again once it looked like the bandits had fixed on his current position. Sixteen left.

He got to the edge of a building and turned the corner. Acidbolts ripped through the bandit he had been using for cover, now drifting over and reaching toward the corner he was hiding around. Some of the goatherds were getting hit by stray bolts.

Some of the goats were screaming in agony. He couldn't worry about that right now. He jumped straight up, caught the roof's edge, and pulled himself up with one hand. Nifty. Another exciting thing his new body could do.

He got to the roof line in a few swift steps and dropped flat. Couldn't be more than seven meters up, and the corrugated metal was toasting him like a griddle pan. Still good enough to give him a covered position to shoot more bandits.

Truth started picking them off. It took them a few seconds to figure out what had happened (the corner of the building looked like it had been eaten by moths), which cost them three lives. They scattered, trying to find cover of their own. Truth frowned at that. It wasn't like there was much cover, but the Acidbolt had almost no penetrating power. It was why he stuck with needlers. Massively more versatile.

Assuming you had spells to lay on them. Which he didn't right now. And the bandits definitely didn't have them, either. *Fuck it.* He worked steadily through his targets. Twelve left. Eleven. They were breaking now—some were starting to count noses. They were sprinting toward the covered wagon. Ten. Nine. EightSevenSix. One made it to the cab. *Nope, can't have that.* The bolt splashed against the door of the cab. *Ah. Annoying.* He picked off the straggler as the wagon started getting into gear. Five.

Truth stood and ran down the slope of the roof. Using the momentum, he took an enormous leap, covering a chunk of the distance between him and the wagon. It was slowly starting to peel away. Even with his speed, he wouldn't catch it on foot. He shot out the wheels. Harder to do than he thought. He kept the bolts going until he saw a tire sizzle and pop. He sprinted for his iron horse.

The bandits were yelling now, sticking their fetishes out the back of the wagon and firing. Not a bad idea, but the wagon's sides were cloth. He started shooting back. He couldn't see what he was aiming at, so his accuracy suffered. They didn't sound happy, regardless.

The iron horse shot forward, the spirit lashed by his will. "Thrush, blind the driver." The demon darted forward, happy to "help." The wagon started jerking from side to side. Truth frowned. He was coming from one direction: directly behind the wagon. Easy to target, even with the bandits' lousy aim. He gunned it, closing as fast as he could while dumping shots wildly into the back of the wagon. It seemed to encourage them to keep their heads down.

He pulled up next to the cab of the wagon. The driver clawed at his face, trusting the bound spirit to keep them on the road. He had the window up. Truth tried a shot, and the acid splashed against the glass and metal, sizzling but not getting through. Truth frowned, then grinned.

Truth sat on the fetish and awkwardly pulled the spear loose from where it had been lashed. He swerved close to the cab and, with a heavy grunt, jabbed it through the window and into the driver. The acid-weakened glass shattered instantly, the spear opening the side of the driver's neck. Truth pulled away. The wagon lurched violently from side to side a few times, then stopped.

He pulled the iron horse around the front of the wagon, dropped the spear, and picked the fetish back up. Sprinted to the back of the wagon, ready to finish the job. The three surviving bandits were all wounded. Kneeling on the ground with their hands in the air.

Truth hesitated. What . . . exactly was he supposed to do there? Self-defense probably stopped when they started running away. He had them down because he didn't want them coming back with friends. Well, they weren't going anywhere now. Did he want to leave them to the goatherders? He couldn't imagine them surviving the captivity if the goatherders dared to take them. Not . . . entirely sure there was a moral distinction between leaving them for the goatherders to kill or just killing them himself. On the other hand, he certainly wasn't going to just let them go.

He took a quick peek inside the wagon. Empty and reeking like a barnyard. This was clearly a raid for supplies. He checked over the prisoners. They had nothing. Basically, the clothes on their back, a few religious charms, and that was it. The fetishes they had carried were no better than the one he was using. He couldn't remember any other bandits looking richer than this lot.

Growling, frustrated, he hopped into the cab and ripped out the connections between the wagon and the chained spirit. Reparable, but not without specialized tools and knowledge. It would be enough.

He walked back to the prisoners. They weren't looking too great. He pointed at the ground where they were kneeling and yelled, "STAY!" in Re'inyo. Maybe they would. He hopped on his two-wheeler and drove back to the intersection. The goatherds kept well away from him. He did the same for them. He stalked into the best maintained-looking building, found a bathroom, used it, found a fridge with cold water, took some, and hopped back on his two-wheeler.

"Well, that was fucked up. Last time I take an intersection." Truth took a swing with some gallows humor. He shook his head and turned east up the A3.

Ten kilometers of brutal, arid desert later, he hit a sudden band of deep green. Huge, lush trees seemed to spring from nothing, and the empty road filled with people and carriages. Homes started appearing. First, shacks and tiny vendors, then more and more developed homes and shops, and soon he saw mattress stores. The blood was still drying on his spear, and he saw signs for discount mattresses.

Yeah. He was in Ressilaud, all right. A wide, slow river, mud brown, was the life-giving artery in the snaking band of green. No fishing boats there, nor pleasure craft. He crossed a bridge, was through the green belt, and suddenly found himself in the middle of a good-sized city. It didn't look like much on the map. It somehow looked like even less in person.

One-story buildings were scattered over who knew how many square kilometers. Shacks made of bundled sticks and discarded pallets, roofed with corrugated metal, or more sticks, or just plastic trash. Trash everywhere. More bald tires stacked for no purpose. Large cloth and plastic fiber sacks filled with who knows what, stacked by little shops selling discount two-wheeler parts or oil for communication altars. Was it still a slum if the whole city looked like that?

There were some better-looking buildings, but not many. Three stories seemed to be the absolute limit, most brown, but some were painted, faded and peeling dusty oranges and pinks. Truth started stopping the better-dressed-looking pedestrians and asking about hotels. He got a lot of blank looks, but he found the words in his phrasebook and kept at it. Eventually, he found his way to the Hotel Anat Gardens (his best stab at a translation). Gated and guarded, naturally, but still open for business and happy to see a foreign face.

"We are quite used to foreigners, you see." The desk clerk smiled, the serpent demon coiled around her neck translating for her. "The airport is right next door. Really, I'm just surprised you came on a two-wheeler. The security situation in the desert is not very good."

"Yes, I had noticed that. Fortunately, I drive very fast."

"Hahaha! Well, not to worry. Our wards are very strong, and we are part of a neighborhood association that keeps things safe. Your two-wheeler will be under twenty-four-hour surveillance, with armed guards standing by. If you want to relax, we also have a restaurant and bar beside the pool. I have taken the liberty of booking you into our deluxe suite, if that suits you?" Her voice was smooth and soft as silk even before the demon translated.

"How much is it a night? Oh, I am only spending the night."

"Sixty shillings, plus a six-shilling resort fee to use the pool. Oil for the communication altar is extra, and you must use the oil we sell here." For an 800% markup on an already-expensive product. She didn't say the last part, but everyone heard it anyway.

"Great. I'll take it." Truth nodded.

The shower felt divine. He didn't have clothes for the pool, but that was fine. He wasn't big on swimming. He just hung out poolside and tried to process the day. It was . . . a lot. The seemingly random kindness and cruelty of people. The freedom of the road, the astonishing food, the baking sun. The shocking power of his body. He reached his hand up and pretended to pinch a cloud.

One day. He smiled. One day, he would find a good place. A place where the garage owner and his wife and the laborers could all live peacefully. The sibs could live peacefully. He could live peacefully. But he would have to be strong enough to keep it safe. And if it didn't exist? Well, then, he would have to be strong enough to create it.

Truth grinned. He couldn't wait to find out what spells awaited him in Siphios. He remembered when he had gotten the Meditations. The System said Truth could beat it up if he advanced the Meditations far enough. Suddenly, Truth believed it. His grin got wider. He was looking forward to it.

CHAPTER 61

BICKERING OLD MEN

Truth sat on a bench in the Agora. He had long since finished eating, but the two old bastards beside him were bickering like champions, and he couldn't bear to go.

"We agree that it is best to live simply and modestly."

"We do."

"And that one should pursue virtue and not fear death."

"Yes, that, too."

"So, why is it that your whole philosophy is just stupid trash?"

"Get fucked. At the most fundamental, basic level, pleasure comes from avoiding pain. That and enjoying what is natural and necessary. Everything else is derived from those two points. And the point of life *is* pleasure. Getting dragged into bullshit by your neighbors and supporting the Polis's mad dreams of conquest just makes you miserable. You only have this one go at things, so fucking enjoy it."

"That's stupid. You are stupid. Look, virtue, real virtue, *which requires civic participation, you little parasite*, is all that we can look to for a meaningful life. You preach moderation because excess leads to pain. I preach moderation because it is, itself, a virtue. Anything not a virtue has no fixed value. Be it good food or a broken leg, it is just a matter of perception and opinion. An indifference."

"Oh, yeah, real fucking indifferent. Hey, fart-knocker, if behaving in a 'just' manner is so fucking important, if moderation is so important, then why are you pricks insisting on paying for new triremes, eh? Or raising more phalanxes to get slaughtered? Where's the virtue in war? Answer me that."

"The Polis demands—"

"The Polis doesn't demand shit. *You* do! You can't claim to be part of the Polis, preach civic engagement, and then shove off moral responsibility when the Polis does something shady."

Truth flagged down a passing waiter. "Another bowl of marinated olives and a bowl of wine. Well watered; I may be here a while."

<< YYYYYIIIIAAAAAAAAAAAARRRHHIVVAMALIII-
WHY!? WHY DOES YOUR SHITHOLE BODY KEEP DOING THAT!>>

Truth stretched and yawned. "Sorry? No idea what you are talking about. You kind of . . . stopped making sounds I could understand for a while. I hope it was agonizing, whatever it was. Anyhoo. Time to be up and at 'em."

Breakfast was not included in the room's price, and it was a bit disappointing. Not bad, exactly, just bland. He sighed. Not everyone could cook like the garage owner's wife, it seemed. The path of the foodie was long. No matter. He would walk it to the end. He packed his things, enjoyed a long shower, and checked out.

"So, how far is it from here to Siphios? I think the map doesn't tell the whole story."

"To the border? A little under six hundred kilometers. To their capital, a little more than twice that. We are both big countries!"

"You certainly are. Anything I should know?"

"Just the usual, really. I would normally recommend you fly. The security situation is really not good. And you will pass through a stretch of desert that is just plain unpleasant for a man on an iron horse."

Truth thanked her, mounted up, and was off. He was determined to have his adventure. Maybe some idea about how to save the sibs would come to him. Probably not. But maybe.

It was a slow push, getting out of the city. Traffic was wretched and not helped by donkey carts wandering the same streets as spellwagons, bicycles, chariots, and seven-legged load-bearing lizards. Once he cleared the town center and started hitting the suburbs, Truth opened up the throttle. If he could keep it at about eighty, he would reach Wajr by lunchtime. He didn't know if the chained spirit could keep up that kind of throughput, but . . . the hell with it. He wanted to go fast.

Watching the green bushes hovering over the baked red soil was amazing. Kilometer after kilometer of . . . nothing much. Land in Jeon was densely settled. As far as Truth knew, people had been living there . . . basically forever. It was farmed, lived on, mined, or preserved as a park. It was all used, in other words. This was fallow land. Maybe it was farmed at some point, maybe not, but in either case, there was a whole lot of nothing going on there now.

It was the security situation; he was sure of it. Even Starbrite wouldn't want to set up a mine there. They would spend as much defending it as they would earn operating it. Just not worth it. He had to swerve a couple of times to avoid trucks loaded with sacks of things, but there would be long stretches where he was the only thing moving on the road.

Wajr was kind of surreal. Truth kept looking around, looking back down the road he had been on all morning, looking around again, consulting the guidebook, looking around again . . . Wajr looked exactly the same as the city he left this morning. No river running along it . . . that he had found. So, there was . . . that. Maybe. But otherwise, it was the same. The same shanties. The same brown everything occasionally livened with bursts of paint and color that must have faded within seconds of drying. The red dust was everywhere and on everything. He was half-convinced he would find the same hotel if he went up the main road. But the restaurant the guidebook recommended was also straight up the main road. Where it met another road. Another intersection where he had to make a turn.

Sinister. Not to be trusted. He firmed his resolve and pressed on. The traffic slowed to an absolute crawl in the city center, but it did keep moving. He almost missed the restaurant, distracted by the shoeless man doing major repairs to a . . . not so much broken as bum-jumped spellwagon. Apparently, the only place on earth it could be repaired was directly in front of the Greenview Restaurant. A brown, bunker-like building with pitch-black windows and a single, austere sign over the door.

Intersections were not to be trusted. It seemed the locals agreed with his deduction.

The food was incredibly unappetizing looking. It was a plate of roast meat and some kind of green-gray-yellow thing that had been smashed into rough patties about the size of his palm. There was also a small heap of salt on the plate. Just . . . heaped. Not served on the side in a shaker; just heaped on the plate. He looked around the room to see what the locals were doing. You picked up the shredded meat with your hand, dipped it in the salt, and ate it. You then ate a bite of the questionable fried-disk things.

Truth sniffed the meat. Goat, he was sure of it, but an absolute barrage of other smells came with it. Onions and garlic and intense ginger, and he was already tearing into it before his analysis could finish. Outstanding! He dipped it into the salt. Also outstanding! Questionable patty? Not as outstanding, but still pretty good! Peas and corn and herbs, probably.

Perhaps he was wrong about intersections. Perhaps the path of the foodie was about finding intersections and embracing them.

One very hearty, satisfying meal later, Truth hopped back on the iron horse and started toward the roundabout. It was at the very center of the city. For some reason, the city was built around a large open stretch of desert. Nothing at all there, just sheer empty space, almost a kilometer square at the heart of the city. Odd. He shrugged and set off for Siphios.

It was at this point he started noticing the demons running loose. First, a few, then tens, then hundreds, and quickly thousands of people were screaming and running.

"Thrush?"

"I cannot say, master. They are of the very lowest orders, insects by your standards. However, like insect swarms . . ."

"I should be somewhere else. Going now!" Truth flogged the chained spirit into screaming activity. He started forcing his way past wagons and carriages as everyone tried to flee the city center. An accident up ahead blocked the street.

"Thrush! Fly up and guide me out of the city!" The bird-shaped demon launched up and flew forward. Truth followed it down an alley and then into a parallel street. There was an impossibly bright green light, almost blinding though it came from behind him. A wailing noise—no, it was too inhuman to be wailing—a piercing cry as something was born into this world.

Truth put his reflexes to the test, driving around running civilians, wagons, chariots, and whatever was in his way. Soon, Thrush was forced to lead him cross-country. Truth could only endure the whipping bushes and bouncing stones as he fled. Driving through the bush, he saw convoys of trucks by the main road. They had set up barricades. Some people were being captured and herded to one side. Others simply executed where they stood, their wagons or carriages hauled away.

"Master! Demons pursue you! Above!" Truth looked up. Far into the cloudless sky, black shapes circled. He got his head down and drove faster. Some instinct caused him to swerve right. This was wise, as he saw a spit of acid slide past where his head would have been.

"They are attacking, master!"

"NO SHIT! Can you take them?"

"Alas, they are too much for me."

"Shit!" They were way up. He still had the Acidbolt fetish, but it couldn't touch them. Not at that range. Normally, he would go for the summoner, but that was impossible under the circumstances.

"Guide me back on the road. Let's see how far they are willing to follow me!"

Thrush did so. No wagons set off to chase him, but those demons were persistent. They kept hovering over him and periodically spit acid. He pushed the spirit as hard as he could and ran flat out for hours. The road was a straight line, with no cover anywhere on it. The demons never quite hit, but the misses were so close that he couldn't relax for an instant. He pushed the spirit as hard as he dared, but the burnout was starting to show. Even the talisman etchings were starting to wear away. He was wearing away. This level of focus: not sustainable. He needed to find a place to go to ground. Take a rest. In the scrub-filled desert between cities.

They were endurance hunters. This was what they did. Exhaust you, then kill you when you were too weak to flee or fight back. And it was working. The road wasn't even paved anymore. It was just packed earth.

"Thrush, anywhere that looks like cover up ahead?"

"Master, there is a village! You could try and find shelter there!"

"How far?"

"Twenty kilometers!"

The demons had spotted it too. They had picked up the speed of acid-spitting.

"Shit! No choice! Can you do anything about the acid?"

"Only briefly."

He stayed low over the handlebars, regulating his breathing. Smoothing out the flow of stellar energy in his body. He could do this. His body could tolerate the strain. He had been sitting all day; the strain was nothing. He could do this. He just had to keep aware of the falling acid. It couldn't touch him unless he let it. Everything was in his control, so long as he regulated his mind.

Trying to keep in that calm state, Truth pushed hard for the village. They didn't make it easy on him. The acid was more clustered now, no longer coming one at a time but in twos and threes. He had to swerve more, even brake momentarily, to throw off their aim. The village came up fast, the villagers running away from the road while others fished out homemade fetishes.

"To your right, a garage!" Thrush shouted.

Truth hit the brakes, turning the iron horse ninety degrees to the road and, while still sliding forward, got power back to the wheels and lunged for the garage.

CHAPTER 62

I WANT SPELLS!

Acid started raining down over the front of the garage, hissing and spitting as it burned holes in the dirt. He could hear villagers yelling and metal clanking, somewhere between a chime and a drum. It started grumbling and rolling. The acid came down harder, eroding the edge of the building. Truth didn't dare imagine the roof.

He started racking his mind for countermeasures. His only ranged weapon was too short-ranged to be useful. The garage had a back door, but that made things worse, not better. He needed a way to retaliate, not keep running. The damn demons shouldn't have so much range . . . unless they were fueled by some damned enormous sacrifice. And whoever those people were, they were slaughtering a good chunk of a small city. So presumably, they had the capability. Damn it all.

"All right, Thrush, you are my eyes. Maximum stealth, slip out and see what's going on."

"At once, master." The bird-shaped demon transformed into mist and slipped out under the back door. Truth took a second to do a blindingly fast touch-up of the worst-damaged cosmic ray channels covering the two-wheeler. He was sure he was missing problems, but in a situation where he couldn't do much . . . he could get ready to run again.

The chained spirit was almost catatonic from overwork. Truth knew they didn't experience burnout like humans, but they could be worn down into almost nothing if abused. And he had been abusing it terribly. Was there anything he could do to help it recover? Maybe.

Truth gave a quick-once over to the garage. In truth, it was almost empty, and many of the tools were things like "convenient log and rock" or "multi-function chisel and mallet." Still, even the most wretched garage must have . . . YES! He dove on the little metal bottle with indecent relief. It might be pissing acid outside. The locals might be making worrying noises that were getting louder and louder. But there absolutely would be a cheap bottle of oil of belladonna in any garage.

Synthetic, obviously. But he'd gratefully take it. He had the oddest intruding memory of a sergeant in the depot during his conscription, explaining why sometimes synthetic is *better* for the spirits. He desperately hoped that the sarge was right.

Popping the little cap off the tip, he squeezed a thin stream of oil directly into the array holding the spirit. It hissed and steamed, then seemed to relax. His old shop teacher back in high school would have ripped his ass in half for running a stunt like this. This was not how you maintained your chained spirit. His training sergeants back at Basic would have stitched those halves back together so they could rip them in half a second time. The belladonna would let the spirit push a little farther and a little longer, but this wasn't the same as a proper rest with strip-down and herbal soak. This was taking the edge off the symptoms without treating the disease.

Bright flashes of electric blue and green started flashing from outside. The metal drumming was now so loud, it hurt. So loud, pebbles and dirt were vibrating across the floor. Thrush drilled back under the door and streamed directly into its control talisman. Truth heard the demon's voice in his mind.

"Master, the local demon hunters have organized the village. They are performing a sacrificial ritual and will likely slaughter those poor slaves above in just a few moments."

"Good!" Truth paused for a moment. "Any chance of all of us talking peacefully, being mad at the people who sent the demons, and having a, you know, good time together?"

There was conspicuous silence from both Thrush and the System.

"I didn't think so either." Truth sighed and got the iron horse ready to go. There was an almighty *CLANG* and a brilliant blue-white flash of light. Truth got the wheels spinning while holding the brake. Once they were up to speed, he launched!

He bolted through the garage door, the last drops of acid burning his skin. He kept accelerating down the dirt path, avoiding angry villagers. Some had hoes out, trying to hook him. Others were running over with chains. Truth stretched his inhuman reflexes to their limit, dodging around them as best he could while clawing toward the main road. The red dust was flying everywhere, wheels kicking up sand and rocks as he spun around outraged locals. He finally got to the main straight and really let the pony run. He didn't aim to hang around and find out what the local shaman could do if pressed.

A few kilometers outside the village, he slowed the iron horse to a gentle, almost jogging pace. It would keep them moving and give the spirit a chance to recover a bit.

So, I think we can all agree this has been a catastrophically shit day, Truth thought. *I've had worse, to be sure. But it really, really draws a fucking line under the limits of the Meditations. No ranged attack. No disguise. It's just not useful for anything other than body refinement. And it fucking says something that the standard-issue weapon in this country is an Acidbolt fetish. Short range, no need for much accuracy, and no need for ammunition. Can't lay a spell over it worth a damn, but if you figure virtually all of your army will be Level Zero, why not? Needlers require actual ammunition, cheap though it is.*

System Hint: You have an outstanding mission to acquire a spell. HINT: Why would your vastly smarter-than-you System suggest such a thing?

Mmm? HINT. HINT.

Oh, get bent. Your brilliant scheme was to knock over rich people's houses until we found what? A safe with the family spell etched on a conveniently pocket-sized crystal? Because I can see that going really well.

The System did not reply. Truth looked back at his packs. Some of the acid had burned through cloth, but things didn't look *too* bad. He would find out tonight, he supposed.

"Thrush, how far is the border?" The sun was edging toward the horizon. On the one hand, camping in the desert was free. On the other hand, driving on a dirt road through the desert was . . . not the best time. He was exhausted.

"A little over a hundred kilometers from here, I believe. We drive through more desert, slowly rising into some small mountains. There is a good-sized town or small city at the pass where the two countries join. It straddles the border. This does lead me to a rather delicate question, master: do you have a passport?"

"Ah . . . no." It took Truth a moment to recall what a passport was. He had never needed one. The lapel pin was all he had ever needed to travel the world.

Thrush cocked its head to the side. "I cannot imagine the border is well enforced here. Something to consider, perhaps."

Truth tried to remember how much cash he had left. Not . . . a ton, probably. Between the books and the repairs to the two-wheeler, much of his available budget was gone. On the other hand, he really didn't want to sleep outside. He wanted a bed. He wanted a goddamn pet cafe. And a cold drink. Food. A flushing toilet. Not waking up to Mr. Scorpion, even if he was really a harmless fellow.

Fuck it; hotel it is. He pulled over and dug into the guidebook.

Truth rolled into Moyle slowly. The city? Large town? Whatever it was, it was squeezed into a valley between two low mountains. The whole city gave a sort of cramped feeling. It also made Truth twitchy.

He was looking in all directions. Checking what he saw against his memories. Had he seen that exact shop before? Because Moyle looked *exactly* like every other city in the Free State. He squinted and really focused. He flat-out refused to believe that, even with his "tourist's" eyes, there were no differences between the cities.

There was a change in hats. The people in Moyle seemed to favor a round, brimless hat that covered the entire top of the head, usually in white. There was more hat diversity in the rest of the country. So. That was one difference. There might even be a second. He kept looking.

The streets were narrower—another difference. Plenty of fruit, plenty of little stores. Paved streets, which were welcome after a high-speed sprint through the desert. Little cafes barely the size of a long booth, seemingly only serving tea and a snack. But the overall sense of beige-brownness remained. It was little explosions of color against brown and gray buildings, not a glorious riot.

There was something he was missing; he could feel it. A subtle difference, even at the edge of the city. Something so ordinary, his mind was skipping over it. He slowly went mad as he negotiated the claustrophobic streets, eventually coming to a halt as a donkey cart blocked the intersection. This was very convenient for the goats who had decided to wander the streets, bleating at innocent strangers.

The nearby construction workers paid no mind and kept their worm demons chewing up rock and laying cement. Trailing behind the demon would be someone working a talisman, curing the cement, and then a second worm demon would lay the second layer, and a second worker with a talisman would cure that, and round and round they went. All that was automated in Jeon, of course. They have infinitely better demon-binding spells.

Wait. Wait just one goddamn minute. His head ratcheted around to look back at the construction workers. One of them was spectacularly picking his nose while using the ring-shaped talisman to direct the worm along the foundation. That was not a talisman a Level Zero could use. Just not enough stellar energy in them to compel the demon to action. It was also a lot more technical than it looked, because the demons were not inclined to be consistent about the ratio of ingredients when they made cement, nor were they inclined to be tidy and level in their construction. Unless compelled by someone who really knew what they were doing. And had the magic to back them up.

Truth started grinning. They were using spells. Utility, noncombat spells. They weren't richy-rich either. These were construction guys. So, spells couldn't be that hard to come by there. Tomorrow. He was too shattered today, but tomorrow. Tomorrow he would slip across the border and get himself some *magic*.

The hotel was fairly basic, but it did have a sturdy gate around its parking lot, and the guard demons looked competent. There was no swimming pool or hotel bar. There was a functional shower ("Only ten minutes of hot water a day, honored guest, and then we have to charge extra"), a comfortable bed, and the sworn promise of the front desk clerk that his aunt would have Truth's clothes washed, folded, and waiting outside his door in the morning.

Truth tried to negotiate a coffee and a breakfast to go with the laundry, but the despairing helplessness on the clerk's face quickly made him give up on that idea. However, the clerk would be only too happy to recommend one of several nearby cafes and restaurants for whatever the honored guest required. Truth drank a liter of clean, talisman water, ate a large fruit he couldn't name and didn't particularly care for, washed it down with most of a second liter of water, and gratefully passed out.

CHAPTER 63

"YOUNG MAN, YOU ARE POSSESSED!"

Truth woke to the sounds of hammering outside the hotel. He had faintly hoped for more screaming from the System, but you couldn't have everything. Worth investigating why his body could torture the System, but . . . it would just have to go on the big heap of Things Truth Does Not Understand. Sooner or later, the mountain would be worn down to nothing. That would be a good day.

Truth frowned. He was so tired; he hadn't cultivated yesterday. Of course, he could cultivate any time, and believing that cultivation worked better at night was pointless superstition. But he did kind of believe it. The sun was just too powerful, its rays too hot to be comfortable to cultivate with so directly. He hemmed and hawed for a while but eventually gave in. The urge to break through to Level Three was just too strong. Even if he didn't have spells for his slots, he wanted the improved strength.

He breathed out, then in, then started moving through the forms. It was childish, he knew. Superstitious. He was a long way from the Level Zero who needed to physically move to do his cultivation. But he just liked it. It made him feel better. So, he would do it, and the hell with people who disagreed.

It was a slow, steady flow of movements. The body stretched, compressed, and stretched again. The form was dancing, exulting, then humble and worshipful. Fierce and meek. The more he advanced, the less he strictly followed the forms of his childhood. The more he let the world talk to him, and him to it. The communion between the universe within him and the universe without, the billions of stars intertwining with the nine slowly being born within him.

The energy poured down, fierce and hot. They were on the equator, he dimly remembered, or just north of it. The power of the sun would be terribly strong there. Still, he could take the heat. Stretching and coiling, then stretching out again. The stellar rays raining down on him, refined along the Nine Worm Path, and then poured like golden water into deep wells. The first aperture, the first star warming from red toward gold. The second star bigger but still solidly orange. And now the third aperture, still closed, the star not ignited. A toasty warm brown. Lightening, turning red as it mixed with the liquid gold of the sun.

The golden light wore away the barrier over the aperture, the star bursting into life. It rapidly swelled, becoming larger and larger. The vacuum formed by the empty aperture pulled in more stellar energy from the other apertures, which in turn pulled in more of the sun's harsh stellar rays. Truth grunted as the rough equatorial rays fell faster and faster into him. Still, he could handle it. His body had been refined beyond a normal mage's tolerance. His apertures were widening, strengthening. The stars were growing brighter. He kept cultivating until he just couldn't stand it anymore.

BODY DEVELOPMENT SHEET
Now Updated for Level Three! Congratulations on becoming a slightly larger ant!
Stellar-Ray Attunement: 90%*
Bone Density: 5.5*
Strength: 4.0*
Speed: 4.4*
Proprioception: 7.4*
Reflexes: 7.7*
Level Progression: 0%
Resistance to magic: Level Zero: 25%, Level One: 10%, Level Two: 5%, Level Three: 1%

Level Three. You were somebody if you were Level Three. Not famous or anything, but somebody. A senior ship fitter down at the shipyard, maybe. A departmental supervisor in a small department. He seemed to recall it was the minimum cultivation for some Army ranks in some countries.

In Starbrite, all the models were Level Three. He remembered that tidbit vividly.

Hey, System. I haven't been practicing the Meditations that much. Isn't that growth kind of fast? And the resistances seem kind of lopsided.

<<First, your stellar-ray attunement is unnatural as hell. I mean, just deeply cursed. You are pulling in almost twice what a mage with a decent foundation should, and it's not only not hurting you, it's fueling everything you do. This leads me to, second, only the spell resistance is the Meditations. Most of your growth is that stupid amount of stellar rays you soak up flooding into your body.

For most not-cursed people, this would result in mutation, liquefaction, becoming a farm for cursed, tumorous spirits, the usual. You just seem to get comprehensive, incremental improvements. Which, and you need to be very clear on this, is not something humans do.

All fucking around aside, this is not human shit. I don't know what you are becoming, but, lucky you, you will be strong at the end of it.>>

Well. That kind of stole the joy from the moment. He thought a moment. There was nothing he could do to fix it. So, for now, accept it. Truth rolled his shoulders and walked into the bathroom. Time to take a good look at himself.

The last few days had been tiring, and it showed even after a good night's sleep. Dark eyes, deep-set beneath strong brows. A straight nose, proportional to his strong face and lantern jaw. High cheekbones, and the face was just thin enough to make them pop. A mass of dark hair . . . wait. Hadn't his hair been brown? Why was his hair black? His eyes were the same color. Why did this change?

He shrugged. It looked good on him. Then he looked a little closer at his eyes. They were the same soft brown as before but were now flecked with gold. Not just gold colored—actual shimmering motes of gold were visible in the iris. You really had to look closely, and the light had to hit them just right, but they were there. Odd. Very odd. He hadn't noticed any major changes to his vision. Well, there was the improved low-light vision.

His body was . . . fantastic. He had always been lean, but he filled out and shot up between the Army food and the Nine Worm Path. He had been just a hair above average height, just a *smidge*, but he was still quite pleased about it.

Now, well. It wasn't just a smidge. He wore his new 193cm with comfortable ease. Long of limb, with the fingers of a sculptor or a surgeon. His muscles were in perfect proportion—not too much or too little of anything. Each standing out like an anatomical diagram. He felt strong. He looked like the better class of God.

And yet the little whispers came into his mind.

You are lying to yourself.

Is that face really symmetrical? It looks off.

The worms made you lumpy.

Even worms think you are ugly.

Even worms don't love you.

You didn't earn this body.

You didn't earn that face.

So what if your face got better, you're still boring.

Murderer.

That's not the real you.

Your personality is still shit.

Nobody who remembers the real you loved you.

They didn't even like you.

Your masters found you a bit useful. Good little rat.

You were never worthy of their love.

Just a thug. Now you aren't even a thug with a spell.

You would ruin anyone you were with. You are poison.

Just like your old man. You are going to turn out like your old man.

Just broken dreams and failure. Might as well pick up the bottle now.

I bet they sell schnapps here. Just fifteen wen a bottle. You can steal that much.

You don't deserve to be with someone.

Nobody deserves to be burdened by you.

You worked your whole life to sell your family into slavery.

It wasn't Mom or Dad. The sib's real enemy was you.

You are trash. Just another slumrat.

Squeak Squeak, little slumrat. See how far you can run. But you'll never leave the slums. Never stop being a rat.

Truth collapsed onto the floor, clutching his head and trying to breathe. He knew the little whispers were wrong. He knew it. The little whispers were echoes of what the System did to him. *But they came in his own voice! It was his own voice telling him these things!*

He hugged his knees and shivered, trying to tell himself over and over again that it wasn't real. That he was loved. That he could love and be loved. He didn't betray the sibs. He was more than a monster of violence. He could be someone safe. That others could be safe for him. He was balled up on the cheap linoleum floor of the bathroom for a long while.

When he felt strong enough, he got into the shower and turned it as high as it would go. He used every second of his ten minutes of hot water. He dried himself, fixing his hair a little with his fingers. Not looking in the mirror.

He started to walk out of the bathroom, then stopped. He turned to face the mirror. Washed away the fog with a handful of water and looked himself dead in the eyes. "I am nothing, *nothing*, like my Dad. I can be any damn person I want to be. I am bigger than my fears. And I am strong enough to love myself." He took a deep breath. "And one day, I will be strong enough to save my family."

Truth was feeling less than fully collected but was prepared to fake it. He negotiated with the desk clerk and won permission to stow his iron horse and luggage in the hotel for the rest of the day, even after check out. When asked why, he explained that, alas! He had lost his passport in the desert, and his flight home was from Siphios. Specifically the capital.

"Ah, you must love that beautiful country. Your Re'inyo is really not bad!" The clerk nodded enthusiastically.

"Thank you. I am practicing." He enunciated carefully.

"Well, it's a minor problem. As it happens, as long as you aren't bringing weapons or drugs through the border, the guards don't care. Honestly, most people here don't have any sort of identity papers, and it's not like the borders are particularly secure. If you don't mind a big detour, you could go around the mountain and drive through the bush. Not fun, but no one would even look at you."

Truth vividly remembered driving through "the bush." "No, thank you. I really like roads. A lot. Very, very much."

The clerk laughed. "All right, all right, don't worry. Ah! But you must speak to your embassy or consulate before getting on a flight. They will need papers there also"—here the clerk coughed and looked awkward—"you will probably not wish to return to this side of the border. Our side is actually guarded quite strictly. You understand that papers are not an issue, but certain fees are imposed. As well as a careful inspection of goods. Many things are found to be 'contraband.' You understand?"

Truth did. "How about leaving?"

"They did try to charge a fee for that, but everyone just went around. They kept trying to expand the guard post, and people just kept going farther and farther around. Eventually, they gave up. Not worth it, you see."

Truth translated that from Ressilaud Free State into "A powerful local family has set up a stationary banditry point and called it a customs inspection, but this is the Free State, so what are you going to do about it?"

Truth knew exactly what he was going to do about it. He went out, had breakfast, bought a new map and a surprisingly comfortable white brimless hat, stocked up on food, water, and toilet paper, then hit the road again.

The "customs station" offended Truth's professional sensibilities. He had experience doing customs work for the Army and then later for Starbrite. Admittedly what he was doing for Starbrite was more "facilitating smuggling" than customs enforcement, but still. This was just bad. There was a roundabout on the main road, with two roads coming off of it to the north. One had a big sign saying KINGDOM OF SIPHIOS CUSTOMS STATION. The other had a large sign saying ONE WAY DO NOT ENTER.

The customs station was just a booth in the middle of the road. They didn't stop anyone. There was just a green haze that fell over people who passed by the booth. Presumably, it would trigger if the spell detected contraband. Truth had severed the functional parts of the fetish, turning it into a sort of ugly stick. He drove right on through.

The change was gradual. The city subtly got more colorful. The people were a little less guarded looking. Fewer visible weapons, though they were certainly around. He could feel a higher level of cultivation. Almost everyone was Level Zero or One, but nobody acted like the Level Ones were anything precious or special. There were actual, honest-to-whoever cops. And they appeared to be doing useful work directing traffic. Incredible!

He laughed quietly to himself and pushed on down the road. It was slow going, as the traffic was still somewhere between "bad" and "actual crimes." Still, no rush. Then he got bored, decided it was a rush, actually, and tried to go around the traffic. This did not work. The traffic went wherever the hell it wanted, and sidewalks were more of a theoretical construct than a physical thing.

Truth finally lost patience and cut right onto a side street. Logically, cities follow a grid pattern, so he could just move up a parallel street. The logic might have worked in Jeon. Six minutes later, Truth was impressively lost. He appeared to be in a residential neighborhood, enjoying above-average quantities of weird looks. Foreigners simply did not come there. There wasn't much *there* there, even if you were a local.

He gave up. It was lunch-ish time. He saw some locals piling into a cafe, decided they probably knew what was good, and followed them in. No hats on these guys, or if they did have one, it was a very small, decorative one. Meh. Not for him.

There are some moments in life where you feel an inexplicable chill. Like you can see the world shimmer a moment, and you realize that the sky is just painted on. If you went around the corner, you would see the wooden props holding up the fake storefronts. You can see the smudged costume makeup on the actors playing the "ordinary people" in your life. Everything is exactly as it was a moment ago, but your perception has changed. Somewhere, someone has written a play and cast you in it. And you only think you know your role.

Truth was no stranger to sudden bursts of paranoia, but this vast alienation wasn't quite the same. The customers were queuing up and grabbing their food. People laughed and cursed and had boring conversations about other people he didn't know. It couldn't have been more ordinary. So why did he have the feeling that these lines were rehearsed? That they were moving according to the blocking given by some unknowable director.

Were these enemies? Or, like him, just actors lost in their parts?

He was waiting in line when a particularly disreputable-looking young man, one of the tiny-hat brigade, tapped him on the shoulder. Truth looked at him. Did he need to squeeze past? Should he run?

"Young man." He looked no older than Truth. "Young man, I see a dark fortune upon you. You are doomed. The case is hopeless. But I alone may save you. Young man, I do not mean to alarm you, but your life hangs by a thread." He put his hand manfully on Truth's shoulder, reaching up slightly. "Young man, you mustn't panic. But you are possessed!"

Warby Picus is a lifelong fan of science fiction and fantasy. One day, he figured he would see if writing books was as much fun as it appeared to be. He hasn't looked back since.